W9-CHT-010

# Feral Creatures

ALSO BY KIRA JANE BUXTON

*Hollow Kingdom*

# Feral Creatures

## A Novel

## Kira Jane Buxton

GRAND CENTRAL
PUBLISHING

NEW YORK   BOSTON

Grand Central Publishing
Hachette Book Group
1290 Avenue of the Americas, New York, NY 10104
grandcentralpublishing.com
twitter.com/grandcentralpub

First Edition: August 2021

Grand Central Publishing is a division of Hachette Book Group, Inc. The Grand Central Publishing name and logo is a trademark of Hachette Book Group, Inc.

The publisher is not responsible for websites (or their content) that are not owned by the publisher.

The Hachette Speakers Bureau provides a wide range of authors for speaking events. To find out more, go to www.hachettespeakersbureau.com or call (866) 376-6591.

Print book interior design by Thomas Louie

Library of Congress Cataloging-in-Publication Data

Names: Buxton, Kira Jane, author.
Title: Feral creatures : a novel / Kira Jane Buxton.
Description: First Edition. | New York : Grand Central Publishing, 2021.
Identifiers: LCCN 2020042932 | ISBN 9781538735244 (hardcover) | ISBN 9781538735237 (ebook)
Subjects: GSAFD: Science fiction.
Classification: LCC PS3602.U9825 F47 2021 | DDC 813/.6—dc23
LC record available at https://lccn.loc.gov/2020042932

ISBNs: 978-1-5387-3524-4 (hardcover), 978-1-5387-3523-7 (ebook)

Printed in the United States of America

LSC-C

Printing 1, 2021

*For Em and Pops*
*Under whose wings a great many feral creatures*
*have found love and protection, including myself*

# Feral Creatures

Maybe it's animalness that will make the world right again: the wisdom of elephants, the enthusiasm of canines, the grace of snakes, the mildness of anteaters. Perhaps being human needs some diluting.

—Carol Emshwiller

# CROWLOGUE

TRANSCRIBED BY A BLACK WIDOW SPIDER NAMED
RA RA

*It is a truth universally acknowledged, that a single crow in possession of a good fortune, must be in want of a Cheeto®.*

Okay, I might have borrowed and bastardized that line a little bit, but it's hard to know where to begin. On a whim and a smattering of Scotch, I am writing my story. I use the term "writing" loosely given that I don't have any fingers (oh, to have the gift of just the middle one). Where are my fingers? I hear you ask. I have a paucity of digits because I am a bird. My name is Shit Turd and I'm a Cheeto®-addicted American crow—not a species known for our literary prowess, but bah stinkbug, we should be.

I've practiced and told this story—my story, *our* story— a bajillion times, because we need stories to survive. Stories suture up our wounds, stitch us back together. They keep our loved ones alive. They connect us all, like the mycorrhiza, the fungal web through which the trees talk. Like baby sloths or Kevin Bacon or actual bacon. Now, where to begin?

*All this shit happened, more or less.*

*Call me Shit Turd.*

Writing is hard.

My story is told often: by me, in the sylvan whisper of old oaks, peppered into misty air by songbird beaks, bubbled up in the breath of beluga whales, and shivering along the frosted strands of spiders. Even squirrels natter about it, those toilet wand–tailed, nut-scrimping, Peeping Tom fuck scamps. It matters because our stories will save us. We must remember and retell them, just like humans did before they all died out.

All of them but one.

In case you are wondering what a human is, they were essentially bald apes that covered their genitals with cloth and experienced incessant outrage. Holy Funyuns, everything set them off—noises, the weather, the interminable celestial mystery of what happened to their socks, but mostly other humans. They were inordinately clever. They invented magical things like pastries with holes in them and the ShamWow, and they got excited over whimsical happenings like a winged fairy who broke into their homes in the middle of the night to collect their offsprings' teeth in exchange for cash slipped under a pillow at varying rates of inflation. They had very, very big hearts and I loved them all. Though I'll admit they had no control over vegetables; I can't tell you the number of times their lettuce was contaminated with Ebola.

I stare out the window and try to channel the deep literary acumen of a dead writer (there are a lot of those now). Come to think of it, I am the only actually alive one, which automatically makes me the world's greatest living scribe and I'm suddenly suffused with confidence. Let me catch you up on my adventures with a little fairy-tale flare...

*Once upon an apocalypse, there lived an obscenely handsome American crow named S.T., which was of course short for Shit Turd.*

*He was given this distinguished appellation by his owner Big Jim, a larger-than-logging-machine human man who once assaulted a sign twirler dressed as the Statue of Liberty and acquired a colostomy bag for the sole purpose of filling it with Peanut M&M's so he didn't have to pay for concession stand candy. Big Jim and S.T., the ravishingly handsome crow, along with Dennis, the bison-hearted bloodhound, all lived together in a gorgeous castle in Seattle. One day, when Big Jim's beautiful ice-blue eyeball fell the fuck out of his head, S.T. (always ready to seize a big adventure) didn't have a moment of doubt or existential terror; he knew just what to do. Being a heroic, intrepid corvid and a goddamned fucking optimist, S.T. fearlessly led his best friend and bloodhound buddy Dennis into the wilds of Seattle to find a cure. There, they discovered that all the humans—whom Big Jim and he had always called MoFos—had contracted a heinous virus. Some believed the virus was transmitted through the screens of technology (the technicalities of this are convoluted, mysterious, and were explained to me by an intellectually enlightened parrot). Others believed the disease was an environmental issue and that the exploitation of nature came back to haunt them. The MoFos that hadn't perished had devolved and changed into terrifying quasi beasts, more pungent than they'd ever been throughout their colorful history, even at Coachella. It was as if Picasso had drawn a collection of animals while handcuffed, on dental drugs, and upside down in a paddling pool of chocolate pudding. They hunted screens, smashing all the glass of the ruinous Emerald City. The natural world began to claim and conquer what was stolen from her with skeletal claws of bramble and a mouth of moss. With no conservation, the crumbling bones of infrastructure were being devoured by ivy and wicked weeds. S.T. set about saving the domestic animals that had become trapped in homes after the extinction of the MoFos. There were great battles between beast and grosser beast. We made friends and we lost friends. I thought I might die of heartbreak. But then—praise to the Cheeto® gods!—we found the last living human on earth and I had a reason to keep hope alive. And, not to brag, but I also bravely overcame a penguin prejudice.*

Stories change every time you tell them. They grow roots, they evolve and shed dull scales for shinier skins, they grow sinuous, sun-striving tendrils and camouflage part of themselves. Many have firm origins in shit (bull or otherwise). This one starts with Shit Turd, the little black bird in a small cabin.

This is my story about the last MoFo on earth.

Are you up for a big adventure? Damn right you are.

*Carpe Cheeto*®.

# CHAPTER 1

S.T.
A SMALL CABIN IN TOKSOOK BAY, ALASKA, USA

A bite is a very sudden thing. Cheeseburgers, Evander Holyfield, Peter Parker, the boat from *Jaws*, and mailmen throughout time immemorial have been ambushed by them. I was powerless, filled with hypnotic venom.

I had been bitten by the travel bug.

I was incurable, plagued by wanderlust fantasies of traversing the big beautiful blue. I was, you see, an American crow who yearned to see the MoFo wonders of the world. I found myself daydreaming about the dazzling Taj Mahal in its tighty-whitey hue, the haunting Incan citadel of Machu Picchu, Lady Liberty with her hostile headgear, the lusty rouge of the Golden Gate Bridge, Pisa's topple-y tower—even fucking Stonehenge to be honest, though it had lost its mystique when Big Jim explained the rocks had simply been plopped there by unimaginative aliens. In the shimmery lagoon of my mind, I'd hop onto the downy back of Migisi, my majestic bald eagle companion and avian chauffeur since I damaged my right wing in a dramatic showdown with a deceptively glassy window. Migisi and I would soar above a velvet tapestry of continents, drinking in the rich MoFo magnificence before the vines, grass, and green swallowed it whole. I'd marvel at how MoFos had dragged their beautiful fingernails across the landscape, before the clandestine conquering of formidable elements—moisture, fungus, bacteria, and the gluey gluttony of insects—demolished it to dust. Before the bird feces corroded it all. Listen, I don't mean to gloat, but I've *always* maintained that pigeon poop will be the end of us. Alas, the jet-setter fantasies were only to be enjoyed in minute-long bursts, because it turns out that having an infant really puts a damper on your travel plans.

You know what else bites? Alaska. Not to be the bear of bad news, but although Alaska is beautiful, it's also quite deadly— like a hormonal honey badger with an Uzi. Toksook Bay was an alright place to be, but it wasn't Seattle, wasn't where the soul of me roosted. A crispy, tea-stained map in our little cabin confirmed my suspicions—Toksook Bay is Alaska's literal armpit. So, I hadn't been in the armpit and our little dusty cabin long, and although I was homesick for the Starbucks logo, my heart throbbed a proud crimson that the Golden Gate Bridge could only dream of.

Because I had Dee.

Oh, Dee. My little Fabergé flower, whose face was an Alpine forget-me-not in full bloom. Dee, whose shy sliver of a smile was a balm for the soul. My nestling—a tiny miracle with breathing skin and Cheeto® fingers and a gorgeous bald head like a dove egg. I had fallen in love with her in a way that made the world shiver with magic. She made the nights warmer and the air smell cotton crisp and fresh, except when she farted, which put the cabin's foundations at risk. She had canny, darting eyes and the lungs of an operatic howler monkey. It was the sort of love that rallies armies and makes one skip and caw in soprano like a helium-filled eunuch. Just imagine—a tiny, silky-skinned nestling with no teeth and no claws. And she was the last.

The very last MoFo on earth.

The snowy owls, Migisi (the wings beneath my wind), and I were doing our very best to provide Dee with what she needed, to keep the last MoFo alive. I was her fierce guardian, her murder, and so, I worked on her wellness, preparing to return to our Seattle safe zone at the University of Washington's Bothell campus where I could raise her with my fellow crows, Kraai and Pressa, and teach her about my beautiful heritage of coffee, rain, weed, Kenny G, more rain, and the Seahawks, whom I've posthumously renamed the Seacrows.

Five snowy owls had been the first to find Dee as an abandoned infant, alone under the strange Toksook trees on a star-stapled night. They'd worked together to lift her bassinet to our little cabin, sending for me (the MoFo-pro crow) to help them keep her alive. The alabaster owls and I spent a lot of time huddled together deliberating about how to ferry the planet's most precious Fabergé flower across Alaska: The Last Frontier, where no man has gone before without freezing his balls off.

It had only been days, but it soon became apparent that MoFo nestlings do not have the esophageal prowess of pelicans and should not have whole blackberries pelted down their throats. There may have been a terrifying choking incident where yours truly had to dangle over Dee's gullet like Han Solo heroically nabbing an imperiled Lando from the Sarlacc pit.[1]

Dee had the resting habits of an insomniac ant, so the five

---

1 This is a reference to a MoFo movie. Watching television and movies is how I became a MoFo expert. Star Wars was a space opera about an incestuous brother and sister who used telekinesis and the help of a green gremlin to get vengeance on their angry asthmatic father and blow up both his balls. I loved it. Two wings up!

snowy owls and I were the most sleep-deprived feathereds in the history of the big beautiful blue. I witnessed The Hook—really a king among snowy owls—fall asleep midflight and smack headfirst into a quaking aspen. And then he just lay there, enjoying a moment's peace. The Hook was an agreeable sky hunter, white as bone. I grew fond of him, even though he remained unmoved by my motion to change his name to Owlfred Hitchcock. The largest owl was Kuupa, a magnificent creature who never took her tutelary stare from Dee. Ookpik and Bristle—hypnotic brush flicks of black embellishing their magnificent bodies—both separately passed out while attempting to feed Dee blackberries (lovingly and sensibly squashed by the toes of an exhaustipated corvid). I saw both owls lose their battle with consciousness and slump onto Dee's tiny chest to her utter hilarity. I learned to sleep on my side while being gummed until I looked like a machine-washed merkin, and even once napped upside down.

Fruit bats ain't got nothing on me!

Little Wik, the smallest of the snowy owls, along with Ookpik, Bristle, and The Hook, was given the task of finding provisions. They'd bring blankets, healing herbs, fresh water, blackberries, and headless red-backed voles no matter how many times I explained this to be a cultural collision. We took turns with diaper duty, being very careful to bury her pellets away from the cabin—away from those whose noses guide glistening fangs.

One day, as I was supposed to be plotting how the owls and I would transport my Fabergé flower to Seattle, I slipped into the warm waters of a daydream. In the dream, I was pressing a brush held in my beak to the peeling artwork of the Sistine Chapel and patching up some of Michael Angelo's unfinished bits with a splattering of Shit Turd flair. I'm happy to report that *The Creation of Adam* was greatly enlivened by substituting my bloodhound bud Dennis for Adam and having the bearded man in the nightdress proffer him a Milk-Bone. In reality, I had nodded off. Because of this, I never heard her approach. It was my fault because it happened on my watch.

Dee had been crying, cheeks salmon pink, salty streams glistening down the sides of her moon face. Just outside the cabin, white-spotted sawyers sang her a squeaky serenade. The owls and I had pulled her makeshift bed over to the window so the air could kiss skin free from the fuss of fur, and those cunning eyes could enjoy the rapturous quiver of leaves and how the light playfully painted the paper birches. She was a watcher, our little Dee. I was so tired, I didn't notice the white-spotted sawyers abruptly silence their song. When my nictitating membranes slid open and the scene pulled into focus, Dee's tiny eyes were on an alabaster head the size of an ottoman, looming over her face. My nestling remained silent, but her tiny chest lifted up, down, up, down, up, down—the beautiful rhythm that meant she still had a chance to survive a world that had obliterated her species.

The polar bear was female, unusually large. Her hunger announced itself on shiny saliva strings that slipped from her black jowls, fusing to the ancient sealskin blanket we had bundled Dee in that morning—a morning when she had hiccuped and giggled, swallowed beak-delivered drops of fresh water, and pulled playfully at my defective wing.

Had I kissed her enough?

"Don't. Touch. Her," I warned the pallid predator breathlessly. I was shaking, perched on the wood table next to the dusty, fat stove. The cabin was small—Dee a few frantic flaps from me—but it might as well have been the Taj Mahal. I was too far away, my speed no match for a polar bear.

"A cub," came the slow response from the female bear, thick and slippery, as if caked in blubber. "A young cub of the

Skinners." Her voice lowered to a shuddering growl. "I thought they were gone." Saliva pooled on the blanket and I felt my ribs constrict, cracking under the weight of the mistakes I kept making with my poor helpless Dee. If I had chosen the fleece instead of the sealskin, would the bear still have come here?

"Back away from her," I warned, my voice a vibrato, unable to steady the fear that snakes around your esophagus when your whole life is in the paw of a predator.

"Why do you want the cub, Crow?" The polar bear shook her massive head. She lifted gargantuan paws onto the cabin's cobweb-festooned window frame. A quick breeze brought her smell to me, a condensed aroma of moss and briny seaweed. *Oh no.* I caught a glimpse of her side and my heart plummeted. Her ribs jutted out in desperate protest, the skin around her neck hanging loose from a diet of algae, berries, and birds' eggs.

She was starving.

I bargained. "There are caribou near here! Many. You can have every last one of them!"

The polar bear's nose wrinkled, drawing in the biscuity smell of my nestling. She lowered her head, coal eyes inches from Dee's button nose. Dee's eyes widened. The bear's mouth gaped open, unraveling a purpled, liver-like tongue. She ran it along a salmon-pink cheek. Dee's face was frozen in shock, eyewhites glistening. I scanned the room for a weapon, a noisemaker, a knife, a gun—oh god, why wasn't there a gun— old boots, chairs, the table, the stove, a broom, old MoFo clothes, pots, there were pots full of Dee's blackberries, black- berries I'd stayed up late squashing, empty pots; I planned to grab one...

And when my eyes flashed back on the polar bear, she had her great black lips sealed around Dee's tiny skull. Her bone-crushing jaw cocooned my hatchling's egg-shaped head.

Between tooth and fleshy tongue, I saw glimpses of a cave seals don't come back from. Ocher fangs were inches from clamping down, and when that happened, there would be nothing left. The world would be scooped out. Emptied. Forever hollow.

"She is my cub!" I screeched, rocks dragging across my throat. "I am The One Who Keeps! I will kill you if you harm her; there is no earthly law that will stop me!"

The polar bear flinched, seeming to recognize something. My heart thundered out an SOS call. The She Bear slowly ran her lips across Dee's face. Dee grimaced from the musty stench, the cold and slimy trail of a tongue. She made no sounds. Five snowy owls—Dee's defenders—burst onto the scene. They beat their wings in fury outside the cabin's traitor of a window.

Glass-breaking screeches sent my skull into spasms. These were not just the screams of our snowy owls. Up in the trees, all around us, was a dappled mosaic of ferocious eyes—yellow and orange—blinking in horror.

There were flammulated owls, with their adorable oversize pupils and Pixar-rendered cuteness (don't be fooled; they'll fuck you up). Northern saw-whet owls, their rain boot–yellow eyes hosting a centrifugal blast of facial feathers. Short-eared owls, intricately speckled, and long-eared owls with ear tufts like a Viking warrior's horns. Great gray owls in their dapper charcoal suits, faces a hypnosis of misty moons. Northern pygmy owls, little crackle-and-pop predator puffs. Burrowing owls, the elusive Mr. Beans of the owl kingdom, frowning quizzically. There were even great horned owls, who are known to snack on other owls, earning them the nickname tiger owl. These sky hunters, many nocturnal and nomadic, had come to this unfamiliar land from faraway places under a bidding. A potent parliament of owls.

Here to defend the last MoFo on earth.

The owls held their breath, waiting for a signal. Kuupa, largest of the snowy owls, turned her head—a satellite dish tuned to pick up the murmur of a millipede—and lasered the polar bear with golden wrath.

"Go, Seal's Dread! Go! Goooooo!" screeched the parliament.

The female polar bear held her ground, sniffing at Dee voraciously. She let out a wet huff. Her growl detonated like a bandolier of grenades—

"There is nothing more dangerous than the Fire Hunter you keep."

"Fuck off!" I said, with some emphasis, puffing my feathers to show her how intimidating I am even though I weigh the same as four sticks of butter.

"The last Skinner cub. She will be the death of you, Crow. *You keep a monster in your nest.*"

Kuupa struck like the Discovery Channel's F-111 Aardvark swing-wing bomber. Her militant talons snatched at wicked white fur, at Grecian column legs. The other snowy owls joined in the mobbing. The polar bear pulled her head from the window, lifting to swipe at the owls. Deterred only by the sheer number of raptors, she lowered, taking a last lazy paw swipe at Kuupa.

The behemoth white bear left in a slow, commanding lumber, Queen Of The Ice Fields. And with her she took our sense of security. Our confidence trailed behind her in clawed tatters. That day, a polar bear stole my hope of returning to Seattle.

My hope of going home.

The snowy owls flew in through the rickety old window that would never be left unguarded again. I hopped gently onto my nestling, dabbing at her with yarrow leaves and smoothing her arms with my beak, inspecting her for damage.

"You're okay, my nestling; everything's okay," I told her, breathlessly. "I'm here." Every feather of my inky body trembled with terror. Never had I so much to lose. Here I was, a crow with a disability—a broken wing that wouldn't let me ride the sky—and lofty ideas, making every mistake possible, endangering this tiny, fragile being. I was the uniformed guard, strained and sweating under an African sun as I stood watch over the very last rhino in existence.

Ookpik and Bristle perched at each side of Dee's bed, their talons scarring the cardboard. Wik nestled on the chubby, neglected stove. Kuupa fluttered her peppery wings—a sound like the flogging of old dresses—atop the table, sending cobwebs into a winged waltz. For the first time, I noticed a small silver band spiraling her leg. The hundred smoldering eyes of a great owl guardianship sequined the trees outside the cabin, and I knew then that it was Kuupa who had summoned them. Kuupa kept her razor gaze on little Dee as Ookpik, Bristle, and The Hook fussed over the last MoFo. But now, Kuupa saw Dee in a whole new way, because the bear had taken one of her golden eyes—a potential death sentence for an owl. She did not complain as Little Wik tended to it. I realized then where Kuupa truly perched, how much tiny Dee had invaded and conquered, burrowing into the hearts of the owls. Dee was not only a nestling but an owlet.

Would a guardianship of owls be enough? I was haunted by the bear's scowl—the raw liver-blue loathing that ran an Arctic chill through my plumage. I thought of what the polar bear had growled...

"*She will be the death of you, Crow. You keep a monster in your nest.*" Because while the last of the MoFos was my miracle, a priceless present to which I had pledged my plumage, to many others she was an unspeakable horror. She was the last of the most violent species to ever walk this earth. Creatures of the natural world called humans Hollows because of their dead-eyed destructiveness. Death in bald flesh. What had the bear called her? A Skinner. A Fire Hunter. The creator of the most feared entity in the animal kingdom, that silver slug—the bullet. They saw her as an incubating killer. Now just a small, beady-eyed pet-store snake, one day she would grow into a murderous predator, taking lives and stealing skins. I often thought of something I'd read by the MoFo T.S. Eliot—"*We do not know until the shell breaks what kind of egg we have been sitting on.*" If only I could tell every being on earth that I was reanimated with purpose because of Dee. If only they knew what I knew, if I could show them the crackling genius of MoFos, the kindness, the creativity. Humankind.

*Human. Kind.*

On grocery store excursions, I never actually laid eyes on the mythical milk of human kindness, but never doubted the existence of at least some version of it—perhaps the Lactaid of human civility? If only creatures of the natural world knew about good MoFos like Elizabeth the First, Chance the Rapper, and Ellen the Generous. But how could I show them? There were no more left. *Aura* confirmed it almost daily, along with other darker happenings that I couldn't allow to dilute my focus on the last MoFo on earth.

And I had more to worry about than what was lurking in the molasses mantle of an Alaskan night...

"The Hook," I asked the great owl, his plumage a brighter white than new printing paper, "what were we discussing a few suns ago? Tell me again."

"Your molting is very bad, so you asked what I thought of the moss toupee you were wearing, and then you asked if I thought your legs looked too skinn—"

"Oh, what? No, not that, the other thing. About the geese."

"The geese no longer make their great migration; they stay here and feast off the seagrasses."

"And the shoreline? What did you tell me?" I said, regretting being so dismissive of him days ago. I had been pretending to listen but actually reading a book I pillaged from the Nightmute library about potty training your young MoFo called *Poop! There It Is!* It felt sensible to get a jump on that shit.

The Hook's face was round and inquisitive. He moved with the confidence of a glacier. "The ocean's angry, coming for us, eating up the distance from the cliffs. We see it all with our watchful eyes. The insect hoards rise. They are destroying the trees and so the ebony forest is spreading. This is the change we see with our watchful eyes."

"Do you know why this is happening?" I asked, afraid of his answer.

The Hook rotated his head 180 degrees. Owls do that shit willy-nilly, but it brought back unsettling memories. "We do. It is the Sun. We can no longer read the big beautiful blue like we used to, because the Sun is nearing. She drinks the lakes. She gives life and she claims it. There is no greater power than Her."

"I understand." And I did. I understood everything. My nestling sat, ocean eyed, learning the peppered patterns that speckled her owls while sucking on heartbreakingly beautiful fingers. It was a betrayal to tell The Hook nothing of a warming world and its cause, but the risk was too great. I would stop at nothing to protect my nestling, and so I would not share that the oily footprints of MoFos were still changing the shape of the soil beneath us. That the symptoms were starving bears and ebony forests.

I was thinking about this—and about how I owed a bunch of caribou a fucking epic apology—when I felt a burning sensation. Someone was watching me with a gaze with more flame than Crunchy XXTRA FLAMIN' HOT® Cheetos®. I whipped my head through the window, pulse spiking. The eyes were a haunted shade of yellow. They belonged to a bald eagle, a magnificent beauty with a wingspan that kissed the horizon and a head as white as the tundra. Migisi's dedication to the tiny MoFo remained as mysterious as her past. Whether danger flowed through her pinions like mountain winds or she saw her own destiny tied to us as clear as a migration map, I was eternally grateful. Migisi and I shared a barbed look we both understood. I didn't speak so they didn't hear—mosquito, skimmer dragonfly, sphinx moth, aphid, blue dasher, locust, mantis, even the leaves—they were all listening. And we couldn't have them listening. Migisi and I stayed silent, but the polar bear had confirmed what we already knew, a knowing of birds from the blue-footed booby to the Japanese quail; *eggs must always stay hidden.* In that moment, by a single look, we decided to keep our Fabergé flower here in Toksook Bay, away from the roaring appetites of the world outside. Where we had protection with binocular vision and heads that rotated 270 degrees. As much as I wanted to take Dee home to Seattle, staying put was the only chance she had at survival. Because, just as with the final Cheeto® of the bag, everything is more desirable when it's the last.

I am The One Who Keeps.[2] It is known.

Migisi had been searching since we got to Toksook Bay, just as I'd asked. And now, I knew by her stare—a look that could debone a herring from the peak of Denali—she'd found something. In her talons, stippled with ruby blotches of blood, unmistakable even from the most ambitious branch of a white spruce, was a piece of paper. I could see that the paper had

---

2  Creatures of the natural world call me The One Who Keeps because I'm the one who keeps the last human and hope alive. "The One" can sometimes be plural; for example, wolves are all called The One Who Conquers. Crows call me Blackwing. I have some other less desirable nicknames like The Legless Half-Breed Made Of Tumbleweeds (I think this was butchered by the avian rumor mill). Earthworms just call me Dickface.

MoFo writing on it, the heart song of a literate crow. Soon the sun would sink, Migisi and I would retreat into the spruce's shaggy canopy, and I'd set my eager eyes on that paper. When, under the cover of night's licorice wings, the snowy owls—day hunters—closed their watchful eyes.

I'd been wrong about things before—penguins in particular—but I could never have predicted what would happen to our little murder. I was wrong about keeping secrets, I was wrong about alliances, and I was fundamentally wrong about my little nestling, Dee.

I should have never compared her to a flower.

# CHAPTER 2

S.T.
TOKSOOK BAY, ALASKA, USA

Somewhere back in the days of healthy MoFos, days distinguished by a chorus of cars and redolent pork belly fumes coughed from the lungs of a food truck, I heard a MoFo compare raising a child to gardening. I guess raising a child is a bit like gardening, if your garden is prone to explosive diarrhea and screaming like an orgy of bagpipes and malfunctioning farm equipment. Don't get me wrong, Dee was the most scintillatingly brilliant thing that had ever happened to me, but I had a formidable parliament of owls[1] assisting me with every midnight meltdown or fistful of blackberry slop lobbed at me, and I often felt like I was stuck in the crow's nest of the *Titanic*.

After the incident with the starving polar bear, the snowy owls and I decided to keep the last MoFo on earth as secret

---

1 I once saw a documentary in which an owl murdered a woman on a staircase and then framed her husband, to give you an inkling of owl ruthlessness.

as a stonefish. Migisi was panicked about the bear disclosing the whereabouts of our nestling, but there is an adage of the tundra and the taiga—*starving bear won't share.* The polar bear wouldn't whisper of a failed hunt. Predator's pride. The owls hung dusty strips of dried baleen over the window, a shield from prying eyes. We had the cover of our beloved trees— spruce, birch, aspen—a strange, small forest in Toksook I couldn't account for because these trees don't grow in the tundra. But I have to tell you, paranoia swooped in. Migisi and I were hiding the contents of the letter she'd found, not just from the little being I loved most in the world, but also from the stately owls who gave of themselves so completely. I was terrified to ask them why, for fear they'd change their minds, unfurl those great speckled wings, and soar to greener Pampers. The prophet Emily Dickinson once said, *"Hope is the thing with feathers."* I was a bird with hope laced through every barbule of every feather, but I couldn't protect the last MoFo on my own.

I was grateful to Alaska's arboraceous armpit and the shelter of our abandoned Toksook nest. Every time little Dee threw back her head and bellowed loud enough to knock Jupiter out of orbit, I leapt into action, tending to thirst, hunger, heat, cold, ennui. I was court jester, doctor, butler, and teething toy. Baby MoFos are like baby birds. They are altricial, hatching soft-skinned and helpless. MoFo hatchlings, however, lack the sense to be silent, screaming like hypo-chondriacal goats in labor (which is called "kidding," I'm not even joking), no matter what predator might lurk nearby. Those skull-rattling, sweaty-pink cries of a wounded animal— we couldn't afford their price. And her smell. That salty-sweet, velvet smell of a MoFo, known across this big beautiful blue. To some, that scent is the first flicker of terror. To others, it is a summoning. Like Cinnabon. And if she caused a fur-lined ear to erect or was breathed into the olfactory kingdom of a creature, word could, would, at any moment, spread on the gossamer filaments of a dandelion, or the casual prattle of a warbler, and what then? In order for Dee to survive, no one, not mite nor musk ox, could know that she was breathing.

I'll admit, I was sneaky. Perhaps it was the MoFo part of me. I'd admired Big Jim's ingenuity when he'd use a voice-changing app on his foredoomed phone to call in sick, which worked even though he sounded like a blow-up doll perishing from a beak-poke wound to the chest. Perhaps it was the crow part of me that learned from watching my crow friend Kraai build decoy nests around the North Creek wetlands to prevent predators from finding where the hatchlings really were. Regardless, every now and then I tuned in to *Aura* and made an inquiry.

What is *Aura*? *Aura* is nature's communication network, a living symphony of sound, where birds and bees and mammals and trees share news about life and love and sometimes tweet about what they ate for breakfast. It's accessible to any living being who is willing to open their minds and earholes, even MoFos, once, before we lost them to technology and their own magnificent minds. Below the lively loam realm, the network is called *Web* and bubbling under the world of water, they call it *Echo*.

I'd tune in to *Aura*, mimicking the owls' doglike bark to ask if there were any healthy MoFos sighted. I did this because I, Special Agent Turd, wanted to know if anyone had an inkling about our Fabergé flower. And because I'm an irrepressible optimist who still dreamed that somewhere out there was another MoFo. That Dee was not the last of her species.

Once in a while, the owls would insist I take a small break.

On my short walks, a creature of *Aura* would jump or flutter toward me. Once, a Seahawks-green buffalo treehopper. An achemon sphinx moth startled me one night. A convergent lady beetle, a differential grasshopper, a dogbane leaf beetle, and a naiad of a dragonhunter—a scary brown larval beast about to burst through its exoskeleton *Alien*-style into a formidable dragonfly-hunting dragonfly. Once, it was, quite regrettably, a brown marmorated stink bug.

"Oh, look, it's The One Who Keeps!" they'd say. "You are a legend!"

I appreciate sycophantic outbursts, but I'd have to shoo them away. Being an infamous legend and (handsome) hero has its perks, but it was too dangerous to enjoy idolatry and autographs. I could not afford anyone finding out about my nestling. I had the owls forward all *Aura* messengers looking for The One Who Keeps to one of my many fake addresses.

We kept Dee inside the little cabin. I couldn't fly and she couldn't walk, so our world was tight as a fist. I traded sleep for running lists of the dangers she faced—Alaska's icicle-sharp elements, the fauna, the flora, and the cherry on my cake of doom—illness. I scanned little Dee obsessively for signs of change. Red eyes. Craning neck. Little red dots. Anything that meant we might lose her to something I dare not speak aloud. I read a lot, mostly about dinosaurs, poetry, and dinosaur poetry (a niche genre), but also about the horrors of smallpox, dengue, Ebola, and the flus—Spanish and avian. The biggest threat to MoFos—as with birds—was not the perceptible but the microscopic. Invisible assassins. What if, much like a sand fly frozen in amber—a sand fly who had sucked the blood of a dinosaur and cocooned a terrible virus—there were still incubators of the virus out there? Inside an electronic orb of amber. Waiting for an *on* button. Waiting for Dee.

This is why I'd taken up drinking.

Feeding her to keep her healthy became a full-time gig. Some endangered provisions were found—tins and tubs of corn, beans, beetroots, peanut butter, and, mercifully, a stash of baby formula. Alas, no fucking Cheetos®. Ookpik and Bristle punctured the cans with their scythe-like talons. I rationed these into tiny portions, hydrating the formula with fresh water and smearing it into her little pink mouth. The owls were rudely insistent on bringing her their kills, and after a soap opera–inspired tantrum, I acquiesced, but under the condition that *all kills be cooked.* In flagrant detail, I recounted the time Big Jim ate a fuzzy Kentucky Fried Chicken thigh from the back of the refrigerator and ended up doing a three-day impersonation of Old Faithful. No, my nestling would not have raw, headless food. She would eat properly, like a MoFo. One day, with fork, knife, and napkin. She would grow up to have manners and cross her legs and say "good afternoon" and apologize when someone bumps into her, like the BBC America MoFos with the exotic birds' nests on their heads.

I found a stash of matches and lit the chubby stove, which spluttered to life, grateful to be reanimated with purpose. The owls—master stealth hunters—brought her fish and squirrels (no doubt caught in various positions of the Kama Sutra, those venereal nincompoops), rabbits, and fucking headless red-backed voles.

Me, every day: What's for dinner?

The owls: Thank the sea and stars! We've found some red-backed voles!

Me: *smacks head onto table*

Holy Hostess snacks, I'd trade my one good wing to never see another nidorous, lumpy red-backed vole without its stupid noggin again. In case you're wondering, red-backed voles taste like the exact marriage of discounted Albertsons chicken and losing the will to live.

I became a bit of a helicopter parent. A sort of persnickety, flightless UH-60 Black Hawk who hovered and droned on about decent education and things being better in my day, like functioning toilets and Taco Tuesday. Dee imprinted on us birds, studying us with retentive eyes. There were gorgeous days like the one when Dee first laughed—a sunny hiccuping of notes that turned flower faces and roused the cricket choirs. Woven into her cloud-climbing giggles was hope for a better world. The snowy owls and I flapped our wings, dancing our delight at all her delicious firsts. She bobbed her head in unison, clever girl—a brilliant mimic.

Soon, Dee started to crawl, and I spent my waking hours guiding her with encouragement or gentle pokes with my beak. I used the fine upbringing I'd received from Big Jim, the training I'd given my Dennis, luring her with treats and treasures—beak blobs of peanut butter or a shiny spoon. I rewarded the good and ignored the bad, which was very difficult when she was jamming her face into the stove or attempting to lodge a fishbone into the sky by way of her left nostril. At the end of those kinds of days, I allowed myself a little of the treasure I'd found sequestered in another Toksook cabin cabinet—my Gaelic giggle juice, Scotch. I fashioned a tiny tool out of paper clip wire and a tea bag, dipping the tea bag into the Scotch bottle's amber neck to sip up its sweet offerings. Come springtime it was easier; I was enabled by the American robins (whom the MoFos had honored with the genus and species name *Turdus migratorius*). The Migrating Turds showed me how and when to eat fermented salmonberries to get shit-faced. According to my library studies, frosts and thawing (which allows in yeast and speeds up fermentation) were happening more frequently thanks to a warming climate. Booze berries galore!² Kuupa seemed disapproving, evinced by how she repeatedly used an upside-down sweetgrass basket as my miniature drunk tank, but jeez—it wasn't like I was going to fly under the influence like the Migrating Turds did. I was a grown-ass crow. If, on my negligible Shit Turd time, I wanted to drunkenly attempt to fly again by launching myself off shelves or express myself through a supersonic reciting of Bon Jovi lyrics, then by Fritos, I would. Big Jim would have definitely high-foured me for it.

Dee started to walk. And thank our lucky gulars we had an enormous parliament of owls to help. The snowy owls became experts at ushering her around by fanning their great wingspans, and believe me, even with one eye, Kuupa had total mastery of that parental "Don't make me turn this head around" look. Seriously, she could go full *Exorcist*, rotating her head 270 degrees. The other owls, flammulated to great horned, took their nomadic wanderings in shifts, many raising their own families on Toksook Bay, which became littered with large nests and planet-eyed balls of fluff, much to the chagrin of the red-backed vole population.

What is it like to live among a giant parliament of owls? It's fairly epic. I enjoyed being the only crow alive who had a window into the world of these magnificent birds.³ I enjoyed their speckled majesty, their almost supernatural sense for danger. The only reason we were able to fend off bears, wolverines, coyotes, and every other one of Alaska's festering fart bags was because of the owls. I will be forever grateful. But if you will indulge me a small complaint? They have these long moments of utter silence—imagine hanging out with

---

2  Who knew the face of global warming would be a bunch of birds forgetting the notes of their love ballads and using *Aura* to send melodramatic messages to their exes?

3  Owls are fledgling thieves, so they are *numero uno* on the shitlist of corvids.

chronic meditators. They just sit there and blink and move their heads like robots, and it's very uncomfortable for a bird like me who is used to a lot of bubbly corvid chatter. I think it's because they hear *everything* and so they're busy taking it all in. Seriously, owls can hear a microbe farting ten feet below a snow dump in the chaos of *Web.* Also—my apologies if you're eating—they swallow those stupid red-backed voles, toads, lizards, fish, or whatever *whole* and then yarf up hideous little pellets, like nightmarish parcels of undigestible fur and entire preserved critter skeletons. Honestly, with these abominations strewn all over the place, Toksook was starting to look like Ripley's Believe It or Not!, so I told the parliament that they had to dispose of their fucking pellets far away from the cabin because it was unsanitary for Dee and was putting me off my earthworms. Typical roommate stuff, I guess.

Then the owls got down and dirty with procreating. This was awkward for me. You can't unsee owl sex—all that biting and gyrating that you have to close your eyes and sing the chorus of "Uptown Funk" to get through. All of them except Kuupa. The great snowy owl never partnered or laid eggs. She had just one owlet whose name was Dee. So, the varied night hunters boned and worked together to fight off predators, to hunt for fish and firewood. They found medicinal plants, and they followed my insistence of finding every last electronic MoFo item in Toksook Bay and hiding them under the floorboards of the Toksook Bay health clinic, covering the boards with clothes and plastic bags. I had never been clearer about any-thing, even the fucking skeleton pellets; if there was only one rule left on this big beautiful blue, it was that *Dee would never go near any MoFo devices.* Was I sure that the virus came through the screens? I'm a crow, not an epidemiologist. Viruses, by their nature, are sneaky fuckers. Had I seen a MoFo physically change because of a screen? No. But I'd seen sick MoFos and

Changed Ones tirelessly, violently hunting for screens, and that made technology the most dangerous element on earth. Dee would never go anywhere. She would stay right here with me. I was The One Who Keeps.

Sometimes I just stared at this sweet, sweet little MoFo, with her hornet's nest of hair, sticky fingers, and electric energy, and I just couldn't believe she was here. She was so gentle, holding me as if *I* were the Fabergé flower, her nose pressing into my plumage. Dee couldn't sleep unless her crow was close. Yours truly became hopelessly tenderhearted, weeping at sunsets and making up bad poetry about my best friend Dennis like a sentimental dildo. Oh, but Dee's walking! My chest burst to watch her lift herself in perfect bipedal fashion. I was so proud, so admiring of her gait, even if she initially resembled a gibbon on drugs. Under the ceaseless watch of feathereds, her walking got stronger. Dee got stronger.

Her education became my main objective—I was obsessed. I lamented that I could never send her to a proper school, that she wouldn't make MoFo friends, or eat gelatinous prefrozen mystery blobs of cafeteria food. MoFos were pack animals, and Dee wouldn't hold a hand or have a prom or a girlfriend or a boyfriend or driving lessons or…don't worry, I never let myself dwell for long, because I'm a fucking optimist and that's what spirituous salmonberries are for. I had the most important job on earth, and I wasn't going to mess it up. I told Dee stories (especially effective when she couldn't walk; a captive audience is best) about her magnificent kind and her slobbery, heroic Uncle Dennis. In *Aura*, there is nothing more important than story; it is how we learn and grow and heal. So, I told her about Big Jim—about the time we had a Beecher's cheese curd, Cheeto®, and Pabst Blue Ribbon picnic at the Skagit Valley Tulip festival; and the time he ran naked under the Space Needle, flashing his figs on King 5 News; and about how his heart was the size of the moon. I collected the books I could find, reading to her, everything from *The Snail and the Whale* to *The Pop-up Book of Phobias* and *Everything I Know about Women I Learned from My Tractor*. I worked on teaching her MoFo language incessantly, using my best Big Jim voice to sound out the names of things.

"Tree," I'd tell her, as she ran her fingers along the flaky bark of an alder. "Birch. Poplar. Spruce."

"Moon," I'd tell her, as she lifted a filthy forefinger to the lunar sorceress who no longer had to battle the neon of cities. "MoFos left footprints up there, Dee. We all used to celebrate genius astronauts like Neil Armstrong and Buzz Lightyear." MoFos, I told her, painted footprints all over the big beautiful blue and beyond.

"Danger!" I'd scream at her as she attempted to kiss a bald-faced hornet. "Dee," I'd say, as she peered at her rippling reflection in the puddled aftermath of a rainstorm, and she'd shriek back at me in perfect owl. "No! *Dee!*" I'd squawk, and her single gossamer thread of patience would snap, and she'd jerk her head, birdlike, and squawk back, "Dee!" perfectly mimicking my strange, nasal tone. What a knife jab, a reminder that I couldn't perfectly provide the variety of sounds she needed to learn her own language. Her MoFo words were clipped and parrotlike. My language was evolving, certainly, as so much was in this new world. I had noticed something strange about Dee from when she was very young, perhaps because she was the sun around which I circled. And I wasn't going to give up until I'd fixed the problem. She didn't like to repeat things all day long. I learned this the hard way when she stuffed me into an old bread bin so she could dance in the dirt and later hide from me in the cavity of a black spruce. The stories she truly enjoyed were the ones about her Uncle Dennis. By the forty thousandth time I'd told her about his heroic luring of monsters with an iPad, I'd have rather been entombed in a shrine of owl pellets than utter another word of it again, but I had to trust. With time, I knew she'd come around; I knew she'd be the most perfectly well-adjusted MoFo that ever lived.

So, please allow me, with excitement in every sparking cell of my body, to properly introduce my Dee, the last MoFo on earth. Many summers old now, she stood as tall as the nearby diamond-leaf willow. Age is relative, and I would guess she was around thirteen (not old for a MoFo, but geriatric as fuck for a banana slug). Her duckling's down hair had grown into a mass of arguing inky tendrils, accented with leaves or an assortment of rude arthropods I'd be forced to assassinate. She sported a white snake of exposed scalp where the hair would never grow again—a pale haunting from the last time she would ever disobey Kuupa. Please admire her smooth skin, a skin that stole the sun's rays in summer and returned them in winter, a skin mired in mud and the frantic footprints of insects. She was unlike the ladies of television with sleek hair and macaw-colored clothing. She wasn't as frail or willowy as the MoFos in magazines and wobbling along runways. The only crow's-feet she concerned herself with were mine, which she loved to inspect up close as I used the opportunity to work on her counting: "One, two, three, four toes!" Dee was speckled like the ink-spattered wings of her owls, brushed with bites and bruises and scars—tattoos of the brave. Her natural stance was a slight squat, charcoal feet clawing into the earth, quad muscles poised for a sprint. Her body was not a canvas to accessorize; it was too busy with the business of healing—fingers and toes bedeviled by dark shadows from a battle with frostbite, entangled roots of sunken scars across her chest, invisible jigsaws where her bones had fused themselves back together. Her body was busy scaling spruce, digging up the earth, and pounding barefoot across frigid waters. It ferreted, tracked, and burrowed. It growled and squeaked and chittered. Dee was a gorgeous atlas of falls and toothmarks and the crystallized peril of ice, earthy and unbridled. Like her skin, she had calloused and had long given up crying. I could barely keep clothes on her, and she wouldn't touch a shoe, sniffing them suspiciously and hurling them into the nearest blackberry tangle, even when the owls brought her every size of sandal and mukluk from here to Nightmute. But my goodness, was she strong and blistered and beautiful in the way she tore into the stomachs of salmon, or how her bewitching fingers danced along the feathers of owls during our nightly preenings. And at this age, she was big enough to host a raptor, which she did routinely. With a perfect fluting of notes or a gentle *Oooo Oooo Oooo* followed by a scratchy *krrrk krrrk krrrk*, she strode like a queen through Toksook. On her arm, our beautiful eagle Migisi or The Hook and his shock of phantom-white feathers. And always, always her eternally devoted crow nearby.

Dee wasn't afraid of blood or darkness or death or fangs. In fact, the only problem with my perfect nestling was that she wasn't afraid of anything. But the Alaskan wilderness was afraid of her. Seals hated her, with stories bubbling through *Echo* about culling and clubbing, red spills on snow. They bobbed above the bay's biting swell and barked colorful insults. Rather understandably, red-backed voles—the rodent equivalent of butt plugs—despised her. Certain insects sent warnings through the fungal network about the creature preened by birds, singing creaky tunes about those who had been crushed by the cruel beaks of her defenders. Fish scattered when she neared. Earthworms all but held up "end of the world" signs at her. Rabbits brought her clumsy sounds into their long ears, sniffing the syrupy scent of her stride from far, far away. Even our extended owl parliament became uncertain of her occasional outbursts and blustering tantrums. It would start with a scowl, a squall blustering inside her, until she bared her teeth and screamed.

"What?" I'd ask her, in desperation. "Tell me! Tell me so I can make it better!" But she was already beating the abandoned ATV or striking a shovel into a brick building with metallic chimes after the latest attempt at shoeing her. She broke things—MoFo relics—in the dexterous crush of her fingers. A tree, the soil, or a plant would never receive her wrath, but her aggression caused a rustle in the leaves. Messages spread on the bejeweled backs of beetles. Dee teetered on a seesaw of delicate and dangerous, an unsettling puzzle no one could solve. And she was regressing. Dee was able to speak MoFo in clipped sentences, but she no longer wanted to practice words. I watched her press her head to the mud or sit motionless in a tree, lips moving as if she were talking to an imaginary friend, and I worried. And every night, her staring competition with the moon. She couldn't sleep until she'd checked its spectral glow. She made up odd rules about things—walk under these trees; touch this, not this. I couldn't stop her from sniffing lichen, tracing the scars of bark, or from following dragonflies on long, winding, and sometimes very dangerous walks. Was there something different about her beautiful brain? The owls watched silently, though I could sense a disturbance among them, subtle as the eye roll of a Brookesia micra chameleon as she gives her very last shit.

So, here we were, Professor Shit Turd and the empress of owls, who had led us to the shoreline on an ambling walk, where she stopped to inspect shells. She trailed her fingers along the foam, cupping her palms to magically form a chalice and douse salty spray onto the fat mats of her hair. I had taught her to collect and cache things, and she had a growing assembly of shells that made her cheeks lift. I projected loudly, competing with the Bering Sea and her wandering mind.

"She sells seashells on the seashore!" I said to her emphatically.

She ignored me, curled in a perfect comma over a suicidal red sea cucumber who was loudly lamenting his terrible, terrible life choices. Dee carefully scooped salt water over him and hummed gently.

"Dee, don't sweat the petty things and don't pet the sweaty things!"[4]

She dove her fingers into the soft, wet sand and smiled at its gentle suction, elated at the hermit crab that scuttled over her plum skin and on to finish the interior decoration of his fine home. She slipped her finger into her mouth, tasting sand. She wasn't listening to my excellent lessons. She was in the mind of a crab, listening to the beckoning of the beach in front of the broken village of Toksook Bay.

"Dee! Again! The seashells that she sells are seashells, I'm sure!" I rapped my beak on a flatheaded rock in frustration.

Dee spun, baring her teeth at me with a low, shuddering growl.

"Words! Speak!" I said to her, but I'd already lost her to a gull's crescendoing cackle, and she lifted her head to laugh back in his throaty language, a shared joke that broke me. My heart was sucked out with the tide. My worst nightmare was crystallizing in front of me.

I was failing. Dee was disappearing into the wilderness.

The Very Last of an extinct species didn't care for my stories or the eminence of her full-flavored history. She was tuning her ears, straining to find the stories of *Aura*, the song of sand and soil. She knew the hidden secrets of owls and to steer clear of the stomach assassins of the Alaskan wilderness—

---

4  Wise words I learned from a funnyman MoFo named George Carlin, who was definitely part corvid.

death camas, skunk cabbage, arrow grass, cow parsnip, queen's cup, snakeberry, devil's club—but she could give a red-backed vole's ass about their names. She knew these devils as the wild knows them—by sight, smell, by a minuscule murmur of her muscles, a silent stir in the intestines, with eyes that shine in the dark. Proper nouns, pictures of MoFos, and the pages of books did not light her up inside. A species devolving. I was terrified. I was losing her.

Dee was becoming an animal.

# CHAPTER 3

ESCAMOSO
ARGENTINE BLACK AND WHITE TEGU
EVERGLADES, FLORIDA, USA

Ha ha! Taste them first.

Lick them in. All of them.

The tongue lashes out, whips the air in pink punishment. I taste the exhale of the steamy swamp, mud bubbling up—*blub blub*—hiding things that do not wish to feel the shiny squeak of my teeth. Leaves of sea grapes, waxy and fat as flattened frogs fear me. Old bald cypresses fear me, those great gray ghosts. Ha! Flatten deer moss and dog fennel with the savage scales of belly. Scales of mine are black, white, black, white—a devilish dance of bone and night. Jaw of mine is to crunch moonlight-pale eggs, their sunny yolk spilling down the savage scales. To savor little lizards and the ivory pebble of soggy rat skull.

Swamp is alive. Breathing and belching. Cicada's symphonic scream. Orb-spider scurries away in golden strings. Grasshoppers bare the fire colors, an inkling of the poisons inside them. Swamp is damp, dark, and full of bite. Here are the hunting grounds of the mosquito monarch.

Clutch of eggs call to me with their sinewy, sanguine smell. Smells of red insides, of hot life. *I'm coming for you.* Wading through green water, pushing ripples aside with meaty tail. Next, bring them into me through rounded reptile eye. And so. Nest is filled with eggs. Ha! But the smell tells me a thing. These eggs are not the eggs of the alligator, swamp's thick-skinned murk. These eggs belong to something else.

Stop.

Yes, I taste him.

The air smacks of slippery scale. Turn and eyes can see the tarry glide of him, this great python of Burma. Longer than a felled tree, shiny as turtle bones.

He wants the eggs. He is coming for the eggs, greasy and slick, rippling through the swampy *blub blub*, no legs just speed.

*Hsssssssssss.* A warning. These are not his eggs, but he claims them. A colossal arrowhead lifts from the swampy soup, midnight eyes and darting tongue.

Nope.

Running, running, I retreat quickly, scampering to safety behind the frantic roots of a mangrove. He can have all the stupid eggs. Python coils and shows the eggs his pink mouth. He will have the eggs all to him. Bah.

Stop.

I taste he is not alone.

Shuddering, low rumble, guttural and cruel, sends the green water into frightened ripples. This is not caiman. Not alligator. Long, wicked jaws are open, she shows python the teeth that will protect her eggs and stop its slither. And her sounds, a slow rolling thunder, the deep, deep roar, they keep coming. They silence the cicadas. This is Nile crocodile, new swamp sovereign from a faraway land. Now she is here in this swamp of mine.

Python's head raises from the pulpy green, coiling her long,

long self, arrow head tree-still and ready. Her tongue *flick flick flick quick quick.* Nile crocodile drags her dark armor, passing her nest of eggs that call to be eaten. She lowers her stony thickness into the liquid green and now they are face-to-face. The swamp has stopped breathing.

Python strikes, faster than huff of hurricane, teeth sinking into crocodile's lip. Crocodile hisses, shaking hard. Python holds tight, needle teeth have got the grip. She thrashes, whipping up water, she clamps deathly jaws down on the muscly middle of python. They are locked, twisty muscle and hermetic hide. Behind the mangrove roots, I will wait until my chance. To come for my eggs.

Thrashing, bite and fight, drifting away from the nest, from my eggs. Yes. I will have them. Now is my chance.

A taste fills the air. Something else is here.

I do not know its smell. This is a dark smell. This is a smell of a last breath, the tight smell of fear.

It stands on hind legs, thick as cypress boles. I have not tasted or smelled or seen this with reptile eye. Scaled feet—gray and shedding—press into mud, long of toe and claw. A twitch of behemoth claw is the only movement.

Stay still. Don't move. I must not be seen. I become root of mangrove.

The back is humped, the head—long jaw that rains a slow saliva—slit of pupil in red eye trained forward on a crocodile wrapped in a deadly Burmese constriction. It throws no sounds. Python and crocodile—in a vicious wet roll—do not know they are being watched.

Enormous thing—not true lizard, not before seen—suffers a shiver along the weblike frills of its craned gray neck. And then it moves, a heavy zigzag, painful swagger until it reaches the water's lip. Python knows now, summoned by the new smell, that dark, dark smell. Crocodile opens her jaw and python slips from her grip, cutting like a whipped ribbon through green water. Gone, gone, gone. The enormous thing slips into the water, winding toward She Crocodile. The crocodile roars, warning that death is near. A row of spines lifts on the long head of the enormous thing. The swamp shudders. It is over quickly. The enormous thing strikes faster than python of Burma, clamping down on the brain of the crocodile. She slumps, life leaving her eyes. The Nile crocodile is now a limp shell, captive in a strange jaw. The enormous thing—not one thing, not another—rotates its sharp slit of an eye to me. I am seen.

Running, running, I am scurrying, gone, gone, gone.

I will find another swamp of mine.

# CHAPTER 4

S.T.
TOKSOOK BAY, ALASKA, USA

Dee's tantrums were excruciating, as painful as when I flew beakfirst into glass over the Woodland Park Zoo and lost my sky privileges. I couldn't stop them—physically, because I am approximately the size of her foot, and emotionally, because I knew exactly what was wrong. It was as if, in an act of utter cosmic shitbaggery, someone held up a mirror as my nestling ripped bricks from a wall until her hands bled, or shredded a yellowing gymnasium banner, her echoed roars bouncing off the walls in lieu of basketballs. She dismantled endangered sweetgrass baskets and launched a frying pan through the post office window, a cascade of endangered glittering glass sending tundra swans into a frenzied flitter. And the owls, well, they saw everything. Let's just say Dee turned a few heads.

You see, Dee was stuck between two worlds. She knew she wasn't truly an animal, the fury of seals and voles and rabbits a stark reminder of her alien presence. My heart broke, watching this beautiful being smack at her rippling reflection in a tidal flat or stare longingly at a herring gull as he skimmed the sky, releasing clams to clatter onto rocks below, a fantasy of the flightless. And when she was feared by little brown bats, marmots, a porcupine, or a lemming, I saw the flare in her cheeks, felt the cruel stretch of heart tendons, the hollow pain of longing to belong. And I thought about how I was neither full crow nor full MoFo but a hybrid, and how it had taken most of my life to accept it.

You see, Dee was in love with the natural world. She spent most of her hours outdoors, preferring the tickle of a breeze to the shelter of walls. She pressed the curling cartilage of her ears to the bark of paper birches, listening to their delicate drinking. The ocean's water winked at her in silver glimmers as she wished upon every wave to sprout gills. She dove her delicious crescent moon nails into the earth, closing her eyes to feel those who toil in soil. She refused shoes because, in the manner of her beloved butterflies, she was tasting the ground with her feet. Dee was connected— perhaps more so than any MoFo that ever lived—tuning in to *Aura*, dunking her head in salt water to spy on fish and learn the bubbling nuances of *Echo*. But her comprehension wasn't perfect. Her calls remained unanswered. It was a party invitation she never received, and though I was glad, since it was safer that she stayed hidden, it was slowly strangling her. Imagine living in a body that didn't live up to the expectations flaunted all around. What had happened to the little hatchling that reminded me of a delicate flower? She was a starving spirit. What I wouldn't have given to be her, and what she wouldn't have given to be me. Each time I saw her furrowed forehead, her fingers dragging the dirt, eyes on the horizon, a nest of brambles in her mind, I knew what I was dealing with.

*When you're depressed, where do you want to go? Nowhere.*

*Who do you feel like seeing? No one.*

*Depression hurts in so many ways. Sadness, loss of interest, anxiety. Cymbalta can help.*

It was The Black Tide, that lapping sadness that came to drown the people I most loved—Big Jim, my Dennis, and now my Dee. But I would *never* let it have her. I got to work, telling her semieducational jokes that I didn't totally understand, like:

Me: What's the difference between a cat and a complex sentence?

Dee: "..."

Me: A cat has claws at the end of its paws and a complex sentence has a pause at the end of its clause!

Dee: "..."

I kept her occupied with explorations around Toksook. I brought her books about the Yup'ik, her people, who told beautiful stories, often through dances and drumming. The dances were stories of animals and birds, whom they believed had spirits, that when those animals died, their spirits inhabited other animals. I imagined Dee's grandmother, her aunt, and cousins licking their fingers while eating *akutaq*—an ice cream–like blend of sugar, shortening (or traditionally, whipped caribou fat), and whitefish, with a sprinkling of raisins, blackberries, or salmonberries. I learned that the Yup'ik word *akutaq* meant "mixing up together." I celebrated ThanksChristmasHallowHanuKwanzaa with her each year—an homage to Big Jim's favorite time of year—and I'd bring her gifts of books, empty take-out cartons, or clothes for her to hurl in the bay as she laughed maniacally. Joy was an imperative element, absolutely necessary for staving off waves of dark thoughts. The Black Tide could kiss my tiny black ass.

Not all nature disapproved of Dee. Many insects adored her in their buzzy, wriggly way. Spiders loved her and she loved them back, watching them throw silks and manifest silvery structures for hours. She befriended a black widow spider she called Ra Ra—a friendship I forbade until I was certain it was truly safe—and she sometimes spent hours catching flies for her arachnid ally, who skimmed across her skin and studied the contours of her face with eight shining eyes. I worried that they'd formed some sort of secret club together, but that was absurd—they had no true way to communicate, the silk spinner and the hominid. Butterflies lit up her very veins by landing on her skin to savor her salt. Bees loved her deeply, dancing in swarming synchronicity around her body. They taught her how to hum. I'd watch, mesmerized, as she gingerly dipped her arm into the sticky palpitating mass of a natural nest, the bees forming her second skin. And the queen bee— a young queen of the free bees—sang to Dee, a serenading like the gentle berceuse of a kazoo, an unparalleled honor, really. I believe the hive thrummed inside her, and it was these connections to the natural world that kept her afloat. She'd lick their honey off her forearms, the sky's dusky powdering of pink illuminating her sly smile. And then of course, there was Oomingmak.

Fucking Oomingmak. We heard him before we saw him. Distress calls haunted thick fog. It was afternoon but pretending to be early morning, cold as a refrigerated can of Pabst Blue Ribbon. Dee had been painting, a favorite pastime for which she used a rock to squeeze the pigments from wildflowers, mixing them with salt water to create various hues. She was putting the final touches on a painting she replicated frequently in different styles and wildflower pigments, inspired by a mural outside of her place of birth—a mural that was part of the great adventures Dennis and I had in our Seattle days. She had finished the evergreen tree and now used her fingers to add more detail to the crow, looking back at me for inspiration. I lifted my melon[1] to the sky, jerking my head around to model for her. I strutted, spread my wings, bobbed, and paraded like a deranged peacock. She laughed at me—a laughter that floated up, up, up on golden wings—and poked at me playfully, branding me with a streak of electric-blue forget-me-not hue.

"Waaaaaaaa!" came the desperate cry. Dee shot up into a low crouch like a mountain lion with a black belt in Northern Shaolin kung fu and a tragic past. I was peeved about the interruption because we were having a really nice moment. The horrible wails started up again—"Waaaaaaaaaa!"—and Dee took off, bare feet thundering across patchy grass.

"Dee!" I called after her.

"Danger!" she yelled back.

"Wait for me! Fuck!" I squawked. Dee doubled back, snatching me in her hands and bolting with me tucked into her armpit. We galloped to the shoreline, where the conundrum unveiled itself through wisps of fog. A lonely sheet of ice bobbed in the bay before us, its captor calling in breathy clouds for its life.

"Baby!" Dee shrieked, pointing. And that's when she launched herself toward the white-capped surf.

"Not with your clothes, Dee!" I jumped up and down and started shrieking for the owls—Kuupa, The Hook, Ookpik, Bristle, Wik, anyone—because when Dee set her mind to something, there was no stopping her, and this is just the same philosophy that hypothermia has. Dee whipped off the

---

1 "Melon" is what MoFos sometimes called their heads, while also what they called a protuberant and impenetrable fruit they injected with vodka. They were a very complicated species; I hope you're keeping a list.

fur-lined parka I'd finally convinced her to wear, her feather-less body swallowed by the bay. She screeched, her lungs gasping at its sucker-punch sting. She flicked her arms, kicked her legs, and thrashed through the salty assault. I jumped up and down screaming because I didn't know what else to do. Dee was an incredible swimmer—part marlin, I'm sure of it—but the frigid Alaskan waters show no mercy, and even from the shoreline, I could see that Dee was turning blue. When she reached the ice floe, she did the unthinkable; her fingers grasped its saber edge, fingers that had already had a deadly dance with the black bite of frost. My gular fluttered in panic.[2] She called to the baby. He inched away from her. She tried again, her voice rattling like an old carburetor as she sang the gentle hum of the hive, the one she used on her cherished owlet siblings. He inched closer. I turned from the ice floe at intuition's sharp call and saw the snowy owls splitting the fog apart like ivory blades. They had blankets in their talons.

"Hurry!" I screamed. "Faster!"

Dee screamed with the effort of driving her arm up out of the water and snatching the thick fur of the tiny musk ox. She yanked, jittery body flailing and fishlike. He resisted, but his hooves had no purchase on the ice, and he slid, braying and wailing, into the glacial shock. I couldn't breathe. Musk oxen are notoriously inept swimmers, and here was this hulking male calf, boulder-like, and I knew my Dee—I knew that she wouldn't let go of the thick ruff of fur around his neck and that he was about to sink, dragging my beautiful nestling with him to the bottom. To where the bones of whales become castles for scuttlers and skitterers, for the armored dwellers of dark.

---

2  Gular fluttering is just me flapping my throat muscles to keep cool or when I get anxious, but thank goodness that never happens, am I right?!

"DEE! SHIT! LET HIM GO!" I screamed. Dee reversed so she faced the calf and started to kick with all her might, treading backward, dragging that forsaken bovine through the bay. She was slick skinned and salt soaked, swimming like a creature of *Echo*, the waterlogged calf bumping along in bursts until they reached the shore. She was her Uncle Dennis's niece, stubborn and silly and brave, and I cursed bragging about his heroic swim in Martha Lake and being so utterly brilliant at storytelling. The owls fussed over Dee, who staggered out of the treacherous Kangirlvar Bay stiff, eyes rolling, her body seizing on her. I had already begun frantically assembling sticks; to hell with my rule about making fires so far from the cabin and the risk of whom a smoke signal might summon. Migisi fell from the sky with two pieces of flint and helped smother the two mammalian popsicles in blankets and the great wingspans of the ice owls.

Oomingmak wasn't in great shape right after the ordeal—neither was I, honestly, my nerves frayed like a cat owner's couch. But he recovered and then he started to grow, and then he never really gave that up. He ate clover and dandelions and sweetgrass, and basically became a Buick. Oomingmak—whom I named after the Inuktitut MoFo word for "bearded one" because Dee kiboshed "Sir Fartsalot"—was obsessed with Dee and discussed it a lot, which got very tedious, as I'm sure you can imagine. And you don't need to know much more about him other than he was humongous and smelled like the Honey Bucket of a highly trafficked dog park. For a long time, she let him invade our cabin, against my very vocal protests, and he behaved, well, like a bull in a small cabin. He sealed his doom when he first crapped in there though, releasing a great steaming avalanche of hot dung. Oh boy, did the owls let him have it, eighty-sixing him for

life. The problem with this is that his unreasonably thick and
unkempt fur brought Dee a lot of comfort and meant that
she could sleep outside, and so she often did, muddy limbs
splayed over the enormous musk ox, her body nestled into
him. And since she couldn't sleep without yours truly nearby,
I had to sleep out there in the frickin' cold as well, sitting
on top of Oomingmak's unsightly gut bucket as the wind
screamed in grief and Oomingmak snored like a hacksaw in
the midst of castration. And I was the MoFo-est of crows, who
wasn't raised to deal with the prickly business of the outdoors
and would have greatly appreciated a roof, a small heater, a
Snuggie—Jimini Crowket!—even a goddamned sock to sleep
on. Dee and I had opposing ideas about what constituted
a creature comfort. But it made Dee happy, so it was what
we did. And yours truly was sentenced to an eternity of the
itches.

There was some comfort in Oomingmak's protection—he
was, after all, a horned wrecking ball with legs—but he was still
a prey animal, a lone one at that. And since we lived in the
realm of the white wolf and Seal's Dread, near the land of lynx
and wolverines, we were helplessly dependent on the vigilance
of trees filled with yellow eyes.

Allow me one more complaint about Oomingmak: When
he got to a certain number of winters old, he became
exceedingly horny, crying out these weird musky tears and
frequently taking out his sexual frustrations on the abandoned
ATV. It was quite unsettling. Such an undignified state of
affairs for a sleek EVS E-Force electric quad. Dee didn't seem
to mind, which speaks to her kind nature and excellent
upbringing.

Having Oomingmak around meant I had less alone time
with Dee, something I resented greatly. So, to vent my frustration, I pulled his tail and found inventive ways to hop on his

back and peck at his idiot mustache-shaped horns. I know it was immature, but it was also very amusing.

So, there we were—me, Dee in the midst of a meltdown, and the great odiferous oaf. Shit, it had been a long time since she rescued that potbellied dingleberry. On the day in question, Dee's meltdown mimicked the coastal storms that struck our bay with increasing intensity. It had started as a nice day. Dee sat atop Oomingmak, as she often did, cruising through the abandoned town in a hunt for additions to her magnificent feather collection and new places to paint. She was running out of good spots to decorate with her portraits of me, the evergreen, and the eight-pointed star, and occasionally of idiot Oomingmak. We had stopped for lunch—fish for Dee and me, green shit for Oomingmak. Dee had seen them up ahead from Oomingmak's broad back. I had been trying to cure my hangover by amusing myself, stabbing Oomingmak in his backside, hopping to avoid the swishes of his tail as he tried to overthrow me. A round of robins suddenly burst into view, flapping erratically over Oomingmak's dump truck physique.

"The One Who Keeps! The One Who Keeps!" cried *Turdus migratorius*. They were twittering and giggling to themselves. The Migrating Turds had drunk like fish and were pissed as newts. Tee many fermented berroos.

"You're drunk! Swizzled! Out of your tree!" I said, not wanting Dee to see this spectacle.

One of the Turds burped and plopped to the ground. This caused the others to vibrate with laughter.

"Go away; we're trying to have a peaceful lunch!" I scolded them, and they left due east as the Silly String flies. I apologized to Dee on their behalf. Some birds just can't hold their liquor.

Then I felt Dee tense. She stood upright, gingerly, arms out to balance, on top of Oomingmak, squinting to translate the shape of a herd of caribou who had neared the bay. A tiny gasp. She slipped silently from Oomingmak, that cloven clod-hopper. Oomingmak and I sensed what would happen with heavy hearts as she tiptoed across a blanket of crunchy leaves and the buzzy world below her feet. She hid her body by crouching low to the ground.

"She is sad," Oomingmak said in his rich, barbecued baritone.

"Well done, Einstein," I said.

"Oomingmak will do anything to better her. Dee looking for more family. Dee looking for more friends."

"Good god, Oomingmak, is it the lichen? Seriously, can you step away to fart? Jesus."

"We have to always happy her."

"I'm doing my best, dude. You, however, should reexamine your diet."

"I like lichen."

"I'm not sure it likes you."

"She is sad too much," he said.

I sighed and repositioned my wings. "You're not wrong there, Oomingmak."

"I love her," he said, and I knew he meant it, and not in the way that he loved his ATV. I darted my head side to side to take him in, the innocence in his watery, soy sauce eyes, eyes that reflected my troubled nestling. I looked at the horns he never used to harm, the inordinate number of flies that ascended from his copper swirls of fur in drunken curlicues. His irrepressible heart that was no doubt the size of a Heineken keg. What we knew would happen then happened. One of the caribou sensed Dee and the herd took off, running like dappled gray clouds on lanky, liquid legs. We watched her body language change as frustration filled her. She was fed up with being cooped up in the periphery of Toksook, of being squawked and shrieked at, fed up with the word "Danger!" and of being constantly supervised. She didn't get to be an animal, but she got to feel caged.

"Dee!" I bellowed. "How many times do we have to go over this? You are not an animal! It's dangerous to be around caribou! You are a MoFo and you need to start acting like it!" It was at precisely this moment that Dee's temper stuck out its thumb and hitched an Uber to a galaxy far, far away.[3] Dee ran all the way back into the village, me and Oomingmak lumbering after her. She was already on the ATV when we caught up to her, which was fine because she sometimes sat on the ATV. But today she flipped the power switch, and the ATV, even to the surprise of itself, lit up and let out an electric hum. Oomingmak snorted in shock. And Dee, who had obviously been paying close attention as I'd demanded she plug in the solar charger while I described the ATV's function to her, knew to disengage the parking brake and twist the throttle. The next thing we knew, she was tearing across the village, jamming her fists to blare its horn, the only vehicle on earth in motion. She swerved past the little shop, the post office and what remained of its windows. She careened over shrubs and an illegal mountain of owl pellets. Then she got in between the spruce trees and I started to panic, Oomingmak unable to keep up with her fingers and their choke hold on a handlebar throttle. Migisi chittered at me from above and I called back to her, urging her to stop Dee. Oomingmak's back shuddered

3 In the time of MoFos, an Uber ride was when a driving MoFo picked you up in his Prius while blasting a Cigarettes After Sex album, and you proceeded to get in a highly inebriated argument with him about whether crows are allowed in his back seat right before you barfed on it. Curiously, no money was ever exchanged.

with ripples, presumably more shock; I'm not sure he realized his girlfriend had this sort of mobility. The last sound Dee made before the crash was a laugh, that golden laugh, and then, with a sharp crack, the ATV struck the solid trunk of a balsam poplar.

Then there was silence.

Migisi was piping out sharp notes of dread as she dropped onto the dented hood of the ATV, calling for Dee to answer. And Dee did, in a thin moan, wiping a hand across her forehead that was painted the red of a nagoonberry.

"Fuck," said Dee. I gasped. I have no idea where she learned that sort of language. She stumbled from the ATV and crouched by the balsam poplar, caressing the bark gently with her fingers, that terrible frown crowding her face. She was horrified at what had happened, horrified that she had caused harm to one of her beloved trees. But she hadn't yet realized all of it. Oomingmak and I had, so we prepared ourselves. I hopped down from his back. Oomingmak trotted quickly to the ATV. Shrieks of horror filled the forest, but one scream in particular cut through our skulls and through the sky and through time itself. A short-eared owl plunged to the grass and landed. Her nest, a bowl-shaped masterpiece she'd carved from the ground herself, lovingly lining it with downy feathers and the grasses of her choice, was flattened, tattooed by the tires of the ATV. Her chicks no longer called for her. She lifted her beautiful facial disk, a porcelain dish of shock and grief, toward Dee, who was just now realizing what she had done. The trees, now filled with all of Dee's guardians, shook with the weight of birds and a malignant heft of sadness. Kuupa appeared, alighting on a branch and catching up on the scene with glowing saffron eyes. A great horned owl cut a cold stare at the silver ring around her leg. Kuupa looked down at it and seemed to shrink.

I was haunted by the shuddering, long-ago voice of a starving polar bear: "*You keep a monster in your nest.*"

There has never been a more terrible sound than the sound of a grieving mother. That sound stole the breath from the obsidian forest.

Oomingmak put his hulking mass in front of Dee with a thud of his mighty hooves. He let out a deep warning, a thundering rumble that sounded so much like the growl of three tigers I once met a lifetime ago. Migisi snatched up Dee's outstretched arm and spread her wings, backing him up. I hopped in front of all of them, readying myself for talons I'd seen rip apart rodents year after year. After a cry from the great horned owl who had never fully accepted our Dee, the owls, every one—from burrowing to great gray to long-eared—lifted into the sky, leaving the branches to mourn them. We would nevermore be *akutaq*, the Yup'ik word for "mixed up together." Dee fought her way past Oomingmak and huddled over the nest, humming to the chicks, show-ing them the rhythm inside her, begging them to beat their hearts. Her tears rained gently down on their tiny bodies. Sad tears taste so different from other types of tears. Just ask the butterflies.

This was the day that Dee lost her guardians—all but the snowy owls, a musk ox, a bald eagle, and me. And this was the day Dee came to hate herself with a perilous passion. The Black Tide crashed in around her, beckoning her to its fuliginous waters where it could wrap its demonic kelp around her ankles and drown her. Kuupa and I looked at one another, acknowledging the unspoken. We were doomed.

I sat with Dee for hours, drinking up her tears.

And it was right there, in a grieving forest empty of guardians, near a nest that ended in tragedy, that I got an urgent summoning. Horsetail stems rippled first, quivering in anticipation. Ostrich ferns were next to spasm in long sways. Then, to the shock of every living organism in that ever-blackening forest, although it hadn't happened for so many, many years, the trees pointed their magnificent branches and called for me.

# CHAPTER 5

S.T.
TOKSOOK BAY, ALASKA, USA

When trees have personally summoned you, it's ethereal, magical, and difficult to weasel your way out of, like quicksand, jury duty, or that head-sized hole in Big Jim's fence.

"I'm not going; I can't leave her," I told Kuupa.

"Go," she said. And then she nailed me with that look ("pissed cyclops") and I started hopping because I value my life. I despised leaving Dee in her vulnerable state, broken and bent over the ground nest, but her inveterately pungent guardian Oomingmak was there. Kuupa, Wik, Ookpik, Bristle, and The Hook were there. Our beautiful Migisi was there on a low bough, her eagle eyes the magnifying glasses of the animal kingdom. And the bees had come to Dee in her despair, composing a beautiful boiling across her arms as if to protect her with another layer. I heard the kazoo chorus of the young queen bee, a humming to heal the heart. She sang about the house of honey and bee democracy. I was reminded of an expression I'd heard on *Aura* from time to time, uttered in reverence by golden tortoise beetle, dwarf dogwood, or reindeer moss: "The future belongs to the backs of bees." I reluctantly yelled to Dee that I'd be back in two shakes of an epileptic snail as I left the ebony forest, scrambling across lonely dirt roads that snake and vine through Toksook, my skin bristling with excitement.

I hopped past Toksook's tired scattering of blue and yellow houses. I skittered past rusting yellow fuel tanks that sat missing their purpose like the discarded Legos of giants. Great white wind turbines spun lazily in front of the bay, totems of another time. Power lines, many now severed and dangling like old fishing wire, loomed above me. Some of their poles leaned precariously, giving them the drooping, heart-singed look of the last barfly. I hated power lines. To other feathereds, they are perching spots. But to me, they would always be the vessel of a virus that destroyed humanity. It made me shiver to think that once upon a time, as we perched birds watched MoFos flit and fuss like ants below, the very thing that would annihilate all but one of them was running along a wire right between our toes.

The wind's glassy calls of "*Come, come...*" filled me. I had chills and not just because the Alaskan coast is colder than a penguin's revenge.

"I'm coming!" I crawked. I followed the green salute of common wormwood and the shy persuasion of Labrador tea. Everything around me trembled with anticipation. As I approached the shoreline, a lone deflated basketball refused to be bullied by the bay breeze, sullenly squatting on the sand as if it had given up hope. The Yup'ik had loved basketball, a sport that Dee could never play due to its collaborative nature. She sometimes bounced basketballs against buildings (yours truly taught her how to keep them inflated with the pumps I found cached in the locker rooms), and after, I'd excitedly show her photographs of her people—perhaps some of them even her family members—dribbling on polished courts that argued with squeaking sneakers. Perhaps the ones smiling fiercely from the bleachers were her family. I know she wondered where they had all gone. I didn't.

An abandoned fishing boat that hadn't been swallowed by the bay sat gloomily in front of the surf, pockmarked by mollusks, partially submerged in sand. I often felt that Toksook Bay missed its MoFos as much as I did.

"Where are you?" I called out. "Also, who are you?" I had been lured to our vanishing shore, a sliver of what it had been when I first came here. The seagrass gave a brittle hiss as if from the tombstone teeth of an old whiskey sipper. Seagrasses can be gruff, as they're salty survivors, but they usually mean well. I puttered along the sand, listening to every earthy clue as to who had called me away from my nestling at such a time. I followed the shoreline, nodding to a western sandpiper whose knitting-needle beak was plunged deep into the sand. Once she saw me, her speckled head shot up, beak suctioned from the hectic underworld of the beach, that wondrous womb of the worms.

"It's you!" she gasped.

"Yes, I am me. Did you call for me?"

She gestured her black beak farther down the shoreline as I heard a bubbling sigh drift from the spume. *There,* sighed the spume, *over there.* It occurred to me then that my summoning hadn't just come from *Aura,* but the underwater world of *Echo* too, setting off Roman candles in my chest. For the last lots of years it had been all about Dee, naturally, but for a moment, I felt a selfish jolt of importance.

I was a corvid on a quest!

"They're calling for me," I told the sandpiper with a puffed chest. "Not just *Aura,* but the aquatic cryptogram of *Echo!* No big deal!" I hopped faster. When my legs started to feel like spent matchsticks, I neared a patch of the bay that was hoarding mounds of salt-bleached driftwood. I caught the tail end of the underwater dawn chorus sung by fish every day. It sounds a lot like the horn section of the Los Angeles Philharmonic orchestra.

And then everything went silent. Even the grizzled seagrass. The bay's face gave away nothing with its gentle rolling.

"Hello?" I said. A tiny pang strummed inside me, which then swelled into a terrible thought. What if I'd been summoned here as a distraction? What if someone wanted me away from Dee? I shook as if sand filled my feathers. I hopped on top of the enormous driftwood log pile and called out.

"Who's there?"

Two pivoting eyeballs appeared between pale driftwood logs. And then swiftly disappeared.

"Hey!" I said. "Hey, I'm here!"

"You're here," said the crab. The eyeballs reappeared, swiveling in suspicion. His carapace was the purple of a dark bruise, his legs pumpkin orange. The crab lifted himself onto the driftwood. This took considerable effort because he insisted on waving his claws around to appear more threatening.

"I am," I said.

"What now?" he asked.

"Did you call me?"

"Call you what?"

"Call me here?"

The crab got irate. "I was called here!"

"Are you pulling my leg?" I asked. The crab's eyes widened in horror and I realized my impudence immediately. Pretty much every entity on earth is after a crab's stems; they are understandably a little sensitive.

"I'm sorry, it's just that the seagrass summoned me—"

"The seagrass summoned *me*!" He was now nervously snipping at nothing with his claws, eyeballs akimbo, and I was beginning to lose my patience with this unstable crustacean.

"Listen, Crab, I was definitely called for—I'm The One Who Keeps!"

"Oooooh. Oh. Oh, this is embarrassing." The crab blushed a deep orange. "I thought I was being called. Thought this was my big moment. Even brought this to celebrate!" The crab's right claw disappeared in between the driftwood and emerged with a small silver fish. "I was under a trench when the calling started, and to be honest, my hearing's quite shitty and sometimes I just get confused in general. I'm called The One Who Creeps."

"I see. Do you know who called for The One Who Keeps?"

Again with the retinal gymnastics. "Wow, what a delight you are! Commenting on my body, rubbing in your cosmic importance! And you haven't said even one nice thing about my fish..." He hoisted the expired fish above his head as if flaunting the Vince Lombardi Trophy.

I stepped toward the crab to get a better look at his fish.

"Whoa, steady! Back off, sand lance swindler!" He was now brandishing his right claw like a rum-addled Captain Jack Morgan. The Dungeness crab then launched from the driftwood with a small splash.

I searched the beach. The bay breathed in and out, bristle worms pinpricked the sand with holes as the ocean sucked back its salt water. Whoever summoned me didn't show themselves. I felt my stomach churn with the tide. Now I was sure of it; this *had* been a distraction. I started a deranged hop, wings splayed in a mad dash for the forest. I'm shit at counting, but I probably got in fifteen hops before I heard an aquatic explosion behind me. I ducked behind a boulder, certain my eyeballs were about to meet a ballistic missile submarine.

It was not a submarine. The creature I saw was walking on its teeth. He stabbed his sword-long canines onto dead wood, using them to launch his gargantuan mass onto the ashen cemetery of driftwood. His movement was peristaltic but magical, blubbery form flopping in jellied inches. He was the color of roast beef. He shook his massive head, tusks cutting the air like Zeus's chopsticks. And his whiskery mustache— if I remember my Nat Geo correctly, his *mystacial vibrissae*— had a life of its own, bristling and pricking its quills to suck up who I was and what I was about. That mustache—holy hot dogs—what a thing of beauty, as if a small imperious porcupine had been coronated as sovereign of this creature's upper lip. I have since written shockingly bad poetry about this mustache. All these years I'd been daydreaming about the Taj Mahal, and here, the eighth wonder of the world had come to me.

I hoped, in the manner one does when facing several thousand pounds of marine mammal, that the walrus had come on good terms. Fortunately for me, I had the advantage of unparalleled stealth, camouflaging myself completely out of sight until I knew his intentions.

"Come out here, Crow," came a voice of thunder. I reluctantly poked my head around the boulder, which was letting off a gentle vibration as if to encourage me. "Yes, yes. There you are." He took me in with protuberant eyes, pale and searching in their center. The eyes swiveled and looked precariously like they might, at any moment, plop out and BASE jump to the driftwood below.

"You called?" I asked, attempting to mask my jittery voice as a rousing vibrato. He responded with a magnificent series of lung-shuddering coughs. Three seagulls that skimmed the sky above us responded in a choking call—*huoh huoh huoh*—a show of respect. I really, really liked this guy.

"I am Onida, The One Searched For."

I met Onida at the ravaged Seattle Aquarium many years ago. Onida was a very giant giant Pacific octopus. An omniscient one at that; she told me that humankind had denied the Law Of Life. That their abuse of the natural world would result in their extinction. She said that *The One Who Hollows as well must return.* Animals believe that Onida takes on many forms, that she is a sort of spiritual embodiment of Nature herself. I don't know what I believe anymore. The only thing I believe in with certainty is Cheetotarianism.

"But you can't be Onida. I've met Onida. Onida is or was a very large oracular octopus."

"Form is as fluid as the ocean. I am Onida and I am many things. I am oracle of the ocean. I am the wisdom of water. Everyone has a journey, Crow. More than just the one," boomed the enormous walrus.

This made as much sense to me as a moose with a hat rack, but I didn't want to appear impolite. "Wow. Well, I like this new look on you. Why did you call for me?"

"You keep the last human child."

My beak dropped. I tried to recover quickly. "What? Pfffft. Don't be ridiculous."

The walrus made a rhythmic clucking with the back of his throat, that magnificent mustache rising and falling like the arms of an orchestral conductor. "You cannot hide the girl any longer."

"I don't know what you're talking about, I live here in the delightful armpit of Alaska by choice, just chillin' with my owl homies—"

"You no longer have the protection of the Taloned Shadows. You know the child has a calling. Crow, you can no longer stay hidden by the lip of *Echo.*"

"Listen, Sir or maybe Madam, you must be confused. I'm

just here, enjoying the buggy summers and numbingly frigid winters. I'm a crow who has lost his flight and can barely take care of himself, let alone a...pppffft! And you know perfectly well, there are no more MoFos, they have all died ou—"

The walrus cut me off. His massive tusks cut the air as his head thrust skyward. He let out a quaking growl that ruffled even the seagrass. I crouched, lowering my head in respect. One flipper flick and I'd be swimming with the seafood.

"Enough," said the walrus in his tuba baritone. "Come." He thrust his blubbery body forward, worming heftily over the driftwood and onto the sand. I hopped to his side, marveling at the hulking beast that blotted out the whole sky. He flung his rippling body across the shoreline, me leaping along next to him, the blundering journey of a flightless crow and the biggest walrus I'd ever seen. We must have been quite a sight.

"Your human is the last. You have done well, your part. She had no chance without you. And now it is time."

"Time? Time for what? We're not going anywhere."

"Your human has her part to play. You can no longer ignore what is happening outside of your tiny den."

"What's happening was and is happening anyway, without her. Before she was even hatched. It's not her fault and it has nothing to do with her."

"It has everything to do with her. Her species is destroying our worlds. You must show her who and what she is."

"She knows what she is. We're not going anywhere." The farther we shuffled along the beach and away from my heartbroken nestling, over the foreclosed residences of crabs, slate-colored stones, and the various salt-blanched casualties of *Echo*, the more I felt my heart muscle pull into tight cramps.

"Do you not care about what is happening? Are you content to be a bystander? You have been listening to the horrors on *Aura*, but you choose to ignore them, keeping your world small and safe. A tide pool."

"How dare you! There has been nothing small and safe about our lives here! Every minute there are a million threats against my nestling!"

"You have ignored the calls of your friends." This stung like a hornet's barb to the heart. Nothing hurts more than the truth. "Tell me I'm wrong."

I couldn't. I looked out at the shimmering ocean, at pewter clouds convening for an answer. There wasn't one. I had been hearing about the exacerbation of horror on *Aura*. For years, it had just been escalation from strangers—the buzzings of the furred, feathered, and flowered—crying out in a worsening world. But lately, I'd been getting messages from my dear old friends—the Seattle murder, Kraai, even Ghubari. The Changed Ones were growing stronger in ways they said I couldn't comprehend. Lives had been lost. They were asking for my help. But to help a friend meant to put my nestling in certain jeopardy. That just hadn't been an option.

It was Shit Turd's choice.

I pressed the great walrus: "Well, what then? We're supposed to run around playing hero against an enemy we don't know?"

"She is one of them."

"She is NOT ONE OF THEM!"

"She has a part to play in all of this. It is known."

"No, this is not some fucking stupid 1980s fantasy movie. This is my life. She is a baby."

"It is time."

"Time for what? What is it that you expect my nestling to do? She doesn't accept herself as MoFo! The only thing in this world that she wants is to sprout wings and grow roots and disappear into the soil and sea. She hates what she is and doesn't even know the half of it! You can mouth off about prophecies and Changed Ones and 'it's fucking time' like some sort of Gandalf motherfucker all you want, but I'm telling you right here and right now, you'll have to kill me before you can even lay your bloodshot, bulging eyes on her!" The silence rang after my yelling. My chest and head feathers were puffed, rising and falling rapidly as I stood in front of the gargantuan walrus holding my heart in my beak.

The walrus made a thudding *whomp-whomp-whomp* sound from the back of his throat that pulsed in blubbery ripples. A sharp belching sound and salty fish spray enveloped me. I ruffled my feathers, shaking off sushi sauce.

"She is the most important being on earth," I told him.

He lowered his mighty tusks and pushed at pebbles that freckled the sand. "She is no more important than a stone. No more vital than bacteria." He paused for emphasis. "Or a virus."

I really, really disliked this guy.

"Listen to me. Do you get this? If she leaves here, she will die."

"Yes," he said with whiskery contemplation. "She will." If I could have punched his jelly ass, I would have, made him wobble all over like pudding in the spin cycle of a washing machine lodged in the ass crack of the San Andreas Fault. He continued, that bolshie, lard-faced sea nut.

"I am not asking you. You are The One Who Keeps. You already know it is time. You are fighting yourself." The truth truly is a swung scythe. "It is time for her to start her swim."[1]

"What *swim*? What is it that you think she can do in a world she's never seen? And where is she supposed to go? If

---

1   This is a tricky translation. What he said did indeed mean "swim," but in *Echo*, it references more of an imperative migration or a life journey.

we leave here and head inland, we must survive the rest of the delightful Alaskan perils. And then what? Huh? She knows how to survive here; we had protection here. She doesn't have the tools for anywhere else. She has nothing but a body she doesn't believe in."

"You are not listening. Listen to *Aura*. Listen to *Web* and *Echo*. Listen without agenda, with every cell of your body."

I hated everything suddenly. Hated the stupid gravelly voiced seagrass, and the pathetic pebbles, and even the ancient washed-up survivalist diaper that made it here despite all these years at sea like some Tom Hanks motherfucker. *Bargain*. "Look, let me raise her until she's fully grown at least. You wouldn't send a pup or a fledgling into what's out...into this mess. She's only probably about thirteen, maybe fourteen. Please, I'm begging you to be reasonable and try to understand what we've already been through. She is prepared for nothing." I thought of my nestling, dappled with bruises and the stridulate steps of insects. My Dee, as radiant as the sun and just as lonely.

The walrus pursed his lips. That wondrous mustache collapsed on itself to release a perfect clarion whistle that cut through Alaskan air. The seagrass shimmied and waved in response. The rocks thought complex things. Distant highbush cranberry shrubs shivered their splayed leaves. The diamond-scattered surface of the water burst with a pearly school of fish. Other fish and kelp and crustaceans kissed the waterline, sending ripples into pirouettes. Like so much of the natural world, it was both beautiful and deadly. It was a water dance, enchanting to the eye, but also a message, the walrus's way to spread word through *Echo*.

I had already made up my mind, and this made things more complicated. Those of the salt kingdom would now know about the last MoFo on earth, where she was, and how to flush her from her den. She would not survive leaving Toksook Bay as such a young fledgling, and so I wasn't going to let her go. I was going to do what is done in the natural world when there is a bigger threat. I was going to build a deeper den. Shame lapped at my shores as I thought of this and of how I'd been silent to the SOS messages of my friends. I'd ignored the Seahawks-green buffalo treehopper, the achemon sphinx moth, convergent lady beetle, differential grasshopper, dogbane leaf beetle, naiad of a dragonhunter, brown marmorated stink bug, and all the others with their pleas from afar. My family in Seattle. My home. The walrus had known I hadn't been honest with even myself about the round of robins who'd shown up before Dee tried to sneak up on the caribou. They hadn't been drunk (that time). They'd been sober and sincere, and they'd come to tell me my family was calling for me. For help. And if there's one thing I'd learned right then and there about the truth, it's that you can bury it as deeply and assiduously as possible. You can even do it with a heart filled with flame. But one day, that truth will germinate and grow and writhe its winding way up through black soil, driven by a ravenous yearning for the light. It will come back glowing green. It will sprout pertinacious shoots, clambering toward consciousness. Rising with all the power of the sun.

This was instantly corroborated by Migisi. She called out in the panicked shrieks of an abused woodwind. My eyes shot to the sky, where I could see her swooping in tight loops below the clouds, directly above our tiny little village. Migisi was sounding out the alarm. Without a glance back at the walrus, I took off like a McLaren F1, earthbound, zooming over the sand as fast as my little twig legs could muster. I tore up and over the seagrass—barely registering their protests of my exit, "*Onida, Onida*"—past the shipping containers, and up the dirt roads of Toksook. I was fast, but not as fast as the trailers of upcoming attractions that flickered through my mind.

*Dee approaching the Toksook health clinic.*

*Dee finding one floorboard's edge slightly raised, a temptation too great to resist.*

*Dee curling her fingers to pull up the floorboard and finding a large rug filled with every electronic item in Toksook Bay that we hadn't dropped into the ocean.*

*Dee leaning over, picking up a long-dormant laptop, and pressing down on its power button...*

I used Migisi's looping flight as my compass and finally found myself under those tormented sky circles, rained upon by terrible, tight warning notes. Oomingmak was standing, hooves wide, an idle Mack truck, waiting. He gestured to me with his great horns. I found myself in front of the convenience store, a place we'd ransacked over the years to feed our Dee. She herself had destroyed some of its treasures, plucking out the rusty keys of its old-fashioned cash register, stripping its wooden walls for fire fuel, and riding Oomingmak inside it, which had a disastrous effect on the china plates. I'm sure there was a MoFo expression about that, but I can't remember it.

I hopped gingerly across dried manure courtesy of Oomingmak, a carpet of glass, food wrappers, and hollow cans of corn. Shelves hung loose on the walls, and in general, it had a post-riot quality to it. Migisi shot in through the open door and landed on the edge of the scarred wood counter. Long ago, a MoFo had used a knife to carve *Ikayurtarluten yullgutev-nun* into its body.[2] Migisi's eyes, cruel sunbeams, landed on something I had buried a long, long time ago. I'd buried it by concealing a latch. I'd buried it so deeply that only Migisi and I knew about it, aware of its presence because of the

---

2  I library-learned that this was Yup'ik for *be helpful to one another.*

contents of a letter we dropped into Kangirlvar Bay many years ago.

How Dee had found the hidden door may always remain a mystery to us, but no one else could have drawn back the concealing layers of hanging muskrat-fur jackets, the red oak spirit bear mask, and the ancient Yup'ik parka made of seal guts. No one else could have used a hatchet or an ax to wound the secret door, using bewitching hands and the power of a MoFo bicep to hack the wood around the latch until the door gave, convulsing open to release smells long buried.

Dee stood a few feet away from us, the ax limp at her side. I couldn't see her face, but I could see her shoulders, tight as drumskins. She had one hand clasped over her mouth because of shock, smell, both. I could see her slight squat, a readying to run. I heard sounds that for many years only came in nightmares, alive but not. A song of sickness burned our insides. Four small steps lowered into the secret room, a makeshift bunker. There were, I think, maybe twelve of them. Twelve MoFos. The only thing I have ever been sure of about this sickness is that it has its own rules. These MoFos had deteriorated but were still in this world. They were blotchy, pale, riddled with worming blue veins from years without sunlight. Their muscles had atrophied. They stirred more than moved, the milky-blue orbs where eyes once were searching endlessly. Oh, how they'd changed since I'd concealed the locked latch of this door all those years ago, Migisi's magnified eyes on me. They had degenerated and shrunk, grub-white and writhing in the darkness. And they had evolved to survive without sun in the manner of creatures who live under stone (and the Irish). A few had more legs than I remembered, adapting uniquely to live in a tight, isolated dark space, a lightless underground landscape. We were all evolving. They were nameless and unnatural. They were once Yup'ik and now they were Changed Ones. And they were Dee's family.

Dee did not make a sound as she took in this unspeakable horror, mirrors from a fun house of night terrors. They were deteriorated but still recognizable to her as her own. Rotted clothing. MoFo shapes. Something lurking in the eyes. Dee shot from the room like a startled caribou, slamming the broken door in her wake. They could not follow. But we could. She jumped onto Oomingmak who ran at her will, away from her past and the horrid reflection of who she was supposed to be, who she might have been. She had heard my stories of The Changed Ones, but they had always been just that— stories. A balm for the soul. Medicine for her broken bones and heart. And here was hard evidence that the monster under the bed was real. She must have been connecting dots, her word-processor mind spinning and sparking. She threw herself off Oomingmak when they neared our cabin. Dee ran inside. Migisi and I followed. The snowy owls fluttered in and perched, flat faces swiveling to catch up with what had happened.

For the first time in her whole life, I couldn't read Dee. She seemed so very distant, as though throttled by the undertow of big black waves. Of course she'd found our secret. She was an incredibly intelligent creature in a tiny terrarium. She had felt her way across every inch of Toksook. She silently reached for the old pair of mukluks that had waited for her by the stove all these years. They fit her. She took a sealskin jacket, forcing her arms through its sleeves. This, for me, was a triumph gilded with thorns. She picked up a book I kept in the cabin— Yup'ik, Our Stories—a book she had hurled at the cabin walls more times than I care to remember and let her eyes land on old pictures of the people in her village. I watched her eye- lashes tickle her skin like millipedes. I yearned to tell her how sorry I was for keeping a secret from her, for destroying the letter from her mother, a woman who had known that hope is the thing with feathers, who'd known her own fate, and who had been brave enough to leave her child outside a darkened shelter whilst calling on her ancestors and the softly swaying limbs of the trees for help. To give her tiny infant the chance the rest of humanity would not have.

Trauma settles in cells. It is a hand-me-down, a corporeal heirloom. A tear slipped down the cheek of my nestling, whose calloused skin could not protect her eggshell heart. She trailed a divine pointer finger along a page.

"Don't touch. Never touch," she said, and I wasn't sure what she meant.

But I would soon find out.

# CHAPTER 6

S.T.
TOKSOOK BAY, ALASKA, USA

The Black Tide was swallowing Dee whole. I tried to throw her a life jacket by reading her stories, the very thing that had kept us both alive all these virulent years. One afternoon, as the day hunters, Ookpik, Bristle, Wik, and The Hook, set out for food and I made a case for anything other than fucking red-backed kebobs or guacavole, Dee lay on the floor of the cabin. Kuupa seemed reluctant to leave, scanning Dee with that sharp, lonely eye before finally submitting to the sky as if it pained her. Dee now wore the parka and the mukluks but never a smile. Fatigue floated off her in lazy blue waves. She had lost interest in food and the sounds from her throat. So, I got busy with my stories, recalling her very favorite.

*"When I first laid my eyes on you is when I vowed to teach you everything I could about how to survive the sharp edges of where we now live. And my big journey, the one I slowly tell you as a bedtime story—along with* The Hobbit *because that's a goddamned classic— is how I know what I've told you is true. About how Mother Nature*

*is not kind, but she is balanced. Every single one of us, from amoeba to blue whale to the tenacious bloom that dares to dream of tomorrow, has their own destiny-fulfilling journey as long as their minds and hearts are open. And we are all connected by a web that looks gossamer and silvery but is stronger than a chain-link fence. And though she is tough, she is always conspiring for your success, encouraging you to evolve. You can even hear her if you listen carefully."*

She wasn't listening with her spine like she normally did. Even the mention of her Uncle Dennis no longer lit her up. It was as if her eyes were suddenly shuttered by windows, glassy and cruel. I gave her matted hair a quick preening and ran my beak gently along her cheeks. Her Uncle Dennis, bloodhound and my very best friend, had taught me that not all heroes wear Spandex and shoot out eyeball lightning; some chew the couch and drink out of the toilet. He was sunshine with saggy skin, heaven in a hound's body. Dennis was the reason I'd survived losing Big Jim, or survived at all for that matter. When Big Jim's eyeball fell out, Dennis and I had to leave our little Ravenna nest, taking on a crumbling world together. Dennis taught me how to open my heart and nose to all the glorious creatures that call it home. He made Big Jim a better MoFo and me a better crow. Dennis died running toward a stationary UPS truck surrounded by sick MoFos. In the end, it had been the siren song of old habits that meant I'd never preen his fawn fur or comfort him during wild doggy dreams again. I didn't think I'd forgive myself or survive losing him, didn't think I'd ever stop thinking that it should have been me. But with every breath and head bob and beat of my little black heart, I was reminded of how fiercely Dennis loved and was loved, and I tried to live up to that as best I could, vowing to live a life big enough for both of us. Dennis would have cherished Dee more than his own life, and maybe it took his tragedy for her to be here. When Big Jim first got sick, I almost lost Dennis to The Black Tide. I wouldn't let its currents drag him away from me. And I would never let it come for Dee.

I had to head to the library to keep feeding little Dee's soul and find a paperback heroine to lift her spirits. Once we'd thoroughly exhausted every book in Toksook, Migisi and I had to make a half-hour flight to Nightmute, where a library sat counting dust particles and dreaming of readers. We'd done this flight many, many times over the years—above a blinding ivory landscape and the muted green meadows and marshes of the subarctic tundra, land of lichen. We soared over the fiery crimson take-over of dwarf birch, over mooses (Meese? Moosees? Dammit, from here on let's just call them gangly Canadian coatracks) and lemmings and black spruces. Even through the worsening storms that plagued us, whose waves pounded us like the fists of impatient gods. We fought winds that could cut glass and hordes of insects that polluted the air in thick, buzzy clouds. Ooming-mak, that gassy fopdoodle, stayed with Dee and therefore never entered the library, so it was the Ritz-Carlton compared to the other dilapidated buildings we knew. It was a palace of musk and dust, a mushroomy museum of words, and holy Hot Pockets, did I love those trips. It was here that I worked very, very hard to evolve my reading ability for Dee's education. I discovered poetry. I fell in love with the MoFo prophet Emily Dickinson, who wrote about birds and knew a thing or two about us.

*An Antiquated Tree*
*Is cherished of the Crow*
*Because that Junior Foliage is disrespectful now*
*To venerable Birds*
*Whose Corporation Coat*
*Would decorate Oblivion's*
*Remotest Consulate*

Oblivion—the end of MoFos! She had seen it coming! She also knew to capitalize Crow because we are obscenely handsome and important.

Mostly, I discovered that poet MoFos knew a lot about the natural world, though some, like William Wordsworth, made it all sound a bit too romantic and had clearly never stuck a boob into a carpenter ant nest. Dee once did this, and she'd tell you that there's nothing romantic about it. I discovered beautiful things, like when Ralph Waldo Emerson said, "Earth laughs in flowers," which was stunning but erroneous—everyone knows the earth laughs in blobfish and Chinese cresteds!

Perhaps the most exciting thing I read about was dinosaurs. I obsessed, reading about dracorex, kronosaurus, quetzalcoatlus, troodon formosus, and my favorite, velociraptor—and discovered that birds evolved from them!

*I discovered that I'm a fucking dinosaur.*

I was always careful to put books back where I found them—mostly; alphabetizing is challenging as crap—each trip affording us one reasonably sized book that wouldn't be too hard on Migisi, which meant *Infinite Jest* would have to wait until we had a better system. This day, I was full of ferrets because I'd found a true treasure. I'd chosen a book about a young MoFo girl who was in love with the ocean and found a magical pearl that, when placed on her tongue, allowed her to breathe underwater so she could visit the world she'd always dreamed of. The girl was made of guts and fire, and I knew Dee would love it. I was also busy thinking about how we were going to stay hidden from fish-face Onida, feeling inspired by the ingenious underground shelter Dee's family had made. I was giddy all the way back to Toksook, clutching the paperback in my foot, crouched low on Migisi's beautiful black back. Herds of caribou snaked in single file below like an ant army. I was worried about Dee, but I was always worried about Dee, and I knew I could fix her sadness—I'd done it before.

Emily Dickinson foretold it.

As we started our descent from the high clouds and the little cluster of buildings that looked like cheap plastic board game pieces, I felt Migisi tighten. She dove, lifting her mighty wings, splaying her talons, pushing her cotton-white head forward. The wind-force was too much, and I dropped Dee's precious book. I screeched for her to stop.

"Migisi, slow down! The book!" I squawked over the roaring wind, feathers on end. "It's about a MoFo girl who becomes a fucking water warrior and takes on a sequestered colony of misogynistic mermen!"

She ignored me. As far as eagles go, Migisi is pretty fucking intense. I frequently encouraged her to join my spiritual journey (Scotch), but Migisi was too full of mercury and lightning and parental obligation. *Butts*, I thought to myself and then said aloud for emphasis. We weren't going back for the book.

A bleeding watercolor of Bohemian waxwings shot past us.

"Wrong way!" they cried.

Snake-necked cormorants followed them. "This way! This way! Go!"

Below, the fleeing of a marten family caught my eye, their bodies like flung Slinkies.

Migisi was a spitfire; I could barely hold on as we dropped low and swooped through the village, nearing the cabin. No Oomingmak. No Dee. Migisi lifted again with a cry, shooting us—a feathered arrow—toward a sinister tendril of black smoke. Smoke that curled from the convenience store. Everything from this point happened in slow motion. It happened without permission.

Dee stood outside the convenience store, hulking ox

Oomingmak by her side. Her eyes mirrored the orange blaze that licked the wooden walls of the convenience store. Dee gasped, and I saw her mind—that clever, clever mind—as it whirled, cranial wires connecting and sparking electric blue as she remembered what I'd shown her about putting out a fire. She pivoted and dashed away from the convenience store, her brilliant mind steps ahead of her, already snatching up her water bucket and filling it from the fresh waterfall from which she drank.

"No! No time!" I yelled to her. She stopped in her tracks and spun at a sharp crack. The fire, its blazing appetite evolving, bit off a panel from the side of the convenience store, hijacking it as it fell. The flaming wood plank made a quick bridge for the flames, which now sucked hungrily on the base of the great white spruce that dwarfed the convenience store. Dee's tree. Our trees, our protectors, who stretched their magnificent limbs to bear the brunt of storms' cruel winds. Our viridescent love affair. A home to her owls. A strange sundry forest of trees that were not indigenous to Toksook, but were somehow here, braving frigid conditions as if they were watching over us. Migisi shrieked, a warning to everything that lived in that tree. Most had already run. For some, mite and moss and mouse and even creatures too quick for an eye, it was too late.

Dee snatched up a battered blue tarp and hurtled toward the fire in desperation, flinging it forward. The fire devoured it, belching its gratitude in orange ember fireflies. Oomingmak bellowed and stamped his feet. Dee did as she was told and backed up, her own eyes on fire with shock and disbelief.

"Don't touch. Never touch," she said, barely audible above the crackle and roar. Her fingers barely concealed two pieces of flint. Flint we'd used for cabin fires, to cause the hot silver skins of fish to spit so that we could shut our stomachs up for five minutes. The silvery flint in her hands shook violently. And then I knew what she'd done. She had set the convenience store on fire to end the suffering of the MoFos inside. There was nothing natural about their stagnation. Sea stars sing often of this natural law in their briny voices: *the doomed and sickly, take them and quickly.* This ambiguous rotting, this *here but not here* was alien to Dee. *Don't touch; never touch* was what I'd told her every time we lit a fire. Nausea ambushed me. Dee had told me what she intended to do, and I had misinterpreted it, hadn't given her credit for her complexity of thought. I hadn't wanted to show her the wild nature of flames; I wanted her to know the MoFo-curated, cottony version, the safer show. I had overprotected her.

I hadn't seen the forest for the trees. I had been so focused on the everyday that I hadn't considered what the worsening storms were yelling at us with their violent insistence or what it meant to live in an ebony forest. What it meant was that the trees were now tinder, brittle, and beckoning. The fire could not have asked for a more hospitable host, and now it leapt from blackened trunk to blackened trunk, roaring in delight. You've never seen a faster fire.

And the trees. My god, the trees. They hummed from their heartwood—the center of their beautiful trunks—a chorale invocation of love and thanks. They shivered their silvery leaves, sipped the final sweet sap through their phloem veins, and took their last breaths. Exhales that gifted us life. They groaned and creaked and sang from their souls. They waved their branches in celebration of the living. Had they known this was coming? Trees seem to know everything and nothing all at once. They did not complain or place blame but focused on their singing, sending each other pulsing messages through their complex neural networks, to the great fungal highway below, together until the very end. Dee watched with furrowed forehead as the fire—a predator with no match—

swallowed our protectors, still hungry for more. Her beautiful forest now blazed black and orange, as if stalked by a smoldering tiger. Paper birch, balsam poplar, spruce, and aspen stood tall and beautiful, pride radiating from every branch. The fire choked them, lighting up their bodies and blistering their skins.

And the trees remembered everything.

Migisi screeched.

"No! Not that way!" I told her.

Running inland meant running into the mouth of a tiger. Several trees, fighting against ferocious orange flames, pointed their limbs in the same direction.

"This way!" I yelled. Migisi fell from the sky, closing in on me. I snatched the dark feathers of her back with shaking feet. Dee threw herself onto Oomingmak's thick back, clawing at his fur. We thundered across the dirt and split hazy sky, heading for the shoreline. Dee's throat filled and was seized by a coughing fit. She slid off Oomingmak and rolled onto wet sand, hacking and retching. Ash fell like smoked snow. Black smoke billowed into the sky, suffocating the clouds. I scanned the beach, looking for a savior.

"Here!" I squawked. "Pull!" Migisi dropped me next to a stubborn little fishing boat. Dee stumbled to the boat, her back to the bay, and started to tug at the fat vessel's lip. She roared and growled and screeched and barked and hung her weight back to release the boat from its sandy shackles. It would not budge.

"Harder, Dee! Harder!" I yelled.

If the ocean couldn't steal it from the shore, how would our little nestling? I called out for the owls, for Onida, even to the trees who had given us their everything, to end this living nightmare. Dee pulled, slate sweat pouring down her face, black tears striping her cheeks. With a sharp yank, she fell backward onto the sand. I hopped up and down, cheering for her to keep trying, because I didn't have a better plan, because we were surrounded by fire and smoke and Dee's lungs were filling, her gasps getting weak and raspy. My vision began to blur.

Oomingmak let out a growl that drowned out the fire's din.

"Move!" I yelled to Dee. She scampered aside. Oomingmak ran at the boat, driving his great horns against its side. He fused the bony base where his horns met in the middle of his head like a bad hair part to the boat's side and pushed. He bellowed and drove ice-breaking hooves deeper into the sand. The boat's side started to rise. The waves crashed, Dee roared, Oomingmak brayed, and the boat lifted from the sand, collapsing upside down but free from its prison. Oomingmak had never been more dedicated to anything, pressing his enormous horns to the boat once more to ram it right side up. It teetered and wobbled. And then he pushed that boat, head down, massive bulk driving our barnacled angel into the beckoning spume.

"In!" I yelled at Dee, and she did as she was told, curled over and coughing up the blackened bodies of trees into her hands. I jumped on top of the oars locked in place in the little boat's belly. Our boat fought the shoreline waves. Frigid water splashed the soot off our skin and feathers. Dee grappled to learn how to row, oars flailing, at first fighting the current and then using her muscles to pull the oars back and into the water, gliding salvation. Migisi screeched and spun above. Dee rowed and rowed, pushing us away from an entity that now terrified her. She turned to face that fire and shook, features ablaze with an angry orange. She had believed that fire was, as it had been for most of her life, under her control. A pot dweller. A creature that lived under stone. She had not known it to be a beast with its own ideas and appetites. Our imprinted nestling sat watching her whole world burn. A world that had fit into the palm of her hand.

A world she had just crushed flat.

Black tears dove from her cheeks. The darkening sky burned an eerie tangerine, highlighted by the bay's black water. Dee—disgraced empress of owls—watched her trees die, knowing that the worlds within, below, and above them would suffer the same fate. She called out for The Hook, for Ookpik, Bristle, Little Wik, and her beloved Kuupa in the sharp shrieks of an owl. It had all happened so fast. They had not made it to the shoreline. And then a deep bellowing. Wet snorts sounded out. A pair of horns were black against an orange sky. Eyewhites flashed, and icy cries of panic sounded out. Oomingmak, too big for the boat, stood on the shore, the fire behind him.

"Oomingmak!" screamed Dee, hysterical.

She did not dive into the water. My gutsy nestling had lost the voltage and confidence that had once sent her, without hesitation, into the frosty waters of this very bay to save the musk ox she loved so dearly. She no longer believed in herself. She believed the seals and voles and rabbits.

Her fire had taken everything from her. And now all that was left was ash, regret, and a tiny boat manned by avian and hominid, floating out at the moon's mercy. Floating toward dangers I was afraid to give a single thought to, dangers I could no longer keep my nestling hidden from.

A series of explosions ripped across Toksook, fire balling upward. Black smoke bloomed.

*Boom! Boom! Boom! Boom! Boom!*

The yellow fuel tank cemetery.

Dee now understood she was a violent creature, born of the most violent beings on earth. Destruction is in the marrow of a MoFo.

She bellowed back at Oomingmak, a primal scream of undying love.

Oomingmak lifted his great horns and called to his Dee. The fire laughed, dancing nimbly behind him.

Night spilled its unforgiving ink.

The moon mourned in orange.

Oomingmak could not swim.

# CHAPTER 7

WAHROONGA QUIDONG
BABY HUMPBACK DOLPHIN
NINGALOO REEF, WESTERN AUSTRALIA

**W**elcome. I want to show you my world of water. My squeals make the sound shape of fizzy foam as I show you to *Echo*.

Fin and Flippers always move because the tide currents say so. They are full of thoughts and power push; they go this way and that way like our whipping tails when we stun a fish—*bap!* Riding them is runny joy. I am always happy—*whirring, chirping in the sparkling shapes of a splash*—I am whole in a big blue place that is always talking.

*Echo*, our house of hearing.

*Reverberating ring. Ripply ting. Hollow boom and rumble.*

It is full of shimmering scales and surprise! stings and warm waves that birth rolling shapes of soft delight. Here is kelp, swish and sway, and, Oh! there, deep down on the yellow bed, is a little red shell with claws, moving sideways slowly so I don't hear, but I do! Its sound is spiny, it makes the shape of *skittery bustle, skit skit snip*. I dive to nudge the smooth shell with my nose and then—*whoosh*—I'm gone, up and up, riding currents that move in eels of cold and warm and warm and cold.

Every day is a melody. Every day is riding the bounteous back of a wave.

*Click click clicks* fill up my body. Clicks and whistles and squeaks, mama sends them to find me. They bounce off my slippery skin like the dappled light and dance back to mama to tell her where am I. I send my name—a song of sunlit seagrass—to show her *I am here, mama, and I am the shape of happy*. I am learning new things. I am here in a sea full of stars—red, purple, sun yellow with five arms—who spit out their stomachs to savor the glossy gray *goop goop* scoop of an oyster and then swallow their stomachs in again—*schloop*— among pallid blooms of algae. Algae are The Ancient Ones. Algae are swishing mystics, life growers, whose outsides sound like the floaty fingers of dead men. I am learning new things. The kelp world is full of magic and silver-finned riddles.

Follow me here, use your fins, and be the shape of joy like me! Let's dance with the white light, ripple over coral—pink and orange, bright as brains and tickly—home and hideaway. Here's a little fish hiding in the swaying jelly arms of anemone. Friends. Friends know one another on the inside and like the shapes they see.

The sounds we make—*chirp, click, whistle, creak, rasp, moan, trill, and grunt*—bounce off the faraway and send us pictures of what is there. In the faraway can be great web-mouth whales who sing songs that bring stories into living pictures, as real as when we chase mackerel into great glittering whirls. In the faraway can be the barking shapes of hunting seals or the lone slice of a sharp-finned hunter. And other sounds.

Twirl to me here; there is a sea turtle combing the waters sun-slow, with shimmery shell and old algae eyes filled with salty secrets. I echo to see, sending out my creaky sounds to fill him up. The sounds come back to me, a full everything picture of sea turtle; I can even see inside him now. He is filled with quiet oval bones and the *shrrrrt shrrrrt* emerald seagrass he loves to graze. I think now I know his secrets. He has come a long, long way, and he carries a great weight on his back—bigger than his polished shell. He carries great worry of things to come. I close up to him and he ducks inside his shell, a shell scarred with story. He can tuck all his bones inside his shell. Everything all tucked up at home where his heart dens.

I blow a jellyfish of a bubble and push it to my family. They show me their tidy teeth and send me sounds and call my seagrass name and drive the bubble with their cloud-colored noses, and we fill the water with squeaky rainbow sounds of bubble skin. We stay together, a together sound shape, because family is *Echo. Echo*, gurgling and glorious.

I am little, but liquid lightning. This way! Swim fast like me to the surface and taste a different world, the world that gives us breath. Up there is where the water is upside down, a kingdom of gray-throat gulls. Where *bzzzzz*-flippered fish can fly. We jump up and laugh to the sun; she is always too busy to play. She sends us her rays and they pour gold on our skins and we thrust our sonic shapes up and over the waves, twisty like sea snakes, slicing fast through *slosh* and *whomp* swells like swordfish. And at night, the sun grows cold and white, spilling liquid pearls and calling to the ocean as a mama and her calf.

I dive below and here is a leaf that has made a long journey from the Up world. I must show you. It has skin and veins and stories. When it lived it was a kingdom to many, bolstered by fungal friendships. What a beautifully weaved world. It listened for the *crrrrrcchh crrrrchhh* of a caterpillar's crunchy jaws and responded with a treacherous chemical cavalry. It flew here like the gulls, on the back of the wind. I am careful with this little dead planet in my teeth, showing it to *scritchy fizzle* sea sponge and *whooooosh* manta ray who glides past, an under-the-water cloud.

Me, I am slippery skinned and smiling. Our shapes glow like midnight phosphorescence, dance like bubbles of laughter. We, the Flipper and Fins, can hum through things and know all their secrets.

Welcome to my world of water.

Welcome to *Echo*.

# CHAPTER 8

S.T.

GOD KNOWS WHERE IN THE BERING SEA

We were in a shitty little boat that bobbed above an alien world. A world of fins and algae and slippery scales. We bumped helplessly above an eerie waterline that taunted us with its secrets deep and dark below. The waves held cryptic messages. Bubbles mocked us as they burst, silent detonations, signs of mysterious movement. Or, as I suspected, farts.

*Echo* was a cruel world I had done my best to keep Dee away from, despite her insatiable fascination with it. Who has time for an aqueous cesspool of a universe with no air and no books—blech! It certainly didn't pass mustard with me. So here we were, surrounded by Black Tide and blue tide, Dee curled up like a sad little Cheeto® in the bottom of our boat as we floated above a fish urinal. Other than shivering, Dee barely moved. We were utterly reliant upon Migisi. She fished for us, draping bug-eyed catches over the edge of the boat. Dee showed no interest, staring into a pencil-line horizon, tortured by the pain of losing Ooming-mak, the owls, her beautiful trees, and the beloved bees that called her name. The only family she truly knew. Was she always doomed to suffer the things I had? I worked quickly because food of *Echo* is to be eaten fresh, lest it become a volcanic laxative, tearing bits of fish belly and popping them into her mouth, gently encouraging her to swallow. I recited lively stories now that we were having our very own ocean adventure. I performed uplifting interpretative dances for her on the boat's lip. I recited Emily Dickinson poetry in a plucky tone:

*"Hope" is the thing with feathers*
*That perches in the soul*
*And sings the tune without the words*
*And never stops at all.*

Even a Shit Turd original:

*The sea is a watery shithole*
*Full of assholes and lots of fish pee*
*The sea is a salty great crap bowl*
*We would much rather live in a tree.*

Our biggest problem fell on us like a tipped Belgian Blue bull. The boat was nothing but an old husk, a haven for mollusks with no snacks or provisions. I asked Migisi to please, for the love of Pabst Blue Ribbon, find us some water. She lifted to the sky without hesitation, knowing—as all creatures on this big beautiful blue know—that without it, we were going to die.

And we waited. We waited and waited. Clouds performed shapeshifting magic tricks. The sun migrated.

Finally, a jellyfish glubbed into view, transparent and billowing in bursts under the waterline.

"Excuse me, sir, can you help us? We need to connect to our friends on *Aura*…"

He didn't respond, ignoring me as he pulsated in diaphanous bursts.

"Sir, please, please help me. My friend hasn't returned, and I need fresh water. Can you tell me how to contact someone through *Echo*?" It was time to name-drop. "Have you heard of Onida?"

He didn't answer because he was a fucking jerk, no better than an arrogant aquatic breast implant. But mostly it was because he wasn't a jellyfish. He was actually a plastic bag.

Dee shivered through a coal-colored night and into the next morning, when the sun elbowed its way through cotton clouds. Her stomach was hollow and her heart was heavy and we had nothing. The odd rude fish would gawk at us, protruding liver lips from the murky unknown, the dark and dangerous that glugged all around us, but I had no way to snag one. Dee could not be roused into action. And now I began to fear that something had happened to Migisi. I hated to surrender in this way, to risk alerting that colostomy bag of a giant walrus to our whereabouts, but my wings were tied. So, I called out to *Aura* in my desperation.

"Help us, please! We need water!" I was very unspecific about who "we" were, settling for "I am The One Who Keeps!" because it seemed to have opened doors in the past.

But the sky remained empty, a steely congregation of clouds. And *Echo* and all its salted buffoonery remained silent to my pleas. Not a blubber-brained marine mammal or a mentally unstable crab responded. Not so much as a fucking coon-striped shrimp answered our calls. There was just undulating nothingness, just painful silence, salt smells, moody skies, and miles of freezing ocean all around us. Oh, and I'd been right about the flatulence. Schools of herring communicate by tooting at dusk, so every day we were treated to the symphonic stylings of *Les Misérables*, if it were performed in fish farts. I knew we were not alone—you are never, ever alone in an ocean—but we couldn't tell who or what was beneath us. And they seemed to want to keep it that way.

I worried about what kind of future Dee had, if any at all. I worried about my plan to get her to Seattle, where we could hide her and be protected by the UW Bothell murder—the only way I could think to keep her breathing. I worried about why I had stopped hearing calls for help—calls that broke me to ignore—from the UW Bothell murder and from Ghubari and his pandemonium of parrots, friends from so long ago. Why had I not heard from them on *Aura* in the last weeks of living in Toksook Bay? I worried about the snippets and flashing stills of the world outside Toksook that *Aura* had played for me before we were forced to evacuate—those terrible, terrible sounds...

I couldn't think about it. A beautifully adapted avoidance mechanism, the MoFo part of me daydreamed when Dee slept. I thought of the past. Me caching credit cards I stole from Big Jim's fiancée, Tiffany S. from Tinder.[1] Me swooping down and stealing pizza from Tiffany S. from Tinder. Me shitting on Tiffany S.'s pillow. Me screeching, "Help, I'm kidnapped!"

---

1   Tiffany S. from Tinder and I had a complicated relationship, and by that, I mean that I didn't like her. Big Jim and Tiffany S. had their ups and downs but also had undeniable chemistry, which was special since most women found Big Jim as sensual as an orthotic shoe. Big Jim and Tiffany S. couldn't seem to stay away from one another. A bit like me and Cheetos®.

every time Tiffany S. was on the phone. Big Jim swaddled in an angry sunburn. Big Jim eating snickerdoodles with Nargatha, who fussed about his arteries and the Pop-Tarts that spilled from our cupboards, playfully jabbing a twiglike finger into his belly.

Nargatha was our neighbor with silvery squiggles of hair and a Rascal 615 mobility scooter. She once rescued her beloved schnauzer named Triscuits, but she rescued Big Jim on a much more regular basis. Before Big Jim met Tiffany S. from Tinder, there had been many, many disastrous dates. Nargatha would whisk Big Jim out for drinks after every failed courtship, which got to be a considerable expense and time commitment. Big Jim was the bowerbird who couldn't quite find the right treasures to decorate his nest or the partner to share it with. I thought about how hopeless Big Jim felt after one night at that fancy restaurant. I'd come along for dinner (bringing Old Hollywood glamour in my dapper counterfeit "service animal" vest). She called herself "Shelsea, like a shell and the sea, haaahaahaah!" and also called herself a goat yogi. She had a very distinctive laugh, like a kookaburra on quaaludes. Honestly, I hadn't thought it a match when she settled on ordering a "beet loaf" but only after asking the waiter for an "egg-free scramble" and loudly announcing that she had "a nut allergy but only in her vagina." She went to the restroom during the stuffed mushrooms and seemingly never found her way out. Big Jim had taken this nail in the coffin of bad dates pretty hard. Nargatha picked us up in her Subaru chariot (a jerky ride, thanks to a spirited restless legs syndrome flare-up) and took us off to a boisterous bar with burgers and beer, clutching a purse full of animal crackers for yours truly. Big Jim pelting darts, finding that booming laugh again. Nargatha dancing on restless legs. Sometimes I think we look so hard for companionship, we don't see that we've had it all along. Like Dorothy and her sparkly slippers.[2]

I remembered how my best buddy Dennis looked as he tore across the yard, fawn skin suspended behind him, his tongue punishing the air like a wind-whipped scarf. I remembered how he would jump onto Big Jim's lap, both of them writhing and laughing and testing the patience of the La-Z-Boy®, me screaming at them to pull themselves together from the top of the flat-screen. I thought of light switches, and Nargatha's golden pies and crazy kitchen dances, and the magical glow of the refrigerator. It wasn't the natural way—certainly not the corvid way—to dwell, but I couldn't help myself. The past is just so very persuasive, these memories a warm bath. How I missed Big Jim and my Dennis with his velvet ears and Frito feet. Grief can slam into you like a well-waxed window. But it means the ones you love aren't lost or forgotten. They've made a home in your heart, which is the most permanent place of all.

Two sunsets had bled when I noticed that Dee's lips were parched and blue. She was still curled, imprisoned in an invisible egg on the boat's floor. Her breathing was shallow. We had encountered no one except a bob of grudge-gripping northern fur seals who had yelled at Dee, "Give us your skin, sweetheart!" which was the cherry on my cake of hatred for *Echo*. I yanked out a long thread from Dee's parka, dangling it over the side of our boat with one foot, anchoring myself with the other. I channeled Big Jim, held my beak high and puffed out my chest, concentrating on the line's movement.

---

2  This is another MoFo movie reference. This movie was about a young MoFo woman who made weird friends (many were missing vital organs), passed out in a poppy field, and was chased by flying monkeys, only to discover she'd hallucinated the whole thing (see: poppies) and to disappointingly learn that she hadn't left Kansas. I gave this movie one wing up because I was pretty offended by the concept of a scarecrow.

I didn't get a bite. For hours I waited, patient as a fossilized cannoli.

I started to get desperate, my calls for help louder and louder, until my beautiful singing voice was hoarse and squawky. Dee was wishbone weak, still coiled like a fiddlehead fern in the belly of our boat. Then I became sick as a sea slug, dry heaving my desperate worry for Migisi. Where was she? I longed for land, for a full belly and a moist throat, for the friendship of our owls whom I couldn't bring myself to think about. Even for the woolly comfort of Oomingmak's back. I missed that Cadillac-hearted oaf and felt a beesting in my throat whenever I thought of him haloed by fire. I even missed the unctuous family tree of flies that deviled him. And I hated this horrible water world.

Finally, we got a response. Not from Migisi or an Alaskan cruise ship of healthy MoFos or a murder of migrating crows or shit-talking seals or labia-lipped lingcod, but from the sky. It lost its temper, frowning in the sinister gray of a gun. It rumbled its complaints and sighed heavily in frigid gales. The scowling thunderheads began to cry, a MoFo mouth and corvid beak desperately gulping in its sadness. And then they threw a full-blown tantrum in the ocean. The waves gathered their frothy skirts, folding into deep rolls. The boat was tossed over their crests, plunged down into the cleavage between swells. I held tight to the bottom of the boat, stomach suspended several feet above me like a thought bubble. The waves got bigger. We teetered over their sharp whitecaps. Dee pulled me into her chest, holding on tight. Her eyes were squeezed shut and under her breath she hummed the song of bees.

"Mmmmmmm, Mmmmmmm."

She was petrified, the winds slicing at her cheeks. She clutched the little black being who loved her most in this world as she uttered MoFo words in her strange crow English, words

I had taught her in a language she hated as she searched for comfort.

"Danger! Danger!"

I couldn't formulate a plan—I couldn't do anything against the ocean's wrath—and so we were battered around in the little toy boat. Water pirated through the eroded holes just under the lip of the old boat. She started to fill, gargling salt water. Dee shrieked and yelled at the winds, "Scrreeeedeee!" And the winds roared back, abusing the sea with the roar of Tiffany S. when I plopped the contents of her little pink pillbox into the seabound water of the toilet, along with her bottle of Chanel N°5. What? It's called *eau de toilette*!

Roiling water fizzed around Dee's feet. She stopped calling out, humming her song of the hive. A great wave gathered its confidence ahead of us. We watched, biting our tongues. The wave lifted high and did its worst. The boat was swallowed in one gulp. Dee gasped as the icy water of *Echo* slapped her skin. I heard a thump, limbs striking wood, and then Dee was thrown into the ocean. I was knocked from her strong fingers. A great gust of wind thrust me into the air, then I plunged into the horrifying world of *Echo*.

It was deafening.

Dark and blue and angry, a deadly washing machine of whipped particles and sand, screaming krill, and the weak wails of bewildered phytoplankton too small to fight it. The currents were all-powerful, dragging their claws this way and that way, ferocious sultans of salt and seaweed. Sounds attacked me—roaring, bubbling, thundering, shrieking shrimp, and a terrifying clicking sound that felt like a showering of bullets whizzing past me. Karma, that green-eyed goddess, flashed her bloomers and both middle fingers. In the stomach of the storm, I was powerless, just one of Tiffany S.'s tiny toilet pills, sluicing along a sewer pipe along with all the lowercase shit turds. I kicked with every ounce of energy I had, flapping waterlogged wings to get *Up, Shit Turd, swim up! Get to Dee!* I punched my beak through the waterline, sucking in the howling winds. A salt river rushed in and I spluttered, vomiting fish pee. I wrestled with the waterline, kicking against currents to stay at the surface to scan for my nestling.

There she was.

Dee's tree-scaling legs kicked and thrashed. She fought an ocean to get to me, snatched me up in the clutch of her hand, punching the sky to keep me above the wrath of a wave. Dee screamed from her spleen as waves enacted white-lipped anger, smashing and spitting around us. An enormous wave gathered itself above us in that slow, steady build, as if calling on the power of some mythical creature of the deep. We had nowhere to hide, both of us screaming like kidding goats, and it was no joke as it crashed down on us as if a ginormous fucking wave was crashing down on us and we were plunged back into that awful, deadly world of water so very, very desperate to drown us. I held my breath, lungs on fire, flapping and hoping because that's what I did best. I opened my eyes in that terrifying underwater world to a sting of salt, and there, in the boiling water, was a great dark mass.

*Oh fuck.*

A great moving mass that carved the currents, slicing through the squalling spasms of a sea storm. My heart thundered out a particular three-note cello theme song that had convinced MoFos they were but helpless chicken tenders in the honey BBQ sauce of the ocean. I squawked in panic, losing the precious air I had left. The horrible bullet shower of clicks whizzed around me, into me. I thrashed my toothpick legs, thrown to the sea surface again by a confusion of currents. Above water I could see again. Against the icy ire of waves and a glowering granite sky was a fin that cut from the chaos and rose to the clouds. I spun, wet wings slapping the ocean's surface, locating my nestling.

"Dee! Gaaluupp gguuulllltthpppp! Dee! Look out, there's something in the wat—"

The knife-sharp fin towered above her like the tail of an airplane.

"Deeeeeee!"

A great predatory shadow lurked under the swell, closing in on her tiny, thrashing body.

"Dee! Dee, look out, swim! Dee, swim—" and the ocean poured into my lungs.

I was bone tired, dizzy from an assault of salt and being flung around like flotsam. The dark shadow was closing in on Dee. I tried so very, very hard to keep my little eyes on her, but the waves were relentless, punching me around the border of their cruel world, and I couldn't see what was happening to my nestling, and I wheezed out a deflated "Deeee—"

And suddenly, I was yanked from the fray, lifted into the air. Water poured from my feathers.

I levitated through the storm's whipping wind, gular flapping like a fish out of water.

"Onida? Migisi, get Dennis!" I said, delirious as my brain churned like spume, upside down and inside out.

My eyes rolled like runaway marbles, and everything went as black as the sinister fin that sliced the water around us.

# CHAPTER 9

S.T.
STILL NO CLUE WHERE IN THE BERING SEA

My nictitating membranes exploded open like the Levi's Big Jim was wearing at Rosita's Mexican Grill on Cinco de Mayo, when he washed down an expresso burrito with five jalapeño margaritas. Warm breath ruffled my feathers. I wrangled my pinball eyes to focus on a giant nose. It gave a primal snuffle, then pulled back so I could see more of its owner's form. The smooth start of a cheek licked scarlet from a fight with the ocean. Sahara-dry lips that emulated calls of the winged and wild. A modest number of eyes that crackled with intelligence. Hair styled as if by leaf blower. Could she have used a little moisturizer? Absolutely. But to me, there was nothing more magical in the world I came from or the world I was now in. She was utter earthly perfection.

My nestling.

Dee clicked her tongue in delight. She rubbed her face against my beak in the distinctive display of affection among owls. The grateful ghost of a recent meal lingered around her. I had a lot of work to do to make her a real-life MoFo, before I lost her to the natural world. But for now, I was a puffed soufflé of gratitude—I hadn't lost Dee to an oceanic storm.

"Hugs, Dee; MoFos do hugs," I scolded her. So much unlocked potential in that furless form. She ignored my request and continued rubbing her nose to my beak.

A scream shattered the calm and some of my smaller ear bones. A horrible, eyebrow-hoisting, pinion-poofing shriek, emanating from someone with the fortitude of a yellow-bellied newt. I quickly deduced the source of the scream. It was me. I'd been swept up by the element of surprise, unprepared for the great fishy rainbow mist that erupted from the ocean's top predator.

*Oh, yeah. The fin.*

Dee gingerly placed me on a slippery surface and surprised me by standing up. Still groggy and disoriented, I took in the scene. We were moving, and fast. *Echo* streamed beside me, calmer after recovering from its midmorning meltdown.

Dee let out a howl, a wild sound I hadn't heard her make in a long time. It had bright energy and stirred the wind. She stood with a straight back, balanced on powerful legs, her right hand curled around the shiny edge of a six-foot dorsal fin. I knew then that Dee had survived not only the wrath of the blue tide, but the beckoning of the Black one. And she was now standing on top of a speeding killer whale. I shot to my feet, too fast; the world wobbled, and I almost slid off waxy skin. Crouching, I steadied. All around us were enormous black fins that shot from the water like skyscrapers. I had very mixed feelings about all of it.

### Shit Turd's Mixed Concerns (a list):

1. Killer whales are the known wolves of the sea.
2. They have the word "killer" at the blatant forefront of their name, in lieu of the less threatening "Mrs." or "Dame." MoFos had not named them Good Samaritan whales or "cockapoos of the sea" but *killer* whales. *Killing* whales that do *killing*. *Killy* whales.
3. We were still in *Echo*, that sloppy-ass septic tank.
4. What happened at the end of *Fight Club*? I know as a rule, I'm not supposed to talk about it, but I never had a chance to finish it before the world went banoony. This wasn't currently relevant, but it did worry me from time to time.

I had to get shit under control, had to make sure that these massive apex marine monsters had good intentions. Utterly at their mercy, I decided that charm was the name of the game. I slid up past Dee and the towering dorsal fin with the grace of a newborn giraffe on a Slip 'N Slide lubricated with Crisco, then rapped my feet on the gigantic black melon of the speeding cetacean.

"Um! Excuse me!"

*Kooooooooooosh*. The blowhole behind me blasted a geyser plume to the sky. It had a distinctive aroma, reminiscent of when Big Jim used to leave lumps of Filet-O-Fish® in the garbage disposal. Then a sound slammed into me. A series of hollow clicks like a hailstorm of bullets peppered my body, arrowing right through my internal organs. I screeched, checking my body for holes, then looked over at where the sound had come from. Another killer whale, this one smaller than the one we rode, had her head out of the water in what the Discovery Channel called a "spyhop," her massive inky head and its clean white eye patch trained on me.

She let out a series of light squeals that sounded a lot like laughter.

"Hey!" I stamped my foot impatiently on the killer whale's head again, forgetting my original plan to be charming.

And then came the most unusual voice I've ever heard. It was deeply sonorous and didn't seem to come from one source but was rather like the boisterous stage act of an overzealous ventriloquist on amphetamines. "He is awake! Welcome to *Echo*," said the voice, bouncing from all directions, vibrational pings coming from everywhere and nowhere to paint tight bumps over my skin.

"Fucking *Echo*," I muttered to myself, forgetting that these guys are sound specialists. The orca let out high-pitched laughter.

"We understand when you enter a new world, you have to leave behind some of your own. I imagine it's very hard." I didn't want to think about what I'd left behind. Ashen memories. A life.

I was guarded, careful with my questions. "Did you save us?"

"Yes." The word swirled around me, then slipped under my feathers and felt like the warmth rising from oven-fresh biscuits.

"Who are you?"

"We are the Black Fins. We are pod and family."

"You're not going to eat us then?"

He laughed, a deep, echoey boom that caused me to slip and smack onto my good wing. I righted myself and flapped my feathers, feeling those rich, warm sound bullets dance and morph into curlicues and tingling twists. To our left, another whale, with its own distinctive dorsal patch like a white fingerprint behind its fin flag, had its head out of the water. Watching me.

The huge male whale continued: "You are full of worry. Full

of pain where you've been hiding what's happening to the world from the ones you love. But you, Bird of *Aura*, have the heart of a blue baleen."

"What in the name of Triscuits are they firing at me?"

The watching whale let out a series of small clicks. They ran up my matchstick legs. I jumped up and down, flapping to swat them away. The big male went on: "We use sound to tell us things, more than what we meet with our eyes. It is our great gift; she means no harm." The killer whale to the right of me lifted her head out of the water and clucked at me gently. I gave her a look mostly reserved for proselytizing deer ticks or MoFos who talked at the movies, puffing myself up to show her I shouldn't be pinged anymore. Just because you have some sort of weird X-ray superpower doesn't mean you should use it willy-nilly. Who knows what the long-term side effects of that shit are? It felt invasive as fuck, reminding me of when Big Jim got in an argument with Sea-Tac airport TSA over the body scanner and yelled, "Quit taking pictures of my schlong!"

"Where are you taking us?" I asked.

"Where you want to go," said the great black sea wolf.

The smaller killer whale was still staring at me as she cruised. I can't help being handsome, but this was starting to smell like a restraining order.

"I suppose she determined that through the sound X-ray thing," I said with a great deal of salt in my throat.

"You told us when you were passed out. You want to help your family. Family is the essence of the pod."

"Oh." I felt another gush of heat, though this time internal. What else had I said when I was unconscious? Did they know my real reasons for wanting to get to Seattle? Did they know I planned to hide my nestling away from the horrors of the new world? They valued family, so perhaps they would understand. Or perhaps—and this was the more likely case—they were agents of Onida. Blubber butt had plans to sacrifice my Dee for their own selfish gains, or as I long suspected, because Onida wanted to seal the extinction of humanity.

The great sea wolf continued: "You must rest, Blackwing. You have been on a long journey. A journey that has just begun."

"How in the name of *Aura* could you know what's coming for me?"

"We feel things. You must rest; the pain in your right wing is worse." I spread my wings, noticing a pulsing throb. What was this meddlesome malarkey? Never in my whole life had I felt so transparent, like a pulpy page of wet newspaper.

I spoke to him whilst using my wings to cover up my bits. "Since you're the boss of the pod, I'd like to discuss how to connect with *Aura* from here and—"

"We have already sent out sound for you. The seabirds, connectors of *Echo* and *Aura*, will know."

The whole ocean rippled with sound bullets, buoyant and bubbly. They softened to a gentle patter, like drumming fingers, then fused together like droplets of liquid mercury in the colors of Easter. I turned to find Dee laughing, a sun-summoning smile drawn on her face, sound bullets warming her skin. Resentment swirled through my see-through body. Despite a lifetime of trying, I'd never made her laugh like that.

"And I'm not the leader of our pod," the killer whale said, a smile tickling his sounds. "Our leader is here." Here, the orca let out a long string of clicks that floated ahead of us like incandescent electric ball bounces—hypnotic and night-club blue—disappearing into the dorsal fin ahead of us. The towering fin that led the pod was graffitied with notches and scratches, the slapdash signature of boat propellers. To my right, the smaller killer whale, who was clearly carrying a torch for yours truly, aligned with the male we rode. She chirped in a broken smoke detector's lonely calls. Dee let out a perfectly mimicked squeal. The pod chuffed and exhaled rainbows in delight. I reeled, stung by the green stinger of the jealousy hornet, stunned from the visualizations, as if on Tiffany S.'s secret stash of marshmallow-flavored edibles. It was a swift and sonorous magic. Laughter pealed, bubbling up from the deep in a colorful kaleidoscope of sound. Dee hummed to them in her song of the bees and the whales silenced themselves, listening in rapture. The salt world she had dreamed of finally welcomed her. She was better than a paperback heroine with a pearl in her mouth. Dee was the pearl.

I suddenly understood that I was expected to hop onto this finned fan of mine. I did it—gingerly so as not to slip in between the bodies of two whales and end up a crowst beef sandwich. Once I was on her back, the whale chirruped with happiness, and I suddenly felt buoyed myself, filled with brassy beading sounds of joy. It was seductive, but I tried not to be bowled over; great danger hides in delight. The female killer whale accelerated, shooting the two of us through a sea that hissed and babbled, carefree foam frothing in confetti sprinkles. We zoomed past other dorsal fins, even the tiny fin of a baby whale. A chorus of complex chatter in a swirling vortex of color and sound made me realize something utterly dreadful. The whales were dumbing themselves down to talk to me.

She slowed as we approached a notched dorsal fin that wasn't as tall as hers, its gloss dulled by adventure. A dorsal fin that stood firm in the face of time, etched with a constellation of tooth marks. I wondered how the massive shark had fared. Shivering seized my body. I didn't need sound pictures or songs or audible hallucinations to know I was in the presence of an ancient greatness.

I hopped onto the body of the magnificent whale. For the first time since I could remember, I was speechless.

"And so here you are, brave as a beginning," came a barnacled voice without an anchor. "With every tide it becomes rarer to find someone who knows. Many of my children only know stories and legends. But you and I, we know. We lived side by side with them. We remember the humans."

My beak rattled, agitated with adrenaline. I had waited winter after white winter to taste this moment. To talk to someone who *knew* the magnificence of MoFos. "You, you remember them! You know how important they are!"

"I have lived one hundred salmon spawns; many stories swim in me. I can tell you stories of great human friendships, songs of fins and feet. Of kindness that came from dovelike fingers. I can tell you about how the humans rounded up my family from great machines with whirring wings, blasting our waters below. I can tell you of lost children and a mother's screams. I can tell you of brave, bearded warrior men who put their tiny bodies between ours and a harpoon's eye. Or perhaps you ask for stories of the brutality of boats and how it is to sing to your loved one, their desperate notes fluttering up over the waves, unable to nuzzle another again or break through the cruel mask of glass. They are stories as varied as waves. None of them matter now. Now, they are gone."

She released shuddering rumbles that swirled into a scene before me. Ahead, rendered by the magnificent memory of a cetacean, were the floating bodies of dead MoFos. Their eyes were stolen, skin suffering a slow escape like the shedding of wet tissue. Hair rippled in wormy tendrils. There were so many.

Fear strummed my veins. "Then tell me why you are helping the very last one ride across an ocean that wants to swallow her?"

*Koooooooooooooooosh*. She exhaled and said nothing.

And suddenly in my mind's movie I saw her leading us to

Onida. I'd watched documentaries about killer whales and the fractious relationship they'd had with humans. Tiny tanks and the kidnapping of pod members, ambushes in coves. I thought of a favorite photograph—the one of Big Jim with sunburnt knees when we caught the big Chinook salmon, also known as king salmon—and how I later learned that our southern resident orcas were starving because they only ate Chinook salmon, which were being unnecessarily overfished by MoFos. Suddenly, I saw this pod acting out of revenge, driving us to Onida so that my nestling could be held responsible for her species. Leading us to Dee's doom.

What animal has had a more contentious relationship with MoFos than the killer whale?

I let honesty speak. "Please, if you know them, then you know what she is and what her chances are. Please. She is good inside. *My soul cannot fly without her.*"

"And that is why we came. Because your love for her is the loudest sound in the ocean."

I lay down on her back, exhaustion taking over. What choice did I have but to trust?

"Rest, and I will tell you a story." She started, releasing pulsing pops, willowy whines. A pattering of low-frequency clicks poured around us like electric monsoon rain. The story came to life with sound, playing out in front of me like a 3D movie. An optical adventure that even the sea-foam stilled to soak up.

*The Black Fins felt the world tighten. They were the first to know, to fear an enemy with a hunger that stretched beyond the horizon and eyes like a glass cage. The Beast had an appetite for salmon, diving from the sky and into the waters to devour more salmon than The Blue could replenish.*

*The One Who Hollows as well must return.*

*The monster vomited its foul bile into the water, choking the lives of those who live through gills. And more salmon were taken, and more, and the Black Fins, one by one, rose to the water's surface with hollow, breathless bellies and skins squirming with bone worms. Soon, the salmon weren't enough, and the Beast began to eat mankind, chewing up their eyes and bodies, leaving their skins to find their own shapes. The Black Fins fought the Beast, but it grew stronger, ravishing pods of Black Fins and mankind alike.*

*But the Beast, in its greed, forgot one human. The last. A raven with onyx wings and great red markings flew down from the sky and brought the last human to the remaining Black Fins. The Black Fins ferried the last human to land, to honor the code of sister species—the code of together. They delivered the last human to the glass-eyed Beast so that mankind could pay back an earthly debt. So that mankind could, in its last blowhole breath, be reminded of itself.*

*Kooooooooooooooooooosh.*

"That's the end?" I asked, wide-eyed. "You realize I'm a crow, right? Not a deuteragonist raven with rosacea?"

"It is a legend we sing."

"If anything, I'm a crowtagonist. And I've never met a MoFo with a blowhole." I was then struck by a memory of a fuming Tiffany S. from Tinder leaping out of the shower, steam rising from her head as she chased after me with a loofah scrubby because I'd feng shui-ed her MacBook keyboard by plucking out its letters. "I stand corrected."

"We have been telling this story longer than the memories of ice mountains. What you are feeling is the pod's excitement, hope's swelling tide. My pod is part of something big, together. This is the power of *Echo.*"

"There are some interesting coincidences with your fairy tale, but I don't believe in this shit. I'm telling you now, and I know you hear this—" I gestured my beak toward the tiny dorsal fin that poked through the surf, shiny and new. "Dee is a fledgling, not a debt." I wondered if they could see right through me, where it was written all over my heart that I wouldn't be handing over my nestling to anyone. My plans to nod my noggin, play along with whopping tales, and then hide her from every living cell on this big beautiful blue, I imagined, were as bright and bold as fresh graffiti.

I looked at Dee, who sang with a pod of killer whales. Once curved and sunken, her spine was now as straight as the dorsal fin she clutched. "You've brought her back, and for that I am more grateful than even you can hear. But that tale doesn't even make sense...the Black Fins deliver the last MoFo to some carnivorous beast? For what! It's not real. It's just a story," I said to her.

I felt her great black-and-white head bob up and down. She filled me with waves of frothy hope as she said, "Dear Crow, it is *all* just story."

And then the Black Fins fell silent. The singing was severed. Colors and shapes vanished.

"What's happening? What's going on!" I spun, hunting the horizon.

*Kooooooooooooooosh.* "Not far from here. Up ahead, we see this." The matriarch made vining, vowely sounds that fanned and flapped like water nymphs, uniting to form a perfect image in the water ahead of us.

It was a recreational boat. A MoFo boat.

# CHAPTER 10

AUGUSTUS
SPOTTED RATFISH
BERING SEA
(REGRETTABLY OVERHEARING AN APPALLING POEM
RECITED BY A CROW HAVING SOME SORT OF
EXISTENTIAL CRISIS AND A BAD HAIR DAY)

*Ode to a Mustache*

I'm enamored with a mustache
With bristles like a broom
A thousand hairs all side by side
A facial flower in bloom

If I had a bushy mustache
I'd comb it with gusto
And wiggle it when thinking hard
I'd be Tom Selleck Crow!

A mustache is a masterpiece
Like the McDonald's sign or Venus

All natural and organic
It's less trouble than a penis


If I were a mustache
I like underpants!
I'd douse myself in honey
And ambush all the ants


If I were a walrus
And had my own mustache
I'd count my blessings every day and
And stash it in my cache!


I wish I had a mustache
That lip-presiding sovereign
That lower-nasal sheepskin rug
What the great fuck rhymes with sovereign?

# CHAPTER 11

❋ ✳ ❋ ✾ ❋ ✾ ❋

PENIPUAN
MYRMARACHNE JUMPING SPIDER
SABAH JUNGLE, BORNEO, MALAYSIA

Open all your eyes.

The air is thick with warm, wet clouds and mischief. Swirls of chemical story puff and plume, warnings from sticky-legged warriors.

The mandible of a mosquito slurps stolen scarlet.

Disembodied howls widen eyes. Leechy appetites abound.

Cicadas screech and blare, from their chests a doomed drumming, and gluey eggs throb with the ravenous impatience of the unborn.

Squeaks of asphyxiation tighten as vines strangle, plants cannibalize one another and exhale rot.

Jaws crunch down on brittle bodies, a crispy rhythm of conquest.

Crystal globes of rainwater burst and bully each emerald leaf.

Feel the magic and malice of mushrooms that tower and terrorize. In the jungle's jaws, predator and prey can be so close as to rub skins.

Truth can take a life.

The jungle is a living thing with hot lungs, an eternal row of fangs. It spits out wings that beat transparent terror. There is no space for silence; every jungle inch is filled with a scream song. Fear fills the soggy minds of panicked quarry. The jungle does not sleep. It does not care about you, not a scritch. Our enemies, yours and mine, lurk. We are always a screech away from death.

And all around, like the churning boil of living soil, swarm the jungle's most powerful army. The Red Soldiers. Militia of ants.

I am not what I appear to be. I play a game of life or death. Shhh. I have changed my body and my mind. I am a morphing trickster, insect imitator. I lift my front legs up to make a Red Soldier's antennae. My eyes have dark patches, a thrilling illusion of an ant's orbs. My body sprouts reflective hairs— what a clever copy—a fantasy of a shiny, segmented body! I must believe I can carry a great stone alone, that I have the two stomachs of a formidable Red Soldier. I do not whisper about my silks.

Shhh. It is a spider's secret.

The stakes? You cannot think about the stakes, about what will happen if a Red Soldier smells your clever disguise, if that Red Soldier calls in chemicals, summoning the power of a million strong. Don't think about the jungle's crushing jaws, the combined muscle and colony mind of the most powerful army on earth. You must not think about how your body will be pulled apart in the segments you have mimicked. And you must never, never allow yourself to think of the greatest threat—their indomitable Queen. You cannot think of these things. In the jungle, there is no space for fear.

A Red Soldier is coming. Two, no, no, three approach. Shhh. One is up close, next to me, his armor shining like sap.

I think ant thoughts. I wave my antennae, make busy business, never-stop-moving because I am a soldier of the Red Army.

For a blink, I am alone. A solitary Red Soldier bustles forth. Recognition glistens in his black eye. He feels me, false pheromones, the truth of me. I strike with the will of war, piercing his body with my hollow fangs and releasing slick venom. Quick as wings, I whip my silks, wrapping the body of a great red warrior and launching us from leaf, and we drop down, down, down on a long secret silver line to where I feast on the body of my fellow soldier, face first.

Eat and avoid being eaten.

In the jungle, you can be predator, or you can be prey.

Or you can be both.

Shhh. I am not a spider. I am an ant.

# CHAPTER 12

S.T.

THE BACKS OF KILLER WHALES, THE BERING SEA

Killer whales can swim at a good clip. My thighs were two walnuts in a nutcracker's vise performing a never-ending squat as a ferocity of fins split the sea. There was something sublimely whimsical about being in the company of whales. I hadn't felt so warm and frothy in years, worry wicked away with the surf. It was indescribably badass. As I stood on the brave back of a whale that had known a century of MoFos, I felt compelled to express my gratitude but not sound sappy. An S.T. original joke was in order.

I leaned forward and projected. "You make us feel that any fin is possible." She responded with a reverse rain of tight teal loops, which I took to mean polite laughter. Hey, I can't please everyone; I'm not a Cheeto®. The matriarch was focused, her mind in the future. I wondered if all this good killer whale karma was how I'd convinced myself that nothing bad had happened to Migisi. I had to trust that my formidable friend was alright. Breathing was not possible otherwise.

A glorious ballet of silky sounds shimmied around us, until very abruptly, they didn't. The whales were so silent, my feathers stood on end. To be this massive and many and to cast a liquid disappearing spell—this, I realized, was why they were so dangerous. This is how a seal never knows what hit it.

We streamed soundlessly through the frigid waters, everything taking on a ghostly eeriness, until it was up ahead of us, bobbing gently against the horizon.

The boat.

It was beautiful. Tooth white and shiny. Her name was *Bering Mind,* evinced by swirling gold letters that danced across her side.[1] My pulse spiked as we closed in. And then it was really, really real; we were right in front of this luxurious vessel that had anchored here, and I could barely breathe, adrenaline sizzling like sounds the orcas had ceased making. Even their breathing was now quiet, controlled exhales through blowholes. They spyhopped, lifting magnificent black-and-white heads above the waterline, letting their eyes tell the story of the bobbing boat. Dee had not seen anything like this, her eyes scanning its ergonomic elegance, the polished lines of design and a bottomless bank account. This was not a tired relic of Toksook. Dee was used to the patchwork of the practical.

And then a sound. Not from killer whale, or crow, or the last MoFo who sat quietly clutching the tallest dorsal fin. A sharp squeak came from the boat. A sound like the protest of a sneaker against a shiny surface.

Someone was on the boat.

The killer whales glided with the ribbony synchronicity of birds, some dipping without so much as a *bloop* below

---

1  Dammit, the guy who came up with that name would have loved my fin joke.

the waterline, others coasting to circle and spy on the boat. I tried to imagine the owner of *Bering Mind*—smart, I decided, to have escaped the mainland and started a life at sea, away from a change that couldn't be outrun. Was the squeak from a one and only? Or were we looking at a flock?

A pack?

Then I had a thought that hadn't occurred to me in over a decade of dreaming about how MoFos loved to meow gibberish at cats, or the particular joy of clapping,[2] or how their emotional state was anchored to whatever song played in the car, or their collective lifelong fear of an imperceptible brute who lives under the bed with nothing but an insatiable ankle fetish. Such a glorious, dichotomous species—some strong enough to survive war, others keeling over at the mere whiff of a peanut. What if this was what I'd dreamed of all these years—another healthy MoFo, that Dee is not the last of her species—and they fall in love with Dee, because of course they will, and *then they don't realize who I am.* What if they mistake me for a brainless bird, and they treat me like Tiffany S. from Tinder or the snooty customers at Walmart did? What if they take my nestling from me, warning me to leave with muzzle blasts from a shotgun?

My heart throbbed in my throat. The female killer whale who definitely had the hots for me disappeared under the boat. Two others followed. I strained to hear them emerge on the other side of *Bering Mind* as they made a 360-degree scan of the vessel. But there was no sound. They weren't going to use their waves, not while they had stealth as an advantage. Dee's chest rose up and down, up and down. Was she anxiously preparing to finally see her own species? Did

2   MoFos smacked themselves to express approval.

she even know? I desperately wished I was on the male whale's back with her.

Another squeak. Movement. The matriarch cleaved the waterline silently with a crow on her back. Someone had left the door into the cabin of *Bering Mind* open, swinging gently like a loose tooth. The doorway's darkness, a gaping cave, offered nothing.

A scratching sounded out. Everyone—crow, MoFo, whale, and water—held their breath. Another scratching sound, then pronounced taps. The delicious footfalls of a biped? Toes swaddled in socks? What would I say to them? Shit, what was it? I'd only been practicing it for a decade, dancing around our cabin filled with enough whiskey to baptize an elephant seal. After every day of adventures and teaching Dee words, after I told her jokes and stories and watched her fall into sweet sleep.

"Hello," I'd rehearse to a fat, dusty stove. "We've been looking for you. Thank god you're alive." And then I would balance on one foot, offering the other foot to shake because that is a polite way to say hello if you're a MoFo meeting another MoFo and I have never been good at fist bumps. And then I would say, "You are not the last one. This is Dee." A MoFo meeting another MoFo—the dream, utopia, paradise. But there was no more time to rehearse the introduction I'd wished for on every one of Dee's molted eyelashes. Because the MoFo was emerging from the cabin.

Red. The color red. Not dark like the moody hue of blood, but a bold, bird's-eye chili red. The red thing thrust from the darkness and pressed down on the shiny white floor of the boat, and I tried to figure out what this could be. A walking cane, I was sure of it. But then another red thing emerged, and then another, and when my mind caught up to my eyeballs, I realized these were legs. Once the red legs had purchase on the boat's flooring, the body hoisted itself through the black door of *Bering Mind*. What we had been waiting for came into full view.

The body was enormous—hot tub sized and just as round. It was a topographical map of hard spines. Beak hanging open, I realized that the spines weren't spines. They were fingers. The hardened fingers of a MoFo, jutting out of something not quite shell, not skin, but some sort of strange amalgamation. On a back leg—as long as our old sunken fishing boat— a piece of material was caught on one of the spiny fingers, fluttering in the ocean breeze like a surrender flag. A snag of denim. The creature had claws—two great orangey pincers. Nutcrackered in one was a black object. I squinted to read "Garmin echoMAP CHIRP" on its surface. Something that belonged inside *Bering Mind* that had pinged and beeped, mimicking the echolocation of the dolphin family. Now it was silent, its face smashed out.

An electronic device. A screen.

I retched, closing my throat to stop sound. I had never seen this creature, but ones like it had haunted my dreams every single night in Toksook and, before then, my every waking day.

The monster—not crab, not MoFo—made spidery, mechanical movements, lifting itself to crawl up the side of the boat in a deliberation of squeaks and scratches. It rested there, gigantic legs outspread to suction itself. It had not shattered *Bering Mind*'s side windows. What a cruel deception, cyanide-covered candy. A cruel reminder that these things didn't play by any rules. What did they play for? Destruction. To win. I couldn't give this creature a name. But the eyes, I knew. They swiveled, searching like security cameras. They were bloodshot, rimmed in red, not the eyes of a crustacean. Round irises, swelling pupils, the murky shadow of memory behind them. They were MoFo. Did the eyes see? Did they know that below the boat, killer whales marauded like toothed ghosts? Did they see the black fins, two tree-trunk lengths away from its hardening red body? Did they know the last MoFo stood nearby on wetsuit-slick skin, her feet frozen white, speckled with salt sores? Did it recognize that it was a hollow husk of the little girl who watched it?

A bristled toothbrush of an antenna on the creature's MoFo-like lips lifted up and down. Armor. Antennae. Claws. A carapace. This desperate thief had stolen the adaptations of an oceanic crab.

I dared to take my eyes off this unnatural thing to focus on Dee. She was standing now, fingers foam white from squeezing the great dorsal fin.

We had to get out of here. Fast. I patted my foot onto the matriarch whale's head. She started an inaudible glide at the sea's surface. I turned to focus on Dee again, to make sure that the biggest dorsal fin was also commencing a soundless exit. He was. Dee wore a frown, eyes flicking across the boat, along the bastardized body of the gargantuan creature. Everything burned bright and new into her retinas. I felt an iota of relief that she would lump this all together—strange white floating object, different from the one in Toksook; strange large crab, different from the ones in Toksook. She would never know what this Changed One once was. What would that do to her?

"Human." The word flew from Dee's mouth without physical shape or color and could not be returned. My eyes shot to the Changed One. The thing's monstrous body twitched. Its eyes swirled on their stalks. The bristly toothbrush lifted, the horrible, rotting lips parted far too wide. And the hideous decapod let out a scream. Skull-shaking, the sound of steam erupting from the body of a boiling lobster. The orcas vocalized in response. The crab made a breakneck scamper down the side of *Bering Mind*. It hurled its enormous shell into the ocean.

"Go!" I yelled to the male whale, Dee coiled at the base of his fin with her hands cupped to her ears, eyes squeezed shut. Killer whales burst from the deep, conjuring great waves that tossed and rocked *Bering Mind*. The crab's legs and claws flapped frantically underwater, propelling it toward us at terrifying speed just under the waterline.

"Quick, go!" I screamed to the whales, but the Changed One was too fast, a few feet from where I perched, thrashing those hideous, finger-covered limbs, screaming loud enough to serrate a skull. Three whales intervened, pinging screeching sounds off this monster's horrible carapace. One killer whale rammed him with her body, holding him back for a moment. He swung the larger of his claws and pinched at her. She ducked, disappearing below. Another whale shot up from the dark deep, snatching an orangey back leg, severing it from its host with a dull crunch. The leg continued to thrash and twitch in between her teeth as she carried it away. Another whale breached, leaping out of the water and slamming down on the spiny red thing. The red creature skittered below the water, shrieking in arrows of pulsing bursts. And it became clear to me then, though already known to the whales.

It was echolocating.

The matriarch and I had shot away from the thrashing limbs, but the large whale, Dee on top, now had a horror with dark red appetites in his face.

"Dee!" I yelled. She dove into the water. The Changed One thrust forward its larger pincer—now devoid of an electronic device—the very best defense of a crab. It grabbed the beautiful black skin of the large orca, clamped the claw shut, and yanked. Dee let out a primal roar. The orca released a sea of sound as the skin of his side was ripped open by the Changed One. The killer whale then snatched the claw that had caused his blood to paint the ocean in moody hues, ripping it from the Changed One's body. The orca pod was stunned, realizing this did not deter the creature. It was already scudding its way to the little girl thrashing at waves to escape.

"Get to her!" I yelled to the matriarch beneath my toes, and she was already doing it, already slicing through blue ocean, around the back of her bleeding son, to cut off a hunter, to get to the tiny being without gills. And the orcas, like waterborne missiles, convened, surrounding the thrashing thing. They released a hailstorm of sound bullets at it. The bullets—the same horrible frequency as the creature's screams, in every color I know—bounced off his shell, some penetrating the weaker parts of him. They were jamming his echolocation. Blinding him. The monster stopped thrashing, MoFo eyes swiveling, their stalks waving, like the fingers pockmarked across its back must have once done. The Changed One was stunned, jerking violently, orienting. Its antennae flailed, toothbrush bristles twitching, hunting in that ravenous way they do once they've succumbed to this rot. The matriarch pulled alongside my nestling. I tugged at her with my beak as she thrust her vigorous arms up onto the body of the old whale, heaving herself up next to her dorsal fin.

"Go now!" I yelled to the matriarch. She didn't. She held her space. One whale, in an ambush at torpedo speed, clenched down on some of the carapace's rigor mortis fingers, flipping the Changed One onto its back. It swung its remaining claw in retaliation, drawing a red wound along the whale's cheek. Upside down, the hideous underbelly, the

rotten plastron of the Changed One showed. Bloody tissue
and clumped algae smeared its pallid shell. Another whale
emitted a deep sonic boom of sound. The thundering force
of indigo hit so hard, algae and wet flesh were blown off
the Changed One. It was some sort of signaling, because I
saw—from the top of the matriarch and the careful confines
of Dee's pulsing fingers—the large male whale, the bleeding
son, charge the underside of the Changed One. He bit down
on a soft spot, where the pod had signaled. He tore the
creature's shell clean off its body. And underneath was a
MoFo body.

Dee stared at the scene from above the waterline. She
gasped. The body was deeply deformed, amputated from
finishing its transformation. Emaciated and maggot white,
limbs like long-lost bones. Feet ripped off by the whale
where they had fused to shell. The feet sank with the empty
carapace, releasing bubbles of protest. The MoFo was almost
transparent. A hole where genitals should have been. Its
imitation crustacean head too big, empty eyes still searching,
it was now silent. It started a slow descent. Sinking down,
down, down to its lowest place yet—the bottom of the ocean
floor.

The orcas circled the matriarch's son, pinging him with
gentle sounds shaped like maple leaves, glinting green and
silver. Dee nuzzled me with her beak, then placed me gently
onto the matriarch. Before I could protest, Dee had plunged
into the red waters, thrashing over to the male whale. She
nuzzled him, running her hand across his skin, careful to
avoid the gleaming raw gash in his side. She lifted herself onto
his back, red rivers running off her. She lay her head onto
his shining skin and stroked her fingers across his back, as
if he were a beloved owlet or baby Oomingmak shivering for
his life. She began the hum of the hive. Hum of healing. The

killer whales started to hum back to her. The pod slipped into formation and began to move.

I looked back, and all I saw were the dashed dreams of a boat and a sad swatch of distressed denim floating on red water.

The MoFo hadn't finished evolving; the weakest part of his shell had left him vulnerable. The whales had known. They'd seen inside of him with sound.

And Dee had known something. The Changed One had gone after her, the implications of this I couldn't bring myself to think about. But she had named her species. And she had not been afraid or let The Black Tide take her. I looked at her, surrounded by great guardians, the sea wolves, and saw that she was busy with her healing, humming to the whale, smoothing her hand and heart across his ivory eye patch. Dee wasn't panicking about who she was and what she might become. She knew who she was. A stargazer. Evergreen daughter. Buddy to the bees. Empress of owls and last legacy. A Blackwing's very best. A healer. My gutsy, ocean-hearted nestling was back. The whales had given her that.

"Crow." The matriarch addressed me in a controlled, hushed tone. "This is what you've been hiding from your nestling? This is the dark truth of *Aura*?"

I nodded as we skimmed the top of an ocean that seemed to be contemplating this too. "There are different types of them. Yes. Many in *Aura*."

"So…now we have met the Beast." And I thought of the orca's algae-covered story.

*They delivered the last human to the glass-eyed Beast so that mankind could pay back an earthly debt. So that mankind could, in its last blowhole breath, be reminded of itself.*

"I fear for your nestling," she said, and my blood froze. I had never told her I called Dee my nestling. Perhaps she read it on my heart.

As we traveled, the pod spoke to one another in a hectic hive of morphing shapes too rapid and ornate for me to fully comprehend, just as their names were. But I could extrapolate. The orcas hadn't seen anything like this. Which meant that what was happening in *Aura* had only just started in *Echo*. It meant that The Changing was not just happening on land. It was happening across worlds.

# CHAPTER 13

S.T.
SOME SLOSHY BIT OF THE BERING SEA

According to one of the books at the Nightmute library, salt water has many beneficial and healing properties. It can be an antibiotic, good for detoxing and skin infections, and apparently MoFos used it for "colonic irrigation," which sounds very sophisticated and I presume it to be some sort of farming practice, perhaps the judicious hydrating of cucumbers. After days and nights of being sloshed around and pummeled with salt, Dee's hair now resembled a homeless Angora rabbit. Yours truly was a bitter old crabstick—cantankerous, not my charming self. I learned that the Ocean is a living being with liquid blue bones. At times she felt like the gentle womb of a benevolent mother. Other times, she was a jade-eyed dragon. And I don't think she liked me very much. She garbled from a moist mouth, gushing an ancient, burbling language that might as well have been Klingon. She had brackish moods and mysterious appetites and seemed frustrated in her search for something, her desire ferocious and foamy. I wished she'd figure it out—my damn legs felt like microwaved Pocky sticks. It was no warm bath in the sink, let me tell ya. Our drinking water came when the sky felt generous enough to urinate on us. Mouth and beak opened to fat clouds, and we'd gulp as if we were crispy lumps of moss desiccated by drought. I was getting sick of all this kumbaya singing that was going on. If it weren't for the endless supply of salmon heads that were lobbed in my direction, I would have asked everyone for a big ol' slice of "shut the fuck up."

Dee, however, was happier than I'd seen her in years, the thrill of the water world glistening in her eyes. One morning, as the ocean mimicked glass, a ring of sea otters swarmed her, paws blooming open like flowers to offer her shellfish. She slurped each like a fine Jell-O shot. We watched the otters hold paws, so they didn't lose one another in the ocean's vastitude, and wrap their little pups in kelp. We swam alongside a pod of narwhals, who were adventuring south into uncharted territory. In this terrifying new world, what a tremendous advantage to be born with a sword sticking out of your melon. They lifted their speckled heads from the water and waved their teeth at us for good luck.[1] We met ratfish and lingcod, spot shrimp and rock crabs. Dall's porpoises, also sensing the temporary truce with the orcas, leapt above the waves and frolicked, calling to Dee, squealing with excitement when she responded.

"She is real!" called a chatty pod of beluga whales, their skin like gloating moons. Even wolf eels, the uncontested winners of the "Ocean's Ugliest" contest (imagine a vacuum-packed Philly cheesesteak, blasted overnight in an industrial-sized kiln, and bedazzled with gerbil turds), showed up. They oozed grimly to the surface to see if what they'd heard was true, that

---

1 Technically that's what those tusks are—an elongated cry for orthodontic work.

Dee was not the tale of a whale. Tiny, globular moon jellies pulsed and strobed nightclub colors in her presence. Great lion's mane jellyfish waved tangled masses of orange-sherbet tentacles among the scaly shimmy of the excited fish that hung with them for protection. Anemones and the scaled, even those venturing up from the ocean's secret depths—longnose lancet fish, mosshead warbonnet, kelp poacher, and krill— pulsed with waves of delight. Dee was an *Echo* celebrity.

"No paparazzi; move along, please!" I told them. No one understood me—story of my life. Dee was finally happy, but I was a grumpster. I missed Migisi and the feathereds. I was worried constantly and had gnarly stomach issues. I'd never spent so much time away from the rumination of tree roots, from the peep and chirrup of *Aura*'s network. From a world where aspens quake and cedars weep. I longed for the sylvan spells a forest casts. I felt like I was withering. Plus, I was molting, so I was the physical embodiment of Gene Simmons's toupee, if it had absconded from a yacht by way of a salty breeze in order to brawl with a boat propeller.

There are no words in any language for the cocktail of feelings that shook inside me when, after donkey's years at sea, shoreline came into view. Excitement thrashed its wings. Panic clamped its jaws on the chambers of my heart. Dread, an anvil inside me, bottomed out. And then, a tiny flicker of butterfly beats. *Hope.*

The dorsal fins, all twelve (I think), cruised like smoke-black spirits through the Strait of Juan de Fuca, land on either side of us calling to me. On one side, Canada; on the other, the United States of America. I had a clear mind map of this whole region from working on the islands with Big Jim! I listened for *Aura*'s call, but the shoreline was still too far. Trees were broccoli florets, buildings hidden by great green beards. And suddenly we were gliding through the familiar, whispery waters of Puget

Sound, passing Port Townsend and Marrowstone Island. Then Whidbey Island was on my left, and I felt a siren song so strong that I finally understood the unnerving inclination to burst into a Broadway number, shared by the black-billed magpie and the Lin-Manuel Miranda. I hopped up and down, longing to feel the tickle of grass and the great rumble of *Web*—that matrix of minerals below. Dee's eyes were large as plates (more tectonic than dinner), drinking in the newness of it all. My nestling stared at the regal, icing-capped giants of the Olympic mountain range with cracked lips parted.

Just when I thought I'd explode from the anticipation, we were there. To our left, a long pier jutted out into the water, where the ferries used to pollinate, dropping off their passengers with a bee's diligence. A sliver of beach hugged the mainland. Driftwood logs for MoFo sitting pleasure. A cement walkway. A wooden statue—some MoFo's loving rendering of a killer whale. In an eerie display of art imitating life, the whale had a chunk of wood missing from its back and the distinctive tattoo of teeth.

Against every earthly and waterly odd we had made it to land. We were in Edmonds.

I cawed out. "Hooray! Hoor—"

The orca matriarch bucked, sending me into the chilly waters of Puget Sound. I flapped frantically, scuttling onto her back like a scolded Suffolk sheep.

Dee turned to face Edmonds—finally, my nestling was here, looking at our homeland—and, oh, I had so much to show her! I wanted to show her where Big Jim and I came in this little city to fix electrical shitstorms, to lay pipes and then lay on the floor after slamming happy hour mai tais at A Very Taki Tiki Bar and Grill on Main. Big Jim met Tiffany S. for a drink there soon after they first met. Through the walls, a MoFo sang about three little birds on his doorstep, and I liked it. Tiffany S. wore a dress tight as sausage casing and Big Jim wore a sunburn so bad he looked like slapped ham. Big Jim's Very Taki advances seemed Very Obvious to me; he spent most of the evening staring at her boobs. I had always found his obsession with them odd—his own chiminea-shaped boobs seemed perfectly adequate to me.

"He wants to get to know you better; he likes you," Big Jim told Tiffany S. as I stuck my beak into her face. It wasn't at all true. I was already on the fence about her after she wouldn't let me pluck the sequins off her purse. I was in her face because I'd seen a spider on her eye, so I snatched it off and ate it.

"My eyelash!" she screeched. Big Jim spent the rest of the date apologizing profusely to her boobs.

Big Jim kissed Tiffany S. goodbye on her nose and watched her wobble away in high heels, contrails of Chanel N°5 trailing behind her. As we stumbled from A Very Taki Tiki Bar, the Edmonds murder watched me from Starbucks's rain gutters. I sat on Big Jim's shoulder as he zigzagged back to the Ford F-150, where we slept that night, Dennis and Big Jim in an Olympic snore-off. An Edmonds fledgling had cried out to me. He'd been quickly shushed by his mother, and I—emboldened by a few sips of mai tai—had squawked, "Fuck you, dudes!" at them in Big Jim's voice, causing him to convulse with laughter.

This memory once brought me pride. Now, it made me want to hide in a sewer hole. I wish I'd known then that a crow is a brilliant being, worthy of the utmost respect. Maybe I'd been riled up after sensing that something was different about Tiffany S. There had been so many MoFo ladies—the librarian, the lawyer, the gastromancer who conversed with dead people via tummy rumbles, the psychic we underestimated (she'd told Big Jim that the human population was about to be wiped out, which had really killed the vibe of mini golf), the body-builder, the one who wouldn't let me steal her earrings, the pet oncologist, the one from Zimbabwe, the one with six children, the one with dead mice in her pockets (Detective Turd eked them out, and she had to come clean about being an Indian python mom). These strange species of MoFo blew in and out of our lives like empty Cheeto® bags. But Tiffany S. and Big Jim had a fire between them. Maybe I'd felt an overwhelming instinct to put it out.

The whales slowed, approaching shallow water. They would not go farther. Dee seemed to understand what was happening. She nuzzled the back of the male whale, his side stolen by the claw of some unspeakable thing now Pepto-Bismol pink. She whispered sounds I couldn't hear.

"Our world is changing as yours has. We all have a part to play. Stay brave, Crow," said the matriarch in a snowing of small sounds, a peppering of purple.

"We will not forget that you saved us," I said to her.

"Our bones will remember one another. We were swept together by the stars and the sounds of the sea. I hope that your heart song is heard and that we hear it before it is our turn to come to the beach. Dee is the last of our sister species. Remind her of the code of together. We all swim alongside one another."

"Um, yes," I answered. I hadn't a clue. Honestly, she might as well have been reciting Shakespeare in Hungarian while wearing a retainer.

And then another sound filled us. Raindrop notes bouncing off clouds. Dee's eyes shot toward the beach. There, on top of a bleached throne of driftwood, was a sky queen.

*Migisi.* Relief broke me open. Dee let out the ebullient call of a bald eagle. She leapt into the sound and started a cetacean's swim to shore, stopping next to the matriarch to allow me to hop onto her head. Dark sails of dorsal fins shrank and disappeared into the horizon. We took a few moments to celebrate and chirrup, nestling our toes into the sand, over-whelmed with grainy gratitude.

Land. Home.

"Migisi! Where have you—"

Migisi fluttered down to the beachfront and gave me a look that could puree a pineapple. Her eyes were the twin daggers of some son of a gun with an ax to grind. I swallowed my question but was so happy to see her that I squeaked. I like to think she noticed how strong my thighs were after an eternity of squatting on a cetacean. Migisi landed—graceful as airborne silk—on Dee's arm. Eagle and MoFo stared at one another, eyes glittering.

But we now had a major problem on our wings. The sooner we got to UW Bothell to reconnect with my murder and get Dee into a safety bunker like the one in Toksook, the sooner I could breathe again. But what lay between us and Bothell remained as mysterious as the contents of Tiffany S.'s purse.

I knew from years of listening to *Aura*, to horrible sounds and terrifying warnings, that whatever had happened, it was bad.

Dee tucked me into her arm. Rivulets of Puget Sound slipped from her face, rolling off my feathers. We began a tense trek up the beach, along the cement trail, across rusted train tracks, and up Edmonds's Main Street.

And holy Funyuns, had it changed.

Edmonds looked like a Jägermeister hangover.

Grass sprouted its revenge between pavement cracks. Jungled weeds looked like magical beanstalks for mice. Vines hung everywhere, draped like Christmas lights that once festooned this city, a city that used to glow with winter cheer. Tree limbs had ransacked storefronts with the Hulk's pea-green wrath. Dee padded catlike in her wet mukluks. Her heart pounding against her rib cage caused my wing to pulse.

"It's okay," I whispered. "We're home." It just didn't feel like it. Dee lay all her trust in me as she strode into a strange, eerie city. Migisi's daffodil eyes ricocheted like pinballs, and we needed them to. The last time I'd tuned in to *Aura*, I'd heard chaos. And now—nothing but maddening silence. Where were the birds?

Ramshackle stores. Busted windows. Emerald ferns bursting in viridescent fireworks. My skin shivered. Dee squeezed me gently in her palm. We passed a theater whose movie posters had been clawed out. Sign hanging like a loose tooth. Caved roof, its belly filled with brick and debris. A Schwinn bicycle being slowly digested by weeds. To the right, movement— creepy curtains of an old '50s-style diner floating like ghoulish fingers. A MoFo mannequin in roller skates severed at the torso. Closer inspection revealed her eyes had been gouged out. Dee knelt to touch the statue's turquoise hat. My heart-beat made my vision throb. What did she make of this? Everything here was new to her. A flash of anger overtook me. Dee wasn't getting to see the real Edmonds—a proper movie theater, the real replication of a 1950s burger bar. She was owed authenticity—clean streets, trimmed grass, the plump smell of a burger arguing with a grill, cheese oozing lazily over its sides. She was given a cheap imitation, a masterpiece ravaged and shat upon. A hollow home.

We crept up Main Street, stepping over debris and a mon-arch of moss. We slunk around a windowless bus in the middle of the street; its side read, "The Most Powerful Network On The Globe, We're More Connected Than Ever!" I tried to do as the orca matriarch had advised—be brave, digest uncertainty, tame fear. Dee avoided deep pools of stagnant green water and kept her wings retracted to avoid mold and rust, that chemical conquistador.

*Where were the crows?*

I looked up at Migisi on Dee's arm, ivory head darting like

a faulty windup mechanism. Flickering panic in her eyes told me she had only just arrived here too. She had no idea what we were facing.

The center of Edmonds had a traffic circle and a desiccated fountain, Jackson Pollock-ed with moss and mold. I looked for answers in the trees but knew better than to call out. When *Aura* is silent, it's silent for good reason, but this desolation was bone-chilling.

Spooked, Dee started to run. She was a gazelle, leaping over the mangled bodies of motorbikes. Migisi skimmed the air above Dee's shoulder; I was in a cage of fingers. We ran and ran, alongside homes once prized for their proximity to Puget Sound, with sagging shingles like sloughed scales. And as we passed our allies—overgrown trees—my gut told me something was wrong with them.

And *Aura* remained utterly silent.

Dee, absorbed with every inch of her new world, was the first to spot signs of a life. She slowed to catch her breath, bending over a blackberry bush crossing a residential street. Dee coiled a leaf up to her nose. She had found a beautiful candy-striped leafhopper, shaped like a miniature shoehorn, belted with glowing blues and reds. The insect's head was a muted yellow. She stared with a terrorized eye. An eye that saw us as winged and limbed demons.

I craned forward to speak to the insect; I saw her legs coil, readying. Migisi let out one sharp warning. The candy-striped leafhopper stayed put. She understood not to mess with Migisi, lest her colorful little body be Benihana-ed into a small mound of glitter.

"Why is *Aura* silent?" I whispered to the cupcake-colored insect.

Frothy liquid waste bubbled from her abdomen, settling like spawn onto the leaf below her. Ah, the call of nature…

"Shhhhh," she hissed. "They're in the trees."

I darted my head to search the crowns. Migisi lifted her zero-bullshit gaze from blue and red stripes to the haunted trees. And the candy-striped leafhopper, who didn't trust anyone and so had survived thus far, leapt deep into the spiraling talons of the blackberry bush. Migisi, enraged, hopped from Dee's arm to take her aggression out on an ancient carton of semi-skimmed milk. When she was done, it was essentially confetti. While we'd been at sea, I guess she'd really been through some shit.

Dee thrust her arm out, summoning Migisi's talons. We took off, our eyes in the trees. What had the leafhopper been so afraid of? I swear to you that what I saw next was real.[2] I saw a tree trunk move. A flicker of movement. Not in the crown, but the trunk of the tree. *Jumping Jamba Juice.* I tried to remember anything from when Big Jim expertly self-diagnosed on WebMD—did I have yellow fever, scurvy, chlamydia? Was there some hallucinogen in the air? Is that why there were no birds here? I did feel sick to my stomach, and it had been ages since my last fish head. Maybe I was losing my mind. Burning the last fumes of sanity.

I jerked my head, urging us to keep moving, eyes on everything. Shit—for now, we had broad daylight on our side. But come nightfall? Then what?

A bouquet of decay suddenly filled our faces. The smell sat in our mouths, pooling like blood. Migisi lifted to inspect, the first time since we'd reunited that she seemed able to leave us. We followed to find her perched on a rusted shopping cart. She presided over plagues of plastic bags, something's scattered teeth, a Squatty Potty, and a jar of Belizean hot sauce. Migisi's

---

2   I'll also remind you that I had, regrettably, not had a drop of whiskey or so much as one fermented berry in a long time.

eagle eyes scanned an oozy mass of liquid that smeared the road. Grayish slime. Small, indistinguishable lumps suspended in goo. Red ribboning snaked in between the gray slime. Surely, blood. And something else. It looked like frog spawn lying on a mountain of mud. The spawn of a freakishly large frog, I was sure of it. One rogue frog embryo lay close to me, between a burst of black knapweed and a junk-mail catalog papier-mâché mess. Dee's frown summed up our confusion. I hopped closer to examine the amphibian embryo. They were not frog spawn.

They were eyes. MoFo eyes. All of them.

The world spun. Tree limbs seemed to swipe at me, my legs like burnt twigs. That horrible memory of Big Jim in our Ravenna yard with the shitty little smug-faced gnome I'd been trying to put out of commission. An image, clear as a glass squid, of Big Jim's icy-blue eyeball as it tumbled right the fuck from his head. Dennis, with his angel-wing ears and his airborne jowls, thundering after the eyeball. Big Jim's very last words: "What the fuck?"

The memory was too much. The pain unbearable. I was exhausted from constantly wishing the world could be better. I fluttered my gular, mouth gulping in air. Dee pulled me tighter to her. We had to get to Bothell, and fast. How else could I keep Dee from all this horror? Keep her eyeballs in their natural habitat? Keep her from becoming what every other member of her entire species had become?

A sound finally spoke to us. The crisp snap of a twig underfoot. Three heads—crow, MoFo, raptor—shot to the tree line behind us. The snarl of overgrowth let us down, hiding horrors. But we knew with the sense and savvy of prey animals; we knew. We were being hunted.

And the hunter was here.

Dee used her magic wand of a finger to point out the

one who'd come for us. And there, in between blackberry brambles, I saw an eye. Not a human eye, not like the ones gathered in a nightmarish heap of slimy trash where we stood, but a spherical orb still attached to its host. The eye stared, unblinking.

Dee raised her finger again, slowly trailing that pearly, half-moon nail. It hovered on another pair of glowing eyes. Her finger trailed once again to where the blackberry bush wrestled a great skeleton of English ivy. There, in among a war of green, was another pair of pupils, dark and terrifying as the ocean at night.

Three. Three sets of eyes. Three brothers. And a great, thorny dragon of a bush whose body hid stripes of black and orange.

# CHAPTER 14

S.T.
EDMONDS, WASHINGTON, USA

Nobody moved. Nobody blinked. Nobody chanced a breath or thought. The solitary eye—the first Dee had spotted—shone with recognition. It knew it had been seen. A glowing ember, it emerged with its partner. Their habitat—a massive striped head—burst through brush. Gnarled, anarchic limbs of bramblebush clawed at black and orange, scratching to hold on to the creature as if trying to help us. They couldn't. There isn't much that can hold back an adult male tiger.

He had changed since I last saw him, grown into his colossal face and body. His coat was heavier, stripes smoldering. Gray scars ran like long-dried rivers, eeling along his cheek and broad nose. Even a tiger had battled to survive a city changed. A growl, the rumble of an idling chain saw, clambered from his throat. It sucked the warmth from the air. From Dee's arm, Migisi stretched her full wingspan to give Dee great dark wings. And Dee's face? I couldn't see it; I was wrapped in her wondrous fingers, ransacking my corvid-MoFo mind to stop the claws of a tiger. Claws and fangs that are drawn to the delicate skin of a neck, to the percussive crunch of a windpipe. And if you know cats, you know that they cannot be bargained with. Cats obey no one. Where prey is concerned, they are puppets, strung into violence by invisible masters. The other two pairs of eyes stayed hidden. For now.

The cumbrous cat that stood several feet in front of Dee roared, a cloud-parting roll of thunder that quivered soil. Migisi was airborne now, flicking out the night-black switch-blades of her feet.

A weapon. Fire. A distraction. A stampede. My mind was like Dennis, rubbery nose sweeping the ground, gangly legs propelling his hunt for an answer. And I remembered that Dennis and I had been in this situation with these tigers before; we'd called for help, and the UW Bothell murder had come, pelting the tigers with a rainfall of debris from the sky. Where were they all now? I stole a glance at pale scoliotic trees, but there was nothing. *Aura* remained disconnected.

Dee, my nestling, opened her mouth wide. She heaved out a roar, a furious bellow from her guts thrown back in the face of the big cat. There was no fear in her voice, not a tremble in the fingers that cradled me. She flung me to the cracked cement of the Edmonds sidewalk behind her—a protective move. I ruffled, shot to my feet, and looked up to the back of her powerful legs, their slight squat. Dee stood tree tall and ready to take on a cat that weighed six of her.

The other tigers didn't stay hidden any longer.

Flash fast, two eyes burst from the bushes. A blur of orange and black flew at me in great leaps. Claws like hot scythes clamped down on my skin and then I was flung upward, suddenly higher and higher, until I was hovering above Dee's Angora rabbit–head and the flame-licked jungle cat in front of her. The second cat, the one that had charged me all those years ago at the Woodland Park Zoo, was below us, baring flesh-shredding teeth and a raw pink tongue. His sabered claws swung at the air, at me, furious to have missed my black body. I cawed at Migisi.

"Put me down!" I squirmed and thrashed, but when a bald eagle decides to snatch you in her talons, there is jack cheese you can do about it—just ask any salmon you know. And so we were far above my darling Dee, watching her standoff with a Malayan tiger in aerial view. The third tiger emerged sloth slow. He was somewhere in between the sizes of his brothers, approaching his largest sibling. The behemoth brother spun to snarl and swat at his striped sibling—a quick flurry of fire.

He'd found Dee first. She was his.

Dee used this territorial altercation of claws to snatch up a fallen branch. I called out to her in the famous unrelenting corvid alarm, the loudest call I knew. I didn't know what was out there, but I no longer cared. I screamed, daring a bigger predator to come for us, to take on these Malayan brothers.

"Caw, caw, caw, caw, caw, caw, caw, caw, caw!"

And then a terrible realization. Dee's branch was rotten; I could see it. It wouldn't host a bushtit, never mind stave off *Panthera tigris*. But she knew this. She knew trees better than the creamy contours of her own skin. She held out that branch to look bigger. She spread her wingspan—a great owl, an eagle—to show them how tough she was. She roared again, flashing teeth and tongue. She puffed her shoulders, leaning in to fight.

The largest tiger placed a paw toward Dee. I screamed from my soul. Dee lifted the rotten branch and pointed it directly at the tiger. The third brother's curiosity was piqued. He gave up swiping at the broken black bird and the eagle in the sky. He circled back to the second brother. All three tigers now faced the end of the branch stump with unblinking fascination. All three tigers facing down Dee.

"Migisi! Fucking help!" I squawked, pleading with her to drop me and go to Dee's aid. My pipe cleaner legs started to quake. Migisi tightened her talons on my wings. She would not see us both die here. The biggest cat placed a paw closer, his whiskers flinching.

"Go for his eyes, Dee! The eyes!" I shrieked, scanning for tools below. But I could read Dee's body better than any book, and I saw all the telltale signs that she wasn't listening to me. She'd tuned out the whole world. Dee was a tiger now. She lunged to poke the tiger's nose. A head jerk. He wrinkled his lips, lifting his whiskers. A sharp snarl, flashing of long fangs. Dee snarled back. The tiger opened his jaw, cavern of pink and black, angling his teeth down to bite the branch.

"NO!" yelled Dee in perfect English. "DON'T TOUCH."

Three striped heads shot up. Migisi flinched. The hair along the back of three tigers rippled into tight shivers. The biggest brother let out a long, melancholy moan. His brothers paced behind him. He chuffed. Dee chuffed right back at him. And then—Migisi flapping great gusts—I got a bird's-eye view of the largest tiger as he swiped the white fur of his cheek against the butt of the rotting branch.

"Don't touch!" commanded Dee in the dying language I'd taught her. "Never touch!"

The second and third tigers couldn't help themselves. They trotted up to her, muscling one another to get close. One rubbed his face against her side. Bicep flexed, she prodded him with the stick.

"No!" she said, her voice thunder. "Mine tree!"

I couldn't. Believe it. The tigers—frickin' cats, I will remind you—obeyed her. Backing up, moaning in submission. Blood would not spill from her throat today, near-extinct sounds would. The once-captive brothers had been raised at the Woodland Park Zoo and hadn't heard the roar of a MoFo in a very long time. Cats hold on to memories like prey in their paws. Their lives had been touched by the magic of MoFos. They'd been curious and found the last one, and, much like this droopy-winged crow, they had fallen under her soft-skinned spell. A trio of lovesick kittens. Tigers don't purr, but I watched them squint their eyes, chuff, rub their scent glands, and behave like obsequious butt badgers. The brothers fawned over Dee, but she kept them at bay with her body language, a crumbling, rotten branch, and instincts more evolved than I'd ever imagined.

It was unreal.

Dee had never seen a tiger before, only heard about them in my stories. I hadn't realized she'd been listening to it all—the stories of a very handsome crow and warnings about the world delivered by bees, or the loamy message of a mushroom. She knew if she'd have shown fear, she'd have been dinner. Dee reached her fingers out like charmed snakes. She ran them along the head of the largest tiger, while he chuffed and behaved like a house mouser on catnip. But Dee kept those shoulders and that branch up. A branch that I now remembered was reminiscent of the target sticks these tigers had been trained with at the Woodland Park Zoo.

The third tiger tried to get close to Dee. He kept his reflective orbs on me, primal urges lurking in their lenses. Cats can never be fully trusted; they wear a call to violence as well as that tongue-lashed coat.

"We know you," came a startling voice. The larger tiger tore his attention from Dee, allowing his brothers to thrust their hulking bodies forward to rub against her feeble branch. His amber eyes bore into me, where Migisi had placed us safely on a middle branch of a Pacific dogwood.

*Oh, you fucking speak,* I thought to myself, further proving that cats are just fuzzy middle fingers.

"You do," I said.

"Is this the last Keeper?" he asked, his voice an earthquake's early rumble. Keeper, like zookeeper. I was right; he had never forgotten his former life, but if there was empathy in his voice, I heard none of it.

"Yes," I told him. "And if you so much as bruise her, I will make a limited-edition poncho out of you." Migisi threw a sharp note into the air. Migisi had my fucking back.

The tiger let out a rumbling chuckle. "I like her smell. Now *my* will keep her."

"'*My*' will not keep her," I said calmly from a ghostly branch. "I am The One Who Keeps."

This didn't seem to register. Or he just gave a negligible number of shits. The third tiger, the smallest—which is relative because he was still the size of Nargatha's 3060 Series Meditub™—leapt toward the base of the tree, thrusting onto hind legs. He vomited blood-boiling roars, raking his switchblade claws down bark.

"My brother wants to open you," said the largest tiger.

"Jesus," I said.

"He remembers." The smallest brother remembered once leaping at me as I fell from a tree at the Woodland Park Zoo all those years ago, back when I still had the privilege of flight. He remembered the crisp, lemony scent of the defect in my wing, a primal calling. A scent subpoena.

I got plucky with the biggest cat. "Tell teeny tiger I'm sorry that the only thing that's shorter than his temper is his legs."

The tiger who wanted to snack on my impressively toned thighs roared louder. But my focus was on how the biggest tiger was in charge, how he kept snapping his head back to Dee. Curiosity and fond memories had caught these tigers by their stripy tails. The big brother snarled, and the tiger on two legs backed down, trotting away from the base of my tree.

I stared that big cat down, black eye to amber. "You remember how they used to be, the Keepers. And you've had to fight The Changed Ones." The tiger kept his burning gaze on me, but for a moment, a hint of exhaustion, frustration, something flickered in those burning eyes.

"We are together stronger than just *my*," he said.

"What is out there?" I asked.

"Death," he said with a snarl. *Fucking cats.* It was then I had to make a quick decision. We could escape these homicidal fur balls and their paper-shredder personalities, and we'd have to chance it to UW Bothell alone. But the brothers' scars told stories; they'd been here at ground zero for over a decade. They knew exactly what was lurking in the shadows.

I flashed back to an image of my salmon-cheeked nestling before her beautiful feet could carry her, of gingerly tucking beakfuls of blackberries into her smile.

I flashed back to an image of a horrible thing—not crab, not MoFo—and how it tore after my nestling, blood and destruction in its eyes.

"If you get us to UW Bothell safely," I said to him, "you can keep her."

Migisi protested in a patter of piccolo notes. She was already having an epically shitty day, and here I was, inviting the mutant orange ambassador of a species that had waged genocide on us egg layers to skip along on a suicide mission. Casually offering to trade our most precious possession. I shot her a look, a sort of "trust me" look, and she took her feelings out on the upper tree trunk, chunks of bark flying like welding sparks.

"Why wouldn't *my* just kill the little black bird and take the Keeper for myself?" asked the tiger with all the warmth of an autopsy table.

I improvised, trying to conceal my quaking legs. "Because of the mouse and the lion. It's...uh...a very well-known jungle story. Once there was a lion who was about to eat a mouse, but the mouse said, 'Spare me! Let me go and someday I'll repay you!' And the lion did. And then one day, the lion was caught in a hunter's net and I think he also had a thorn stuck in his paw, and the mouse came to his rescue by gnawing through the hunter's net, plucking out the thorn and freeing him. And he said, 'Now you see that even a mouse can help a lion.'"

"This is a boring bullshit story," said the tiger. "There is no *my* in it."

"But you are like the lion in this story, you see?"

"Hm. And you are like the mouse?" asked the tiger.

"Yes," I told him.

"*My* is the lion in this jungle story?"

"Yes. And maybe also a little the thorn."

I wish I could tell you what was going on in that large feline skull. The lead tiger looked back at his brothers. The marginally less violent one was rolling on his back, grumbling with padded paws in the air as Dee ran the branch across his belly. The other was attempting to headbutt everything within a six-foot radius.

"Where do we prowl to?" he growled. And I told him. He wrinkled his nose to snarl. "No. Not there."

"If you want her"—I gestured to the most novel prize on this big beautiful blue—"you'll have to take us."

So that's how we ended up here.

Picture this: A once-residential street in Edmonds wrapped in greedy weeds, frozen in time. Where cobweb-coated houses wear crowns of moss, and all around, ghostly pale trees hold their breath.

Picture an overcast sky filled with the most magnificent bald eagle, her wings like water. Picture the inky silhouette of a crow (super fucking handsome) perched on her downy back. Picture below them a streak of enormous male tigers in Halloween colors. Triangular trio of flame and ink. Picture, at the helm, the smallest of these three, a predator with quick claws and a grudge like Gorilla Glue. Behind him a few paw-prints, picture his brother, a cat with memories of MoFos and milk bottles, wearing a slinky stride and a sandpaper tongue. To his right, picture the biggest tiger of them all—the biggest you've seen—a cat who pounds the perishing asphalt, whose shoulders undulate with the ascendancy of waves. And striding in-line with the two largest tigers, picture this—

The last MoFo on earth, an apex predator above them all. A being so heart-crushingly beautiful the clouds part for her, enamored of her upright elegance. Look at how she balances on toes swaddled in mukluks once handcrafted by the dancing fingers of her family. Picture a peony-cheeked being with intelligence blazing behind bonfire eyes, stars beneath her glabrous skin. Picture a girl, the last girl, who survived because she was stitched together with stories and the hope they held.

Dee clasped the branch, swinging it to keep the cats in-line with a jab to their hulking bodies. She knew, my clever MoFo, about the tidal pull of invisible instinct, and so she knew never to turn her back on a tiger. She pressed on, passing houses speckled with bullet holes, bushes the size of woolly mammoths, a bulldozer with a broken nose, the rusting debris of her kind's legacy, stains of bombs and smoke and fire. All alien sights to Dee, an immigrant to humanity. And she always, always kept the spots on the back of black feline ears, like surprised eyewhites, in her sights.

But what was so terrifying about all of this—other than the obvious idiocy of putting our trust in three tigers—was that there was almost no life. I had been so afraid of encountering another degenerated MoFo or a Changed One like the one on the boat, but I hadn't expected this. There were no Changed Ones. Only horrifically yucky eyeball soup. The occasional insect and dweller of *Web* bugged out at the sight of the formidable apex predator gang—tiger, MoFo, bald eagle, and badass crow—and honestly, who could blame them? We looked like a fucking Salvador Dalí painting.

Migisi and I watched from the sky, making sure nothing ahead could surprise us.

"What is wrong? What has happened to you!" I asked stagnant maples and evergreens. I attempted to tune in to *Aura* and never took my BB-pellet eyes off what the felines were doing, mentally adding "cat herder" to my résumé.

"What has happened here? Tell me!" I yelled down to the largest tiger.

"Fight rules now," he said. "Claw is king."

"Can you be more specific?"

"Silence!" he roared.

We were quick to learn that tigers are not only vague as crap but they have the attention span of Instagram addicts. They bounded after anything that twitched, which in this hollow suburbia was every skittering leaf or evacuation shelter pamphlet with lofty dreams of elsewhere. They got bored and destroyed things for no apparent reason, taking out tantrums on trash. Endless claw sharpening. Incessant yawning. And they peed on *everything*. We had to perch on a mailbox, perishing of boredom, while they played hockey with a hubcap or "groomed" by saliva-sliming themselves with a tongue covered in the thorns of some death-metal desert plant. Inevitably their treasures lost their luster and would be peed upon in corrosive yellow signatures. The worst part? They inspired Dee to pee willy-nilly!

"No! Dee, discretion, for the love of Pete! *Behind the tree and hide your pee*, remember! Bury it in leaves!"

This was a major setback. The tigers had inspired her to defy the fundamental nuance and classic literary virtuosity that is *Poop! There It Is!*

Alas, big cats are as annoying as small cats, though instead of cat scratchers they used fir trees, and instead of stealing socks they pillaged the rear-mounted tires from Jeep Wranglers. They were taken with whacking things off other things, then staring disapprovingly at Dee as if she were responsible. And most irritating of all, they were unreasonably obsessed with boxes. Upon finding the rare box that had survived—whether Walmart or Amazon—the tigers would fight over who won the right to squash his box of fart into box of Amazon, only to then stare into oblivion awaiting knighthood. And every few steps, a black-and-orange snake would lift into the air, and a tiger would expel an epic mist of urine like a Glade automatic air freshener with scent "Autumn Ammonia." Even from the sky we were choking; Dee smelled like the dumpster of a San Franciscan Olive Garden. With every spritzing, Migisi screeched in despair. She took to strategically positioning herself above the trio and releasing a colossal white streak from the sky. After striping a tiger in white, she would chuckle fruitily over infuriated roars below. You had to admire her perversity.

The advantage of all this uncertainty and feline funny business was what I had hoped for—the tigers didn't miss anything. Tigers are normally solo striders, but these brothers had been together for years, changing their normally nocturnal hunting habits and honing their sixth sense for survival. Keen instincts meant getting to see another sunrise.

After a long walk and squatting in a shitload of boxes, we found ourselves at a crossroads. To our right, a residential street, darkened by twisted, fingered foliage. A war of weeds fought over a handwritten sign that said, **Ignoring my student debt like there's no tomorrow. suck my monthly statements, sallie mae!** To our left, an overgrown park surrounding a lake.

Dee lifted a mukluk toward the house-lined street. Three tigers let out strained moans, pacing side to side. Dark ears lay flattened on their great heads. It stopped Dee in her tracks. Migisi landed on a DEAD END sign, far enough away to prevent Teensy Tiger from making a corvid canapé of me. Dee froze, watching the largest tiger's stripes flicker with ripples.

"Death down there," he said. "*My* will not go." He let out a reverberating shudder that made my feathers stand on end. I squinted down a long street and saw silent trees, mired in shadow. Something about them was scaring the shit out of three tigers.

"Eko," Dee called to the largest tiger, who went by the name his MoFos had gifted him. The middle tiger was Liem. Liem liked to swim and had about as much personality as Big Jim's fatty lipoma. The small, homicidal one was named Olan The Asshole. Alright, it was just Olan, but that was an oversight. Dee pointed her stick at the park in the opposite direction of the trees and Eko got it. The tiger trio raced to the water and plunged themselves into the lake, ignoring my protests. Dee ran in after them, chuffing like a big cat.

"Dee, wait! Slow down!" I felt a barb of frustration at Dee's carelessness, her constant charging about the place and acting like an animal. She never listened to me. Migisi's eye roll felt like seismic activity beneath me as we soared over them. And then, from the middle of the lake, concentric circles emerged right behind Olan's bobbing body.

"There's something in the water!" I yelled to Dee and the tigers, paddling across grimy green that hid the horrors beneath. "Quick, get out! Get out!"

From the circles emerged a blanched and bloated back, skin poppled with petechial hemorrhaging[1] and red, roving eyes. A

---

1  I'm a forensic pathologist, thanks to fifteen seasons of *CSI*.

Changed One swam after the smallest tiger. Dee shot from the lake and yelled for the tigers to follow.

"Come! ZzzzZZZt!" she called.

Eko burst from the green water. Then Liem. The Changed One, bulbous eyes ballooning above the waterline, slithered across the lake. It gained momentum, closing in on Olan. Inches from having his tiger tail clamped down on, Olan sprang from the lake. The Changed One watched from the water. We prepared to flee but quickly realized that the monster had become a creature of the lake—it could no longer walk. It had atrophied, its skin slack and pulpy. Enormous and bass-like, it didn't have the energy of the other Changed Ones we'd encountered. A horrible reminder that these things were as unpredictable as cats. The creature watched with tumefied eyes from its aqueous prison.

Migisi and I met Dee and the tigers at the end of the lake as they shook themselves of the slimy green. I practiced Lamaze breathing for my pulse, which was now in the late stages of an African jazz number.

Olan The Asshole was extra snappy, unnerved by his close call. Eko looked up at me as Migisi and I whirled above him.

"The mouse saved the lion." He was contemplative. Very un-catlike.

"You're welcome," I said.

"*My* would have eaten the mouse!" roared Olan.

A very wise MoFo once said that you should never work with children or animals, and if his species hadn't succumbed to a hideous technological virus, I would have bought him a beer.

Dee was thrashing water from her haystack of hair when Liem lunged at her. He knocked her flat to the grass. In a second's snippet, he'd snatched up her wrist in between his fangs. Migisi and I dropped from the sky, bit down on his tail, and wrenched it with violence. He spun and roared. Dee shot to her feet, roared, and threw herself at his body, pushing him with all she had.

"No!" she yelled. "Danger!" He lowered his head and chuffed at her, whilst I made a small prayer to whoever might be listening that I would give up dreaming of Pabst Blue Ribbon–dipped Cheetos® and my old collection of those hilarious monkeys that dangle from cocktail glasses if we could please just get to UW Bothell with most of our appendages.

The Changed One in the lake slowly dipped down, disappearing into a sinister boil of bubbles. Migisi chirruped, alerting us to ducks that burst onto the scene, flapping like windup mechanical toys.

"Is that what I think it is? She's real!" one quacked. "Really real! I see the shadow she paints!"

"Can we stop for a minute, Meryl? I ate some rocks to break up lunch and I think I overdid it..."

"Focus, Rick! It's one of those bread-throwing things!"

"What's bread, Meryl?"

"I had so many options! The pick of the waddling! How did I end up with someone so uncultured?"

They were joined by more ducks blaring, "What is that?" "What happened to its beak?" "Rick's throwing up rocks!" "Never pick a partner for his plumage!" "How do we get it to throw bread at us like in the stories?!" until they were all chased away by a tiger with a rampant Napoleon complex and my chance to ask them questions became yet another thing doused in urine.

The closer we got to UW Bothell, the less playful the tigers became. By the time we actually reached Bothell and my chest fizzed like shaken Pabst Blue Ribbon, they were agitated and more than a little terrifying to be around. They skulked through neighborhoods, growling at the shadows of trees and the bowels of old Bothell buildings. And when we reached

UW Bothell, they were picking fights with one another. Dee's leg was caught in a crossfire of claws, red tears streaming down her calf. Migisi dive-bombed the big cats in fury. Our adventure eagle was soaring headfirst into some sort of ontological crisis.

"Quiet!" Eko snarled. "*My* have brought you here. This is where you chose," he said, as if coughing up a bone.

Mushroom-colored clouds darkened, frowning at my former home. I heard a crack that must have been a chamber of my heart.

UW Bothell looked like it had been hit by a hurricane.

Trees lay severed and splintered, ripped from the earth, their roots exposed nerve endings. Great swaths of grass had been uprooted, uncovering soil as soft as spleen. Blood stippled broken walls. The college's roofs had partially collapsed. Barbed wire lay in haphazard spirals like sun-dried worms.

And everywhere—feathers. Pewter gray. Pigeons. Bright cocktail colors and the soft pastels of a new nursery. Parrots. And most prevalent of all—panther-black feathers strewn everywhere like lonely ink quills.

Crows.

No bodies, but the delicate decor of birds everywhere. Dee lifted me to nuzzle my beak. Three tigers paced in silence. An agitated eagle swooped above. An urge to run gnawed like hunger.

What had happened to my murder?

I had promised my nestling to an unstable predator because I'd known I'd have support at UW Bothell, because hundreds of the taloned kind would have my back so she wouldn't end up in the possession of three tigers. What had I done?

Rhythmic whirring filled my ears. A blue body materialized at the tip of my beak. An ancient insect, nature's drone, a winged master of flight and sight.

"Come," said the great blue skimmer, his voice the crisp crinkle of a gum wrapper. He was the haunted blue of a wrist vein, eyes like faraway worlds. "Come, quickly, light as flight. You must move like shadows and you must not, none of you, make a sound!"

# CHAPTER 15

S.T.
BOTHELL, WASHINGTON, USA

Dee ran. Tiger paws conquered tired concrete with a spring of uncertainty. Migisi sliced through cold air. It was silent but for the breathy ruffle of feathers and silvery snaps as we broke through gossamer arachnid silks. The little spiders hid. It was a smart move; they were at great risk of drowning in a deluge of tiger urine. I hoped for wooded wisdom from the trees—maple and dogwood, plane and oak, cedar, pine, and sweet gum—with bent bodies and arthritic limbs, trees that had seen and suffered everything with the curse of sentient cells and deeply anchored roots. I needed their guidance more than ever. Still, nothing. Their silence felt like a burn, my feathers on fire with betrayal. And we had no choice but to trust, to follow that great blue skimmer as his glassy (and, from experience, frustratingly indigestible) wings whirred along deserted Bothell streets. The area was abandoned bones, a russet world, grimy and gun colored. We skulked past a thirsty gas station that had been ransacked. A yellowing poster that showcased the finest of roller cuisine broke my heart, my stomach yowling in sorrow.

"Hey, buddy, remember me?" the gas station hot dog seemed to say, still the radioactive pink of an unsheathed dog doodle after all these years. "Remember how fucking delish I was? And dude, you could've had three of me for a buck! Fuck yeah!"

We passed a giant prophetic mural of animals running—elephant, giraffe, wolf, ostrich, lioness, and the ubiquitous penguin—that said:

### STAMPEDE TO THE WOODLAND PARK ZOO!

Individual coffee stands, Seattle's little caffeine islands, sat in varying states of disarray. I got a jolt of joy from a quick memory—Big Jim and me driving his Ford F-150 up to the tinted window of Latte-te's. The glass would squeak aside and two breasts would bungee jump from the shack, thwarted from hitting pavement by the bikini equivalent of dental floss.

"Mornin', Big Jim!" Ashley would sing, as if surprised to see him.

"Ashley! Hell of a fine day!" he'd say, though he'd just spent the drive over there cursing Punxsutawney Phil.

"The regular?" the bikini barista would say with a flash of blue-white teeth. Her long hair always needed fondling when she asked questions.

A slight crack in Big Jim's voice, "Hold the sugar though; you're sweet enough."

Her fuchsia lips would lift into a smirk. "You sure? You usually take a shit crap of sugar—"

"Uh, yeah, sugar, no, the regular way's great." When she turned to froth the milk, Big Jim would smack himself in the head, leaving me to ponder how her Golden Globes hadn't been parboiled by the steamer nozzle.

"A treat for your parrot?" she'd ask, and he'd nod vigorously.

"You know him so well!" he'd say, which wasn't true, evinced by the fact that she still thought I was a parrot. She'd laugh, exposing her molars to the shack's roof.

"You're so funny, Big Jim," which was a vulpine move because it always fed her tip jar. And Big Jim would rev the engine excessively, cloaking her little coffee stand in F-150 fumes as he whistled Bon Jovi all the way to work. And as always, this parrot was left in awe of the striking similarities between the courtship rituals of the MoFo and the blue-footed booby.

Soon, night would seep its dark oil, and I didn't want us to be caught out here—wherever the hell we were—in these horrid haunted streets when that happened.

"Where are we—"

"Shhhh!" the great blue skimmer shushed me. Migisi's back muscles clenched. Dee and the big cats crept along a long yawn of a street with a sneezing of dormant vehicles—one Nissan Rogue, a midlife Chrysler, and an obscene number of Subaru Outbacks.[1] A minivan with the bumper sticker "Watch out for the idiot behind me" sat dust caked and dreaming of destinations. I surprised myself. In Toksook Bay, I had never expected a MoFo to suddenly materialize. And yet here, after all these years, I held my breath as we passed each bumper, in case a bright-eyed being poked their head through the glassless window and hollered in a bright voice, "You're here! I knew you would come! I never gave up hope!"

A great scholarly brick building loomed above us. The great blue skimmer kept its compound eyes on this building.

"Here," said the dragonfly.

Dee was already face-to-face with brick. She ran her fingers— fingers that had coaxed a newborn owlet from its frangible egg,

---

1 The Subaru Outback was the rusty steed of the tattooed, flannel-clad hipster MoFo, second fiddle only to the bicycle or an actual fiddle.

fingers I'd really come to count on—along a foreign barrier. It objected with a squeak under the pull of her skin.

A window. *Glass.*

I was dumbfounded. "How is this poss—"

"Shhhh!" spat the skimmer, shushing me for the second time. "Not safe here. Not yet." He hovered in the air mechanically, wingbeats like summer rain.

"Wait here," I said with great authority to Dee and the cats, who all proceeded to completely ignore me. We wound around to the side of the old school, which opened up to a grass field. Dee gasped. The tigers' warning growls slipped under the soil. Migisi chittered in shock. My eyes beheld bodies. Great moving mountains with hearts bigger than homes. Noses as dexterous as MoFo arms. Smoke-stained skin with wandering creases that rippled under the frolic of a fly. We were staring at a large and healthy herd of elephants.

I lifted my good wing. "You all stay back while I—"

Dee was moving toward the herd as if in a trance. Her hand, a hand that had lovingly dabbed yarrow across the dark hole where a beloved owl's eye used to live, reached out to the herd.

"Dee, wait!" I hissed and when I realized there was no stopping her, I addressed the herd. "She is safe! Please, she's just a calf!"

Eko's roar burst out of him. The largest elephants stepped forward, trunks lifted. Gray ears fanned like the great leaves of jungle plants.

"Dee, stop!" I yelled as she moved like a woodland sprite toward the enormous proboscideans. Disobedient Dee had placed herself between perennial enemies of an Indian jungle. And as the herd tightened their protection circle, a female elephant exposed her side and I saw words. MoFo words. She'd been branded by a species who used fire and metal, so that now her tattoo was a darker gray than her own skin. It had happened long ago, but elephants carry everything with them—they live closer to tree time than we do; memories reside in the soul of them—and all I could think was that if these elephants had suffered trauma, then little Dee could be a scapegoat for the deeds of her species. A present-day punching bag for the sins of the past.

The female elephant's burnt scar read:

CDC LYING! DON'T GO 2 QUARANTINE CENTERS!

The largest elephant trumpeted so loud, endangered glass rattled. The tigers flattened their ears, growling. Dee froze. The blazing cats paced with fury. Protests bugled from the herd. The large male charged toward Dee. I ran as fast as I could toward Dee. Puddles rippled under pounding steps. In a few great strides of tree trunk–like feet, he dwarfed her.

"Wait, wait, wait, wait, wait!" I yelled as I anticipated fangs clamping down on my body, for Olan The Asshole to do what tigers do when you turn your back on them. I made it to Dee. I crawked in gratitude as she snatched me from the ground.

"She is not like them!" I said. "She is good and kind!"

The enormous bull elephant lifted his trunk into the air like a bullwhip. He brought it down and brushed it across her delicious cheeks, over hair like the crispy noodle nests of a Chinese restaurant. He let his great trunk slide down the length of her arm as her eyes glittered like a sky stabbed with stars. A low rumble rolled from inside him as he swayed from side to side.

"This way," he said, turning. The herd turned at his beckoning and suddenly they were walking to the red brick building.

I looked back at three tigers who simultaneously flashed a great many teeth.

"She is mine!" roared Olan. "Mine for bringing her here!"

"Silence!" trumpeted the bull elephant.

"The Keeper is mine!" Liem roared, setting off minor earth-quakes in Guadalajara.

The largest elephant's voice lowered to an earthy rumble. "You will not place a paw closer. You have shown that you cannot be trusted to keep a truce. And we will speak of it no more." He turned to me. "They know the rules. They cannot pass this threshold."

We left the tigers pacing in a tangle of snarls on the sidewalk. Dee reinforced the elephant's orders by calling out to the tigers with a nasal, "Stayee! Dee come back!" Migisi did a victory lap in the air, laughing like a maniacal Disney villain. We walked toward a door, away from tooth-rattling growls, shrill whimpers. I felt a little bad about lying to the tigers, but not that bad. Olan and his stripe-spangled buttocks would have had me for breakfast. A quick bowl of crowtmeal.

"Phew," said the skimmer as he whizzed past me. "Wasn't sure if they would get you smush smush." I felt my fondness for him dwindling.

Dee turned to face the herd of elephants before committing to the red brick building. She lifted her arm to mimic a trunk. The male elephant lowered his great head toward me. "You have protected her all this time."

"Since she was a hatchling," I told him. "She's the very last."

"I remember. I remember you and your friend." *Dennis.* "He is very proud of you." If a crow could cry, I would have; I'm man enough to admit it. In his wise eyes, I saw the baby zoo elephant I had watched chase a murmuration of starlings all those years ago. He had made it. He'd grown, beaten over-whelming odds to adolescence. In spite of everything, his herd had thrived. A female elephant, the one with a sentence of scars, let out an insistent rumble like a machine's tired sigh. They wanted us to go in through a door too small for them to follow. A door wearing a sign that said "Tavern on the Square." And so, we did.

And the first thing that hit us was a smell that would quell the consciousness of a devout dung beetle. Dee sneezed. Deafening alarm calls echoed across a building that used to be a large restaurant. Dee thrust one hand up to an ear to curtail decibels on par with a Guns N' Roses concert—if it were held on an erupting volcano and Axl Rose had been replaced by a blue whale. I looked up to a spectatorship of birds, passerines perched on dusty chandeliers and ledges, wings outstretched, throats keening. Migisi surprised me by sitting on a once-gold railing to catch her breath.

Dee tipped her head back, staring at a grand bird ball. She spotted an owl and called out to her in a feathery, pitch-perfect tone. The birds, shocked to silence, looked like they'd flown into frying pans. Dee responded with a gentle hum, the drone and bumble of hive dwellers.

"No, Dee, speak *properly*!" I whispered. Once again, I was ignored, treated like a pungent plate of diced liver. The birds bobbed their heads for a better view. Many did not have a name for the witchcraft below. They'd been born into a world without MoFos; they were never-persecuted dodoes, glistering eyes agog. They were blissfully unaware of her violent history. It was as if they were witnessing the coruscating dance of a ghost. A bending back of time's hands. They stared at a unicorn, mythical in her motion. They were looking at the impossible. A one. An only. The birds stared with trilling hearts at a rising from the soil, from history, from horror.

They stared into the lonely eye of the sun.

And it wasn't just birds inhabiting this mildew palace. A puppy yawned. Its parents pointed at Dee with wet noses, tails and ears erect. Cocaine-faced possums blinked. A tortoise craned his neck to aid ancient eyes. Newts with glassy skins twitched. Chestnut-eyed elk sat frozen, their legs folded beneath them in a wooden booth that may have once hosted brunch. A snake fly waved her antennae, guarding eggs that glistened from the emerald leaves of a sprouting fern. Banana slugs painted velour furniture in silver. There was a bevy of brown—mule deer, beavers, moles, and marten—all watching the bipedal the elephants ushered in. A knot of garter snakes pulsed with anticipation. Ant and termite stilled their skittering. Dee captivated a constellation of creatures. And when they awoke from their shock, I didn't know what they would see. Whether they would see my precious nestling or a predatory ape.

I realized then that fauna that should have run from her had not. They could not.

What had happened was that we had walked into a zoo.

A starless zoo where none of the animals were caged. My head darted—back, forth, repeat—scanning the makeshift zoo, looking for who was in charge, hunting for the MoFo who had created it. No one—not skunk nor salamander—made so much as a soup slurp.

Every entity stared at Dee as though she were an exotic animal.

And then movement. Emerging from what had once been a bar and where a sign said "No Minors," a shadow slithered toward us. Its caster stepped from the blackness. He grew as he lumbered closer and closer, until he was towering over us. Waves of recognition and relief broke on me. He smoothed a hand over his long ginger cords.

*My god.* Orange the orangutan.

Orange, legend and hero, had helped me many years ago in Seattle. He helped us infiltrate MoFo homes and free the domestic animals who had been trapped inside when their owners succumbed to the virus. Without opposable thumbs, homes were impenetrable to us feathereds. It had earned him the nickname The One Who Opens Doors.

Dee wore an expression I'd never seen, her eyes suffused with starlit admiration. Some force of nature had waved a wand to conjure her closest living relative. Her heart pulsed like a moon jelly, the horizons of her world stretching with possibility. With hope.

Dee sat down in front of Orange with an involuntary *oomph*—the breath knocked out of her. Each finger trembled, her heart thundering in my ear. Her nostrils were the wings of a butterfly as she sucked in Orange's musty smell. She mimicked his movements and gave the cracked chirrup of a happy owl. Orange studied the water in her eyes, the great gray plate of his face lit with wonder. He snorted—cautious excitement, a colossal creature maneuvering as if he were made of delicate folds of rice paper. He lifted a blue banana finger and pointed at her leg, where the tigers had opened up her calf. Caked blood and mud painted her skin. A tear tobogganed down her cheek. I will never know what she felt in this moment—what it's like to see yourself reflected in another for the first time, to suddenly not feel utterly alone in the skin you're in. This was the closest to a Magic Kingdom moment she'd ever get, the heart-billowing joy and magic, the chance to witness a beloved beast rising from the pages of a fable. She twisted her leg to help him examine the wound. He kept his burnished brown eyes, stagnant pools of euphoria and sorrow, on Dee and her injury.

Dee gingerly slipped the sealskin jacket from her shoulder to show him a scar, an old tattoo from the Toksook days. He ran a rubbery digit across its slim white road.

Orange thought very carefully, reaching back into the recesses of his memory and his heart. He lifted his beauti-ful leather fingers, floating them in a dance as delicate as cottonwood fluff. He repeated the polished motions with the utmost tenderness, concentrating by pursing his lips. Orange put every ounce of energy into a long-dead language. Neither Dee nor I understood sign language, but we watched him paint the air with words, and for a moment, I felt like I could fly again.

"Can she understand me?" Orange asked me in gentle grunts.

"Yes," I told him. "Use your body and your eyes. She's listening."

"You are...you are different from the others," Orange said to Dee.

"She is very special," I told him.

He reached out slowly, wrapping my body in his fingers and pulling me toward the great gray moon of his face. Dee's muscles said no. They wouldn't allow him to take me. Her fingers whitened, tightening on my chest. Orange's eyes were gentle, full of fondness. He placed his finger on her shoulder scar again to convey empathy and that raspberry-flavored treasure—trust. In the animal kingdom, there is no greater gift. Dee released me.

"Old friend," the great orangutan said to me as I studied the rutted terrain of his faceplate up close. "Welcome home."

"Orange, I'm so very glad to see you." He looked fantastic, apparently one of those beings that gets mysteriously better with age, like Stilton cheese or Diane Keaton.

A terrifying voice elbowed out from behind the enormous male orangutan: "Get the fuck out of my way."

Orange turned, and we all watched a tabby cat swimming in scars saunter in like he had a saltwater fishing rod lodged up his rectum. Arthritic and acerbic, he was as feisty as fire. He minced toward us in saucy steps, glaring as though mentally rehearsing a plan to assassinate us all in our sleep. The cat brushed past Orange, rubbing against him possessively.

Dee instinctively stuck out a finger for the cat to smell. He cautiously sniffed the digit and rubbed it across his cheek. With a great deal of sass, he forced his way onto her lap.

"Fucking finally—I sent the tiger brothers to find you and bring you to me, even though they're shit at following orders," he said as he lay there, purring like a Harley-Davidson.

"How did you know we were coming?" I asked him.

"A little fish told me."

Dee attempted to pet him, which worked 50 percent of the time. The other 50 percent, Genghis Cat swatted at her with claws like prison shanks. He closed his eyes, purring in rapture, only to open his lids and ask her if she'd brought him any "fucking cheese." I felt the tigers had been excellent training for this moment. Good old Genghis was another badass from our Seattle past, a ferocious tabby who'd forged a fierce and unlikely friendship with Orange and his family. Dee started to purr, the cadence of a cat, of a creature who had *finally* been accepted by wild things. This, I thought, was where we could hide. Yes. Dee could be safe and happy here.

"Who is in charge?" I asked Orange, whose family—both orangutans and feral cats—was surrounding him, choking on their curiosity. Dee excitedly pointed a finger toward a window, where a flutter of newspaper-colored feathers had emerged.

"Goobarry!" she said. Genghis purred louder at her words. Orange touched Dee's lip with his leather finger.

An African gray fluttered down to the crap-adorned carpet we sat on. "My dear old friend!" he said to me in a voice like a cascading waterfall. A voice I'd missed as much as Cheetos®.

"I cannot tell you how good it is to see you, Ghubari." I tried to play it cool and hold back a dam of emotion but still managed to sound like I had a northern red-legged frog in my throat.

Ghubari studied Dee, how she mimicked Orange's gentle

movements, how she avoided the unprovoked swipe of a cantankerous old house cat.

"Goodness gracious. How on earth? Just...look. Here she is. You've manifested miracles, Shit Turd. Look at this young lady before us, alive despite so many odds. A little seedling determined to reach the sun. The tiny turtle determined to taste salt water."

I beamed, I'm sure of it. "Where is Kraai?"

"Kraai and the crow murder are the night eyes; you will see them in the morning."

"What is happening?" I asked him, gesturing to all the eyes upon us.

"Come, we must talk in private." Ghubari—a parrot who puts the RAAAAAAAA! in brain, truly a suppository of knowledge— didn't miss the tension that suddenly filled the air; he could feel my resistance. "She will be safe here. Just advise her not to touch Genghis's belly. Or his legs. Or anywhere around his back. And also, not near his nose."

I looked up at Dee, and down at Genghis Cat who was audibly rehearsing a plan to assassinate us all in our sleep. "I'll be right back, I promise." Dee made to stand, but Orange placed his finger on her shoulder again. I nodded at her.

*You're okay, my nestling; everything's okay.*

I looked over to the railing at Migisi. Dee had adventure eagle eyes on her.

"Come, Shit Turd," said the wise old African gray. "I have much to tell you."

# CHAPTER 16

S.T.
MCMENAMINS, BOTHELL, WASHINGTON, USA

Ghubari and I hopped out the building through a gap between bricks. Night began bruising the sky, the clouds claw marked. I saw no sign of the elephants or tigers. I marveled at Ghubari's pewter gray, the bold crimson quills of his tail, flashing on the last time I'd seen him, all those years ago. It was in our Toksook Bay cabin. We'd made the long journey there from Seattle with Pressa, Kraai, a sharp-shinned hawk, a northern harrier, and a Steller's sea eagle with a beak like a stand-up paddle board. We met the five snowy owls who came to be like family to me as they huddled defensively around my little nestling, tiny Dee, who was starving and in desperate need of someone to love her. We were so busy, eschewing sleep for days on end to help the last MoFo on earth. I remembered the conversation like it was two hours ago.

I hopped around the dusty cabin planning Dee's salvation, pelting words at Ghubari like spit seeds. "We need to gather more food; she's still malnourished, and her skin is too cold! We can probably sort out a better shared living situation and take her care in shifts—"

"Steady, Shit Turd, steady. We came here to help the owls, to answer their plea. We must share our knowledge, teach them how to keep her alive, and then we must return home. A lot of lives count on us."

"But Ghubari!" I couldn't help my voice from leaping an octave or two. "Look at her! She's the last MoFo on earth! She's here with us! We have to stay here and care for—"

"S.T., bless you and your big heart. The owls have imprinted on her, it's too late for them. She's too dangerous."

"She's not dangerous! She's a tiny hatchling! She's a miracle!"

"A miracle? Or a Changed One in a different skin?"

I looked to the raptors for support. Stern faces, each resembling the sphincter of a fretful shar-pei. It communicated an alliance with Ghubari and his big brain.

"Pressa?" I pleaded.

"I know this is hard, but it isn't safe, S.T. Let's finish teaching them everything we can, give her every fighting chance. Then we must return to our own nest. Please, S.T."

Kraai said, "S.T., you must come back with us. I cannot leave the murder and I cannot bear to leave you here. We don't know what she'll hatch into. Come home, my friend."

I looked over at Dee, shivering and helpless. I marveled at her pink fingers, counting them as my heart filled. I was already home.

Ghubari was gentle with his words, but they still felt like they were shot at me from the muzzle of a rifle. "We cannot stay with you here. We have a responsibility to those who have come to depend upon us—those whose species have a chance at a future. You need to separate yourself from this creature, because one day what happened to every one of the humans, what happened to Rohan and Neera[1] and Big Jim, will happen to her, and S.T.—it will destroy you. If not your body, then worse—that big heart of yours."

The last time I saw Ghubari was as he lifted into a silk-scarf sky with Pressa, Kraai, and the magnificent birds of prey.

Big brain and big heart had fought. Heart had won, but it didn't mean it hadn't been broken in the battle.

Ghubari and I hopped along a dark dirt path toward a small shed. The door was propped open, so we squeezed through. I was cloaked in dark until I heard the familiar chafe and hiss of a struck match. Suddenly, I was in heaven.

The shed was ornate, untarnished by hoof or claw. A sifting of dust added to its general charm. It had stood the test of terror. There were a few chairs, a tiny little bar, and—slap my bad wing and call me parrot—rows and rows of intact whiskey bottles.

"Okay, I've died, and this is the afterlife, right? Macallan, Buffalo Trace, Glenmorangie, Johnnie Walker Blue? In glass bottles? This is it. I'm dead. I know it."

"This is The Shed. It used to be a whiskey haven for humans. Now it's where I go to contemplate." Ghubari's eyes traced the quaint chandelier, a lamp held by an iron bat and snake sculpture, warm flickers of light that danced along cobweb-free curtains, delicious old books, a sleeping fireplace, and a Persian rug with minimal feces on it.

"How on earth is it…this nice?" I asked.

"I've done a lot for our community. I've been granted one private space."

"I've always admired your ambition, Ghubari!" I blocked out a thought of our little cabin in Toksook, the good memories we made there, our owls, Oomingmak. I was getting good at blocking the pain.

---

1 Rohan and Neera were Ghubari's beloved MoFos.

Let me ask you this: Have you ever been around someone so intelligent you feel you have the IQ of a congealed blob of refried beans? That's how I felt around Ghubari, Plato of parrots. And here was the perfect opportunity to finally showcase all the (sometimes drunken) learning I'd done at the Nightmute library.

"It reminds me of a quote I once read, '*Intelligence without ambition is like a turd without wings.*'"

"Bird."

"Where?!"

"'*Bird without wings.*'"

Goddammit fucking shit fuck.

Three sharp raps on the door. I dove into the fruit bowl.

"No need to panic," said Ghubari. "My esteemed colleagues are here."

*Esteemed colleagues*—how did he know so many clever things? I tried to commit it to memory for later use. The door creaked open. A head bragging in Caribbean blue and buttercup yellow poked through.

"*Raaaaaaaaaaa*, hello!" came a bright burst of a voice. Enviably MoFo. The blue-and-gold macaw sauntered in, her lengthy tail dragging in a brush stroke of crayon colors. Her face was white, skinny zebra stripes framing her limpid eyes as if applied with Tiffany S.'s eyeliner. Behind her, a yellow-crested cockatoo strode in and whipped out his wings, waiting for something. I suspected applause. Ghubari gestured first to the macaw and then to the cockatoo, who had fluttered up to the bar top next to me to admire himself in the cloudy mirror.

"Shit Turd, it is my pleasure to introduce you to Calliope"—the macaw bowed—"and Tom Hanks."

Calliope bobbed her bright head, gingerly lifting a foot and its mosaic tiling of scutes.[2]

---

2   Like scales, but way cooler.

"We've heard many stories," she said. "There are even songs about you."

The cockatoo's yellow crest fanned up at the mention of songs. "Oh, a song! What joy! What shall I sing for you?"

"Tom Hanks is quite the performer; he specializes in dance," said Ghubari. Tom Hanks broke into an enthusiastic shimmy on the bar. It was very leg-centric, his slim limbs snapping up and down cancan high as he performed a sort of hectic Irish dance. I didn't know how to react. Beings who burst into song and dance have always made me anxious. Tiffany S. once dragged Big Jim and me to a theatrical production of *Mary Poppins* and I hoarked a Doritos Locos Taco all over the man bun in front of me.

Ghubari turned his attention from the jig, pupils pinning as he focused on me. "I thought you were dead, Shit Turd. We stopped hearing from you."

My heart rate galloped. "I couldn't risk anyone knowing about her."

"I want you to tell me how you kept the girl alive. And how on earth you got her here without wings," he said, calmly.

I gestured to the lines of whiskey behind the tiny wooden bar. He nodded. I wrestled the waxy top from a bottle of Maker's Mark. Someone had ingeniously left a pile of tiny stones on the bar top. I dropped stone by little stone into the bottle until whiskey splashed down its neck and sides. I dipped my beak into little whiskey puddles, filling my belly with fiery gold.

"Hey!" Tap. Tap. "Is this thing on?!" quipped Tom Hanks in perfect MoFo between wing splays and jumping jacks. And then I told Ghubari, Calliope, and Tom Hanks what I've told you—everything. They listened calmly, except Tom Hanks who was busy blowing kisses and moaning "hubba-hubba" at the mirror. And when I was done and the whiskey felt like lava inside me, Ghubari started to talk.

"It is very grave news to hear that *Echo* is now affected. But I suppose that was to be expected. The Changed Ones are a cancer on the earth, and cancer spreads."

Calliope screeched and recited from memory: "*Raaaaaaaa!* 'The Hallmarks Of Cancer!' By Douglas Hanahan and Robert Weinberg! One! Cancer cells stimulate their own growth. Two! Resist inhibitory signals that might otherwise stop their growth. Three! Resist their programmed cell death. Four! Multiply indefinitely. Five! Stimulate the growth of blood vessels to supply nutrients to tumors. Six! Invade local tissue and spread to distant sites!"

Ghubari continued. "The Changed Ones have thrived. They have changed in ways we could not have imagined," said Ghubari.

Calliope flapped her turquoise wings and spoke in an old MoFo voice, so raspy I envisioned a ghost of blue smoke coiling to the ceiling. I saw yellow moons for fingernails and the way that time had drawn a beautiful map onto a MoFo face, etched evidence of a life. "*Raaaaaaaa! 1 Corinthians 15:51–52! Behold! I tell you a mystery. We shall not all sleep, but we shall all be changed, in a moment, in the twinkling of an eye, at the last trumpet. For the trumpet will sound, and the dead will be raised imperishable, and we shall be changed!*"

"What do you mean, 'changed'?" I asked Ghubari. "Like The Weavers?"

Ghubari continued. "There are many more types. We have been watching a species morph and evolve at an unprecedented pace. They are mimicking the natural world around them, developing survival adaptations—"

"The Bassian thrush uses farts to hunt prey!" I don't know why I blurted this out. Nerves and whiskey were in a vein-popping arm-wrestling match over who could embarrass me the most.

Ghubari continued. "They are growing and changing on a global scale. They are conquering territory. They have driven species—predators even—from their hunting grounds. And so, the Sky Sentinels banded together and came here. We are safe for now. We live here in symbiosis, in strange habitat homogeneity. Each creature can stay here during the night hours and when The Changed Ones are active."

I nodded. "We must be carefully circumcised."

"*Circumscribed,*" Ghubari corrected.

A peek under my feathers would reveal I'd turned the ceremonious red of the Japanese flag. "When are they active?"

"It varies. They seem to go through periods of dormancy. Conserving energy, like a state of torpor. And then they are everywhere, gaining more ground, destroying creature, land, and soil—"

"Is that what happened to the trees?"

A hard sigh. "The Masticators. In areas they have ravaged and hunted, they have eaten the trees from the inside out. The trees are hollow. That is why *Aura* is no longer effective everywhere. They have shut our great connectors down. S.T., we're watching an evanescence of nature. Most biological warfare happens at a scale that we cannot perceive. Not this. The Changed Ones are taking advantage, annihilating what was a growing abundance of species—a testament, really, to the creativity of evolution. Does it choose to take a thousand years or a day? The evolutionary theater of the living world is fascinating. They are stealing from us, transforming through rapid speciation, genetic mimicry, phenotypic plasticity, who can say? I fear this play will end a tragedy."

He squawked loudly and then mimicked Rohan's voice,

flawlessly: "'*Adaptive radiation is a process in which organisms diversify rapidly from an ancestral species into a multitude of new forms, particularly when a change in the environment makes new resources available, creates new challenges, or opens new environmental niches.*' Humans are more dangerous in death than they were in life. As their territories grow, the silence of *Aura* is spreading. We are facing a Darwinian War."

"My god. Are you sure about all of this?"

"No, not really. I'm a parrot."

"Then...why is it safe here?"

"Because The Changed Ones have not yet taken this area. Because we have a herd of elephants, a thousand birds, and a great many species that defend this area. But as more of them become active, as they gain strength in their transitions and adaptations, we will have no choice but to run. And hope there is some habitat left for us."

Tom Hanks, sensing the discomfort in the room, launched into another lively round of Riverdance while singing Michael Jackson's "Smooth Criminal." I raised my voice to be heard over his theatrics.

"Ghubari, I saw some terrible things. I saw a great mass of MoFo"—I swallowed discomfort with a slurp of Glenlivet— "MoFo eyes. Like a collection."

Calliope ruffled her feathers and spoke. "The Changed Ones come in different forms. Some mimic birds. Others mimic spiders or larger predators. They are all degraded humans, a virus-ravaged body's violent struggle to survive. *Raaaaaaaaaaaa! Calliope! We've got to go outside! We've got to find help!* I believe the ones that are out there were all once healthy humans, the ones that didn't rot and perish. A species cannot survive if they cannot reproduce, and what you saw was an attempt at that. Parthenogenesis—that's the word for reproduction without a—"

"Mate or a turkey baster, yes; I got it, thank you. Virgin birth. Solo sexy time."

Ghubari looked disapproving. "That was one of a great many failed attempts. They cannot reproduce."

I hopped in excitement. "This is great news! So, the fuckers will die out at some point!" The whiskey was talking. I felt a hot poker prod of embarrassment. *Keep it together, S.T. Be super smart and stuff.* "Ghubari, I can't tell you how good the relief feels. To be here, to have somewhere to hide her. Ever since we were in *Echo* and that crab thing tried to kill her—"

"I don't think it was trying to kill her."

"Uh, no offense, Ghubari, but you weren't there with its weird-ass eyeballs on stilts and the way it went bat-turd bananas when it saw her."

"I told you they are trying to reproduce. They have been hunting for a female."

The room spun and I'm pretty sure it was only partly the Macallan.

Tom Hanks picked up on the tension and started head banging while mimicking his bubblegum-voiced MoFo, who I quickly ascertained must have been in the performing arts. "*Why yes, I'd love another glass of wine,*" he said, followed by, "*Do these leggings give me camel toe?*"

Ghubari continued, louder. "It's only a matter of time before they find her. We must prepare her for an attack on them. I'm certain that the answer is war, and she's the only one of us that can operate human weaponry. Dee is the only one capable of the reciprocal, necessary violence."

Calliope channeled her old MoFo again, and suddenly we were sucked back through the waves of time, plopped into the middle of a nightmare. "*Raaaaaaaaa! The gun cabinet, where are the keys, they're at the window, GET BACK, GET BACK, my god . . . Calliope, what have you done with my keys?*"

That even shut Tom Hanks up.

Calliope's MoFo came to life, materializing in our minds through the muscles of her banana-yellow throat. "*Calliope, go girl, go on, through the window—get help, I can't hold them off...go to Daniel, girl. Tell him to barricade the windows, Calliope, they're banging on the windows! Oh no! Windows, Calliope! Tell Daniel barricade windows!*" I saw a desperate old man, cut off from the world when technology went down. Who was Daniel? A son? A brother? Calliope's MoFo had no way to call for help other than his beloved parrot. Calliope started preening, a self-soothing act.

My breath became ragged. "They will not come near Dee. They will not know what she is and that she's here. She will not fight anyone's stupid war or go near any weapon on this big beautiful blue. Do you understand me? She is the last MoFo on earth. She is my nestling. She will hide out here and I will teach her things and help her become a grownup MoFo."

"Bravo! Bravo! Encore!" cheered Tom Hanks, perfectly mimicking the sound of applause.

Ghubari laughed. "My dear friend, all these years and you've never given up your hankering for the old days, the times of Rohan and Big Jim. She is not of that world or that time. She, too, is changed."

"No!" I'd spent a decade wishing to hear Ghubari talk, and now I didn't want him to speak anymore.

"Take her unusually long toes, or the shape of her. Though young, I can see how strong she is. Her legs—"

"No!" I told him.

"She has a tree climber's hands and a body that survived a virus none of her species could."

"Enough!"

"She has the eyes of a night hunter. She sees better than we can in the dark, can't she? How is her sense of smell?"

"STOP, GHUBARI!"

"What deal has she struck with the mosquitoes that they haven't eaten her alive? She sings the bombination of bees and knows how to read the language of the natural world like no other human has ever done. I sense she knows it better than you or I."

"She is MoFo—she is better than the natural world!"

"She *is* of the natural world, S.T. Humans were never exempt or separate from nature. She is a survivor, seventy percent water, just like the planet she hails from. She is not from the old world. She is a wonderfully wild thing and she belongs in nature. You cannot trap her this way. If you drive a pin into the back of a butterfly, it will never get to taste a life."

"She's not a stupid butterfly—"

"That's a metaphor—"

"Yes, I know what a fucking metaphor is! I'm not trapping her! I want her to live a safe life; I want her to be what she's supposed to be—what's wrong with that? Everything on this planet might want to gawk and poke at her like an endangered zoo animal or destroy her for being born, but I won't let that happen!" My gular fluttered so hard I was almost panting.

"*The hiiiiills are aliiiiiiiiiiive!*" Tom Hanks sensed he was losing his audience. He added a peppy, "*I can cry on cue!*"

"My dear, heart-strong S.T., the only one who is treating her like a caged animal is you! Humans kept themselves from the outside world by encasing themselves in terrariums. An inch of glass to keep nature at bay. You are doing the same to the last human by cutting her off from a world she belongs to. She is not in your possession any more than she is in the possession of The Changed Ones. And you couldn't control her if you tried—she's female."

I thought of Tiffany S. from Tinder's Beelzebubian wrath when I cached her fake nails. I thought of the bikini barista's power over Big Jim and how the female wolf spider, black widow, scorpion, and praying mantis murder their male counterparts. I remembered how the female mosquito, never the male, was the one who sucked Big Jim's plasma, and how after copulation, a male drone bee's genitals are ripped off and he dies for his queen.

He had a point.

"You can't hide Dee away from a life. They will come for her. You can't stop them. But you can prepare her to fight. Maybe the last human can be the one to end this." He hopped to the tiny table where I was perched, candlelight illuminating his scarlet tail feather. He took a short sip of spilled whiskey. "Her being here, you being here, is giving us great hope. The creatures here are invigorated. They'll come to love her. They will help protect her as best they can."

I felt crushed. Broken. Stupid. Drunk. I thought about the words of a walrus: *She has a part to play in all of this. It is known.* I thought about the female MoFo I had known best, Tiffany S. from Tinder, and how the last time I saw her she was lying unconscious in a white hospital bed, machines chirping like sparrows, tubes snaking up her nose. She'd been attacked on the street for having the audacity to walk alone. Because she was a woman. Because she was prey. And even in a changed world, it was the same for Dee. She was being hunted.

But I didn't have to listen to Ghubari, planetary as his brain might be. I was quickly formulating a plan. Dee and I could not stay here; this was not the shelter we were looking for. Millions of MoFos sought shelter when the virus hit. Many must have made underground bunkers like the one Dee's family had hidden in. I would bargain once more with the tigers, with the elephants, the orangutans, with whomever I needed to for short-term protection, and Dee and I would find that shelter.

And we'd live there, my Dee and I, together, happy, and safe, for always.

Tom Hanks was now hosting a pity party for one in the corner of the bar. His yellow crest hung like a collapsed sail as he stared mournfully at his toes. A MoFo word finally made perfect sense to me—*crestfallen.* He had not managed to keep the party vibe—he had not shared the joy of his spirit, and so he had let down his MoFo, a consummate entertainer. Ghubari and Calliope took notice of his dejected state and shared a look.

Calliope opened her curved black beak and projected up to Tom Hanks on the bar top. "*Raaaaaaaaa! I see a little silhouetto of a man...*"

The yellow crest shot into the air. "*Scaramouche! Scaramouche! Will you do the fandango!*" Tom Hanks resumed his zealous Irish prancing. I was reminded that it took a team to keep The Black Tide at bay.

Early-bird light fluttered against the shed windows. We had talked all night. "Ghubari, my bones are burning. I need to rest. We can discuss more later. Please take me back," I pleaded.

Tom Hanks took a deep bow after finishing off a weird little ditty about milkshakes enticing young men to visit his property.

Ghubari gestured silence as he snuffed the candles with great wing flaps, and we, three parrots and a crow, started across the dirt path lit by a haunted moon. Then the night screamed. It was a hawk's summoning to hurry, but so much louder than any hawk I'd ever heard. Ghubari bodychecked me, slamming me against the side of a rock. Tom Hanks hid under Calliope's great teal wing. Ghubari raised his head to the sky. I followed suit, and what I saw made my brain melt.

Great bodies with gray pebbled skin and oily feathers sailed above. Things that were neither birds nor MoFos, but some bastardized imitation, cruised with wingspans the length of a Subaru. So large they hid the moon. I knew them instantly, remembered my best bloodhound buddy Dennis tearing along a road as they thundered behind him with ostrich legs and barreled chests. Fuliginous eyes. Malformed faces. They had changed. Smaller, lighter legs. Elongated heads. Full beaks. Functioning feathers.

They were *flying*.

Once the overhead horrors had passed, Ghubari whispered, "Go, quick as you can!" We tore across the dirt path together.

When we entered the Tavern on the Square through the brick gap, most of the animals were asleep in their tiny territories across the dilapidated restaurant. I couldn't process what I'd seen. My gular was break dancing in my throat. Calliope and Tom Hanks watched me with worried eyes.

Ghubari whispered, "It is shocking; you must breathe. A lot to take in all at once, my friend. You must not be sad about all this, about your altricial girl, S.T. You know, your beloved MoFos would call you a hero for what you've done." I cringed, guilt spiking up my spine. "In terms of your interpersonal human relationship, so little has changed. You had a mutually beneficial relationship with Big Jim, and look at your relationship with Dee—it's pure symbiosis."

*Symbiosis?!* I stopped him. "Ghubari, you're not wrong often, but about this, you're way off base. It is not symbiosis. You have forgotten how much you once loved a brilliant MoFo named Rohan. In this wild, wild world, Dee is the reason I open my eyes; do you understand me? Her heart opened mine, its beat is the soundtrack of my soul. She is the feeling of flight. She gives me back my wings. I will tear the sun out of the sky to protect her, and as long as the ocean breathes, I will love her with the feather and fur and ferocity of every living beast on this big beautiful blue."

That buttoned his beak.

Dee, Migisi, and I made a temporary home there among a refugee menagerie. I can't tell you for how long, only that we saw quite a lot of sunsets and sunrises. While I was uncomfortable around so many animals, Dee was revitalized. She was living in a storybook come to life. For so long, she'd heard my story of Orange and Genghis, of elephants, dogs, and the bravest birds on this big beautiful blue. And here many were—crawling up her arm or attacking her ankles or chewing on her flock-of-seagull hair.[3] She loved every second of running around in the story that helped grow her bones and brain. She loped around with Orange and his family. She befriended more eagles—bald and golden. She mimicked the sounds of insects, reptiles, and amphibians. It kept my hoyden of a girl in one place, levitating with happiness, but I hated how this was furthering her jungle etiquette as she learned about life from skunks and rats and horses. I worried most about the inordinate amount of time she spent crouched among flowering plants, humming to the pollinators who skittered across her skin. I was trying to raise a MoFo, not a cub, not a pup, not a kit. Why couldn't she try harder to be who she was supposed to be? How could I get her to listen and see the magnificence in her species?

The tigers stalked the sanctuary perimeter to be closer to her, and pachyderm protection meant they couldn't get to her. And it wasn't all sunshine and salmon roe. We were under siege, hiding indoors when The Changed Ones were active and flew above us, showering us with horrible screams. We could only relax when they were dormant. And those windows seemed to be getting smaller and smaller. I have just one

---

3  Her hair was not like the MoFo band, but rather a literal flock of seagulls wrestling over ramen.

more complaint—the crows. Our reunion was beautiful, but brief. I barely got to spend time with my beloved murder at all because they were our sedulous eyes in the sky, and they spent all their time on the roofs keeping watch or being heroes while tracking the movements of Changed Ones. The Sky Sentinels didn't have time for play or the whiskey shed. I'd watch them streaming above, seasoning the sky with their onyx wings—but they were above me, so high above me. How I wished I could join them.

It's hard to be a hero when your wings don't work.

Maybe they hadn't truly forgiven me for abandoning them— for breaking the code of murder.

And then one night, I may have put a few too many stones into the bottle, if you catch my cricket, and I'd been trying to convince Ghubari that I understood complicated things like Schrödinger's cat and Higgs Bosom. Ghubari exhibited saint-like patience, gently suggesting we head back to Tavern on the Square since the sun was rising.

I hopped over to where the orangutans slept, draped around filthy velvet furniture. Clone-like clusters of stripy cats and kittens had filled themselves in between woolly orange bodies. Orange snored gently while clutching an enormous stack of well-worn Victoria's Secret catalogs. I beak-prodded him. Genghis Cat sprang into action, hissing at a stubby urn of Grey Poupon and then me once his eyes had adjusted.

"Where's Dee?" I asked. Orange hastily shoved his catalogs behind him and pressed on leathery knuckles to lift his great body, ginger cords trailing.

"She...she was sleeping here," he said. Green-cheeked conures woke and shrieked, rousing skunks and moles, am-phibians, reptiles, and insects whose eyes became searchlights hunting for the unicorn they must have now felt they'd only dreamt of.

Migisi was awakened by animal sounds, chittering in panic. She'd been asleep and hadn't seen what happened to Dee.

Ghubari looked at me with citrine eyes, feeling the knife slice of my terror. "A MoFo whose movements don't wake a menagerie of creatures on high alert. She is quite miraculous…"

I couldn't hear the rest of what he said because my heart was pounding a jungle-drum alarm.

Dee had vanished. Taken by a night filled with horror. By an enemy who wanted her for unspeakable things. And I was getting ready to tear the sun out of the sky.

# CHAPTER 17

MATIAS
GRIFFON VULTURE
AÑISCLO CANYON, SPAIN

Death tells us a lovely story. You know this, don't you? Pay attention, my son; hear it in the snapping of sinew, see its slippery elegance in the bubbles of blood that escape from an open throat. These canyons have always been our home. The limestone cliffs, the icy retch of glacial waterfalls. Here the sun beats the faces of rocks. Tattling turquoise rivers mock the lush greenery. They claw at rock and swallow soil, a steady and stony slaughter.

The One Who Hollows as well must return.

We must always listen for death to tell its next story. It may sing a twisty song, percussive panting, and final notes. Undersong of the Underworld.

Kettling in great warm loops under a cloud kingdom, Death summons us with a smell. The smell of a heart in stop. Snapped bones. Beatless blood. Last exhales. Shiny rivulets of freed fluid. A spill of soft, glistening organs. Escaped tongues. There is bluing, delicious dampness, new holes become new homes. An exquisite swelling. Brave, billowing gas and a pie-bald rainbow pleasuring the skin. Stiffen and soften, repeat. Death is the most impossibly beautiful transition. There is no sweeter smell. There is no greater calling.

Falling in flight, we touch our talons to tenacious moun-tain grass. Among its gentle blades—sibilant sighs—it tells us the story of a rabbit. The grass knows what happened. The grass always knows. The rabbit has not been in Death's lung long. Death's sweet, sweet scent has called the others to her bidding. Blowflies—always female, happily ballooned—entrust the rabbit's fulvous fur with their precious eggs. Bacteria mimic the river's confidence, drenching themselves in glowing glory, changing Rabbit's inner climate and welcoming the mighty families of *Web*. An army of ants has arrived, a great black river, invading the rabbit's frozen eye, a sightless delicacy. We all dream of juicy marrow and the full-flavored strings of the heart. We wait to hear the birth of maggots, who buzz and shriek with joy, delighting in their great Feast Of Meats. They are at home in a palace of worms; they know they will go on to greatness. Below us, the greatest power of all—the fungi net-work, that great tentacled wonder. Pulsing with pleasure. We honor the almighty connectors of *Web*, the secret messengers of the soil, with the richest of the feast. And then we admire what is left, an astonishing art of bone, cartilage, and fur. Rabbit sustains a tiny Universe. An homage to life, the master-stroke of death. We all play our part in the music. Life and Death hold hands and dance.

Death is certain, my son, as certain as your father and I knew you were ours when we found you, the lone porcelain sheen in a nest of crushed shell and yolky slime. Your father and I knew you were ours. A lady vulture had loved you, incubating you in a twiggy nest before her wings were ripped from her mantle, before something's teeth yearned for her downy chest, leaving a gentle shower of taupe feathers. Another lovely story.

We tell our stories again and again to remember, son. You will remember when the sweet scent summoned us, when we first laid eyes on that great pile of human corpses. You will remember how we touched down on the grass and they told us in a sharp whisper, "RUN." You will remember how the smell was different, the sweetness cloying. You will remember how the sun pointed to the giant eggs that lay nearby, so close, too close, in buttery gleams. You will remember how we circled the five enormous eggs, unsure, vomiting our doubts, hopping and calling for answers.

"Run!" screamed the grass.

You will remember the first sharp crack in that colossal egg, like the sound of crunching spines. You will remember the strange, sick beast that bared its nakedness, its bluish skin sticky with gungy white fluid, its horrid, misshapen beak. Its one human eye—round and roving—pink as a fresh brain. It was hunting. We knew, already hunting. From shell but not of shell, with twisted limbs, sickly wings, and a craned neck. This creature, who shrieked in Death's cold warning, is not in the dance, neither Life nor Death. These things do not share or give and so do not belong in a tiny Universe. You will tell this story again and again so that we all remember. We remember to run.

Change is as constant as the shadows that lick and tease our limestone canyons. And when Death comes for us, we will be grateful for the chance to play in its generous spectacle. There will never be a greater honor.

Death can be soft or sharp, a moment's kiss or a hero's odyssey. It can be quiet or colorful, violent as talons on soft-bellied fish or as stealthy as a long-leaved butterwort using its delicious stickiness to trap a gullible fly. Death has eyes and ears and that smell—that sweet, sweet smell. It is, in all its shifting ways, utterly magnificent. And the best part about Death is that it is all of ours to share.

These canyons have always been our home. You, son, have always been our home.

# CHAPTER 18

S.T.
BOTHELL, WASHINGTON, USA

I stood outside the crimson-bricked citadel of Tavern on the Square, life robbed of its nectar because my precious nestling had been taken from me.

*Use your head, Dee; it is the best advantage you've got,* I thought, as if she could hear. *Use your MoFo mind to survive.*

Snow was falling from the sky. The crisp morning air beaded with beautiful black bodies. My mind was mossy, running on fumes of fear. I hardly cared that I smelled like A Very Taki Tiki Bar's urinals or that I was still molting and resembled an electrocuted echidna. My chest felt scalded. It's hard to breathe when your heart has been stolen from your body.

An inkwell's spattering of crows stained the roof, magic carpet bushes, Narnia-esque lampposts, the stately corn dog silhouettes of sweet gums. Migisi watched me from the red building's rain gutter. It was so unlike her to have fallen asleep while keeping guard of Dee, but I couldn't criticize. To quote an infamous avian proverb about hypocrisy, *"Birds on lofty boughs should be wary upon whom they shitteth, for they may endeth upeth on a less lofty one the following night and be shatteth upon themselves."*

Crows touched down on the snow with dinosaur toes in battleship gray. I scanned for familiar features in satin silhouettes. Most of them were young—a crèche of crows—and I didn't know them.

Warning calls sounded out, the foretoken of corvids who were hyper aware of the enormous raptor on the rain gutter, but confident in their numbers. Migisi, ruffled, watched the inky invasion, her eyes narrow and vindictive like two escaped anal beads.

And then a voice like cool water trickled from above. "S.T.!"

She landed like sifted sugar, flashing the singed underside of her wing, a place where feathers could never grow.

"Pressa."

"You look—"

"Yes," I said, standing before her like a Spirit Halloween wig that had been repeatedly brutalized by a Segway.

"What has happened, S.T.?" She was shiny as latex, her eyes the last lambent coals of a dwindling fire. Four crows, each with large, sleek bodies and beaks that sloped into sharp points, touched down around her. Their heads darted back and forth as they took me in, assessing, sporadic wing flaps serving as warnings.

"It's okay," she told them. "He is murder. This is S.T."

Sons, I thought. Pressa's strapping sons. They hopped on anisodactyl feet,[1] assessing the crow equivalent of a turd in with the Tostitos.

---

1 Three toes forward, one toe back.

Hundreds of black feathereds mantled the edifice. My neck strained from searching for the most beautiful crow of all, and the danger of these night watches dawned on me. Had something happened to Kraai? Guilt sat in my belly like a hunk of freezer-burnt venison. Heroes didn't last long in a world like ours, and Kraai could never have changed who he was.

The last crow fluttered from the sky, spilled confetti. We all watched the feathered embodiment of courage, a miracle dressed in black wings.

"Kraai!" My voice was something ragged, a ship fighting through ice and rock.

"Tell me," he said, feeling panic pour from my plumage.

"It's Dee; she's been taken." I pointed my beak toward the red brick palace behind me. "Ghubari's inside. He says you'll help me."

There were a lot of things Kraai could have said to me, things about abandonment and the tangled fishing lines of friendship. How I'd fallen silent in the murder's time of need. He said none of them. Instead, he peered right inside of me, right at the hole where my heart should have been, as though not a decade but a day had passed, and he said, "We will find her. We are the eyes in the sky."

Forgiveness is the ultimate act of strength. I bobbed my head in gratitude.

"The last human can't be difficult to find," he told me as he gestured to hundreds of glistening eyes.

"Don't count on it," I said, remembering Dee when she was several springs old, how she would crouch, blending in among bursts of monkshood, marsh marigold, cotton grass, and fireweed. How she learned to pad, soft as a lynx, evolving from the mistakes of a Sitka black-tailed doe— the twig's crunch that gave her away. How she snatched fish from the water world with falcon-fast hands. How she learned the prickly lesson of patience, stalking me as I sipped from a fresh puddle. She pounced, snatching my body in quick pink fingers and laughed, a sound like rain-drops pattering bluebells. How I told her she had to find a new practice subject unless we could locate a functioning defibrillator.

Migisi dove from the rain gutter, snatching a talon full of snow and soil, unsettling the dark crowd. She lifted her clasped talons to investigate and revealed a tiny, panicked head. It was desperately trying to bite her with miniature, knifelike teeth.

"Ach, let me…let me go!" He screeched, and she squeezed tighter. There were no protests. Really, no one felt compelled to challenge a raptor in the midst of an existential meltdown.

The shrew's pinprick eyes were closed with the exertion of escape. "No, no, let me, get, go, ugh—"

"Wait!" I said to Migisi, who shot me a look colder than moonlight on a penguin's ass. The eagle's death glare suddenly morphed into a large flat-screen TV and a cozy craftsman living room long ago, where I sat, stabbing my splayed toes against a remote to change the channels. I located National Geographic, then nestled into the La-Z-Boy®, helping myself to a little beakful of the warm Pabst Blue Ribbon Big Jim had orphaned due to having fallen asleep naked on the coffee table again. I stole a Cheeto® from its bag gingerly to avoid a rousing rustle. Dennis, all velvet folds and jowly slime, lay at the base of the La-Z-Boy®, dreaming about something vivid. His gangly legs thrashed, whacking the legs of the coffee table, and his tail mimicked a rudder. He emitted shrill moans and porcine snorts. I rolled my eyes at the slimy, half-eaten bull pizzle that lay next to him. The Nat Geo special, my late-night treat, had been about shrews. I watched the Bugle-nosed rodents skitter across the screen, learning about their territorial nature and impassioned battles. About how shrew moms venture out with their babies by having each of them clench the base of a sibling's tail to form a shrew safety conga line. I learned about the venom they inject through grooves in their teeth, a venom strong enough to kill two hundred mice. They use echolocation to find prey, determine where enemies are, and navigate space in a black underworld. What I learned from that Nat Geo special is that size is relative, and this little guy was worth more to me alive than as Migisi's protein bar.

Brilliant thoughts unleashed from my mind, thundering forth like the supreme athletes of the Canterbury Park corgi races. One idea careened across the finish line. I yelled out to the shrew, explaining what I needed.

"She'll let you go if you'll help us," I added.

Migisi squeezed him so that his phallic nose inflated, and his eyeballs looked like steamed pork buns.

"*Migisi!*" I squawked at her. "Do you agree, shrew?"

He nodded. Migisi reluctantly flung him to the ground and started beating up a mound of snow-covered sword ferns. The shrew prepared to dart, and then saw all the eyes in the trees.

The shrew sighed heavily before doing as asked. The crows tilted their heads in confusion. I hoped this would work because I wasn't sure how else to stop Migisi from snacking on Special Agent Shrew. The shrew burrowed underneath the soil there and then, emitting sounds—tiny, crystal bell–like tings—through the world of *Web* as he went. He moved fast enough that the birds fluttered to the nearest tree when necessary, tracking him from the sky. Twitter and skitter, twitter and skitter. I felt I had begun to lose my audience; I could feel Kraai pulling in the air, needing to tell me to leave the shrew and get to hunting the best way possible—

from the clouds. But then, *eureka*. The little shrew struck gold.

"This one?" he asked, whiskers twitching. His eyes were no bigger than a needle's.

Under the lip of a rock was a haphazard silver web and its creator, a black widow spider.

"Yes!" I shrieked. "Thank—"

But he had already vanished into a dark tunnel network beneath the sparkling snow, tiny obscenities echoing in his wake.

Pressa fluttered down and jutted her beak. "How did you know he could find the spider?"

"Shrews are the only rodent who can echolocate," I whispered. "I learned it from the MoFos. I've seen the magic of echolocation up close; some good friends showed me."

"S.T., why are we spider hunting? How will this help find Dee?"

"The spiders will know who took Dee; they've always watched over her. But spiders are hard to find unless you have a bond with them, right, Spider?"

The black widow—a defensive female with the telltale scarlet hourglass painted across her body that translates as "don't fucking eat me" in bird hieroglyphics—sat watching with eight skeptical eyes.

"I'm a friend of Dee," I whispered. Her body relaxed in recognition. I asked her where Dee was.

"A hunt," she said, lifting several arms. "Find the tigers."

It wasn't much, but enough for me. "The tigers! Quickly, we have to find them!" I shrieked.

"I just saw them!" called out a crow with one backward-facing feather. "I know where they are!"

Kraai dropped to the ground next to me. "You are tired; we can find her for you." As if the black feathereds hadn't already been patrolling these treacherous streets all night, unheard of for birds who instinctually huddle from hidden frights and nights with grabby fingers.

"No," I told him. "I have to be there; I'm the only one she listens to." I warmed myself with the costly fleece of a lie on the coldest and bleakest morning in memory.

Migisi spread her chocolate wings, a hundred crows looking on in utter horror as I stumbled onto her back.

"Rise!" called Kraai, and hundreds of wings lifted with the grace of Pabst Blue Ribbon bubbles. The red brick building and the gray hulls of elephants shrank to pebbles. A tower of giraffes ambled near them, from this height now wandering pencils. Ivy-smothered buildings had drunk the drink-me potion and a greatly changed Bothell looked like a train set swaddled in snow. And we set out to find my heart.

Kraai and Pressa aligned themselves with Migisi's smooth flaps.

"Dee!" I called out. "Dee! Dee!"

"NO!" snapped Kraai. It was the first time I'd ever heard him lose patience. The crows, busy birds of constant chatter and a whole Reddit thread of opinions, flapped silently, the air stitched tight between them.

"There has been so much change since you left," Kraai told me in a velvet voice. "*Aura* has been sabotaged. It is spotty at best, the connectors unable to reach one another through the hollow trees. It is dangerous to be out here in the great numbers of a murder. But to be alone..." We both let the sentence trail like the landscape in miniature below.

I searched desperately for the weathered ruff of a sealskin parka and hair like a back-combed Peruvian guinea pig. I looked for dexterous limbs and a strong, agile body.

I just wanted her back.

From the sky it was easier to see the barren spots The Changed Ones had claimed, gloom gray and poxed by rust's slow war. I caught glimpses of scurrying creatures—rat and rabbit and raccoon—as we soared across a white kingdom.

*My Dee. My best thing. Where are you, Dee?*

"Kraai," I reassured myself, "Dee can handle herself, even among tigers. She's a MoFo; she has the traits of them. I want you to get to know her, Kraai. I want you to see how much potential she has—" I stopped. It was too hard to go on.

"I don't doubt she is a marvelous creature. But you should know that this is no longer our world. The Changed Ones have taken over. They are destroying our homes, feasting on our bodies. They are caging us, and our cage is shrinking. We fly when they allow it, when the skies are clear. Which is only when they are dormant."

"They are dormant now?"

"Of course. There are lone ones, some that seem to be struggling to change and survive. But most of them—thank flight—are dormant."

"They are becoming more active, aren't they? Getting… stronger?" The temperature dropped.

He tucked dark thoughts behind a cheery tone. "Let's focus on your nestling. Keep your eyes wide-open. We're almost there."

We flew in silence, hundreds of eyes in the sky. The birds scanned a fondant landscape for movement. Packs of dogs gilded the ground with pawprints. A white blanket shrouded the rusting relics of extinct MoFos.

And then, as if the sky had heard my desperate pleas, thanks to the luminous glow of snow, I was able to clearly see streaks of orange and black as they thundered between trees, across an ivory quilt.

"There!" I cawed.

Migisi lowered, streamlining her body into a bullet. The crows plummeted with us, calling out the location. Orange and black zigzagged between the bulbous crowns of trees. From above, the scene was spotty as they ducked in between foliage, vehicles sleeping in snow, across treeless patches. But I knew. They were hunting. Chasing something down.

*Dee.*

"Get to them, Migisi!"

My shivering legs squeezed tight as we swooped down, licking in between tree trunks, narrowly missing scratches from skeletal boughs. Speeding snow blinded me. Rocks blurred below like rivers. The crows called for the tigers to abandon their hunt. A rabbit vanished into the wrinkled pockets of a cotton landscape. Migisi lowered to hover above three orange-and-black cats.

"You owe me a rabbit," Eko growled at me.

"Dee's been taken!" I told him. "Taken by one of . . . them."

His roar was a living thing. His brothers growled at him, biting at the air. He was putting them in danger, calling unwanted attention to a trio who stood out like a crow in a coffee shop.

"Silence!" said Olan, licking his lips. "We will find her. Come!" The tigers broke into a run. The eyes in the sky followed.

"You cannot trust them, these cats," Pressa said, appearing next to me.

"I don't trust them, Pressa, but they say they can find her!" I said, huffing clouds of cold air.

The snow blurred the lines between areas green and thriving, and the urban patches ravaged by The Changed Ones. We could no longer clearly see the delineations, the boundaries of safe and not. We reached a clearing ringed by Douglas firs. They held out their arms in a welcoming manner, and

we filled them with our bodies, clutching to their lichen-
licked branches. The tigers started sniffing, rubbing against
bark.

"Where is she?" I asked the firs, feeling their faint heart-
beats. They didn't answer. Only a few clung to life, sacrificing
bright pulses and nourishment they couldn't afford to give in
a determined quest to revive their loved ones. Trees would
never lose hope, and they would not stop gifting their own
vitality in magnetic messages and deep, earthy altruism. I tried
not to imagine their suffering, and instead imagined what else
was out there and where Dee might be in a world I had no
mind map for.

A cluster of glowing eyes with pupils like pinpricks stared at
us from a hollow in the fir.

"Who are you?" called Kraai, flapping from his branch.

"Raccoons, I think," I whispered to him.

Faces poked out of the dark abyss. It became clear that they
were not raccoons.

"What are you doing here?" I asked, stunned.

"Trying to live?" said one of them, peering from their
huddle in the hollow. There were a cluster of yellow eyeballs
and a crowding of long, striped tails. The creature's voice was
pleasant, a musically tropical tongue in a strange land.

"Ring-tailed lemurs," I said to Kraai. "Zoo survivors."

The lemur extruded a skinny finger from the hole in the tree,
pointing below. "Tell them to fuck off, please." He gestured
toward the cats being cats at the base of the Douglas firs.

"Please, I need you to tell me if you've seen a Mo...a
human."

The lemur looked at me as if I'd slapped one of his wives.
"They're everywhere, those beastly creatures, tearing up the
trees and preying on everything that moves—"

"No," I said. "A real human. Like they used to be."

"He's been at the fiddle-neck, Tahiry," said a sharp voice from the Madagascan huddle. "Hear that, Felana? It's asking if we've seen any healthy humans around!"

"Crazier than a bag of bark beetles," said another lady lemur.

"What is it, Hanitra? I can't see!"

"Some sort of grubby parrot. Lost all its fancy colors. Might have been on fire at some point. That reminds me, Felana, I have a lump I'd like you to look at—"

I didn't take it personally. I refuse to be insulted by a species that practices "stink fights" by rubbing scent glands from their wrists over their preposterous tails, then flicking them at one another like nut-bag perfumers. Tahiry lived with so many partners because lemurs are polygynous (one male mates with several females in a breeding season). MoFos were also sometimes polygynous, but most tended to have just one wife, which they called monotony.

The tigers were sniffing for scent marks. Liem rolled in powdery snow. I looked around this forest clearing gently nuzzled in white and saw other eyes in the trees. Things were hiding from us. Other things were surviving here, and I felt the stabbing ache of wanting that for Dee so very badly.

"Kraai, what if we split up? We'll find her faster," I suggested.

"No," he said. "We never split up. We are more powerful when we work together because we look out for one another by being one. That is the code of murder. You are..." And then Kraai spoke MoFo, which I'd never heard him do. "*Family.*"

"Kraai, please, we have to keep moving; I have to find her. Every second that slips by...How much area is there to cover?"

"S.T." He paused, took his time. "I want you to understand that if she is taken by a Changed One, we may not even see her from the sky." The air suddenly seemed poisonous, burning my lungs.

"This way," came a low growl from Liem. The tigers padded like forest phantoms, leading us to a stand of western hemlocks.

We feathereds landed, silently, sensing a presence in our pinions, touching onto wintry limbs. And there, splayed across the bough of a great blue-green beauty of an ancient evergreen, was my nestling. My heart.

She wasn't moving.

# CHAPTER 19

S.T.
BOTHELL, WASHINGTON, USA

Dee's body was prone, slung across a thick, mossy bough half-way up a Sitka spruce. Her legs and mud-speckled mukluks dangled. Her arms hung, lifeless, from the branch, precious hands mottled, stiffened by snow. The clumped fur of her sealskin parka's hood was pulled partially over her head so I couldn't see her face.

Migisi and I were on the same page of this horror story—*get to Dee, now.* Our eagle lifted her warrior wings. Dee's head snapped toward us, baring the *back off* warning grimace of a big cat. It worked, halting Migisi's flight, her talons strangling the branch.

I looked down at the real big cats, who were crouched side by side, watching Dee as if waiting for something inevitable.

Tension filled the urban forest around us. I felt my black brethren all around me but kept my eyes on Dee.

A porcine snuffling filled our heads. Below, emerging between the lifeless bodies of once great spruces, a being came into view. It lumbered on four legs, its back arched into a horrible bulging protuberance. The being drooled and snorted as it prowled in between the hollow trees, a halo of barbed wire embedded angrily into its gruesome hump. Small udder-like breasts swung underneath collarbones as sharp as an ulu. Twisted twig fingers held a dirty cord. The old cell phone charger dragged in the snow behind it. This was a loner like those Kraai had described, a label-less misfit. Not MoFo. Not animal. Its clothing had long rotted off, revealing dappled gray skin. Its scarlet eyes rolled in an endless quest. From the side of its horrible head grew a tumor, long and misshapen. It had the look of an experiment from a lab run by drunken squirrels, or an amateur portrait by a juvenile proboscis monkey using the medium of mayonnaise. This one seemed forever doomed to be an in-between. It was stippled with scars, defying a decade of decay, and perhaps, still searching for a screen.

I had to get Dee out of there. I looked down at the tigers, expecting them to attack in their signature explosive, 260-pound, sixty-mile-per-hour ambush, but they were lying in wait, watching Dee with a familiarity that made my pinions stand on end.

Dee's parka hood had slipped back, exposing her fixated stare. And I knew by the lively fire in her eyes that she wasn't here because she was lost or because she was taken. She'd snuck away and come here because she'd been freed from her Toksook cage. Because she had to see what had become of the rest of her species.

Because she had the curiosity of a crow.

*Oh god. Dee knows what she is, and she sees herself in this hideous thing. She's going to want to get close, to have contact with one of her own.* A close encounter with an orangutan, however magnificent, hadn't been enough. And here, right in front of her, finally—dear god, finally—was one of her very own species. How on earth could she resist?

A young hominid, a vestige of the greatest species to walk the earth, looking at a fun house mirror. A hybrid creature. She was searching for answers. And Dee was being watched by me, another strange hybrid, neither full corvid nor MoFo, but an in-between. Painful implications hit me like a Slim Jim® to the eyeball—the horrid thing and I were *both* composites, imitations of real things. The broken hybrid had come for Dee in lieu of my bloodhound best friend, in lieu of the screens that broke it. Trying to take everything I loved away from me. Its very existence was too much for Dee to deny— a ghastly siren calling her to the rocks. I was filled with an unspeakable rage. I decided then and there that I was going to kill it.

A scream flew from my beak. "Get away from my nestling, you rancid shart bag!" I readied to launch from Migisi's back and take this abomination on myself, even though I weigh the same as a packet of spaghetti.

The creature's head snapped toward me. And then something happened, so fast I could barely make sense of it.

A muffled crunch signified Dee's swift drop from the fir tree.

"Stay!" Dee snarled at me.

The Changed One's lab mouse–red eyes widened, exposing an intricate dream catcher of bloodshot veins. It lifted onto two legs, displaying an ancient scar, smiling in the letter C. The creature screamed—a shrill expulsion from the abyss of a rotten body.

The crows did not call out their trademark alarms. The ghosts of trees stayed silent—they had no choice. The Changed One's jaw slackened with an audible crack. A sizable rock had struck it. The force of stone knocked the creature to the ground. Dee flung the rock aside and leapt flea fast to the malformed creature. She snatched the tumorous growth in one hand, flattened her palm against the opposite temple of an egg-shaped head, and with one ferocious thrust of her arm, one sound like a branch snap, the hideous screaming stopped. The creature slumped to the snow. Its body with its warped breasts and smiling scar faced the tree crowns. Its head was backward, submerged in snow. Dee spun, locating my eyes among hundreds of black bodies. Her expectant gaze locked directly onto me.

Her eyes were smiling.

She was waiting for my response.

The crows had stopped breathing. I felt Migisi's talons extend, her head snap from side to side as she assessed their reaction, waiting to learn who she'd have to kill if they came after her girl. Dee waited, salamander still, for my response, hope lighting up her face. I didn't dare move, not sure of what would happen next or what a murder of crows might do after the violence they'd just witnessed.

There wasn't a chance for them to react. Dee was in action again. She checked to make sure her victim wouldn't rise. Running fingers along the elongated tumor, she grasped it and shook it hard. And that's when I realized that it wasn't a tumor, but a malformed attempt at an antler. Dee studied the Changed One with animal instincts. She hovered over its hideous form, darting her head and taking in its abominable smell in quick sniffs. Then she whipped the phone charger from arthritic fingers and grasped it tightly like a snake. I opened my beak to yell, "No, Dee! Danger!" at her, but before I could, she'd flung the cord onto the snow. We watched, breathless as she sidled up to the nearest Sitka spruce and its blackened, crumbling trunk. Her fingers danced a beetle's scutter across bone-dry bark, tenderly stroking the blackened bodies of moss. Dee placed her lips close to the brittle bryophytes.

Since I'd very first found Dee, her skin had always craved moss's velvet caress. Moss was her particular passion, a cushion on which she often slept, the lining of her diapers when she was just an owlet, its fuzzy face always her first source of comfort when she was in a temper that would impress a bull elephant in the grips of musth. I waited for her eyes to well, for tears that did not come. Migisi's head shot up. Suddenly, Dee was tearing at the bark with her fingers, ripping off great chunks of the tree's skin. Moss flew. Splinters ricocheted. Panic bit me. Dee would never harm her trees, not even a dead one. I began to fear what the contact with this Changed One had done, whether something had happened when she saw the phone charger...

As broken bark took flight, something came into view. Inside the tree was a gleaming white. She worked quickly, dispatching tree skin and exposing what looked like ivory mucus, a pseudotransparent jelly. The crows nervously shifted their weight, silently unsettling the snow from branches. Dee grunted as she split off a skunk-sized slab of bark. She stepped back to give us a clearer view. All above her, a dead forest full of corvids leaned in to make sense of the senseless. The pale, gelatinous goop had a ghostly sheen to it. Its transparency revealed the form trapped inside and the thudding whomp of a heartbeat. Dee used the sharp claw of each fingernail to tear at the jelly. The more mucus she flung to the ground, the more we saw. Inside the jelly was a being whose skin had hardened, frostbite black. Its eyes were closed as if in a trance or state of dormancy. The beginnings of appendages protruded from its side and it was covered in a carpeting of fine, spiny hairs. A MoFo. A MoFo in the midst of an unprecedented transformation. There was no doubt in my mind, this creature and its kind were hollowing the trees. And though I was born from the chasm of an egg—a passport to the kingdom of nature—Dee had known before I had.

Dee slumped onto her knees, several feet from a neck she had fractured. She looked at me one last time, waiting. I gave her nothing, afraid of what the slightest sound might summon. She pressed a shell-like ear to the great trunk of the spruce and raised her fist to its dark bark. Then, the crow who raised her watching in horror, she smacked her knuckles against the wood. The tapping was rapid, a hollow echo sounding out. She thumped hard and I watched her knuckles glow pink and deepen into an angry scarlet.

*Stop, Dee. Stop,* I tried to tell her telepathically, hoping that our constant contact had afforded us that luxury. She persisted. I made motions to leap from Migisi's back, hop to the branch, and stop her from harming herself. From summoning something. Migisi's back muscles tightened— *don't move,* they said. As Dee rapped her fist against the dead wood, she hummed her song of the hive, the nasal, buzzy song she sang the most. The crows shot each other frightened glances. They hopped on slaughtered branches, poised for flight.

And then, out of a chalky sky came a showering of airborne missiles, black and white with crimson streaks. The speckled bodies landed in the decaying arms of the tree, Dee kneeling below them. They appeared confused by who had summoned them, but sparks of excitement soon filled their glossy black eyes. There was a troupe of them—a gang, a descent—and they got to work quickly, drilling their beaks into the weakened wood of a sad spruce cemetery. The feathereds made fast work of the surrounding trees, boring quick holes in a buckshot pattern, exposing the horrible white within. The trees were all filled with encased MoFos.

And what was happening hit me. These MoFos were in larval form, transitioning into fir tree's sworn scissor-mandibled enemy, insects that could hungrily ravage thousand-year-old giants, devouring them from the inside out. The MoFos were becoming bark beetles. What had Ghubari called them? The Masticators. And by some miracle, Dee had known how to summon the enemy of an enemy.

The birds drilled into the gelatinous goo and started greedily consuming slimy larvae, a delicacy in the woodpecker world. More woodpeckers in a dizzying bedimming of black, white, and red arrived, answering the indefatigable percussion of the last MoFo on earth. They drilled her beats back to her. They fused themselves to fir tree corpses and filled belly and beak with imitation beetle.

And before any of us could catch our breath (except the tigers, Olan yawning loudly), another swarm arrived. A drone-like buzzing made our beaks vibrate as dark clouds swirled around us. We watched, incredulous, as insects of the order *Hymenoptera* descended on the trees, membrane-thin wings like mechanical things. We witnessed one of the most feared predators of the insect kingdom—virtually every insect on earth has a wasp species to haunt its exoskeleton—arrive en masse, humming an answer to Dee's song. A sea of wasps squeezed their way into the exposed bark, seeming not to care about the presence of woodpeckers. Thousands of fertilized queens used their stingers, drilling and plunging their ovipositors into the changed bodies of MoFos. I gasped. What would happen next was one of nature's darkest happenings. The wasps were going to lay their eggs. And their larvae were going to eat the MoFos. From the inside out.

Not only had Dee summoned the predators of bark beetles, but she'd somehow summoned the egg layers among the wasps. She'd called on queens. She had conjured wild magic before our eyes—a symphony of superparasitism.

A sound louder than the rumble and purr of wasps and the drill of specialized beaks cut through our skulls. We all knew this sound. Perhaps Migisi knew it best. A hawk's scream, the aerial call, the cry before talons rip through skin. Only we knew it wasn't a hawk. More calls sounded out. They were on the move. Dee shot up from her kneeling position. Scarlet teardrops dotted the snow below her knuckles. She lifted her arms, gesturing to her corvid crowd.

"Caw, caw, caw, caw, caw!" Dee mimicked the corvid alarm. And she didn't need to repeat herself. Black bodies took heed and shot from deceased branches. Dee broke into a run underneath a winged blanket of black. The tigers erupted into a run to join her. Migisi and I leapt from the Sitka spruce, casting an eagle's shadow on the nestling who ran like a startled caribou below. Kraai was suddenly by our side.

"The fledgling," he said, and I flinched, waiting for his verdict. "She is our greatest hope."

I exhaled. The violence that had gotten Dee exiled from her beloved community of owls had become an invitation to a murder of crows and an improvised sanctuary of animals. They'd watched her use cunning, patience, stealth. With a cat's kill skills, she'd gone straight for its neck. And lastly, she'd done the unthinkable, this one who got lost in the wonder of sea stars, who lived to tickle salmonberry-stained fingers delicately in soil, craved the spongy stroke of moss on her skin, the kisses of rain and butterfly feet, this MoFo with a lifelong yearning to fly. She'd drawn on passion. She'd used what she learned from the natural world against her own species.

"What do you mean?" I asked him, feigning ignorance.

"She is so…wild. She's a weapon." Excitement trailed off him as we sped across a wintry sky. "And she'll do what you tell her. She was waiting for your approval down there, waiting to see what you thought of what she'd done. Ghubari will be so thrilled to know about—"

"Ghubari will not know about this," I cut him off, my voice shaking to hold back anger. "Kraai, you have done nothing but show me kindness. You are murder to me. But I will ask one more favor of you. Ghubari must never know about this, about what you saw her do down there. Dee is not a weapon or a tool or something to be offered up to The Changed Ones. She is mine."

"Yours?" he asked, taken aback.

"She is my nestling. I'll keep her safe. I'm The One Who Keeps."

A kettle of hawks screamed in the distance. Another lie I told myself.

"I, I don't understand why—"

"Just do it for me, Kraai! Perhaps if you had your own nestling, you'd understand."

"I have around eighteen of my own—"

"Dammit, Kraai! Please!"

Kraai looked at the MoFo below, bounding across a white world. In bird's-eye view, a hooded heroine lunged alongside three enormous tigers. They growled. She roared back. Midrun, she stooped to snatch up a rusted golf club which she used to bait them. Dee raised her head to the sky, hood flopping back from her flushed face. Migisi wheeled above her. The last MoFo raised her arms like outstretched wings, a look of jubilance lighting her from the inside. She smiled, waiting for my approval, for me to tell her she'd done good. I wouldn't. I hated what she'd done. This was not how I'd raised her. She was not a wild and violent thing.

"Astee!" Dee yelled. "Astee!" Nonsense. Gibberish.

From my high spot in the sky, I gave her nothing but a glare of disappointment. I looked away.

"Faster, Migisi!" I yelled, urging her to keep up with the murder. Mukluk and tiger paws pounded frosty ground. One upright MoFo, proud on fast legs, and a trio of *Panthera tigris*, capricious beasts of stripe and stature. They painted a white world in animal tracks. Behind us, something terrible was gathering like sinister clouds. Sharp screeches were multiplying, as if breeding in the air.

"S.T.," Kraai said, "it's one thing for me not to say anything, but I can't guarantee the entire murder won't scream about finding French fries." A corvid expression, and he was right—crows are not known for their subtlety. "I'll do as you ask, for you, friend. But I don't know how you're going to avoid involving her. I know you can hear them. You know what's coming."

When you've told yourself one lie, it's a slippery piece of bologna. It's a gateway to fabricating a whole new sparkling reality, one you'd prefer. One in which no one you love can get hurt. But I could hear them. The hawks were not hawks, but imitations of raptors. They were Changed Ones who'd no doubt been dormant. Now, their screeching conquered the airwaves, their strained calls to one another rattled around my skull, and I had to face the truth. The Changed One Dee had killed now lay motionless in the snow. But before the bones in her neck cracked, she had screamed the scream a species had been waiting for all this time. She had let them know. Of course she had. It was the driving force of evolution, of every living thing on earth, wasn't it? Survival. They had been looking for their final chance at living, at reproducing. They had been looking for the last.

Haunting hawk screams battled one another. Closer and closer. A crescendo of chaos.

"S.T.," Kraai said, "you must prepare. They've been awakened. They know she's here." Migisi let out a cirrus-high screech of fury.

The great hunt had begun.

# CHAPTER 20

❦ ❋ ❋ ❦ ❋ ❦ ❦

## NUBBINS THE DONKEY
## LOCH LOMOND AND THE TROSSACHS NATIONAL
## PARK, SCOTLAND

$A$ye, there's nothing like the wee hours of the mornin'. *Rise like the grass, don't be an ass*—it's a wee motto of mine.

Routine, discipline, regimen, vigilance.

This is how, when many of our cloven kin have perished, I—Nubbins, donkey of the Strathpeffer wilds—am a survival expert. They laughed at me back in the day, so they did. Called me stupid. Paranoid. A numpty. An utter tube. But back on our beautiful wee farm, in the great green fields, back when the luxuries of ear scritches and poop scooping were aplenty, I was preparing. I was rolling around in shite as a stealth tactic—to hide the smell of my hide. I stockpiled a sugar cube survivalist stash. I ate sweetie wrappers to build up an iron constitution, elite training for my donkey body. I apprenticed with the foxes as they used earth's magnetic field to hunt, learning to (mostly) distinguish between inner guidance and gas. I mimicked their nocturnal territorial screams, which resulted in an inconvenient stint at the vet's and a time-wasting head scan. I practiced hunger strikes and melee attacks on our feeding trough to the bafflement of my human.

I knew my time to shine had come the day our human didn't come to the field. She always came for us, whatever the weather, and we've got a lot of that in Scotland. My survivalist senses kicked off.

I rallied the troops. Hamish the Hebridean sheep. Gregor the goose. Esme the Scots Dumpy hen. Bone Grinder the barn cat. And my battle buddy, Angus the Highland cow.

It took six misty mornings to convince Angus to leave our field once I discovered the electric fence was off. Angus, a spoiled show cow, had been used to fancy shows and cameras and pedi-pedis. Bovine models aren't much for adventure. That and he'd finally scored with Margaret, our human's other Highland cow. The affair was fast and furious—and quite gross, actually. Angus was totally exhausted; he's pretty used to having it all done for him through artificial insemination. That jammy wee sod.

But eventually, I shepherded the troops out into the wild world (minus Margaret the Highland cow and Shelly the Shetland pony, whose faith is firm in the belief that the world ends at the bottom of the hill and that we would all plummet over the edge like plums off a wee tree). They were wrong about that. We wandered for a long time, encountering some collies, a few sheep, and some Ayrshire cows (a huge time suck as Angus fancies himself a wee Casanova—for the record, I hate having to listen to cow sex, but it's marginally better than Angus's poems).

Then we ran into humans. They were poorly—I suspected swine flu or mad cow disease, which is something I can't mention around Angus; he's a jessie, such a big girl's blouse. I cannae convince him to get with the program and roll in his own shite. Angus is just too vain—he finds mud offensive and I have a hard time tearing his ginger arse from admiring himself in puddles, so I do. The humans we encountered were incredibly aggressive—especially when they saw Angus who's a big ginger target, and they'd come flying for him and I'd have to kick 'em in their noggin or exact a melee attack. Despite having been born with two massive weapons attached to his heed, Angus was no help. He's a cowardly custard, and unfortunately, a pacifist cow.

Sometimes you look back on your life and realize you were in training all along, and everything was preparing you for this moment. I looked back to when I was a wee donkey getting whipped within an inch of my life while ferrying fat-arse tourists across the beach. Every day my hooves bled, and my back felt like breaking. I got beaten for stealing the chocolate Flake out of a fatty tourist's ice cream cone— I was doing her a wee service; she was the size of a barn! And then I took a wee nibble out of a young tourist who stuck his finger up my nose and that was the last of it. Wee Nubbins got the death penalty, headed for the glue factory. In the nick of time, our human rescued me, brought me to our beautiful farm in the countryside, and gave me home-grown apples. She put soothing creams on my knee scars and fetlocks and put me in a field to keep her prize High-land cow, Angus, from getting melancholy. Angus was prone to loneliness and afraid of other bulls. I saw it as a very noble job.

As we traveled over the years, I saw a lot fewer humans than in the beach tourist days. I don't know if they died or fled. Once in a while, we'd see one emerge from a nuclear shelter like a pale wee mole, but they never lasted long, and I couldnae trust them with Angus—he's essentially a mobile Big

Mac. No, I had to channel my fatso beach tourist anger and scare them away.

The Brave Beastie Bunch weren't to last long. Bone Grinder the barn cat was excommunicated the second time he attempted to eat Esme the hen. We lost Gregor the goose in a storm. Hamish ran off with a flock of sheep looking to start a utopian commune in Cornwall. Esme the wee hen eventually went a bit off her heed, clucking a load of nonsense. She died of natural causes. We'll miss the old lass.

We traveled great distances—the landscape is increasingly quiet, which is tough for Angus who loves a bit of gossip, but there's loads of grass everywhere now, which is a nice perk. Deer and foxes have taken over. I once smelled a wolf and redirected us by telling Angus I thought I'd heard the band of Her Majesty's Royal Marines who perform at the Royal Highland Show. I've followed the sun, gone the opposite way, up, down, back, forth, around, and I keep getting stuck in front of ocean. I'm actually beginning to think we might live on an island. I wouldnae tell Angus that—he's a wee bit claustrophobic. We've been to Brighton three times and I have to creatively pretend it's a new town each time to ease his mind.

If I'm honest, I don't totally believe our human's still alive. I just don't think she would have given up on us. I'd never tell Angus that. I've said I know with great certainty that she's out there, that she just got lost on her way back from Sainsbury's. It's only a wee fib, like when I told him hamburgers were made of squashed daisies. Hope seems more important than the truth, and I have a job I've been sworn to do. Och, he's a wee naff, Angus, but he's my wee naff, and he must never get sad or lonely. Such a massive great oaf, but one wee word and he'll crumble like a chocolate Flake.

After a great many mornings on the road, we're headed back

to our wee farm in Strathpeffer now, to see if our human came back for us. Maybe she'll be there wearing her wellies and a smile. Maybe Margaret and Shelly will be there and some big wee Anguses to play with. Until then, we hoof on and Angus will never be lonely because I made a promise. I'm Nubbins and I'm a survival expert. I've been preparing my whole life.

Routine, discipline, regimen, vigilance.

# CHAPTER 21

S.T.
BOTHELL, WASHINGTON, USA

Dee's eyes were two frightened fish as she ran. They flickered, watery, darting up at a halo of crows. Kraai manifested by my side, beating his wings in active flight.

"Blackwing, are you sure? I just think it would be better for you to come with us. Please, I can't persuade you—"

"It must be this way. I have to hide Dee away," I told him. Migisi caught her breath as she perched us on top of a toppled billboard with a snapped neck. The billboard was covered in dirt, bracken, and siftings of snow, but you could still read its original Christmas advertisement. Santa rode with reindeer through a velvet-blue sky as he delivered a sack full of cell phones. Peeling letters peeked through—*Peace on earth*—and hectic red graffiti over the top of it: GUNS AND AMMO SEE ERIC IN WOODINVILLE IF YOUR SICK WELL SHOOT. And smaller green scrawl: UR GUNS WON'T HELP U NOW.

I know what you're thinking, and you're right: this was empirical evidence that the very first casualty of the apocalypse had been grammar.

Migisi sat watching, wings tucked tight, head camouflaging with the snow. Her breathing felt labored.

"Please, Kraai, this is the last favor I'll ask of you," I begged him.

He bobbed his head, though it pained him. Then his cool gaze lingered on my nestling. We could all feel the longing of his corvid companions, how they wanted to be close to her.

"Rise!" he called, and as they lifted farther from her fingers, Dee wailed. Dee had heard stories about these crows, longing to be part of the murder her whole life. She was getting abandoned again. They left like a gust of airborne leaves. Dee fell to her knees, her arms stretched high. She turned to show me her pleading, tear-streaked face. I heard my heart crack. I knew this bitter feeling, what it's like to be the only one, an outsider that never fits in. She'd wanted to be a part of this family, but, just as with the owls, she kept getting shut out. Did she think she'd done something wrong? I looked away; I had to stay strong. The One Who Keeps was doing this so that she'd live. Because keeping her alive was a nonnegotiable goal, because the murder was headed back to warn Ghubari and the animals at Tavern on the Square, and they all saw Dee as a weapon. They were biased and blinded by their own fear. They couldn't see her for what she was.

Nestlings are not weapons. Dee was not born on this big beautiful blue as a "resource," existing solely for our convenience.

Migisi's breathing still seemed raspy, even after her break on the billboard. I peered down to make sure she was alright, and she snapped at me. Something was up and she clearly didn't want to squawk about it, so <u>Shit Turd's Mixed Concerns</u>

(a list) was growing by the minute. It was possible she was on her moon time. Tiffany S. from Tinder used to sometimes get this way, and once Big Jim said, "I get it! It's shark week!" and Tiffany S. slapped him so hard his beer hat fell off. Tiffany S. then kicked the La-Z-Boy®, screaming something about respect and a period. A pretty dramatic response over a punctuation mark if you ask me.

Our heads filled with the ghastly cries of hollow creatures.

"We need somewhere to hide, Migisi, quickly," I told her. "Away from everyone and everything. They only see Dee as either a weapon or prey. That's not what Dee is. She is my nestling. We have to keep her to ourselves."

I told her my great plan. Migisi read the UV patterns that pirouetted across the snow in northern lights colors. Her chocolate feathers ruffled as they felt the earth's magnetic vibrations flow through her, strumming her heart. This is how the creatures of *Aura* navigate the sky; we create mind maps by using light and the planet's percussion. This was how we would stay one step ahead of The Changed Ones, whose distant screaming was a thick, smoggy pollution. Migisi sensed the world around her and used the skill of sky dwellers—from merganser to arctic tern—to plot our great flight. We agreed on the final location. Our beautiful eagle had a lifetime of using mind maps, but as much as I tried, I was still better at navigating with landmarks like Dick's Drive-In and Five Guys. Um, yum.

"Dee! Come!" I said to her in Big Jim's no-nonsense bass. Dee gestured to the sky, toward where a constellation of sooty speckles seasoned the air. She placed her hand on her chest. *It hurts*, said her eyes. We both filled up with the sorrow and loneliness of the day we lost our parliament of owls. The crows left our heavy hearts, printing the sky in V's and lowercase m's. *V* for valor. *m* for murder.

"Danger, let's go, Dee!" I told her. As if in response, a scream—closer than the others—shot through our skin to scrape bone. The tigers growled in harmony.

"They come. They come quickly," said Liem, his pupils swelling until they eclipsed his eyes.

"They come for the Keeper," said Olan. "They hunt her." Dee leapt over to me. She held up the cupped castle of her palms. I launched myself from Migisi's broad back, landing in the exquisite cage of Dee's fingers. I would not let her be ground-bound alone. Migisi would direct us from the air, keeping watch for sky-shrunken predators. My MoFo and I would stay together—always together—and find a home of our very own.

Migisi lifted, and from below, I could see that her flaps were missing their fluid power. Still, she glided with the beauty of the white dunes she cast in shadow. Dee ran, powered by frustration and the flint-tipped slice of pain. She chuffed, the tigers running along beside her, though always a little ahead. I kept my beady eyes on a bouncing Bothell.

The screaming became more and more distant, and I wondered if The Changed Ones had been led a different way by Kraai and the murder. Wonderful—another skewer of guilt for the Shish Turd kebab. And then, Dee and the big cats stopped. The cats moaned, their whiskers fanning like porcupine quills. Dee, then, as if to defy me, squatted right there and peed, daubing the snow in lemon yellow.

"Christ on a Cheese Nip, Dee! Toilet time is private!" I scolded. You'd have thought she'd been raised by an incontinent corgi-poo, not five snowy owls, a bald eagle, and a staggeringly cerebral crow! The tigers were agitated, pacing, leaking groans. Dee chuffed at them. Olan let out a roar so ferocious it bullied the snow off branches. Dee roared back at him.

"No! Go!" she yelled.

The tigers paced and snarled and chirped and moaned but seemed to be pinned in place, unable to go any farther. And Dee was stern as she bared her teeth into a sharp snarl.

"Go! Run fas fas!" she told them with a growl. And then she took off.

"Dee! We need those sentient trash liners!" I squawked in protest.

"No! Danger!" she spat back at me. I watched the tigers pummel white powder in frustration. Dee shushed me and focused on her flight across the snow.

We ran along a road. Lake Washington loomed to our left, still and silky. Dee avoided the flooded parts of the road. The trees that lined the road were alive but silent, skeletal as winter-white goblins. Dee ran swiftly, doe-like. There were no sounds but the eerie sugarplum tinkle of ice drips. She stooped every now and then to squat and urinate.

"Dee, pull yourself together! You don't pee willy-nilly like this! Where do you think you are, Chuck E. Cheese?!"

I rattled my disapproval at her squatting—I'd worked exceptionally hard on her toilet training.

It happened enough times to make me wonder whether she had a bladder infection, which was one of the many, many things I learned about after Dee's little teeth started falling out, and I didn't know that was a thing so I was in a total tailspin and thought she was Changing and I read every medical book Nightmute library had to offer, which had horrifically graphic pictures and eventually made me want to impale myself on a chopstick.

"Hamburger help us! Dee, what is it? A menopausal anterior prolapse? Oh god, it's benign prostatic hyperplasia, isn't it? It's a prostate issue, isn't it? I've always feared this. Talk to me, Dee!"

Dee stopped on a dime, startled by something. She put me down to circle a cluster of bags that looked to have been the treasures of a MoFo. Migisi's shadow swam across the bags.

"No! Come on! We have to go!" I yelled.

The burlap bags gaped open, their wares spilling out, mantled with siftings of snow. Dee darted her head at hoarded shoes, gold coins, cigarettes, and what looked to be seeds. At the very end, things that became the most valuable to MoFos were the glittering things crows had always cherished.[1]

"Dee! They're coming for us!" I begged of her. "You're unwell and making terrible decisions; your prostate problem is more serious than we thought!"

But something had grabbed Dee's attention. She approached a mound of MoFo garbage in the manner of a crow. Small hops forward. Swift jump back. Cautious head bobs. Sidling closer. Dee used her fingers in lieu of a beak, snatching an old wrist-watch and flinging it to the ground in case it was a biter.

"DEE! For shit sakes, come on! We have to get to somewhere safe!" I chided her. I had a big problem on my pinions— I couldn't physically force her to do anything, not even with my impeccably toned thighs. My nerves were fried, and I was losing patience. She prodded at pulp that had been a book in a past life.

"Dee! *Please*, we are in serious danger!" I told her. "Danger, Dee!"

Dee snatched a spoon—she'd seen those before—using it to sift aside snow. She unburied a shoe as I had a conniption fit, stomping and high kicking. She rummaged quickly, arm darting like the willowy neck of a swan. Sequestered in a filthy

---

1  Except toilet paper. In the midst of their pandemic panic, American MoFos hoarded unfathomable mountains of toilet paper. It has never been clear why they needed so much, and I imagined them salivating over their stock-piles like Smaug, if he'd had irritable bowel syndrome.

ballet slipper was a tiny square bottle. I recognized it instantly. Dee lifted it to her eyes to study the golden liquid.

"DEE! NOW! I'm sick of you not listening to me!" I screeched in desperation. As if in response, a Changed One's scream sounded out.

She twisted the top, put her nose to the bottle's delicate little neck, and retched, succumbing to an attack of the sneezes. Dee snarled at the miniature bottle of Chanel N°5 but tucked it into the pocket of her parka. She picked me up and resumed sprinting. A rattle of relief flew from my lungs.

"Good girl, Dee!" I yelled. "Finally, a little fucking culture!"

I was pleased. This made up for her horrible habits of pissing all over the place and dumpster diving. I actually knew a lot about Chanel N°5, Tiffany S.'s sworn favorite and the choice of many—a bottle was sold every thirty seconds around the world in the time of MoFos. It contains some weird shit to give it its signature scent, the so-called "scent of a woman"—including moss scraped from the bark of northern hemisphere trees. Originally, in 1921, Coco Chanel needed to add some musky base notes, and so she procured the obvious—sexual pheromones from the anal glands of the Abyssinian civet cat. In 1998, this was replaced with an imitation of the sex pheromones in cat piss, but still—it's a hell of a smell to the non-MoFo nose, reminding me of the time I mistook Nargatha's platter of potpourri for trail mix. Not to be outdone, Dior's Poison contains a synthetic version of whale barf, while other prominent perfumes feature the aroma of beaver balls, deer dicks, and the fossilized feces of hyraxes.[2] MoFos stealing from the pigpen of nature. How do I know all this? Big Jim

---

2  A hyrax looks like an inflated animatronic guinea pig but is actually an African rock-climbing mammal who is somehow most closely related to the elephant.

and I researched it all in a fruitless attempt to get Tiffany S. to switch to something cheaper after she'd discovered that I'd been pillaging her Chanel N°5 and caching it in Nargatha's compost bin.

"How come you always smell so fancy and French?" Nargatha asked Tiffany S. one time while kneading her arm like defrosting dough.

"It's Chanel N°5," Tiffany S. whispered to her, and from then on, the women in Big Jim's life both smelled like a libidinous leopard. Bad taste, it turns out, is highly infectious. I figured Dee kept the vial because of the moss scent, but I hoped that somewhere inside, Dee felt a call to be French and fancy.

She squeezed me gently to silence me. And then she froze.

Why weren't we hearing the distant screams of The Changed Ones? I looked up to an empty sky; Migisi had flown ahead of us to do recon.

Dee crouched. Her nose sucked up sharp air. A frenetic quilt of mice skittered across the snow. They were fleeing. Dee looked behind us, tracking, a lovely popping of cartilage the only indication of her swift movement. She launched us over a partially frozen puddle. She ducked behind a huge, anarchic mound of sticks piled next to the water. Hidden in between the sticks was a cluster of watery brown eyes. A family of beavers huddled together, nut-brown paws tucked into one another. Too frightened to breathe. Dee frowned. I worried because that was the face she pulled when I told her not to dig gigantic potholes all over Toksook because it was starting to look like a large lump of Emmental cheese. And that face usually led to a Salish Sea storm.

Dee's heartbeat pulsed through her fingers and into my black body. She peered over the stick mound, taking in sights I couldn't see, and once I started silently poking at her palm, she gingerly lifted me to witness. Some things are so horrible, your mind sews itself shut. The Changed Ones moved quickly. They raked their fingers through the snow, exposing a jumbled junkyard of things the snow had buried. One of them used scarlet eyes to scan the snowscape. Only it didn't have to rely on two eyes. It had grown multiple heads, all of them competing for space with grayish skin stretched tight over bone, mouths gaping as if about to speak. Most of these heads were clustered on its bowed legs. It had too many veiny arms sprouting haphazardly from the sides of its torso. Another MoFo jittered as it tracked, its back so arched that pearly nubs of spine had split through its skin. Another was larger, its muscular body covered in large, burl-like growths. The smallest one, with tooth-white skin, had only half a body, severed off at the belly button. It used scraggy, jutting, backward-jointed arms like the wing bones of juvenile birds to haul itself across the snow. These things were unspeakable. I would have no way to reconcile these entities with the MoFos I'd known and loved if it weren't for the giant John Stamos tattoo. These creatures were hunting, releasing grunts that morphed into rancid clouds in the air. I prayed that they hadn't learned animal instinct, didn't have Dee's heightened senses, that they were still MoFo enough in their tracking. I still couldn't see our beloved eagle. I didn't know where Migisi was. And then the creatures caught wind of something.

A solitary mouse, Snickers brown and lagging behind his companions, burst into view, racing for his whiskered life. The Changed Ones focused on the tiny, terrified being as it wrestled an endless white tundra. Dee didn't breathe. The Changed One tilted its many heads to watch the rodent. The mouse scurried on. We watched, praying the beavers could stay as still as the sticks of their home, that our bodies wouldn't betray us with their noises. We crouched in agony near The Changed Ones. Then, the one with many heads lunged. A whiplike tongue—long as a rat snake—shot from one of its gaping mouths and lassoed the mouse. It sucked back into a gaping mouth hole. The little brown mouse vanished. Scarlet foam hung from the creature's sickly pink jaws. And then it did something unthinkable.

"Caw! Caw! Caw!" Strings of red flew as it called out in the perfect pitch of a crow. It was telling them to keep searching. *She is out there.*

The creature then—a study in the unexpected—growled. The growl of a mighty cat from Malaysia, a perfect mimicry of Eko, Liem, and Olan. Then it let out a gull's salty laughter—a language that borders and connects *Aura* and *Echo.*

These abominations were mutants, thieves stealing from the natural world—amphibian, reptile, insect, mammal. I didn't care about Onida or prophecies or the delusions of marine mammals; Dee needed to be somewhere safe. Somewhere with impenetrable doors and iron locks. With me.

I felt Dee stir. Her free arm stretched out, her fingers slipping into snow. She clutched something tightly. I looked up at her to tell her to stop—*no, no, no, don't be stupid, Dee*—by bulging my eyeballs like a rubber chicken caught between a rock and The Rock. She gave me a slow blink—an affectionate gesture in cat. And then, in a lightning move, she lobbed it. The thing—rock or ball, I'll never know—sailed through the air in a high arch at the mercy of Dee's throwing arm, an arm that would have done the Seacrows quarterback Russell Wilson proud. Sickly heads shot to attention, and The Changed Ones scrabbled after the *clunk* of the projectile slamming onto the ground.

Dee's eyes squinted to focus between the sticks to connect with the beady brown eyes of terrified aquatic engineers. She gave a bow—a sign of respect in crow—and launched us from the beaver hideout. Dee bolted across slush, and once her mukluks touched firmer ground, she began a turbocharged sprint. I kept my beak trained on the vast sugaring of snow ahead. In Dee's tight grip, I couldn't turn back, couldn't see if The Changed Ones had seen us and what they would look like once they'd seen Dee—the very MoFo they'd been hunting.

*Where are you, Migisi?* I searched the sky for chocolate wings.

Dee didn't stop her long-distance sprint as the road curved, and then, in a most shitty turn of events, the sky began to scream again. They were flying fast, faux-hawk screams swelling between our ears, and Dee picked up the pace, feet barely licking the snow. She flew across a parking lot and past an armored Winnebago with an "I ♥ Uranus" sticker on it and a disemboweled lawn mower and through great glassless doors and up a sleeping escalator and then we were under a roof with busted skylights, and after interrupting a cluster of squirrels who were fornicating loudly on top of a sign that said "Self Help," we stopped.

Dee didn't love to be indoors, but she had no choice. By using Detective Shit Turd's superpowers of deduction, I could tell Third Place Books used to be a bookstore. Now, it was home to those who sew silks. Pigeons had left abstract impressionist murals in alabaster shit. Brave troops of mushrooms bloomed here and there in the drippy, dank, and damp. Raccoons had perfumed the place in pee, molesting everything with their creepy miniature wizard hands, those bank robber–faced bunions. The bookstore's Honey Bear Bakery had long been ransacked. Something had been dragged across the floor, leaving a gruesome red S trail. The books, much like their authors, were no longer upright. They were littered everywhere. Pages had been torn to make nests, munched upon by ravenous insects (it appeared that a Very Hungry Caterpillar had literally gorged on his eponymous classic). But, somehow, it still held a quiet magic. I felt crepitating genius that flared from the minds of MoFos, now secretly sequestered across the crisp leaves of broken-backed books. It gave me hope that they were still alive in the pages of those books, woven into words.

Dee crawled under a table, pushing aside a delightful tableau of rat droppings. The rodent's equally delightful skeleton (at the time of his demise, I suspect he'd been winning a lively game of Twister) sat near us, among a colorful cemetery of building blocks and a copy of the book *Why Mommy Drinks*, which seemed like it was winking at me. Fatigue weighed on her like waterlogged boots. She placed me on the tiles. She picked up a piece of moss something had tracked in, rubbing it for comfort. We waited. The screams got louder and louder, and then—thank our lucky Fritos—they started to wane, as terrible creatures shrieked about finding the *running She One* in the language of hawks. Then—more sounds. Close. So close.

*Tap tap tap.*

*Tap tap tap.*

*Oh, for Starbucks's sake, we're not alone.*

# CHAPTER 22

S.T.
THIRD PLACE BOOKS, LAKE FOREST PARK,
WASHINGTON, USA

Dee looked down at me. Her eyebrows lifted like two flannel moth caterpillar jump-rope champions in perfect tandem, and I knew we were both hoping it was our adventure eagle.

Tap. Pause. Tap. Pause. Tap tap tap tap tap.

The tapping continued, emanating from behind a counter with a sign above it that said "Sell Us Your Used Books." The curious crow in her just couldn't handle it.

"Gisi?" It was how she said Migisi's name when she chose to use MoFo words.

I stomped my foot, furious at Dee for giving away our location.

There was a thick, sticky pause. A voice bounced back to us, "Gisi?" identically to the way Dee said it. Dee shuffled backward on the floor, shocked, *shuffle shuffle* until her back was up against an old trash can. Every cell of me wanted to believe Dee was not the last. But if I was honest, even if a healthy MoFo stood up behind that counter, I wasn't ready to share her.

Dee was mine.

Both of us were choking on our curiosity, but I couldn't risk anything happening to Dee and I didn't know where Migisi was, and we'd planned to get Dee to Whidbey Island. I'd decided the island was our best chance because Dennis and I found a note a long time ago that said: *Cash, canned food, flashlights, water.* ~~*Find H.*~~ *Find Sarah. Find a way to Whidbey.* Maybe we could make a home there, underneath ghastly streets where scarlet eyes prowled. That's what Ghubari said the pregnant MoFos had done when the changes happened—they'd burrowed underground like rabbits. That's what Dee's family had done with the very best intentions, cutting themselves off from everything. And that's what we would do.

I gestured toward an escape route—the top of the escalator.

"Gisi?" came the terrifying echo again. Dee's cold fingers wrapped me in a safety shell. I lifted into the air as she stood.

SLAM!

Dee spun to see a book's pages flutter after its plummet from the sky. Above the book, perched on old pipes that slithered along the ceiling, was a big black bird.

My nestling let out a soft rattle. The bird mimicked her. Dee used the crow sounds for what the bird was, and the bird responded in crow. Though it was no crow. The raven let out a crawk, ruffling the leonine mane of feathers around its neck.

Dee pointed up at the raven. "Asshole!" she said, and I coughed to shush her. I had perhaps been a bit too vocal with my disdain for ravens. But wouldn't you have been, if you were constantly compared to a bird who was revered for his larger size and allegedly bigger brain? I was always mistaken for a raven when out with Big Jim. MoFos would approach me, behaving as if they were about to rub eyeballs with a unicorn, only to discover a herpes-stricken donkey. Crows are the pleather to raven's leather. Ravens get to be creepy cool, crows are just seen as Creepy McCreepertons. Ravens are shy forest dwellers, good with secrets, and where's the fun in that? Seems selfish not to share them, if you ask me. They're more in tune with the melodies of the wildest woods, and some say, the afterworld. The great black bird stared down from the top of old pipes.

"What do you want?" I asked.

The raven ruffled again and lifted his contour feathers. This asshole was really rubbing those larger wings in my beak.

"Isn't the question what do *you* want?" asked the raven. His voice was deep and rough, the sound of a stone. Ravens speak many languages—forest, river, sky.

"Great. A raven with riddles, what a fucking cliché," I said.

"What do they call you?" asked the raven.

"Turd," I said, puffing up while envisioning a Tom Ford suit, an Aston Martin, and a martini shaken like a San Franciscan bartender. "Shit Turd."

"Alright Turd Shit Turd—"

"No, it's just—"

"What do they call *her*?"

Dee was staring at his sleek beak bristles, mane, and the cloaking wings with boogly eyes, and I didn't like how this trouser sprout was giving my nestling the old bank-camera eyes.

"Why are you here? This doesn't seem like a raven haven," I asked.

The raven didn't answer; he was studying Dee, wings still splayed.

"Hey!" I said, hopping on the spot. "Did you hear what I said?" This guy was swiftly becoming a turmeric stain on the tie of my existence.

Dee stepped lightly toward the raven, one arm extended. She was offering him her piece of moss. It was a clever move, to be so utterly surrounded by crow treasures—socks, greeting cards, and those delightful novelty candles in the shape of cacti—but to offer a forest bird an olive branch from his world. But fuck all that sentimental shit; this was a nightmare.

The raven let out clicks and notes like a bell ringing under-water. He eyed Dee, his mind a bustling ant farm. And then he let out a call I hadn't heard in a long time. It was painfully familiar, a tune that used to haunt subways, hotels, streets, and homes.

"Duh duhduhduhduhduhduhduh."

A cell phone jingle.

He repeated it. My beak flopped open, tongue rolled across the floor like a toilet roll gone rogue. And then he watched Dee, ink-black head craned forward.

Dee opened her beak and called back: "Duh duhduhduh-duhduhduhduh."

"She is not Hollowed," said the beautiful bird.

"Of course not, you coprophagous spoon!" I spat. "How dare you test her! She is the most magnificent and dignified creature you will ever lay your eyes on!" We both turned our black beaks to Dee, who was peeing all over the floor.

"Flaming Fritos, Dee! No! How in the name of Pete Carroll is your bladder not empty by now? Bad, Dee!"

The raven watched, seemingly undisturbed by Dee's re-gressed house-training. "The One Who Keeps The Last Human," the raven said to me. "She is a strong one, your little bird."

"She can snap a neck like the head of a myrtle spurge."

"Yes, we've seen her."

"We?" *Oh no.* If I possessed the privilege of sweating, I would have done a great deal of it. From within a fallen Jenga tower of broken tables and chairs rose a being. Dee gasped. Another raven whipped the air with its wings, eyes on Dee. It had the same hawk-sized body as the raven on the pipes, the same letter-opener bill and ruff of mane feathers. Its wings were the velvet drapes of an old opera house. But this raven was as white as cream. Dee squealed with joy. The ravens of Toksook Bay had become nothing but shadows as they hid from Dee, afraid of the flightless body that had changed the world. Neither of us had ever seen a white raven. Kraai once told me fireside stories about how the white ravens of Vancouver Island loved to communicate with the busy beings of *Web*, that mysterious and wondrous world below the soil. Some crows believe the white raven is a ghost, a chalk-winged guide along the river of prophecy.

"What do you want from us?" I spat.

"We've been summoned," said the white raven. "All of us."

"There's been a lot of fucking summoning, hasn't there?!"

And then I felt every feather of my body rise. *All of us.* I hopped in a circle, scanning the bookstore. We were completely surrounded, and I wanted to punch myself in the cloaca for not realizing this would happen. Ravens are criminally cunning. Ravens are blade-beaked mimics. And ravens are also known for something else. They are the eyes in the sky to another.

Many call them The Wolfbirds.

And all around us, in between bookshelves and among the chaos of clutter, were the glowing eyes of wolves.

Erect ears swiveled like searching satellites on fulvous heads, peering from upturned tables. A jet-black wolf—enormous and imposing—stood at the top of the motionless escalator. There were wolves at every exit, on every counter, beside stacks of books—more than I could count.

I looked up at the black raven and unleashed a corvid insult at him that roughly translates as "I hope your anus is set on fire and your wings get caught in a high-powered ceiling fan."

It didn't seem to faze him, that avian traitor. The white raven landed gently on top of a sign that said "Information" with a giant question mark. Fuck yeah, I had questions, starting with "How does it feel to be a weak-winged cheat? A snail-hearted snitch?"

She didn't have time to answer me. A body vaulted up the escalator, mouths of the many heads that sprouted from its skin gaping. All its eyes widened, and the heads gyrated. The Changed One had tracked us. It locked all eyes on me. I knew this look. I'd seen it in bars and doctors' offices, many restaurants and grocery stores, and most especially from Tiffany S. from Tinder.

*You do not belong here,* it said.

And then my arteries dried up. The creature's horrible mouths slit into a gesture I knew, a gesture that is not from the animal kingdom.

It was grinning.

A chorus of lupine growls shook the bookstore. The Changed One's horrible crop of eyes landed on Dee and it let out a predator's victorious bellow. Then came its vicious scramble, the twitchy scuttle of a tick. It was coming for Dee. I hopped in front of her, puffing out my wings.

"Run, Dee! Run!" I hissed.

Wild as rapids, a pack of wolves lunged for the Changed One's warped torso. Wolves—bonded by bloodline—sank their canines into too many heads and tore the thing apart. It was a seasoned kill. A choreography of decapitation.

The warrior wolves dispersed again, taking up strategic positions between the bookshelves. I had not yet caught my breath when all the wolves who had snuck up on us like a fanged blizzard turned toward the bookstore's entrance near the Honey Bear Bakery. Wolves standing in the yawn of glassless doors stepped aside. Four winter-white wolves padded into the bookstore. Their tongues released small saliva drips, breath clouding icily. When my nestling reflected in their shining eyes, they froze. And I can assure you, nothing is more intense than the gaze of a wolf.

So, this is how it would end for us. Not with the horrors of what MoFos had become, but with the wolf superpack that had grown much larger than when we had fought it in Bothell Landing, when we had unleashed a motley crew of mutts to drive the wolves from our territory. And they would remember, these winter-white sisters, once of the Woodland Park Zoo. Now, having dispatched the Changed One that had come for their kill, they would exact revenge on the limp-winged crow and his nestling. Dee was a two-legged warrior, and she may have been able to take on that Changed One, but she was no match for a wolf pack. And this one had a vendetta. It was all my fault.

"You don't have long," came a whisper of wet, a voice like the braiding rustle of a creek after rain. Wolves speak in the language of rivers, in fluid riparian sounds that carve out the shape of their thoughts. A white wolf padded forward. Her pack—wolves of silver, brown, black, white—kept their smoldering eyes on her pale glow. Three white sisters padded beside her, her equal in grace and power. White paws dipped into a slippery spill of red. They neared Dee, then stopped, the fur along their spines lifting.

Dee dropped to the ground. She rolled on her back like a schnoodle luxuriating in a putrid duck carcass.

"Dee!" I yelled. "Get up!" She ignored me. I pecked at her arms. She brushed me aside, keeping her eyes on the filthy tiles. I lost my temper then. If we were going to die, I needed it to be dignified. I needed the wolves and their unctuous raven lunatics to know what it was going to cost our world.

"Dee, for fuck's sake! Get up! Listen to me for once!" I

screeched. And then to the ravens and the wolves, "You dip-shits, you will answer for this! I am The One Who Keeps! The blood of the last human on earth will be on your paws, and you will answer to Onida and to the Great Sky King!" There is no Sky King, I made that up. I was very distressed.

The inky raven let out a low croaking. "We were summoned here—"

"Oh my god with the fucking summoning! The truth is that you just do whatever these mangy mutts tell you without a thought about the big picture."

"No, Crow. Open your understanding. We know who you are."

The white raven ruffled her mane, which was infuriatingly beautiful and stupid. What does a bird need a mane for? Honestly. "You are The One Who Keeps. We were summoned here by her." She gestured toward the floor. I stared at Dee, who had stopped rolling and was looking at me with that expression again, belly exposed, that desperate longing tugging on her face.

"What do you mean, she summoned you?" I asked, anger rising in my throat.

"She marked the boundaries of the wolf pack. She called them to her."

I looked at the four white wolves, beautiful as the moon, deadly as its tide. And I remembered that wolves keep other animals out of their territory by marking a chemical fence of urine and scat. Like our mind maps, but less sanitary. And then I thought about how, as we'd run, Dee had squatted and pissed all over the place—and goddammit, summoning them is exactly what she'd done. Dee had been leaving a calling card for a wolf pack I had no idea she'd known was there. She'd been biofencing. How did she know how to delineate territory using urine, or summon wasps, or talk to a tree? All I wanted was to instill a little culture and refinement in her! All I wanted was for her to pick up a book or brush the oversize dust bunny on her noggin or recite a poem or paint her goddamned fingernails and fart discreetly. Dee had called the predators to us. She'd trapped us in a wolf den.

"Goddammit, Dee!" I screeched, stomping in a tight circle, my legs marching in obscenely high steps. "What are we supposed to do now? Beat them to death with *The Joy of Cooking*?!"

Her eyes lowered, face reddening.

"Bad, Dee! Terrible, Dee!" I issued a violent kick to a crispy copy of *How to Win Friends and Influence People*.

"Fear," said the white wolf, a wolf who had been raised by MoFos. "I smell none of it from her. She is fearless, this night child."

"Night child?! What does she mean, night child?!" I squawked at Dee. "You've been leaving the sanctuary? Sneaking around at night? Dee, no! Danger, Dee! Danger, *everywhere*!" The feathers on top of my head were puffed like an oversize Russian *ushanka*, and I was three hops beyond furious but not blind to the body language in the bookstore. The white wolves were curious, tails held high. The other wolves were crouching, light on their feet, their eyes as wide and shiny as parking garage mirrors. The fear came from them. They were frightened of the MoFo in the room. Wolves are moon howlers who live on legend and story. The ones who had never seen a MoFo had no doubt been listening nightly to howls about the boogey monster. And here she was, *standing* tall, beckoning them to her. What animal has had a more contentious relationship with MoFos than the wolf?

"What does she want from us?" asked another of the white sisters, a front paw lifted.

"Yes," the ravens croaked in perfect chorus. "What does the last human want?"

I looked at Dee, madder than a pissed-on pigeon. "Well?"

Dee studied the hulking lupine bodies among a bounty of books. And before she could respond, the shelves shuddered with low growls. The wolves bared flashes of white fangs. A hideous yowling shot through the windows, arrowing through our bodies.

One of the white sisters turned her muzzle to me. "They're here. RUN!"

Ravens, black and white, sliced through the bookstore. "This way! Now!" they called. Before I could process what was happening, a blur of silver fur flashed and blazed around book mountains as the wolves leapt into action. Moon howlers move with the power of water; now I felt a dam burst around me. Dee snatched me and bolted toward the entrance of Third Place Books, guided by the wedged tails of two ravens.

The world bounced up and down. Suddenly the air had a cruel crystal bite and I heard the crunch of thawing snow under speeding mukluks.

I caught a glimpse behind us. The ravens levitated like magical things, watching us get smaller. They dove back into the bookstore, tethered by an ancient bond with the wolves.

Dee didn't look back, couldn't afford to see what might, at any second, burst from dark windows.

# CHAPTER 23

S.T.
LAKE FOREST PARK, WASHINGTON, USA

Dee veered off Bothell Way and along the tree-flanked Burke-Gilman Trail. She ran until her lungs rattled. Dee dropped underneath the dark bodies of young poplars and Douglas firs. Something was haunting about their sepia color, as if they'd been trapped in a Victorian photograph by black magic. I'd read about these trees in Nargatha's copy of the *Seattle Times*. Wrapped in the cloak of night, a MoFo had snuck toward the gentle giants. The MoFo drilled holes into bark skin, pouring herbicide into the trees' wounds. Murder by poison. The motive? The MoFo wanted a better view of Lake Washington. These trees were replacements for the slain who once watched over the lake like old woodland wizards, granting the wishes of the living with every exhale. The horror of it added to my swelling fury, the poison in my own old wounds, and the pain of the past. I was pretty fucking livid as I hopped from Dee's reddened fingers, steam absconding from my nostrils. Still panting in cold clouds, she pointed up at a crispy brown Douglas fir.

"No! Look at me! Look at me, Dee!" I yelled at her. "Focus!"

Dee kept her eyes up at the crowns, let out a scratchy sound. Crow for "friend."

"Listen to me! Listen, Dee! You never listen!" I was fuming, a Shit Turd flambé. "You're too busy launching us right into danger's mouth! Chasing after caribou! Peeing for predators! Sneaking off into the night! Recklessly alerting Changed Ones to our whereabouts at *every turn* when you know damn well how to be stealthy! Stop trying to be something you're not! If you don't listen to me, how the fuck can I keep you alive?" I hopped in front of Dee's crouched body and puffed my head feathers so she knew I meant business. A small figure fluttered from the sepia Douglas needles. Pressa. She had followed us. Where were Migisi and the rest of the help I needed? I didn't have time to acknowledge Pressa as she touched down on a mound of snow. I was consumed.

Pressa's voice was soft, the fluttering of a flag. "S.T., I—"

"Wait, Pressa," I snapped, turning to Dee. For Dee's entire life, everything I'd ever done was to keep her alive; why couldn't she fucking see that? Animalistic anger inside me had incubated long enough. I had encased it in a hard sweep of shell, but it wouldn't hold any longer. It was about to hatch— teeth, talons, and all.

"Dee!" I screeched. "Enough is enough!" Dee frowned. Pressa darted her head, trying to make sense of the scene.

"This is not a playground! You cannot tear around calling on predators and dispatching things like some sort of monster!"

"Assholes!" Dee excitedly referred to the ravens. "Woolwes!" she said, appealing to me with MoFo language, her words like the babbling banter of a chicken.

"What do you know about wolves, Dee? Nothing. You know nothing at all!" As my nestling grew, the wolf packs around

Toksook Bay had all been warned. "Come near her and she'll skin you alive!" I'd told the most hunted animal in American history. They never came anywhere near our cabin. It became a refuge for caribou.

Dee snatched up a hubcap, freeing a dusting of snow. She placed it on top of her head, bared all her teeth, and raised her eyebrows comically—a pretty convincing impression of either Orange or Jim Carrey.

"Put that down! There's fucking nothing funny about this!" I snatched a small stone peeking out from the snow and spat it on the ground for emphasis.

Dee dropped the hubcap and let out a small rattle, an appeal to Pressa, who opened her beak. I cut her off—

"No, Dee! Look at me! Only me! It's time you fucking start listening to me! I've had enough! I'm trying to keep you alive and at every single turn you behave badly! Destruction! Monkeying around! Peeing all over the place! Calling on predators! YOU ARE NOT AND WILL NEVER BE AN ANIMAL. YOU ARE A MOFO AND YOU BETTER START ACTING LIKE IT! YOU'RE GOING TO GET SOMEONE KILLED AGAIN!" The next words tumbled from my throat, free from their tinny cage, years of pent-up emotion bouncing off the bark of inchoate trees.

"You're a fucking disappointment."

Dee flinched, darting her head, listening to *Aura* in case I'd attracted attention. And this made me even angrier, that she *still* wasn't listening, that she moved her head like a bird, as if her eyes were perched on the sides of her head. She had to understand what was at stake here. That acting on animal instincts would get her killed. If I had broken Dennis's habits, then he would never have chased after a UPS truck and my heart would still be in one piece.

Dee kept her shining eyes on Pressa, her brow stitched tight.

Her cheeks blooming crocosmia red. She clenched her jaw, her nostrils flaring like wings of a feeding butterfly. Her lower lip trembled. She padded away from me to sulk under a young poplar tree. She parted a frosting of snow with her fingers, unveiling a monarch of moss. She made the heartbreaking cries of burrowing owlets. She called for Kuupa and Oomingmak in owl and ox. She was the last of a species who needed to learn how to be human before she made one more mukluk print in the snow.

A great force struck my side. I slammed against the buttressing roots of a silent Douglas fir. I opened my eyes. Pressa was on top of me, a flurry of feathers, screeching as her feet raked at my chest.

"Pressa?" I screamed my surprise. "Ouch!"

Her assault was a never-ending flurry.

"Hulk Hogan!"[1] I squawked. I shielded myself with my wings and struggled to get away, and just when I thought I'd have to burrow underground to escape her, she stopped. She stood over me, gular bouncing like a frantic fruit fly.

"Are you done?" she yelled. "Look at me!"

"I'm looking at you, Pressa!"

She walloped me with her wing. Crows are capable of great violence.

"What's wrong with you! You've lost your damn mind!" I screeched.

Pressa snatched two foot-fulls of snow, launched into the air above me, and pelted me with them.

"What is your problem?!" I shrieked, stealing a glance at Dee, who had blocked out the bickering crows, focusing on the spongy fleece of moss.

---

1   This was the "safe word" Big Jim used to sometimes shriek from the bedroom; even not knowing exactly what a safe word was, it was worth a whirl.

"What is my problem?" she asked, from above. "*My* problem?"

"Why are you assaulting me?"

"'*What's my problem*,' he says! I don't have a problem, Shit Turd; you have a problem—and until you get your beak out of the suet feeder, so to speak, you don't get to leave this area."

"What in the Frosted Flakes are you talking about?"

She did another very rude and nasal impersonation of me. I hoped it was very inaccurate. "'*What's my problem*!' Wake up! Why do you think I'm here?"

"I don't—"

"You have no clue! You didn't even acknowledge me because you are completely blind. I came here to save you from yourself! I flew after you because, though Kraai might grant your every wish and enable your flighty ideas, I'm not going to stand by while you make another deadly mistake. Marching off by yourself to hide from the entire beautiful blue! *No feathered may return to the egg*, S.T.! You can't hide like Big Jim with pizza and internment—"

"Internet—"

"Beak down and listen! The code of murder, S.T.! We are stronger together! Think back on everything that's happened to you, how you've stayed alive! You had help. We all worked together. You don't stand a chance racing out into the jaws of the jungle with no one. You're hollering out for help on *Aura* and what you've been completely oblivious to is that the trees are all dead! Look at them! Look around you! Look!"

She was right. They were silent. Evergreen needles ever-brown. Sepia bodies, hollow husks. Their throats ripped out. The bark beetle creatures—The Masticators—were ravaging our gentle giants. Dee had known before I had, her head hung low in respect for a cemetery—a forest of the dead.

"Trees *have* been talking to you, S.T., helping you, singing to you, and you've listened when it suited you! TREES! And where were you when they were screaming? Everyone is trying to help you, S.T., and here you are, running away from us all." Her whole body fluffed and puffed until she was an airborne sea urchin. "That MoFo is the last of her kind and you're so busy yelling at her to be something she's not that you broke her." Pressa landed. She jumped in place, her wings batting the air like tennis rackets. Hopping mad. And suddenly, as if her anger was a spell, hot air rising, she lifted again, suspended above me.

"Everything Dee does is for you! She tries so hard to gain your approval and you yell at her, pick on her, and tell her *she's a disappointment*? She cannot change who she is, S.T.! How do you not get this? You, a bird who only ever wanted to be a MoFo, can't see that she's in your reversed predicament, that all she wants to be is a crow! All her movements and sounds and the way she looks at you—my god, S.T., the way she looks at you! Your hollow little MoFo brain is missing all of it! Why do you think Dee is sitting over there, lost and alone? Because you crushed her. I just watched you crush your own egg. She's trying so hard not to be herself, and that means you have clipped your nestling's wings. Now Dee doesn't know how to be in the world, has no one to identify with, and the being she loves more than life itself is disgusted with what she has become. What a lonely, lonely life. Congratulations, S.T., you've raised a caged bird."

"I've never been disgusted with Dee! I just want her to rise to her full potential! I love her!"

"When have you told her that?"

That shut me up. My heart sank, a stone.

Big Jim told me he loved me every time he drank whiskey,
which was very, very often. He never once tried to make me
into something I wasn't. I remembered him swanning around
A Very Taki Tiki Bar, his crow on his shoulder, glacial-blue
eyes alight with pride. How he'd answer the endless questions
MoFos asked about me in a tuba voice. He was proud of me
when he showed off the trick where I'd shell a peanut and
offer it to a lady MoFo, or when I'd swear like a substitute
teacher, but he was just as proud of me when I ate worms in
the grass. Sometimes, when his sweat-filled nights diluted into
foggy mornings, I'd find him in our dew-beaded yard with
the early birds, his big palms filled with wiggly pink spaghetti
strands he'd collected for me himself.

"She never listens to me!" I whined to Pressa.

"She's your nestling! My life for an earthworm, S.T., I have
eleven sons and they never listen to a single squawk I have
to say. Get over yourself. And the eagle who has given you
everything insisted I come after—"

"What's wrong with Migisi?" My rib cage constricted. "Where
is she?"

Pressa walloped me with a rock the shape of Texas. "Migisi—
you whipworm—is losing her mind because she can't keep up
with you; she's tired because she's about to lay eggs, but you
haven't noticed because you're stuck in Shit Turd Kingdom,
stuck in a MoFo mind where everything is about the past and
the future. Wake up, Shit Turd!"

A mind stuck in the past or the future. It *was* very MoFo, I
thought.

"Eggs! When?" I screeched, remembering how tired Migisi
had been lately and when we'd met up with her on a sliver
of Edmonds beach after our great *Echo* journey. I had never
asked her if she was okay. I'd just expected her to ferry me
all over the Pacific Northwest willy-nilly, to be our eyes in the

sky. To just up and be an adventure eagle. "Is she alright? Is she safe?!"

"Are any of us?! You have a lot of making up to do, S.T. You're not the only one who has problems."

"I'm sorry," I said, deflating. "Dee is my—"

"NO!" she screamed. "Dee is not yours! What MoFo reasoning to think you own her! Dee is a wild thing, and once a wild thing is owned, its spirit is no longer free, no longer true to itself. When you're owned, you're stripped of your autonomy, your unique, original essence. She's perfect just as she is, and she doesn't belong to anyone but herself—say that she's yours one more time and I swear on my salmonberry stash, I'll—"

"You're right. You're right!" I bobbed my head at her. "You're right about it all."

Pressa's voice calmed, each word a wispy cloud. "It is not your job to change her. It is your job to love her."

I looked over at Dee, sifting through ivory powder to free the green beneath. She was humming gently, a song especially for the ravaged tree above her. A poem popped into my head.

*He who binds himself to a joy*
*Does the winged life destroy*
*He who kisses the joy as it flies*
*Lives in eternity's sunrise*

I'd never understood it before, but ol' Billy Blake was right.

"She's not mine, and I haven't done a good job of showing her how special she is. That she's the reason my heart beats."

Pressa touched back down to the ground. Her wings tucked back into her sides. Dee was still lost to the world of bryophytes—moss, hornworts, and liverworts. Crows squabbled all the time, and I suppose since I was constantly picking on Dee, it was background noise to her.

"Imagine the pain and loneliness she feels. We've seen our kind die, we've suffered together. But always together. None of us have been The Last, The Only." We looked at Dee, curled under a tree trunk, humming her sad and gentle song. "You taught me a lot about MoFos, S.T., and I'm as enamored as you are, but as the wise poet once said, 'Oh, you're a loaded gun, oh, there's nowhere to run.'"

"Bon Jovi," I said, inspired.

"And that's why I'm here, S.T. You are that gun and you cannot run away and hide."

She was so right. How had I been so wrong? I looked back over to Dee. She was gone.

"Dee?" I called.

Pressa and I hopped over to where she had sat, curled up and disgraced. Mukluk prints painted a portrait of movement away from the trees. We followed them until they disappeared, suddenly swallowed up by ash gray of pavement and road. An abandoned street. The street's silence hammered inside my head. Anger and shame were kicked aside by terror.

"Dee?" I called out. "Dee?"

"Dee?" Pressa called out.

"Pressa, what have I done?"

"Keep looking, S.T., I'll search from the sky!" She shot into the air and looped above, scanning for the last MoFo on earth. I was sick with worry and the lung-scorching fumes of regret. Where would she go? She had left the trees, walking toward the road, toward tired buildings and urban decay—so unlike Dee. I read signs for a yoga studio, a coffee shop, a place that sold discounted tires. And the next storefront sign I saw shook my bones.

"Pressa!" I yelled. "Down here!"

She dropped from the sky. We stood in front of a dilapidated shop, its sign showcasing the most terrifying words I'd seen in an age: *Phones & More.* I already knew—a *Corvus* knowing—Dee had gone inside. I'd forced her to go against her better nature. We raced into the store and froze.

The shop's guts had been ravaged by hundreds of twisted hands. Blood-smeared surfaces, smashed desks, floors tattooed with claw marks. Dee stood in the middle of a mountain of broken plastic. On the wall behind her were the remains of a poster. It was faded, but there was no mistaking its advertisement—MoFo lady laughing, a cell phone pressed tightly to her head. My gular fluttered.

Dee had a cell phone in her hand.

I don't know how she'd found it among this rubble, but she had. Fuck it. She had. My neck feathers spiked.

Its screen was intact.

Pressa was suddenly by my side. Would it turn on after all this time? Did it have to turn on for Dee to be snatched by its spell? I had no answers. Just everything to lose. Dee had never been near one of these before. And now she held a bomb, a gun pointed at her face, an infected needle whose virus hungered for her species. And it was all my fault. Dee held up the cell phone to show me, her eyes seeking approval.

"Don't. Move." I told her. Pressa's breathing hitched. Dee's eyes flicked to the cell phone in her hand.

"No!" I said. "Look at me, Dee! Look at S.T.!"

Dee frowned in confusion. Pressa let out warning caws. *Danger*, she told Dee in five piercing notes.

"Dee is MoFo!" Dee said, lifting the cell phone up into the air, her plastic smile mimicking the MoFo lady on the poster.

"Put it down, Dee. This is not who you are. Walk out of here with us. Slowly, Dee. Very slowly. Don't touch; never touch. Danger."

I started to back up gingerly, willing her to follow. Dee looked at me long and hard, suspicion shining in her eyes. Slowly, she lowered the old cell phone in her hand. She chucked it onto a tangled nest of phone chargers.

"This way, Dee. Very, very carefully. Come out here. Follow S.T."

She padded gently from Phones & More. I had so much to say, so much relief billowing from me, I could barely stand. But before I got the chance to utter a caw, something else happened.

The screech was an amplified raking of nails. Dee pivoted. Pressa's head bobbed. We waited, sure we'd misheard. But there it was again, a sour scream from the forest. Dee and I shared a sharp glance. Dee snatched me from the ground and into a coop of fingers. We knew this call. It was woven carefully into the strings of our hearts.

"Wait! Hold on!" Pressa's protests were dampened by Doppler as we sped across the road.

Dee ran, and we channeled our inner orcas. We found ourselves in a clearing, ringed by a necklace of trees. We listened for the siren screech. The distress call of an owl. Where was she? Dee called out to her, hooting the "*Who cooks for you? Who cooks for you?*" calls of a barred owl.

"Friend!" she assured the mewling night hunter in its own tongue. And then silence. Dee tried once more, soft as silk. And the screech came back, arrowing through the trees. I searched every snowy branch. It came again, Dee flinching at the distress of a beloved bird.

Dee placed me gently on a bench. She padded into the center of the clearing. She kept her wingspan halfway splayed, ready to fly. Pressa caught up and touched down on the bench next to me.

Dee flinched and spun to face a poplar tree. And then, as if born from the darkness, an enormous thing emerged. Head suspended from its torso, its body was covered in spiny bristles. Its eye roved, red as the insides of things. It moved mechanically on too many legs.

A Weaver.

Not a spider, not a MoFo, but some horror in between. The owl's scream scratched the sky behind Dee. She spun to face the night bird in distress on the other side of the clearing. Oozing out from behind blackened bark was the bird. It stood in a puddle of thawed snow. It was not an owl. Here was the creature that Ghubari and I had scuttled underneath in the cover of dark, the thing that had grown grotesque wings. Here, up close, illuminated by silver sky and the shock of snow, I could see that the dark holes of its face held two eyes, a shining black menace. How large its body was—it would have dwarfed Big Jim—its pallid skin stippled with greasy feathers. The creature stared motionless, a bony growth-like beak sprouting from the middle of its elongated face. Each of its leathery legs clenched a talon like an industrial steel hook.

Two of them. Two creatures that might have slithered out from under H.R. Giger's bed. One mimicking a bird, the other mimicking a spider.

The bird creature darted its head from side to side. My stomach started demonstrating its balloon animal repertoire. The creature's eyes were on the side of its head and I involuntarily thought of the halibut, a flatfish whose eye migrates to join its partner on the other side of the fish's flat head as it matures. The Bird Being let out the distress "*screeeeeeeeedeee*," the piercing cry of a barred owl. The betrayal smacked Dee squarely in the chest, winding her with its blunt strike. Her face collapsed. Color drained from her cheeks, her powerful legs buckled. Dee dropped to the ground.

The Weaver and the birdlike being closed in on Dee. Four more Weavers appeared, silently stitching tracks into snow. More of the gargantuan Bird Beings came up behind the beaked creature. More and more Weavers filled the blackness behind Dee. I hadn't seen them creep like this before. Slow, calculated steps. They surrounded her. Every memory of these things was suddenly challenged—their blundering greed, chaotic violent acts, the palsied movement of spiders on fire. Now, they were feral creatures with the quick movements of birds, the hydraulic shimmy of arachnids.

But this was good; yes, it was good, because there were two types of Changed Ones. This meant that they would fight over her, they'd be possessed with jealousy, and we'd sneak away. The violence that hissed inside them was what I now counted on.

"Stay away!" I said, in the coarse corvid call known to every creature on the big beautiful blue. The birdlike being closest to Dee—now on her knees—spun toward me, snake neck rippling back and forth like a sidewinder. The eyes—oily shards of coal—burned into me. It would come for me. I had seconds.

The Bird Being lifted its head to the clouds and spilled out my warning caws precisely—a copycat. It mocked me. Those cruel eyes found me again. A flash licked across its lids.

*Nictitating membranes.* I gasped.

"Crow," it said, in a deep bass of a bronchial beast. This time it wasn't in crow. It spoke MoFo. Pressa and I were paralyzed. Dread burrowed in my bones.

And then the Weaver reached out one of its spidery limbs, pressing the sharp point of a once-MoFo arm against Dee's skin. Dee flinched.

"NO! SHE'S MINE!" I yelled.

The Changed Ones circled like vultures around Dee. Two sounds—one from Weaver, one from Bird Being—two hawk screams, call and response.

*Fight, dammit, fight each other for her. Get up, Dee. Get up.* I spoke to Dee in my mind, willing her to lift from her crumpled heap. To straighten the rounded shells of her shoulders. Activate those beautiful fingers. She had a plan; I knew she did. She was playing opossum, coiled like a spring.

The Bird Beings all screeched in raptor's shrill summoning. Everything happened so fast. The Weavers let out a quick sibilant hiss.

I could do nothing as the closest Weaver snatched Dee in two enormous spiky limbs.

"No! Put her down!" I yelled, racing toward the abominable spider that had captured Dee. A force clamped down on my bad wing. I glanced up at the towering arachnid leg that had pinned me to the ground. Four pairs of eyes loomed above me like hostile planets. The Weaver lifted its leg and I felt the pressure release from my wing. The leg hovered above my head as the Weaver readied to bring it down on my skull. Another force, this one plowed into my body, launching me into tumbles. I was pinned now by Pressa, breathless from her dive. The Weaver's leg struck the ground where my head had been seconds before. I looked up just in time to see the Weaver carrying Dee. It skittered away into a black labyrinth of trunks. The Weavers all dispersed like spiders erupting from a broken nest. The Bird Being turned to face me.

And then the rush of reality crashed into me.

*They had worked together.*

"Do it. Go after her," I read in the sheen across its black corneas. Daring me to my death. Another wiper-wash of nictitating membranes. And those eyes. Behind them a malevolent mind—I knew, without a doubt—was thinking. Then, with a stretch of the bony growth, behind a cage door of saliva strings, it spoke again.

"NO! SHE'S MINE!" it screamed, and my heart seized. Cruel mimicry, a thief of my MoFo words. A simple parroting. The absurdity of claiming her, Pressa's chastising, all of it thrown back in my beak. The Bird Being sprung into the air, angular wings catching its weight, and I caught a glimpse of its knife-like wing joints, the flight feathers hefting it into the sullen sky. To fly, this creature's very bones must have hollowed. The other Bird Beings leapt to the air.

"They took her! They took her!" I screamed, erupting from my stupor. "They took her! Quickly!" I threw myself across the clearing, stumbling over the craters left by mukluk prints, deformed bird feet, and the skittish scars of spiders. I called out to *Aura*, screaming for someone to help us—bird, insect, tree, fungi, Onida, help us, help us, please, anyone, help us.

"They are going to kill her, Pressa, and I will die too."

"S.T., try to breathe. If they wanted to kill her, they would have already done it. They want something else with her," said Pressa.

I felt my body ball into a fist. I remembered what Ghubari had said—

*"I told you they are trying to reproduce. They have been hunting for her."*

"We have to get help. We have to get back to Ghubari and all the domestics and the elephant herd—"

"And we have to do it now," said Pressa.

"But with *Aura* down, all these dead zones, how will we get a message to them in time? How will a crow with a broken heart—"

"Try to keep the bees in your head calm, S.T."

"But how will we get to them in time?" I held up my weak wing. "They won't know where we are!" I looked around at the bodies of the replacement trees who never made it to adulthood, who suffered the same fate as their predecessors at the hands of humans.

"Yes, *Aura* is shut down. And I'm not strong enough to fly

you. But I have an idea. And I'm just warning you, you're not going to like it one bit, but also, I don't give a hooting hoverfly because you've behaved very badly, and frankly, S.T., you've given love a bad name."

I momentarily regretted all the late nights answering Pressa's every fawning question about MoFo life. I'd loved it, but damn. "You're right," I said, trying to stop my mind from its scribble scrabble into the future on hamster feet.

"Follow me. And keep up," she said, hopping across the clearing like an inky angel. Kind and clever and brave. As strong as Tiffany S. from Tinder. I scampered behind Pressa.

The very last time I saw Tiffany S. standing on two feet, I'd been perched on the back of the La-Z-Boy®. Big Jim was draining the one-eyed lizard (an elusive reptile I'd never been able to locate). She approached me slowly. I expected histrionics from her, seeing as I'd just refashioned her pantyhose into a Superman-style cape for myself. It suited me. She wore an Easter-yellow dress and pinched her anxiety between fuchsia lips. Her makeup was adventurous and her hair that of someone who had recently escaped an insane asylum by way of a category five hurricane. This is because I had sabotaged her hair iron.

"Shit Turd. You and I have to work this out, honey. I'm not here to take him away from you. You've got your thing, B.J. and I got ours. I'm trying my best here. Can you cut me some slack?" She extended a peace offering in her long pink talons.

A Cheeto®.

"Can we be friends?" she asked, a tremble in her voice.

I weighed the pros and cons of the delectable orange treasure. The pleading pooling in her eyes. That feather boa– tickled tease, hope.

Then I launched myself through the window, dropping a

stream of shit over her head. Really, the perfect metaphor for my terrible attitude.

If you're not careful, history is a perennial plant. Tenacious roots hide themselves so that things can once again burgeon in bright colors.

*I'm sorry, Dee. I'm sorry, Tiffany S.*

# CHAPTER 24

MARIPOSA
SCARLET REEF HERMIT CRAB
BONAIRE, SOUTHERN CARIBBEAN

I have spent my life hiding
   I carry my home and the weight of the world on my back
   And outside, the whooshing world roars
   Waves thrash their mighty arms, conducting current moods
   Perhaps I have missed the aqueous dance of anemone,
   That the sea stars sing of survival in a constellation of color
   That every bubble strives to reach the sky
   And I tuck myself tighter into my shell, pale and shy as sea-foam
   Maybe I've missed that the giant clam is a brave mollusk, a silky-lipped secret keeper who will tell you if you ask
   Nothing will awaken the life within you as the silver switch and slice of a shark
   The electric energy of an eel can change the currents of your story
   Leafy sea dragon dresses in seaweed, a private show

And the jellied globes of fish eggs shine with potential, glistening from the fizzy frenzy for life within

The sponges open themselves to every passing plankton, for your pleasure, life flows through pinprick pores

(Minuscule beings can hold the hearts of lionfish)

Parrotfish parade their paints for your eyes, not their own

Algae brave a thousand salt-stung mouths

The anemone feels its friendship with the clown fish, holding back the sting of its tentacles for a greater gift

And now, the end is near. I must leave my home

Did I fill my life with color and sense and sound?

Or did I miss the brilliant blue spectacle?

I made a shape for myself,

A shell shape

Tiny, hidden, satisfactory, and safe

But now I am sorry that I didn't stretch to take up the entire ocean


I spent my life hiding.

Come out of your shell.

# CHAPTER 25

S.T.
BOTHELL, WASHINGTON, USA

It was like looking through Big Jim's mug of beer. I used to do this as Big Jim swiveled on a barstool, slinging back peanuts. He'd engage the nearest pod of MoFos, demonstrating one of his slick bar tricks or bewildering them with a human beatbox freestyle. I'd hop from Big Jim's shoulder, along the fuzzy slope of his arm, and onto the bar top where I'd shred a few napkins (a subtle comment on the unequal distribution of peanuts) and then peer at the scene through the glass mug. The world was bathed in psychedelic amber. A busty bartender swam around with a ballooned head as if she'd been stung in the nose and misplaced her EpiPen. The bar's bottles were wonky props from the Mad Hatter's adult tea party. This is what everything looked like as Pressa and I ran, sun melting snow. Exhaustion and heartache can skew the world into a fairground fun house.

"How do you know they're this way?" I frantically asked Pressa, who galloped like a roadrunner, taking great leaps where her wings would catch the air and she'd force herself back to the ground. Because of me.

"I don't, I'm following my inner map, feeling where the murder might be; we've got to try—"

"Pressa, we can't just guess! We have to—"

Pressa stopped short.

She stood over enormous mud marks. The hollow prints of hooves.

Changed Ones had thundered past here, uprooting the burrowers—taffy-pink worms, silver springtails, ants, and rotifers. Beyond the blindness of the eye, I heard shrill screams from the world Dee loved so deeply.

*Dee*, I thought, *Dee, Dee, Dee.*

The world of *Web*'s protozoa, water bears, nematodes, and pygmy creatures had scuttled to safety as their mansion of moss was ripped apart. A universe of microorganisms had experienced their big bang.

Our beaks were drawn upward by the crisp rustle of wings. We ducked. More Changed Ones—the oil-feathered flying things and their vulgar airborne bodies. Once they'd passed, Pressa gestured to the hoofprints, then the sky.

"They're all heading east," she said.

"Shit, you're right. But where? How far?" I asked. "Pressa, I'm holding us back. You have to go ahead and get help; we have to get to Dee faster than I can—"

"No. We don't separate. We go together. That is the code of murder," she said. The look in her eye—a look I'd seen Nargatha give a Bieber-haired teenager who called her a "denture diva" right before she plowed over him with her Rascal 615 mobility scooter—told me to drop it. Pressa was risking her life for me, and holy Hostess snacks, I don't know if there has ever been a more crowmantic gesture.

Another hailstorm of wingbeats rained down on us. We

ducked behind a tree trunk. I glanced up and felt the mug of Pabst Blue Ribbon lift from my vision. Hope sharpened everything into crystal focus.

"There! Look! Look!" I gestured up to a streaming rainbow ribbon. Pressa called upward—five throaty caws, "We're here! We're here!" And then—thank the entire cast of *Law & Order*—streaks of Carnival color spilled from the sky. A feathered form descended, gray as Gandalf and just as wise.

"Ghubari!" I shrieked. "Ghubari! Listen, we don't have time, we have to spread word, summon every esteemed colleague on earth—"

"That doesn't mean what you think it does," he said.

"Dammit, then summon *every creature on earth*—The Changed Ones took Dee! They took her! Right in front of me! And Ghubari, *they spoke*! They know what I am! They called me 'crow'!"

"I see," said Ghubari, calm as a Buddhist cucumber.

Ghubari and Calliope clutched the branches of black cottonwoods. The parrots surveyed the devastation. Resin that bled thick golden tears from tree trunks. The cottonwoods breathed out a sweet balsamic aroma—olfactory grief. It brought swift scent-summoned memories—Dee gingerly dabbing her cuts with crushed cottonwood buds, Dee with her bees as they emerged from the frigid fist of winter, gathering resin from cottonwood to make a homemade glue for the hive. I shook to escape the needling pain of missing her, a crush that was steadily collapsing my lungs. *Dee. Dee. Dee.*

Tom Hanks, the cockatoo, joined us on a nearby cottonwood branch, giving a dramatic high kick with one leg.

"Hellooooo!" he sang. "It's me!" His mezzo-soprano was so good I had to double-check that actual Adele hadn't survived her species's extinction by squatting in a tree this whole time.

The three parrots peered down from above.

"Where's Kraai?" I asked.

"I don't know," said Ghubari.

"Where are the elephants, the dog packs, we need to—"

"Perhaps, Shit Turd, we do nothing."

I stared at the round, inquisitive faces of parrots. "What?"

"Perhaps, Shit Turd, she is exactly where she needs to be."

"No, Ghubari, it's The Changed Ones that have her; we need to summon all the animals—"

"They are gone," said Calliope, the macaw in Hawaiian hues.

"Gone where?"

"I sent them away," said Ghubari. "I told them to leave our territory. All of them. They have started a great migration, to find somewhere safe to call home. The Changed Ones have Dee, and while they have her, Shit Turd, every other living being has a fighting chance to escape."

Everything began to bulge and bloat, beer bubbles and glassy distortion. "Ghubari, I don't understand. Are you hearing how important this is? *They have Dee.*"

"Shit Turd, she is with her kind now. They have the very last of their own and now you get what you wanted too. The species will not die out if there is a female to produce young. Think of it."

Pressa took over for me. I was too stunned, a legless half-breed made of tumbleweeds. "Ghubari, listen to yourself! You can't sacrifice a nestling; it's not the code of murder. These beasts can't be allowed to continue their reign of horror—"

"Speciation reversal, Pressa. It is a natural notion—we've seen it in ravens, and there is a chance The Changed Ones could breed themselves back, to combat the devastation of the virus on the human anatomy. Imagine reversing Darwin's tree! Breeding back the traits of humans that are missing in these mutated beings. You said it yourself—one called you 'crow'! Marvelous! They are still in there somewhere! And then you, anthropocentric S.T., you might finally get your quixotic dream. Don't you see? They might not be what they once were, but they will be something closer, thanks to Dee. All thanks to the genes of your nestling."

"I don't have time for YOUR GARBAGE PARROT SCIENCE! I have to get to Dee!" I yelled upward, shaking with anger. "This is not her destiny. I am The One Who Keeps!"

Betrayal is a hard, hot poker to the heart, quick scars and scalded soft tissue. I wanted to yell, "Shame!" and throw tomatoes at him, but there was no time for that. I'd had enough. I ran on, passing lonely houses that posed for the lake. Shadows blackened the pavement as bright birds chased me from the air.

"Hypocritical!" said Ghubari, slowing his flight to stay above a sprinting crow. "What about the rabbits, voles, salmon, and deer Dee has eaten to survive, the creatures she has destroyed? In nature there are always sacrifices—"

"Dee lives her life in gratitude of those gifts!" I screeched, my voice bumping along for the earthbound ride. "She's respectful of nature! She receives gifts and gives them. She knows that in order for life to continue, she cannot overfish. She would never hunt the last salmon. It's all a web of reciprocity; you know this, Ghubari, The Changed Ones don't give back! They will obliterate the planet if no one stops them! Of course, some animals become prey—MoFos called it the circle of life, remember?! They held up baby lions as Elton John sang about it!" From shaggy arborvitaes, a pair of Steller's jays watched a trio of parrots in pursuit of earthbound crows and questioned their fermented berry intake. "But The Changed Ones are dominating, hell-bent on destruction. This is not a natural balance."

"Nature has always been building biological superweapons. This is not new."

"Go away, Ghubari!" I was experiencing acute déjà poo—the feeling that I'd heard this crap before.

"What about the human hearts?" projected Ghubari as we navigated around a filthy old couch squatting in the road. "Those hearts are still in there somewhere! They still beat, Shit Turd!"

"I've made my peace with the extinction of the MoFos. It's better that Dee is the last MoFo on earth than we allow them to continue as they are. What the hell has happened to y— No, I don't have time for this. Dee needs help!" Here, I tripped over a stone and face planted, but we won't dwell on that.

Ghubari was suddenly at my side, skimming the pavement with a perilously low flight. "It's worth a shot! They are killing every living being, and if we don't try, we will all be extinct. Shit Turd, The Changed Ones are mimicking the natural world, harnessing the powers of nature. I have seen them using the traits of animals, but what if, instead of returning to their humanity, they tap into those with the greatest powers of nature?"

That stopped me dead in my tracks. The parrots hovered above.

Hard bumps across my body told me he was right about one thing. There were much greater powers in nature, and I couldn't think about what would happen if The Changed Ones adapted those.

Ghubari landed on the lakeside street with galling elegance. "It is better that we have them back, S.T.! It's what you've always wanted!"

"Ghubari, you're wrong!" Words I never thought I'd say, much less scream, tangy on the tongue. "Can you hear yourself—procreation with those monsters? We have to rescue Dee; we have to work together. If we stop caring about one another, then we're no better than them. A great poet once said that 'we've got to hold on to what we've got, it doesn't make a difference if we make it or not.'"[1]

Ghubari searched the vast caverns of his mind, finally at a loss. "That's quite beautiful. I've never heard that poem before, S.T."

"That's a damn shame, Ghubari," I said. "Now get the hell out of my way!"

I heard their parting wingbeats. I didn't have time for my pending emotional meltdown; we had to find Kraai and figure out how to get Dee back without the herd of animals I was counting on. We were flying solo and unfortunately not flying at all. Suddenly, Tom Hanks dropped directly in front of Pressa and me with all the grace of a ripened coconut.

"Get out of my way, Tom Hanks!" I shrieked. "I'm going to find Dee!"

Tom Hanks splayed his white wings and cleared his throat. He projected beautifully, and suddenly, instead of a theatrical cockatoo, I saw a young MoFo actress, holding her audience. I pictured the youthful glow of her skin, hope and the light of a stage shining in her eyes. A MoFo with the bones of a bird, but the brave of a bear.

*All the world's a stage,*
*And all the men and women merely players;*
*They have their exits and their entrances;*
*And one man in his time plays many parts*[2]

---

1 To be clear, the poet I refer to is the illustrious Jon Bon Jovi, who was a magnificent MoFo with the voice of a rose-breasted grosbeak and the hair of a Silkie chicken.
2 These were beautiful words from a play by William Shakespeare, who was also known as the Bard, which I like to think was just a drunken Early Modern English pronunciation of "bird."

Tom Hanks bowed his head, signaling deep respect, the feathers of his crest like bright yellow fingers.

"Look for the lake house with *alive inside* written on the roof. You'll find help there; tell them I sent you," said Tom Hanks in a hushed tone. He shared a mind map with Pressa by letting out a sharp squawk of sound. Before he vanished into a curtain of clouds, he sang, "The show *must* go on."

And on it would.

"Can we trust him?" Pressa asked.

"What choice do we have?" I said, sensing we both felt that Tom Hanks was telling us the truth, that he'd never forgotten the young MoFo who'd taught him how to be an entertainer. Tom Hanks would have given his right wing to sing one last song with his MoFo. Pressa and I ran alongside lake houses that hugged Lake Washington. And then I stopped.

"Oh grubs, what is it?" whispered Pressa.

"That. Do you hear it?" I asked. A ghost of a sound. But I listened to the flutter and flare of my veins, the way little Dee had done since she first started to engage with the worlds around her. The way Dee knew to listen to the warning calls of a *Turdus migratorius*, how the trees rustled and tightened before a storm. Instinct. And while a large percentage of my insides told me I needed a Big Mac, a smaller part told me I needed to follow this sound. I took in the faces of lake houses, the mouths of their letter boxes rusted shut, front lawns choking on weeds.

Pressa lifted up into the sky, soaring over the roof of the lake house.

"S.T.! There is writing on the roof! MoFo letters! I think it might be the place!"

I heard the faint sound again and ran toward a battered fence.

"Bird your loins, Pressa!"

I heard Pressa mutter something about only understanding me a fraction of the time and then heard her hijack the wind above me as I squeezed in between a gap in the green wood planks and tore across the lawn—a great green labyrinth of sword fern and salal and wood sorrel—

"Shit Turd, careful! We don't know what's down there!"

And then I was leaping past a cobwebbed statue of a mer-MoFo and approaching the door, a hand-carved MoFo masterpiece in knotty alder. The door—a Haida scene of orcas in battle—had seen its own fight, a sharp scar rivering down to its base, ending in an estuary of a hole big enough for a handsome crow to fit through. I stopped, Pressa hovering above me. The springtails in my belly told me I was in the right place. I slipped in through the crack in the door.

It was strange to be inside. Dee never trusted the insides of houses—a ceiling meant she couldn't read the sky. The once-modern lake house was spacious, dark. Dank wet smells slithered across old chairs and shelves, a tableau of MoFo life. Gaping windows surveyed Lake Washington, eerily calm as if reflecting a memory of glass. Old footprints told tales like the ancient etchings of a cave wall. I would describe the house's decor as "bog nouveau." The greedy salt smell of sex hung in the air. A definite sign of squirrel sexcapades.

"There, through the windows!" I launched myself through a gaping floor-to-ceiling window, and then Pressa and I were running beside patio furniture, across a stretch of grass, up to the placid waters of Lake Washington. And there, at the lip of the lake, was a waddle.

A waddle of Humboldt penguins. They had survived despite being zoo animals, and they had grown in their numbers. The younger penguins had less of the Humboldt's signature pale salmon face mask, pink patches of skin that help the penguin stay cool in the warmer temperatures of their native Peru and Chile. I marveled; the Humboldts were adapting to the chilly Pacific Northwest.

"We are looking for the crows, please, have you seen them?" asked Pressa, our diplomat. "Tom Hanks sent us here!"

"Tom Hanks! We love Tom Hanks!" penguins honked excitedly.

"The Changed Ones took my fledgling!" I squawked, unable to help myself.

The penguins, like a rack of bowling pins decked out in evening wear, elected one penguin to come forward. The penguin with the largest pastel pink mask used spatula feet to waddle a few steps in front of the others and said, "The One Who Keeps! What a great honor to be in your presence! You are a legend!"

The penguins raised their little black flippers up and down, honking a kazoo's chorus of joy.

I'd always felt that penguins were sophisticated and intuitive beings.

"I need help," I told the spokes-penguin. "The Changed Ones have taken my—" I looked over at Pressa, whose eyebrows would have been in the stratosphere if she'd had any. "The Changed Ones have taken Dee, the last human. She's everything to me. And she needs my help. I have to find her. I have to protect her."

The penguins shuffled and shivered on the spot. "A Keeper! Alive! Alive!" they cheered. I felt their giddiness and an excited exhale from the surface of the lake. "We have heard of her! Yes! The Keeper who rides the sea wolves! *Echo* knows of her."

"The seabirds speak of her!" honked the spokes-penguin.

"Yes! That's Dee! Please," I begged the penguin, suddenly motivated by a MoFo movie, "I'm just a crow, standing in front of a penguin, asking him to help me rescue the last human on earth."

"We want to help! We want to help our kind!"

"Our kind?" I asked.

"Yes! Yes! Earth birds!"

Pressa had already gleaned their meaning and was raking at the grass with her toes uncomfortably.

"Grounded birds! Birds who cannot ride the sky!" clarified the cheerful seabird.

"I see," I said, feeling a prick of self-consciousness. "I need to find the crows, I need allies; I've got to find out where The Changed Ones have taken Dee…"

"You need to travel fast," said the main penguin, in the sounds of a smile.

"Yes!"

"Hooooooray!" cheered the waddle of penguins, hopping up and down excitedly.

"Come, come, come!" they all chanted. The penguins waddled up the unruly grass of the lawn, so tall they were barely visible. They stopped where the property line ended, where a fence lay in splintered fragments. Pressa and I stared at the neighboring lake house's jungle of weeds and brush. The house was derelict. It wore a moss wig and a tired expression. It was slowly being digested by vegetation.

"Um…where?" I asked.

"There!"

Pressa and I squinted, darting our heads. There was nothing but bramble and a lively battle of sword ferns. Old prejudices began to rise up within me. What did these aquatic tampons know about anything? They were just strangers drowning in a strange land. Perhaps the happy-go-lucky thing was all an act, they were high on hope and herring. Maybe they'd all lost their minds in the quest for somewhere to belong.

"Our friend is one of us, an earth bird. Penguins are friends to earth birds and *Echo* birds."

"I really don't have time—"

The penguin raised his sugar-pink face to the sky and let out a honking bellow so loud I leapt into the air: "Come out!"

Brambles started to shimmy like the jingling hip scarf of a belly dancer. The first thing we saw was an enormous leg, the steely gray of a gun. Then three enormous talons.

A Changed One. A setup. I knew it! Those Oreo-colored butt plugs!

"No need to be shiverish!" the penguin said to me. "Come on, Budiwati, don't be shy!" The penguins peeped and gurgled excitedly. With a swift stride, the rest of the being emerged, towering above us all at the height of a tall MoFo. Not a Changed One, but a striking reminder that every manner of creature camouflaged itself in the jungle of Seattle in order to survive. Things were hiding. Everywhere.

"Holy taquito..." flew out of my mouth.

I'd known Pressa for a very long time, and this was the first time I'd heard her swear.

"Oh, fucky!" she shrieked amidst panicked wing claps. She shot onto the top of a kayak shed. "What the ass shit!"

She wasn't very good at it.

"Don't run!" the main penguin warned Pressa. "Never run from her!"

"What the helly bitch is that thing there?!" said Pressa from the safety of stacked kayaks.

I stared, utterly mesmerized. "It's...a dinosaur."

"A what?" Pressa appeared to be having a panic attack. Her gular thumped like nightclub bass.

"I don't understand," I said to the head penguin. "How did it get here?"

"They," said the penguin, and the gigantic bushes of evergreen huckleberry and red osier dogwood split aside, and out strode other impossibilities. Other enormous entities with towering necks and reptilian legs.

"We, the penguins, went up north, swam ourselves an adventure." Here, the penguin described the area, and as he did, he released a babbling sound, a reverberation from *Echo* that strummed inside me. Its vibrations painted a picture—a port, I was sure of it, up north. Canada's once-bustling Port of Vancouver.

"A great gray nest arrived at the Port of Vancouver—"

"Hoooray! Hooray!" honked the penguin posse.

"Keepers had put lots and lots of wild creatures into the floating metal nest. It sailed the waters from oceans away and made it to the port."

"They made it! Huzzah!" honked a tiny penguin. More honking and flipper flapping ensued.

"That is how we came to know Tom Hanks! Tom Hanks arrived on the floating metal nest!" cried the spokes-penguin.

"Huzzah! Huzzah! Huzzah for Tom Hanks!"

"Not a floating nest," I told them. "They called it a boat, or a ship, or a vessel." A collective "Ooooooooooooh" from the waddle.

A penguin shaped like an award-winning eggplant shouted, "The One Who Keeps! A genius!"

The head penguin continued. "They'd been at sea for a long time; the Keepers held on as long as they could. We greeted them—Welcome! Welcome!—as they released all the living beings onto land and tended to the sick and the ones with weak legs. But then..."

The penguins bowed their heads and mumbled, short huffs and honks. I could picture it. The MoFos had been in isolation for a long time. And then they weren't. The virus worked swiftly.

The enormous being let out a Jurassic screech. Pressa's eyes impersonated those of a Black Moor goldfish. The penguins leapt up and down. MoFos, I thought—always so very, very clever. A cluster of them had had the foresight to load up a boat with animals and send it out to sea. MoFos had even volunteered to chaperone. Suicide saviors. In an act of hope and faith, they really had built an ark.

"The earth birds look out for one another. She wants to help; they swam a long way to get here," said the peppy penguin.

"They swam?" I asked, incredulous.

Pressa now had the stupefied look of a sheep who, while minding its own woolly business and chomping innocently on a clump of grass, suddenly remembered a nefarious past life. "I don't know, S.T., I don't know what she is; I'm still not even sure we haven't been poisoned," she said, breathless.

"Can she run fast?" I asked the penguins.

And then the dinosaur spoke. "Can *he* ask questions directly?" Her voice was as deep as Lake Washington, a guttural combustion with a tropical twang. A colossal gray leg swung out, those treacherous toes thumping down on the earth. The other leg crashed down after it as she strode toward the tiny crow and a cheerleading squad of flightless birds in formal attire.

"Can she run fast, *tsk, tsk tsk*. Faster than you can fly, little weed," the enormous creature said to me. Her arched body—suspended on those gargantuan legs—was covered in a sumptuous shag of black hair, the cloak of a 1970s pimp. That great toe whomped down in front of me, and up close, I understood the terror of this specialized tool used for disemboweling. Suddenly, an enormous beak hovered close to my own. I was mesmerized by the electric turquoise of her bald, wrinkly head. Her face, an inhospitable mountain range, conjured images of another time, a time when giant reptiles ruled supreme in *Aura, Echo,* and *Web.* When the very first birds descended from theropods, the dinosaurs with three toes and hollow bones. A great bone helmet postured like a war weapon on the seat of her skull. Her intricately wrinkled neck started in stop-sign red, dribbling into two pendulous wattles that swung like ancient scrotums. She scrutinized me with orange eyes—burning planets. We both knew that in that moment, if she chose to kill me, nothing could stop her. One peck. A headbutt. Quick swipe of that lethal toe. Even her eyelashes were treacherous spikes of doom. I bowed to the towering tropical being of Australia and Indonesia, a primordial beast of a bird.

The cassowary.

She peered at me, burning planets flaring, this living fossil full of fight. I felt it simmering just under her cowboy-boot skin.

The cassowary's creviced beak opened, snatched me by the wing, and flung me into the air.

And suddenly I was on the back of a fucking dinosaur.

# CHAPTER 26

S.T.
BOTHELL, WASHINGTON, USA

Penguins cheered and clapped their flippers below. Pressa gawked at me with her beak open. I instinctually resumed my expert squat on top of Budiwati the cassowary, clutching lumps of the shaggy pimp hair of her back with my feet. Budiwati's huge electric-blue head swiveled around to peer at me, suspended by her ophidian neck. The wide-eyed beak-to-beak inspection seemed like an infringement of my personal space, but I wasn't sure what social etiquette was like on her tropical home islands of New Guinea. Or what on earth had happened there.

The five other cassowaries huddled together, staring at the black little earth bird with more than a modicum of confusion. One cassowary, who I quickly discerned as the male partner to the bird upon whose back I squatted, fixed his gaze on Budiwati. His approach was sheepish. He cautiously tip-taloned toward her. She dwarfed him.

"Budiwati…"

She swung her burning eyes to meet her partner's, her neck coiling skyward—a roused cobra—to her full height.

"Perhaps, darling, you should reconsider this," he said with trepidation. "We could stay here near the lake where it's safer and—"

Budiwati let out a scream that blew her partner's red wattle scarves into the air behind him.

"Have a lovely time, darling!" he said, shuffling back to the cluster of cassowaries who seemed unsurprised by this exchange.

That great helmet—the peak of a barren mountain— swiveled back to me.

"For whom should we hunt first?" Budiwati's diesel voice was laced with menace.

"The crows," I said. "I need to find my family. The crows know everything about The Changed Ones. They'll help me find Dee."

She paused. I imagined Mr. Budiwati's words sinking into her skin, the realization that being the Uber driver for a total stranger was a potential death sentence.

"Inside you, are you a slow loris?" she asked. It took a minute to think about what she meant as I flipped through images in my head, scrolling to a National Geographic documentary on the slow loris—an adorable, gong-eyed Indonesian primate that covers its face when frightened.

"Yes, I'm afraid," I told her. "But inside, I'm a dinosaur."

"Which way?" she said, and I felt her enormous leg maneuver underneath me, her three toe-daggers fashioning grand canyons into the world of *Web.*

"Honestly, I don't have a clue," I told her, exasperated.

"This way! This way!" chorused the penguins, as they threw out blares and peeps and shuddering honks. The sounds swirled and pinged against our skin, forming a mind map inside us. "Go this way!"

"We believe in you!"

"You can do it!"

"Find the crows! Find the Keeper!"

Budiwati's eyes lingered on me, the oasis of each pupil swelling. In the sheen of her eyes I saw the reflection of a little black bird with a broken heart.

A crocodilian rumble shuddered free from her throat. "I do hope you can hold on," she said. I was skewered by a cold spear of fear. There was an unbridled mischief in this voice, and the terse exchange with her partner told me that creatures did not fucketh with this bird. Budiwati was leggy and lawless. And she was calling all the shots.

She liberated another primordial roar, raking the earth with her toes. I turned to the kayak shed.

"Press—"

Budiwati rocketed into motion. A few muscular strides brought us to the cruising speed of a hipster's well-maintained Subaru. I barely got to hear the penguins' honking vibrato song about The One Who Keeps: Very Handsome Legend. Trees and foliage whizzed by in a speeding train of greens—chartreuse, olive, emerald, bottle, shamrock, sage, crocodile, and pickle. Houses were a brick blur. My face felt like it was being lambasted by a large industrial fan. Above us, Pressa flapped furiously, riding the sediment stream of aerial plankton.

I jolted up and down on Budiwati's back, flung about like a show-jumping stallion's sugar lumps.

*I'm coming, Dee. I'll find you. Or I'll die trying.*

It was a suicide mission to leave one of the only safe areas left in Seattle. To put my trust in an emotionally constipated dinosaur.

I was experiencing acute déjà death—the familiar feeling that we were about to snuff it.

I knew why I was doing this, but why was Budiwati doing this?

Pressa sliced the sky to keep up with Budiwati. The trees that surged beside us were scooped out and hollow, their slow rhythms stilled. Some surely sat with bodies inside them. Incubating—what did Ghubari call them?—Masticators, imitation bark beetles waiting to unleash their horrors.

*Focus, Shit Turd. Focus on hope. Find the Sky Sentinels. They'll know what to do.*

Budiwati skidded to a halt, my beak slamming into the back of her leathery neck. Her head darted in a reptilian manner. The draping black feathers of her body started to vibrate, accompanied by a throaty, blood-chilling hiss. I peered around her snaking neck. In front of us—Changed Ones.

Pressa's wingbeats drummed out a panicked solo.

"Run! Fall back! Fall back!" yelled Pressa.

"What she said!" I squawked.

A Changed One swiveled to face us with a horrific crack of bone. It was fused to the side of a dusty food truck, glued by sticky finger pads and a transparent webbing between its joints. Moody gray skin, body slippery and muscled in the manner of a reptile. Branded with burn marks and the silver ghosts of scars. Rusted barbed wire coiled tightly around her muzzle. Chains embedded into her calloused skin trailed behind her— jewelry of the damned. A jigsaw piece of her skull was missing to expose a swath of glistening gray brain. Clumps of moss had affixed to the exposed gray matter, literal moss on the mind— it was revolting, I hope you're not eating. A screwdriver stuck angrily out from the compacted snake of brain tissue, and I suspected then that at some point, a long time ago, this Changed One had been tortured and terrorized by MoFos. Treated like an animal.

Her sleek body shimmied from the food truck with a gecko's precision. Dart and stop. Dart and stop. She paused in a large oily puddle in the road. Bloodshot eyes absorbed a hissing cassowary. The other Changed One was as white as bone, on all fours with backward joints and the fleshy tail of a sun-starved thing. Its white hair hung like limp straw, pointed ears erect. Its face wasn't visible because it was stuck in a large metal coffee can. Fading words blazoned the exposed base of the can—RECYCLE. Stealthy and silent, these Changed Ones were working together, as each other's eyes and ears. The one with a can stuck to its face angled its pointed ears back and forth, listening to paint the picture in front of it. I didn't know how it had survived and I didn't fucking care. I had a black belt in running away from things and I wasn't afraid to use it. I felt Budiwati's muscles ripple underneath me, the comforting squeeze of a pending retreat.

Nope.

Budiwati let out a battle cry and ran straight at the Changed One with the Phillips-head lodged in its noggin.

"No, no, no, no, no!" I yelled as my little black body jock-eyed up and down. Trees bounced. Pressa screamed. I swear I heard an earthworm laughing, that sadistic fuck crumb. The Changed One shimmied across the puddle as if also liquid. As large bird and large beast were about to collide, Budiwati's power-pylon legs catapulted us into the air. For a moment, we were flying. She thrust her mighty legs forward, jacking them into the chest of the lizard creature. The force of the kick sent the lizard flying, slamming into the side of the food truck with a metallic clang.

Budiwati shrieked and the coffee can snapped toward her. Three muscular strides and Budiwati was can-to-face with Can Face. She kicked the can upward, a neck snapped, alabaster body flipping into the air. It landed in the puddle. Budiwati pummeled it with those enormous feet, stomping and huffing in low growls.

The reptile creature recovered from her colossal kick, lifting onto two legs, memory of muscle. It ran like a frantic basilisk lizard toward us.

"Chain lizard incoming!" I screamed in the soprano of a Bee Gee.

Budiwati's bone helmet lifted. And as the Changed One with its scars and chains and tightly bound muzzle was almost upon us, lizard legs readying to pounce, Budiwati swung her weapon-like second toe diagonally down its chest. A bloom of bright red entrails splat onto the road in front of us. Budiwati turned her attention to the pale, can-faced Changed One. She bobbed her head and brought those legs down onto its pallid body, again and again and again, not totally unlike a more violent version of Tom Hanks's Riverdance.

"I think you've extinguished it," I told her, noting that when *Aura* was back up, I'd need to locate an emotional support animal. Surely the right peacock was out there...

I turned to find we had more company. We'd attracted the attention of a huge festering clot of sick MoFos.

"Fuck trinkets," I said, eloquently.

A gang of them, rotten imitations of earthly things. There were too many for even three dinosaurs. In unison, vermillion eyes rolled into focus, widening at the colossal bird and its plucky passenger. Budiwati let out a hiss that was missing steam. She knew we were outnumbered.

"Oh no..." dropped from Pressa above us.

A heavy feeling sank all my organs.

And then, a frenetic whirring sounded out in the boisterous hum of Tiffany S.'s mini vibrator. A fun-sized bird darted past Pressa while letting out staccato *drt!* notes. It stopped on a dime in midair, wings in a blurred flurry of motion, its throat magenta and opalescent, shimmering like a sequined scarf. An Anna's hummingbird. We stared at her in a slow-motion stupor, and I swear I heard Louis Armstrong's "What a Wonderful World."

Budiwati hissed at the encroaching gang of Changed Ones. The Changed Ones kept rapt focus on the miniature bird hovering above them. Hummingbirds have great healing powers; those burring wings will heal a wounded heart, beat for beat. Was it the gossamer fairy wings? Those hypnotic figure eights? The dazzling metallic rainbow of color? Was there something deep inside The Changed Ones that recognized the wonder of nature's exquisite imagination? Could this glittery miracle have done the impossible, warm candy colors searing through festering skin to restart the human heart?

Pressa lowered to my side, eyes filled with terror.

"There are too many, S.T.," she whispered.

The hummingbird materialized in front of Pressa's beak.

"The bees! The bees sent me! Don't worry! I'm here!" chirped the Anna's hummingbird. This wasn't terribly reassuring—a bit like we'd shown up to a sword fight with a carrot. Or a miniature vibrator. She threw out more chip notes. The Changed Ones became enraged, leaping and swiping at the air around her. And it dawned on me. Those *drt, drt, drt,* sounds were *exactly* like the typing taps of an iPhone.

The sick MoFos burst into palsied lunges, triggered by the taps of an iPhone, limbs raking at the sky to snatch the hummingbird. The aerodynamic jewel dove and wove around them, a shimmering will-o'-the-wisp, out of reach.[1]

"Fuck. You. My. Flowers!" The Anna's hummingbird shot down to a gooseberry flower for a quick sugar hit. She darted

---

1   It's tempting to worry for a bird that only weighs four grams, but fear not! They're whimsical little warriors with jabby nasal knives, strong enough to lift the soul, merciless while hunting life's sweet nectar. They hum with the bidding of their beloved flowers and belt out a little "fuck you" anthem that will make you think thrice about trespassing on their territory.

into the air again, almost too fast for an eye to follow. Then the Lilliputian bird dove—faster than a fighter plane—right at a Changed One. She poked it squarely in the eye before rocketing up to the height of an evergreen. She whizzed back past the disoriented cluster of Changed Ones, who lurched like old machines to locate the airborne iPhone. Budiwati used the distraction to escape. We owed our lives to an itsy-bitsy bird with so many secrets in its prismatic plumage.

And we ran and ran, buoyed by a bird the size of Big Jim's house key.

Budiwati broke into a freedom run. Pressa weaved above. For a moment, fear released its talon-hold on my neck. Budiwati's feet pounded a rhythm. I started to hear excited whispering among living trees. I tuned in, and even while traveling at Subaru speed, I heard the crisp crunch of many-legged beings inspired by our boldness, stirring in soil. I heard the halcyon rhythms of the natural world crescendo into an oratorio of liberty, as if the sounds themselves were on a great adventure.

I didn't know Budiwati's past, but she was writing a new story with each footfall. Fear would not map her course. She was feral, free, and possibly a few flamingoes short of a flamboyance. The sun shone on her tropical-lagoon-to-fire-engine colors. She unshackled a paralyzing roar. Sure, tonally, it sounded like the backfiring bowels of Hades, but it was also one of the most magnificent things I'd ever heard. With that oratorial firework of freedom, I knew I had been wrong to try and hide Dee. Because what kind of a life is a life lived in fear? What kind of hollow living meant you couldn't stretch your wings and scream the song inside of you? Dee knew a caged life, clipped wings, slinking in the shadows. She knew what it felt like to be ashamed of who you are, to be herded into a skin that doesn't suit. Dee deserved to sing her own songbird's aria, to push up from the dirt, to reach for the sun. I had to show her that I hadn't been listening and that now, I had tuned in and I could hear everything.

Budiwati's call was the eruption of an ancient volcano, a celebration that rained down in fiery liquid. I remembered the orcas, the shrew skittering through soil. I thought of what the big male orca had said—"We use sound to tell us things, more than what we meet with our eyes. It is our great gift"—and if this Indonesian dinosaur had the courage to break away from her chains, then so did this little corvidosaurus. The sea wolves used sound to seal the intimacy of their pods. Tribal tones. And I remembered a gift that I'd always had. One of the most heeded calls in the animal kingdom. MoFos inspired crows—their avian shadows—to evolve alongside them, challenging us to compete with the boisterous bedlam of MoFo life. To lift our voices to the blare of the bulldozer, police siren song, the seismic tease of a subwoofer. I opened my beak and freed a sound recognizable to every being on earth. Five sharp caws.

The corvid alarm.

A pause. And then, buoyed by flipping the bird in the face of danger, I let out five more. I was a crow and this was my song.

"Caw! Caw! Caw! Caw! Caw!" My calls filled the spaces between the trees. I cawed for the family of crows who made me proud to have fought for life from the chalky chamber of an egg. I imagined what the orcas would see—neon bursts of prismatic color shooting from The One Who Keeps, up and everywhere like a bioluminescent sea of electric-blue stars. Budiwati fucking loved it. Having savored the flavor of her own freedom, she was guzzling up mine. She threw back her casque—that great bone helmet—dangly wattle swinging. We roared the roar of dinosaurs, calling back to primordial things we once were. Bird-boned beings that had navigated a treacherous environment, supervolcanoes, an ice age, and a colossal ball of fire on the horizon that broiled everything to crispy critters. We were things that knew how to survive, then and now.

A feeling—one I hadn't felt in so very, very long—sparked and spit and sang like a mini meteor inside me. Freedom. Purpose. Passion.

This is the feeling of flight. This is what it is to fly.

And so, three fucking dinosaurs screamed across the never-ending stretch of an extinct road. And it didn't take long before we were heard. Sound traveled on the wind, across the crowns of faraway trees to reach us.

"Caw! Caw! Caw Caw!"

"A crow! A crow!" yelled Pressa. She called back.

Budiwati roared in delight. Pressa and I upped our game, spilling out the alarm. Louder. Faster.

The crow called back again. And then another. Stentorian sounds pinging through the air like rainbow rockets. Then came a *how how how*—a jungle jingle—another animal, inspired to blow its bagpipe lungs. More and more crows joined in the cacophony, *Aura* reconnecting, spreading an emergency call to action.

We were kindled by the sonorous calls of the crows, and other birds joined in too. Ants cheered in chemical chorus. Lemurs and golden lion tamarins—old funny-faced friends— swung into view in the trees beside us, spaghetti limbs and Silly Putty bodies that weren't going to let fear suffocate them either. They added whistling clicks to the symphony—the *eeeeoooooooooow, eeeeeoooooooooow* holler of the lemurs, bewitching the air. Because when you're courageous, it is an invitation to others. The sky surrenders before those brave enough to leave the branch.

"It's The One Who Keeps!" I heard them call.

"The One Who Walks With Tigers!"

"Hero! The hero is here!"

"The One Who Rode The Mythical Stallion Of The Canine World!"

"Look! It's The Legless Half-Breed Made Of Tumbleweeds!"

I wasn't thrilled that certain nicknames had stuck.

And then the sky was a pointillism of crows—"They're here! They've found us!" cried Pressa. Crows settled gently all around us like siftings of gunpowder. A sea of beady black eyes shone down at us from a patchwork quilt of leaves. I spotted Kraai. He stared at me, opened and then closed his beak. Kraai was speechless. He hadn't predicted that I'd arrive on a dinosaur. Old Shit Turd is full of fucking surprises.

"Kraai! I need your help! They took Dee!"

"I'm so sorry, S.T.," he said, his voice thick in his throat.

"Do The Changed Ones have a den?"

"Yes," said Kraai, thinly masking his stupefaction at the almost-seven-foot bird eyeing him like something that had been peeled from the shoe of a landfill laborer. "This way— where the sun wakes."

"We have to hurry."

"S.T., you must prepare yourself—" and then he stopped. Maybe he could see through my black breast, right to the big little heart inside, tattered and frayed, desperate pleas for Dee in its hollow beats. "Quick as we can! This way; follow our sky path!" yelled Kraai as he shot into the air with the grace of light.

The path we followed was twisty to avoid floods. Fire-singed buildings with delicate bones. The territories of terrible things. We saw deer, galloping wild horses, dog packs in homemade dens, Frito-toothed beavers, the glowworm eyes of feral cats. My heart fought with my rib cage, as if trying to burst through my chest and find Dee itself. I didn't know where we'd find her, whether we'd get there in time...

But the crows—birds with guts and gumption—and the wattled gladiator who charged through a glaucous ghost of a city kept my heart beating.

*I'm coming, Dee. Hang on. I'm coming, Dee. Hang on.*

And I don't know how long we ran, but every second felt like a life sentence without the being who was born to love bees, the little miracle who had been ushered into my life by owls and had made the whole world sprout sense.

The crows signaled silence. Budiwati carefully trotted along a bucolic road, lined with old wineries and snaking vines. Abandoned tracks daydreamed about the touch of a train. And then we passed Woodinville Whiskey and the Hollywood Tavern, where Big Jim and I would perch by a blazing firepit and share a whiskey and peanut butter milkshake, and the hypnotic blue of the flames and the amber liquid inside us made the world seem like a womb.

We caught up to the crows. They made a blanket of black in front of enormous wrought-iron gates.

My feathers stood on end. Algae-stained stone and swirling letters spelled out *Chateau Ste. Michelle.* A once-upscale winery with imposing gates, shackled in rusting chains and austere-faced locks. Two signs flanked the Chateau's main entrance. One said, "It's The End Of The World. Please Join Us As We Drink Every Last Bottle For A Smooth Finish." The other was in funny-font graffiti and said **EAT LOCALS**. We all turned to the trees across the street, wizened maples swaying with scoliosis. They were alive, flanking the sign for the Columbia Winery, their limbs stretching through a blurry fog of time to show us.

"There," said the trees with their beautiful bodies and their sweet-sap souls. I heard the frangible *skir skir* of crisp-shelled insects, thrumming support for the trees. We were listening.

The trees' sharp branches pointed beyond the wrought-iron gates of Chateau Ste. Michelle with feather-raising insistence.

They routinely raided ours, but we had never been at the frothing mouth of The Changed Ones' den. The heart and home of these warped and violent things. Kraai had evaded their cavernous jaws by the grace of being airborne. I, an earth bird, would not have the defense of flight. With a tormented look in his eyes, Kraai stared at a bird with only one wing.

A wing and a prayer.

A shiver snuck up Budiwati's spine. I looked at the twisted metal of gothic gates.

*I'm coming, Dee. I'm coming.*

# CHAPTER 27

S.T.
CHATEAU STE. MICHELLE, WOODINVILLE,
WASHINGTON, USA

Crows hopped through gaps in the gothic gates. I followed. A cluster of rusted locks glowered at us, bleeding tangerine tears. Most of the murder lifted silently and touched down on the patchy grass of the Chateau grounds. Budiwati—legs made of electrical springs and the intensity of the Napoleons (Bonaparte and Dynamite)—leapt effortlessly over the wall of the Chateau, snatching me up in her beak and flinging me onto her shaggy back with manners akin to a coupon-clipping hippo at a Walmart on Black Friday. Her head snaked high, darting side to side. I gasped at the scene stretched out in front of us.

"Houston, we're not in Kansas anymore," I whispered.

The long path that bisected once-beautiful soft green lawns hosting rustic vine rows, gossiping geese, and a receiving line of white mulberry trees was desecrated. I saw tattered signs, phantasmal decorations from when the winery had turned fifty years old. Piles of trash sat in moody lumps across the muddy grounds. Car parts, filthy bathtubs, rusting things that once had the value of gold, when gold had the value of gold. A huge oil spill brooded like a dark rainbow lake. The shells of dismembered trucks, plastic, six-pack rings, straws, and the skins of burst balloons made a grotesque cemetery of MoFo waste. But I noticed a pattern to the trash piles. One pile, a Jenga tower of rusting rifles and guns. They had organized. Stockpiled weapons. But what good were weapons without the fingers to man them? Nothing but gawdy tinsel for a septic landfill.

The crows were terrified. Tail flicks. Wing flaps. Everyone's feathers lifted from their skin. Smells fought with one another—sharp metallic slice, the cloying stench of rot. We didn't need to stare at the rotting corpse of a Changed One, at the slack jaw exposing a mouth full of deformed body parts. Too-fat fingers, a nose, a lump sprouting hair and milk teeth, more of those ghastly eyes. A sickening spectacle of failed reproduction. We didn't need to see blood trails and giant ghostly cobwebs woven by horrible things to know—this was a very dangerous place.

*Dee. Where are you?*

The hollow ache in my chest was unbearable. My lungs were collapsing sails.

I felt the wind stir my wings and found I was flanked by Pressa and Kraai. The look in their eyes—a look that said whatever happened, we were all in this together, code of murder, code of crow—filled me with a pride that fizzed in my bird bones. Kraai gave a nod and we all committed to the path ahead, the murder slipping into stealth flight above us.

Budiwati padded the crumbled asphalt and starving soil. Tufts of animal fur flitted across the ground like tumbleweeds. Bones glowed, riddled with the indented signatures of their calcium sisters—teeth.

"Hssssssssssss." From the base of her neck to the tip of her beak, Budiwati was a hooded cobra. I felt melancholy exhales and couldn't believe that the two rows of white mulberry trees that lined the road were still living. Living, but victims of violence, etched with scars. More garbage mounds, and then we were under a giant sequoia, a variegated western red cedar, an umbrella pine, and what was once a place for MoFos to park their cars. Budiwati tensed as she maneuvered her enormous feet up stone steps.

And then we were in the heart of the Chateau.

Across from us, the winery's biggest building. An old dairy barn with a mansion facade, its windows were glassless, oversize doors still intact. Victorian lampposts had their glassy heads smashed in.

Budiwati rumbled, an internal boom like thunder caged by ribs. My eyes followed the arch of her neck. Her beak pointed to crowns of the estate's massive interspersed giants—red oaks, a European copper beech, firs, fern-leaf maples, Japanese Stewartias, and twisted-limbed London planes. They were up in the trees and on the Chateau buildings' roofs. Changed Ones, imitation birds, some brown and hawkish, others with bald, bluish heads, sinuous necks, and the daggerlike bills of herons. All of them gruesomely grotesque and squatting in the tired boughs of trees. They were dormant, some eyes closed, some open but captive in the middle distance. *Torpor*, I thought, to conserve energy.

My murder looped above, a black cirrus cloud that wheeled and swirled around the crown of a mighty copper beech tree. Their kaleidoscopic dance surged and poured around the ancient tree and then balled into a fist. Then a quick burst—a jolt of energy—as they shot back toward us, landing all around Budiwati gently, as if ground from a pepper mill. Pressa and Kraai landed on Budiwati's back, next to me.

Budiwati swung her head around with an expression that would shear a sold-out stadium of overgrown sheep.

*This is my family,* I told her with my eyes. When I was sure she wasn't going to pulverize them, I focused on my murder.

"She's there," said Pressa, her voice paper-thin, tied tight with fear.

"Is she—"

"Yes," she said, saving me from the pain of asking. I pictured Dee's nose pulling in oxygen, releasing carbon dioxide in a steady stream. A hominid mirror to our beloved trees. Pressa's beak gestured to a large mass. There, in the arms of a hundred-year-old European copper beech tree, was a hideous construction. It looked to be some sort of nest, a jumbled mayhem of plastic bags and metal parts and rusty weapons and, predominantly, glass. Shards and shards of glass, the glittery, tinted, and dull, all in a monstrous mosaic.

And poking out here and there were things that would make you crap on your cassowary. The metallic bodies of dormant electronic items. Broken laptops. Cell phones. Speakers, cameras, projectors. They still coveted the very cause of their extinction. I shivered. And from the center of the humongous nest, peeking out from behind a ledge of broken toasters and motherboards, I spied an Angora rabbit, Dee's ShamWow of hair.

Adrenaline coursed through me. I wanted to cry and throw up and scream out to her, "I'm here, Dee! I'm here!" and get her away from these irritable bowels of hell. Hunched in the forbearing arms of the nearby giant red oak were more of the bird Changed Ones. One of them, with its tar feathers and strange canoe of a beak, I recognized. It was the one who had seen me with a grisly eye and called me crow in a dying language. In the critically endangered words of a MoFo.

I looked up to the nest, willing Dee to let me know she

was alright, to wave her strong arms and show me she'd been buoyed by the swarm of crows above her. Pressa sensed this.

"Don't call out," she said through the ruffle and puff of her feathers.

I stayed silent and made out more of the flotsam of that strange nest—a chain saw, strips of corrugated metal, a rifle. Some sort of sticky secretion held them together, suspending the coppery-penny patina of bullets. The rifle had my attention. Dee knew how to use a gun. I'd taught her because I'd watched Big Jim, and Big Jim would have loved this little MoFo with all his gigantic heart, and he would have taken her under his wing and taught her how to protect herself. And then a memory, swift and beesting sharp, drove into my mind.

A dry day in Toksook Bay. I stood on the ground next to Dee, who'd woken up in the pube labyrinth of Oomingmak's fur that morning as if summoned, quietly trotting across the dew-kissed grass. She had stooped to examine bent twigs and flattened grass. I hopped along after her as best I could, as always unable to sense what she could. She listened to what a hungover *Turdus migratorius* had to say and eventually hid behind a tree to watch an arctic fox washing herself in a patch of sunshine. Time spent watching the paper-white fox had put Dee in a very good mood.

"Finger off the trigger until you're ready, Dee," I told her, eye on the basketball she'd chosen as a target. The rifle looked enormous in her arms. "Focus on the basketball. Dee?"

Dee was staring at the azure-blue box of a house next to us. A line of pudgy willow ptarmigans studied her from the roof. On the rotting railing of the house's steps, Dee fell under the spell of a male bluethroat—a tiny ornament of a songbird. The petite bird was a bit of a trickster and had stolen a song that wasn't the kind a bluethroat sings. But Dee was enthralled by this saucy little being, lost in the cornflower-blue of his music-box throat, his pumpkin-orange bib. He was curious and playful, a kindred spirit. Dee made an O with her mouth, instinctively mimicking the shape he made as he sang.

"Dee! Concentrate!" I scolded her. "The goddamned gun is loaded!"

Dee's eyes were smiling when she turned to focus on the deflated basketball. In a state of blue-throated bliss, she squeezed the trigger. The rifle blasted, bucking back into her shoulder. Our heads rang. When Dee recovered from the shock, the ptarmigans were gone. A floating white feather was all that was left of their fleeing. The bluethroat had vanished. Dee wailed and flung the rifle aside (I dove into our old toilet-training bucket for cover). She ran from me and I had to let her go, to scream at the ocean and scale trees and lose her fingers in the moss kingdom. To tell the bees what had happened. The ptarmigans never came near Dee after that. Much as she searched, listening to the wisdom of the world around her—"*here is fresh water,*" says the red-throated loon; "*here are the berries,*" says the jay; "*here are the clams,*" say the merganser and the spoonbill—Dee never saw a bluethroat again. From then on, I couldn't get her to touch the metal menace of a gun. And here she was, trapped in a nest adorned with them.

Kraai leaned in close. In whispers like wingbeats, we deliberated.

"We need to do this in silence, while they are dormant. We are enough crows to fill the crowns, but there are many Changed Ones here. If we can help Dee shimmy down the arms of the copper beech—if we can do it silently—we can sneak out of here."

As we stood there, in the heart of a desecrated winery, from the back of a cassowary, I felt something. A swelling beneath me that I couldn't pin down. I chalked it up to the overpowering reek of rot that washed over us in dizzying waves. I nodded to Kraai. We had to be quick about it.

"I'll fly up to her and let her know you're here. That we're all here for her," said Pressa. And I pictured what she was about to do, how she'd flutter up to Dee and Dee's beautiful cheeks would lift, the waterlines of her eyes would fill and glisten in that way that they do, and Pressa would reassure her with a very gentle *Kkkkr*. Crow for *friend*.

I realized too late what the growing pressure was. I was sitting on a proverbial pressure cooker, a barn stuffed with flatulent cows and no ventilation. The dinosaur with a crow perched on her back had been slowly absorbing the horrors of this lair, a place that wasn't her home but perhaps had been ravaged like her tropical island on the other side of the big beautiful blue. She was furious, displaced. Perhaps she'd had her nest raided, her eggs and hope crushed, chicks snatched away from her by things with craning neck bones. And I felt it—like the snap of a taut rope—Budiwati couldn't be small or silent anymore. She had, at last, been free and there was no wrangling her back into the jar. I was sitting on Mount Vesuvius. And my ass was about to get Pompeii-ed.

Budiwati let out a roar that shook the leaves of the hundred-year-old copper beech, gnarled London planes, and giant oaks. She charged. Pressa and Kraai shot into the air. I snatched up shaggy, pimp-cloak hair and we were suddenly galloping straight toward the giant red oak and the horrible, monstrous clone of a hawk on the lowest branch, now awake, red-ruby eyes wide and trained on us. It leapt onto the ground, screaming at the other Changed Ones. Budiwati—shrieking back—leapt into the air. We were suspended for seconds, and then I felt those lethal legs swing forward. The Changed One dodged. Budiwati's legs slammed into the trunk of the giant oak. Screeches rained down from above as The Changed Ones felt the impact, launching themselves from the mighty oak. Budiwati—the last primal echo of the velociraptor—faced the Changed One. They circled one another, a string of red drool hanging from the beak of the horrible creature.

The crows sounded out the corvid alarm.

"Run, earth bird! Run!" They had lived in hiding from these things longer than Budiwati. "Look out! Look out! Look out!"

The Changed One flung its beak—giant forceps—toward me, leaking blood. It missed my bad wing by the length of a ladybug. An eye flared as it registered me, pupil tightening. I leapt from Budiwati's back and started a mad dash across the grounds, away from the giant red oak, eyes on the copper beech tree and the abomination that held Dee.

Brave crows dove and mobbed, their valiant cries sparking in the air. I turned to see the Changed One snapping at their inky wings. Budiwati screamed and swung her toe across the Changed One's breast. I focused on my run. Behind me, I heard the slimy slip of internal organs loosed from a broken body.

All around me, dropping from the great trees, were more winged Changed Ones. Caws crescendoed—loud as a jet—and then a mass of crows was all I could see. And Pressa was next to me and Kraai in front of me, and this was my family, screaming at The Changed Ones.

*We are more powerful when we work together because we look out for one another by being one. That is the code of murder,* I heard Kraai say, a lifetime ago.

"Go! Go to Dee!" I yelled to Pressa and Kraai and the booming black tornado of crows. "Go to her!"

"We won't leave you, S.T.!" said Pressa. Two crows, strapping young crows I recognized as Pressa's sons, grabbed me by a wing each and I was hoisted into the air, a blizzard of black swirling around me. My feet snatched up the low branch of the maple where they placed me. And I didn't know what we would do, now that The Changed Ones were awake. They knew we had come for Dee and they were all around us, some on the ground now, stretching out their warped wings. Waking up to intruders in their lair.

Two more of The Changed Ones dropped down and began to circle Budiwati. Their necks craned forward, horrible shrieks dragging across our skulls. But the crows were already calling out the alarm for another danger. Something had emerged from the mansion of the Chateau.

Fear stitched the air into an impenetrable knot.

It was upright. Tall as a lamppost.

The crows were stunned to silence.

It stood on many thin, vitreous limbs. The Changed Ones—those still in the trees and the two circling Budiwati—stared motionless at the being. Budiwati was stretched to her full height, staring at the eerie enigma that had slipped from the mouth of the mansion. Only one sound now—the susurrus of wings.

The creature had an exoskeleton, smooth and shiny, perfectly transparent. All of its insides were on display. Visible through a pellucid shell was an unmistakably human jigsaw of bones, as if a MoFo skeleton had been cocooned by the shell of an insect. It looked like an animated X-ray. Claws had conquered the territory of hands. It had a mandible in lieu of lips. Languidly waving antennae. Its torso was bisected like an insect. In its compound eye, bulbous and beelike, there was authority that everything in the Chateau felt. An icy intelligence. I spun around to see birdlike Changed Ones waiting for this towering Changed One. For movement, a command—I didn't know. And when I took my eyes off the Changed One's glassy torso, its eerily narrow waist and exposed organs, the way it was assessing the environment, I realized that there were actually two more of these things standing by its side.

Budiwati broke the silence with a sharp snort. And the largest of three Insect Creatures, towering at the oversize wooden door of the mansion, opened its pellucid mandible. Four sharp clicks fell out. The response was instant. The bird Changed Ones circling Budiwati bolted in that deformed scamper—an abomination of twisted limbs, beaks biting the air. Budiwati thundered after them, racing past the London plane trees, disappearing behind more trees and trash and into a territory none of us knew.

Seized by panic for Budiwati, I turned back to the Insect Creature. It had just used a command to lure Budiwati away. This see-through creature, with its human bones and its glassy insect exoskeleton was calculating. It was in charge. I didn't know what it was capable of, but all the internal squishy bits of Shit Turd were screaming.

From the maple branch, I saw that we were still surrounded by Changed Ones. Crows screamed from the sky, out sized and outnumbered. And Dee was still too far away from me in that lethal nest. She couldn't be left alone a second longer with these abominations.

I would not leave Dee.

The crows would not leave me.

We were not enough to take on these violent creatures. We were black lace and silken scarves, dangling over barbed wire.

I had known it as I hopped through those gothic gates. Kraai had known it looking at his friend, the crow with the wonky wing and the hole where a heart had been. Shit Turd, the little black bruise.

This would all end in a stubborn suicide.

But what could I do? I was at the mercy of something so much stronger than the virus that wiped out Dee's species. Love is the sun. It burns tiger bright, illuminating the heart and searing away sadness. What a beautifully brave act to hand over a heart. To risk the burns of a blister-skinned sovereign. Dee was my sun. Just as bright. Just a one. Without her, the world would turn black. Without her, I would wither and die.

And I had something of vital importance to tell her. Even if it meant sacrificing my own life. And I was ready.

I had to make it right.

More sounds. A wailing protest. A spine-tingling cry. All eyes landed at the steps that lifted up into the heart of the Chateau, where another creature strode into view and my beak hit the floor.

# CHAPTER 28

✴ ✳ ❋ ✤ ❊ ❦ ❀

GENGHIS CAT
GRACING WHATEVER SHITHOLE THIS IS,
WASHINGTON, USA

You can all relax now, because I am here. What did you think? I'd run for safety at the whim of a fucking parrot with under-eye bags like pinched scrotums? Did you suspect I—a ninja with feather-wand fastness and laser-pointer focus—had the spine of a banana slug? Then you are a shit-toned oink with the senses of a sniveling salamander.

Then you don't know Genghis Cat.

I look around and can see that we are surrounded by The Bird Beasts, those crepe-faced, hair ball–brained fuck goblins. I intensely dislike these lumpy whatthefuckareyous who straddle between the Mediocre Servant and animal worlds, trying to be one thing and really not being, like imitation crabmeat in a sushi log that is really just fucking whitefish and WE ALL KNOW IT.

"Would you like a little of the crabmeat, Genghis?" my Mediocre Servants seemed to ask with their blobfish lips and stupid faces.

"THAT'S FUCKING WHITEFISH, YOU REGURGITATED MOLES!" I'd yowl, and then I'd steal the sushi log and run off and growl very much so they couldn't have it back, and later I would pee on their night pillows for good measure. I cannot imagine their lives before me. We mustn't think of those bleak dark ages.

But the Beasts are dangerous. I have watched them morph and chew into a house. I have seen them with spider legs and second stomachs and camouflage skins. I have seen them tear the legs off a horse and steal flight from those with feathers. Orange and I have lost family to their fuckish appetites. But they are still fakish faking beasts and I'm fucking Genghis Cat. They are imitation crab and Genghis is filet mignon Fancy Feast, bitch. Probably I should come clean here and tell you that I'm immortal. I always suspected it but can confirm it now that I have surpassed the allocated nine lives. I'm somewhere around life 884, give or take seventy-eight. Some mousers have called me a god, but I insist on modesty. I also don't deny it. I might be a god. It seems to fit. It feels right. A stealthy, striped god with an exotically spotted tummy—it seems certain, doesn't it to you? I'm 186 percent sure at this point.

Orange insists we stay away from the Beasts all the time, but I only let Orange think he's in charge. Orange is incredibly sensitive, despite being the size of a Winnebago. He hand-raised each of my kittens and has terrible nightmares, and I have to knead my paws on him to calm him down. Orange and I have a deal. I will kill anything that comes to harm Orange and Orange will continue to be the reason I purr.

I am the god Genghis and I am not afraid. I have at least 990 lives and my memory is impeccable, and I'm not afraid to be here in this strange place decorated like an overzealous suburban garage sale, or whatever those things were called— I can't remember. A couple of head rubs and a vigorous spritz of my lethal urine and now this place that has old smells of spilled wine belongs to me.

I followed a smell here, a smell that made me think of concentrated mouser piss and also my Mediocre Servants. And she is here.

I'm here for the one they call Dee. I'm here for the Mediocre Servant with the warm lap and the soft earth–smelling skin and probably also a lot of fleas. I'm here because I remember one or two good things about the ones I used to live with—the one with the skin drawings and the one with the long mane who liked coffee and chemistry. Dee is the last living memory of old-time back scritches and head rubs and how I would offer my magnificent belly with its breathtaking spots and the Mediocre Servants would go to touch it and—ATTACK! I'd snap at their dildo fingers, slicing at them with my scimitar paw weapons, which was hilarious and delightful for all involved. I'm here because all the lizard hunters, jumpers, long-haired assassins, night kings, mousers, shadow stalkers, tree scalers, and even that one that doesn't have fur and looks like a rejected P.F. Chang's dumpling—they might not know the living smell and touch and sounds of Mediocre Servants, but I do, and I hold on to memories like prey in my paws. They have been raised on the stories of the Servants and their Mediocrity. I tell all my kittens as I pummel their tiny heads with my sandpaper tongue that smells like an eclectic medley of fish. They hear of scratching posts and leather furniture and catnip and Science Diet and the extraordinary pleasure of yarfing on a Persian rug and the magical *kkkkkkrrrkkk* of a can opening. Because we tell our blue-eyed kittens what to fear and what to love, what is a warm sun spot and what is sinister and menacing, like cucumbers. We must remember the Mediocre Servants when they were less rotten.

Dee stroked my head and allowed me to chew on her arm. I

claimed her by rubbing my face on her finger. This is a binding contract of ownership, throughout the universe, in perpetuity. I feel change coming in the way the wind whips against my whiskers. I see playful patterns in the rainbow light. I will Dee to live on, the last, the one with eyes that see everything like Genghis. And frankly, one day Dee will be all grown up and able to make cheese. Really, it's all about the fucking cheese.

Mediocre Servants have never been perfect, but they were once a damn sight better and I'm god enough to admit it—I miss them.

So now I'm here and I'm not afraid of what's next. Oh, and I brought some fucking backup with me.

# CHAPTER 29

S.T.

EITHER CHATEAU STE. MICHELLE OR THE TWILIGHT
ZONE, WASHINGTON, USA

In a once-beautiful winery that was now a den of doom, with
fur fizzed up and an arched spine, stood a domestic shorthair
cat. A fire starter. The Bruce Lee of felines. A tabby that had
sired an entire generation of Seattleite cats—generation FU—
and was probably singlehandedly responsible for the eradica-
tion of at least one entire songbird species. There was Genghis,
with greasy punk rock fur and an arthritic gait purchased at
heavy discount from the Ministry of Silly Walks. There wasn't
a bison brave enough to tell him that the earth's twirling had
caught up with him. Genghis yowled and hissed, and to be
honest, every carbon-based life-form from the gothic gates to
the stiff skyline was confused into silence. Every pin-pupiled
eye couldn't believe the balls on this cat—metaphorically and
literally—they were like two pool balls lodged in a wad of
taffy. I readily averted my eyes from Genghis's profiteroles and
looked back to the ancient copper beech tree, up at the nest,
where I could no longer see the top of the Angora rabbit.

"Dee! Dee!" I called to her from the pit of my stomach on the low maple branch, but she couldn't hear me.

Genghis hissed and spat, showing off the prickled ridge of fur along his spine and the glorious guts of him. The glassy-bodied horror watched and gave a minor tilt of its head, a hauntingly MoFo movement.

Then all around, emerging from bushy bursts of English and Portugal laurel, from beauty bush, Osmanthus, azalea rhododendron, holly, and the ever-present Himalayan black-berry tangles were more cats. They were marmalade and panther black, tortoiseshell, calico, flowing-furred and short-haired, those with poofy poof tails and those with kinky scuts like stubbed cigarettes. Eyes—green, yellow, blue, red—all shone like the reflectors of Satan's bike. These felines were collarless, fur adorned with sticky burrs and a furry forest of prospering parasites. These were not the dough-bodied domestics I used to torment back in Ravenna. These were hardened street cats that had outlived the MoFo race. They were wall scalers and pipe dwellers, tenacious from the lines of their square jaws to the worms inside them—tape, hook, whip—that sang soldier songs about their in-credible interspecies pilgrimage. A true testament to the virility and sexual prowess of Genghis Cat, there were an inordinate number of tabbies with distinct gofuckthyself faces.

The cats had come for the birds.

But these birds, with their hybrid sizing and appetite for annihilation, were not the song sparrows of the streets. These "birds" made a mockery of the natural world.

The towering collocation of bones scanned the scene. I watched its motherboard mind at work, terrified of what it could execute. I scoured my own mind for how to get past The Changed Ones and up to that nest, to Dee.

The cats all slunk in like apathetic ghosts. And—be still my shivering spleen—shadowing them were the great lumbering bodies of the orangutans.

"ORANGE!" I squawked.

Orange and his family, more than six of them—maybe double or triple that but who in the fuck will ever know because of my shit counting—pressed their knuckles to the ground, feet shuffling to keep up. And the bird Changed Ones hastily retreated into the high trees and rooftops, their panic buzzing like flies.

Orange, The One Who Opens Doors, great Man Of The Forest, Savior Of The Domestics, the Orange of Genghis's eye, looked larger than he had when he sat with Dee at the old McMenamins oasis. His great gray faceplate lifted up to the nest in the copper beech. He was looking for Dee.

A chesty bass bounced out from behind Orange like a resonant throat clearing. Our eyes pulled a dark mass into focus. A masterful lumber on four legs. A domed barrel chest, eyes and forehead laced with a beautiful embellishment of wrinkles. The peak of his steep boulder of a head was a steeple worthy of worship, sporting a crop of reddish fur. His ferocious arms thick with fur, as if he wore winter sleeves. I gasped, struck stupid by his beauty and arresting power. A western lowland gorilla. I once had the extraordinary privilege of sitting with a gorilla as it died. I had been wholly captivated and only ever dreamed of seeing one living again.

"Yes!" I yelled. I was turbocharged by the image of King Kong, here to pluck Fay Wray from the rusting skyscraper. And more of them arrived. The massive frown-faced male gorilla turned to usher others forward with a gentle gesture. As he turned, he showcased the marvelous silhouette and deep dip of his back, stippled in moonlit silver. There were young gorillas among them. Awkward adolescents, bowl-eyed babies and their watchful mothers, even elderly aunts. A mother knuckle-walked with a rubber-limbed baby Velcro-ed to her leg. Panic lanced up my side at the thought of a baby in among these hideous creatures, but that is the way of great apes—they stay together no matter what they must face.

"The apes came," I heard myself whisper.

They all came for Dee. Even those who had never laid an eye on her. Memories are inherited; they live in the dancing double helix of our DNA. The stories of MoFo kindness had survived extinction, sinking deep into skin and cells.

And the apes remembered.

Old Genghis had brought the hominids, the last of Dee's kind. And realization struck me—she had not been truly alone in this world. Family had been here all along. And they'd come to help her.

I looked up to the nest, desperate for Dee to know big beautiful Orange was here, the cousin who had tasted her tears and soothed a leathery finger over the winding tributaries of her scars. And gorillas! Creatures she had never even imagined in her dandelion-plucking daydreams.

"Look, Dee! Look who's here!" I shrieked. "The great apes of wrath!"

There was still no movement from the serrated nest.

The creature with the crystalline shell watched the apes arrive. It saw through a compound eye that looked like the skin of a speaker and gave him an insect's 360-degree vision. Through its transparent dome, I could see right to its human skull, into the empty black sockets that used to house MoFo eyes.

The air was stitched tight with tension. Too much tension for a young male orangutan, who let out a desperate holler

and barreled toward the creature with insect vision. Orangutans hooted, hysterical. The young orangutan released a rock
from his right hand, launching it at his towering threat. The
enormous insect dodged the incoming assault, stony projectile
sailing past his strange head. It lunged, snatching a shaggy
ginger arm in its right claw. The orangutan yelped. Apes leapt
up and down, cupping their hands to their mouths to amplify
their outrage. Two more orangutans ran to the defense of
the young male. The insect held tight, the orangutan thrashing and screaming. And then the insect made a swift, sharp
move.

The orangutan's arm was torn clean off. The insect dropped
the arm on the ground, palm cupped upright in a begging
gesture.

The two orangutan defenders recoiled in terror, scampering
back to the others. A one-armed orangutan hobbled back to
his family and was swallowed up by their protective bodies. The
apes turned fury to action, grabbing from piles of MoFo trash,
using the vices that had made these monsters against them by
hurling laptops, printers, glass, metal, and plastic.

I had been so absorbed by the horror, I only then realized
that the other two transparent Changed Ones had vanished.
And this powerful insectoid with its glass aquarium for a
body stood in front of the Chateau. The gap in its mandible
widened. I braced myself for what it would do next.

A word leapt from its face like an alien thing, ricocheting
across the Chateau.

"Come."

The gorillas, orangutans, and a colony of cats spun on light
legs, hunting for the invisible. My eyes shot to the nest. The
avian Changed Ones, high up in the branches and on the roof,
screamed in unison. A calling to them.

More hawk and heron creatures arrived, cresting over the

trees. The Changed Ones lost all inhibition, targeting the felines with renewed ferocity. Cats were snatched by gnarled talons, lifted into the sky.

A black compound eye watched, unflinching. The pale insect slowly lifted its antennae like some sort of chitinous king. A twitch of its right claw—a spasm of anticipation, pleasure, I'd never know.

*My god.* It was assessing, manipulating. I was staring at the hard shell of an insect that cocooned the spongy mind of a MoFo. And that was a calamitous problem.

The summoned bird creatures attacked the apes. Orange and the orangutans threw up their arms, ginger cords swinging wildly. The gorillas stood on their hind legs, the great male thumping his hollow chest.

The great apes scattered into the welcoming arms of the trees. Some of the smallest shot up lampposts. An older female gorilla had made it to the base of a tree when a hawklike Bird Being clamped down on her face. The hawk slashed with a bloodthirsty beak until two beautiful arms hung limp by her side. It afforded a young mother gorilla a distraction. She escaped up the tree with her tiny baby as the hawk thing dismantled its prey below them. In the chaos, Orange swiftly snatched Genghis—frothing with an arched back in the center of it all—and hoisted them both into a London plane tree. The birds unified to dive at the remaining cats.

The great apes whooped in warning, but the cats were clawing the curtains of survival, already catapulting from the scene like hurled lawn darts.

Panic, adrenaline, and terror make a potent cocktail. I shook my head to stabilize a whirling world.

*Come on, Shit Turd. Do something. Be brave.*

*Are you the windshield or the bug?!*

In front of me, a lumbering fawn body materialized. A ridiculous brown bulk I'd know blindfolded in the dead of night. A body that had taught me how big love could be. Saggy wrinkles, plodding paws, and a wattle that hung like the Cryptkeeper's balls. He let out a bugle call.

"Ooooooowwwww! BooOOOOoowwwoooo!" *Dennis*. He barked twice, a hero's beckoning, as he danced on skittering black nails. Then, a deep play bow. *Come on*, he said. *Let's get her! Let's get Dee!*

"Come on, buddy, you can do it!" said Big Jim, coaxing me along the tip of the Japanese maple branch, big hands at the ready as he offered me the whole sky. "I got you, little buddy! You can do this! It's time to fly!"

I looked up to a sky filled with mobbing nightmares, hawk-like birds that dove at a panicked mass of crows. Below me, Orange's wife cradled the young orangutan who only had one arm. She made desperate sounds, incanting an irretrievable spell to bring him back to this world. A being neither MoFo nor bird scratched at the soil under the tree closest to me. It lifted red eyes to me, snapping at the air with a misshapen beak. It started a heavy hop toward my tree.

*Time to fly.*

It was now or never. Shit Turd was about to go down in a BonJovial blaze of glory. I leapt off the branch, gliding down, down, down to the mud below. I fixed my eyes on the ancient copper beech tree and the abomination of a nest that sat like a tumor in its chest. And I ran. I ran as fast as my twiglet legs could carry me, veering around gaping holes in the soil, stubborn trash piles.

Gorilla sounds. Screeching. The keen of crows. Horrible screams.

RUN.

*Hang on, Dee. I'm coming.*

Eyes on me, I felt them. To my left, another abomination of a being.

Flapping above me, higher, higher, it was gathering power, readying to strike.

RUN, SHIT TURD, RUN.

A black wave of crows swarmed around it, mobbing it from all angles, beaks and claws aimed for its red, red eyes. I heard its beak clapping at crows. Two beautiful black bodies lay motionless on the ground in front of me. Fallen crows. My heart felt stuck with a needle.

RUN.

*Go, Shit Turd, go.*

I ran on, the copper beech roots bumping up and down in my vision, my heart in its limbs. I was a black-winged bird risen from the ashes. And then a voice in my head—*I'm just an earth bird; how can I do this?* I blocked out doubt and pushed harder, Dennis and Big Jim running beside me—I could feel them.

"Come on, Shit Turd! You can do it, buddy!" boomed Big Jim in my ear.

"Booooowwooooooooo! BoooowwOOOOOOO!"

I reached the roots of the copper beech and looked up to the skyscraper, a challenge even for King Kong. My legs shook and I flapped my wings.

"Come on, Bad Wing, we have to do this!" I commenced a determined climb using my beak and the plucky part of me—dinosaur DNA. I scrambled up the slope of the bark, flapping like a fledgling, feet scraping for purchase.

*I'm coming, Dee. I'm coming.*

I made it up to the limbs of low branches, my legs on fire. No time to stop. I ran along the branch, picturing Big Jim clapping below, Dennis racing around the base of the tree in jubilance, and now I was King Kong, heart bigger than Manhattan. I tackled the hurdle up to the next branch, bark splinters biting my feet. I bit the rounded nub of a burl and used it as leverage, shimmying up onto a higher branch, and another. Even Kong scaled the Empire State Building bit by bit, but I felt like giving up, the effort too much for my brain and heart and body. But the leaves around me shivered out a rallying rustle. I felt the old copper beech willing me to go on, rooting for me. Conspiring for my success.

"Gooooo," I heard her say. And I gave it everything I had, flinging myself up to each jutting lump of the copper beech's bark. I made it to the next level of branches.

And I slipped.

My foot swung out from under me. I rolled off a branch. The last thing I saw as I tipped was the distance I was about to drop. Bone-hard ground, stone, and roots below.

The wind blew my feathers upward as I plummeted.

*Dee, Dee.*

The fall stopped. My stomach stabilized. My back had support.

I opened my eyes. I was in a bed of fingers.

Dark, soulful eyes stared at me, squinting to make sure I was still breathing. Dexterous fingers that paint one-of-a-kind prints smoothed the feathers of my chest. I looked up to spectacular strong arms, dark hair, and a brilliant mind, filling with relief, wonder, gratitude.

The young gorilla let out a soft grunt and tucked me into her armpit. She moved nimbly, with careful placement of each foot and hand, and we ascended into the tall branches of the mighty copper beech. Up and up we went, and I didn't dare look down, since a bird admitting to a fear of heights is a shit fest I'd managed to keep pretty quiet since I'd crapped out my wing. And then we reached the horrible nest, a tumor in the copper beech tree. Cruel lumps of metal and an empire of rust. And she let out another gentle "ooff ooff" and placed me on the end of a broken tentpole sticking out the side of the nest. She gave me a last look. Maybe she knew from the social groom-time stories of her family that once, it was almost her kind we lost.

"Thank you," said the inky bird reflected in the shine of her eyes.

The gorilla looked down at a war and bravely started her nimble descent.

I hobbled along the squalor of metal and glass in shambles. Dee was in the middle of the nest, her back to me. Her sealskin parka was partially shredded. She was bone-dry but caught in a current, staring into bleak sadness. The Black Tide crashed violently inside her like an *Echo* storm that once nearly killed us. She was drowning.

A memory sank quick fangs into me.

Big Jim, me on his shoulder as he slumped from the Ford F-150. The driver's door swung lackadaisically. Big Jim shuffled to our front door on lead-pipe legs. We had just left the hostile lights of a hospital—lights that had confused me with their cruelty; why were they interrogating such delicate bodies?— but Big Jim was still there. His mind was grappling with how Tiffany S. was just a shell, lying in a white bed with lights all around but none inside her. He was replaying what the doctors said.

"Coma." A word that sounded like a faraway state where they grow juicy corn and raise chickens. "Her family has asked that you don't return. They're dealing with a lot now—Tiffany's sister is—well, we don't have concrete answers. She's been flown to D.C. to see a rare treatment specialist. She's contracted something...unusual. Both daughters need full-time care. I can appreciate that, but the family is going through an exceedingly difficult time; I'm sure you can understand? No, you can't come back here. Tiffany's coworkers are due to arrive. Sir, it's time for you to leave! Sir!" Big Jim was being banished from the chambers of his heart.

*Tiffany's coworkers.* Big Jim sweated even more than usual around them. Their shiny Boeing badges seemed to make him shrink. They were MoFos who laughed a little too hard when he called champagne "fancy beer" and at the way he pronounced hors d'oeuvres ("whores dooves"). It didn't matter how much Tiffany S. squeezed Big Jim's arm or steered the conversation back to him, he never felt like he was enough for her. Big Jim was always Pabst Blue Ribbon—he was never going to be fancy beer.

When we got out of the truck, Big Jim was still time traveling, infiltrating a dark night when Tiffany S. had wandered the street alone. A late trip to a Walgreens in Ballard, streets slick with rain and the pulsing glow of neon reflections. Hair done, dress nice, always heels. There had been three of them, three hungry predators lurking in the shadows. Three splintered souls who felt entitled to take things that didn't belong to them. To whom fine bones and a flair for the feminine is an invitation, fruit ripe for the plucking. And Big Jim knew that if he had just been there, he could have taken three of them on, ten of them, twenty of them for her. That's what his big hands were good for—to protect the ones he loved. In the gutter, under neon glow, the pregnancy test she'd bought soaked up tears from the sky.

Big Jim fell through our front door and stared at his big beautiful hands, hands that hadn't been there for her, big hands that had no purpose—what good were they? He dropped to his knees and sobbed. A tsunami of Black Tide crashed into him and he fell apart, his body quaking with pain. Dennis, who usually greeted us exuberantly by peeing in a mighty McDonald's golden arch, watched for a moment. His droopy eyes registered the broken bits of Big Jim. He disappeared calmly into the kitchen with clicky claw plods and returned with a favorite toy, a squirrel Big Jim imaginatively named Sqrl. Dennis carried the toy up to his favorite being on this big beautiful blue, sat so close there was no space between them, and dropped slobbery old Sqrl into Big Jim's lap. Big Jim flung his arms around bloodhound bulk and he wept from somewhere so deep I thought we'd never get him back. And I carefully preened his unwashed hospital-smell hair and the new harvest of stubble that had sprouted on his face. I checked his ears and swallowed up some of his tears. We took care of him the best way we knew how.

Big Jim didn't drown that day. And Dee would not drown this day. It was so easy to forget—she was only human. And they are not unbreakable.

"Dee! Dee! It's me!" I cried.

Dee lifted her head to face me, the edges of her mouth curled down like parchment paper. Her eyes were filled with salt. Her arms were covered in angry slices, bruises like the ones a banana suffers. Some of the cuts were swollen and angry. How silly of me to worry about infection and invisible assassins when the real deal was at our door.

"I'm here, Dee!" I called, hobbling over metallic lumps, inelegantly tripping over the butt of a glass bottle. I rolled down the side of the nest into its palm. I felt sharp nicks in my skin and I didn't care. Dee hung her head, tears streaming down her sweet, muddy cheeks. I pushed my head up into her hand and felt a flicker of fire in her finger. I peered at those fingers, the magic of her entire species distilled down into the half-moons of her nails. I ran my beak along her palm, where the lines were. MoFos could read futures in those lines, and I wished I could have drawn hers longer, so that she could have more of life. She sat there in shards, stuck in a glass nest, because I had broken her. I knew these were my last moments with Dee, so I was careful not to tangle up my words, make thorns and blackberry snarls of them.

"I am so proud of you," I told her. "Dee is perfect." I made a guttural crow sound for gratitude. I smoothed my beak along her fingers, and I hoped she could feel even an acorn of what was inside me.

She spoke. "Dee—" she stopped, struggling with the words that splintered on her tongue. A tear splashed onto my head. She pointed a swollen finger to the terrible creatures below.

"No," I told her. "Dee is like S.T. I am proud of you every day." I puffed up my feathers to show her just how big my pride was.

Her eyebrows huddled together like gossiping caterpillars. "Dee is crow?" she said, looking for permission. Her hunger to belong broke me.

"Dee," I told her, "is the best crow I know." I stopped talking to her in MoFo, a language I had mostly forced upon her. I talked to her in crow, a language of body and sight and sound altogether. Another tear slid down Dee's cheek, only now her cheeks lifted, the corners of her mouth rising like oven-baked bread. She lifted me to her face. I nuzzled my cheek against hers. And she knew how much I loved her. It was warm and shone bright and bathed her in a spider-spun gold. It scorched off the darkness and fucking barricaded the waves of The Black Tide. And she forgave me in that way the pure of soul and the very courageous can, the way her Uncle Dennis would. I was an idiot for taking this long to figure it out, to tell her. *I'm sorry*, I told her with tail pumps and gentle rubs of my beak. *I'm sorry. I was wrong.*

I wished for more time. I'd lived a very big and bushy life, but Dee was the future and I yearned to do better for her. Was I ready to die? Fuck no—I hadn't seen the Taj Mahal or Machu Picchu, or even that penis museum tucked away in the thigh folds of Iceland. And I wouldn't get to see what Dee looked like as she grew up to be Big Dee. When she got to use her wings and fly. But it was worth everything I'd ever been through to get here—even that terrifying *Echo* storm and when Big Jim's eyeball bungee jumped from his head—and I was grateful for the moments I had left. For every flicker in the day's colors I got to spend with her.

The sounds around us intensified.

Dee stood up, flinching as something punctured her foot. A nest, by nature a sacred and softest place—even that, The Changed Ones had made hostile and barbed. Dee padded gingerly to the edge of the nest and lifted me so I could see over its saw-toothed edge. I got a bird's-eye view of pandemonium below. The crows mobbing the bird creatures. Primates in the trees around us. A horrifying insect in control of it all.

"Danger," said Dee. She let out the corvid alarm. "CAW! CAW! CAW! CAW! CAW!"

"Yes," I said. "Dee, we won't hide anymore."

She made a sound, that clever, clever mimic. The clattery *clack tack* of antlers colliding. The sound of Toksook caribou sparring. I spread my wings in answer: *Yes.*

"Show them, Dee."

Dee paused and bent over, wrapping her fingers around a neck that stuck out in a nest of nails and jagged things. The moody barrel of a gun.

"No," I said to her. "Show them Dee's way."

It was my turn to coax my nestling from the nest. Down the stoic arms of the copper beech.

Dee lifted me to her face. And if it was the last thing I ever saw, well, as the old adage goes, the light of heart is free to fly. Picture the last MoFo, the apple cheeks and sparkly space-dust eyes. What a bright and brilliant star. Look at her ears—auricles, they called them, just like pearly seashells or the *Auricularia auricula-judae* hugging the hardwood of an old beech tree. Survival suits her. Look at how alive she is; doesn't the world seem better with her in it? Supernatural. Super natural. Notice that power in her, those natural instincts. Look at how she wears that fierce glow. She is lit up from the inside by the sun.

# CHAPTER 30

※ ♣ ❋ ♠ ⚜ ♣ ❀

WEST COAST TRANSIENT ORCAS
PUGET SOUND, WASHINGTON, USA

We stream through the salt world in black and white. Emerald kelp bows as we pass. Silverfish dart for cover.

Urgent sounds—thousands of pings against our slick skins—sharp and small as shrimp have summoned us.

The Beast is here.

The Beast of our legend has shown himself. He is borrowing skins from the creatures of *Echo*.

We swim past a hybrid hagfish, coughing up sludge. Its sound is thick and pink. *Glub. Glub. Glub.* Pints of pink slime fill the salt world around us. We slice through its cloggy goo. Other creatures—seal and Dall's porpoise, cod and rockfish—float, aquarium-eyed and belly-up. They have choked on pink poison. The hagfish are coming up from the deep. The Beast has many forms.

We have no time; we race to follow the sounds. Never has there been a call like this.

All sea wolves heed the call. It has come from the resident

orcas of Puget Sound. We transient orcas, orcas of the deepest ocean, the traveling sea wolves, the ones who feed on seal, walrus, and otter, go to them. We speed through the salt tunnels, sending back bright rays of sound in bold colors.

*We are coming. Fast as we can.*

Other great black-and-white bodies are here; other orcas flank us. We speed together, speed of sound. More orcas and more.

Up ahead. There. The resident orcas huddle together close to the waterline.

Incandescent colors swirl and spike, spin and shimmer; the ocean glows with bioluminescence.

It is Tallulah. The great matriarch floats on her side. She is black and white and red. Her pod is still. Their whines are sharp as fishing wire. We are all caught in the net of grief.

Tallulah was the oldest among us. She lived one hundred season cycles. Tallulah held us all together with her tales. Tallulah is gone from us now. Taken. We have lost time and love and her gentle guidance. We have lost her voice, the feeling of it flowing through us, wrapping silkily around our bones. Her fluke and fin will wave no more. She has gone where the water goes.

Her majestic son—glowing sounds dappling his great black-and-white body—opens his rubber mouth wide. We see his necklace of barnacle teeth. The bubbles he releases are steely blue and storm silver, slick as a wolf eel.

"The Beast," he says. "The Beast has come."

# CHAPTER 31

S.T.

CHATEAU STE. MICHELLE, WASHINGTON, USA

Dee placed me on the edge of the nest. She studied the scene below. I had the impulse to tell her that after we'd descended the copper beech, we should slink away, just Dee and me, safe shadows. But those were old inclinations, the sentiments of a yellow-bellied marmot. We had to help the hominids in the trees and stop a pending carnage of crows, black beauties who mobbed with ferocious agility. The MoFos didn't name one of their greatest fighter jets Blackbird for nothing.

Dee made a high-pitched fluting sound.

Could it be? A chittering bounced back from the clouds and burst around us. I called her name out in joy. "MIGISI!"

And there she was, like a McDonnell Douglas F-15 Eagle. Head in winter white and pregnant as fuck. She looped around us, detouring to dive and unleash her talons on the eye of a Changed One for the shit of it. Our adventure eagle shot back up and landed on Dee's outstretched arm with as much elegance as one can when incubating a clutch of tennis ball–sized eggs.

"What are you doing here so pregnant?" I asked her. She stuck her face in mine and screamed supersonically. I bowed my head in apology. Listen, I'll always be a work in progress. She bumped my chest with that glorious buttercup beak.

"No," I told her. "I've missed *you* more." Migisi and Dee then shared a look whose meaning I didn't comprehend until I was snatched up in Migisi's talons, dangling in the sky next to a glass nest and the fuckity plummet-drop to below. My view—little black crow feet and the bird Changed Ones, orange and black apes in the trees, and crows whirling and diving, everything in miniature from up so high. Migisi set me back down onto the maple branch for safekeeping. She thrust her salmon-filleting beak into mine and shrieked. *Stay put. I mean it.*

Migisi was airborne again, gliding over the fray, returning to the branch that held part of the great nest. Near Dee.

The two horrible transparent insects emerged from the doors of the Chateau. My liver quivered thinking about what the tall one in front of the great doors was capable of. What might three of them do?

"SCRREEEEEDEEEEE!" All eyes up at the nest. Dee was standing, her torso and the imposing look on her face visible. She lifted the metal pole she had dislodged and struck it three times against glass and metal. A hauntingly hollow sound.

The crows instinctively retreated to safe spots in the trees.

All eyes on the feral creature. A lively young animal standing tall on two legs. A species that once roamed the plains of this big beautiful blue. Now, she was the last. A burning sun.

I looked at the Insect Creature. The compound eye was trained on Dee.

Dee screamed, "FUUUUUUUUUUCK!" No one, not primate nor wood louse, made a sound.

"Astee!" she yelled. That's me. I'm Astee. That's how Dee says my name, the name she never uses, a name like a too-big apple in her mouth. I never told you that because I was ashamed, desperate for her to say it properly like Big Jim and Nargatha and Tiffany S. did. But now, it was the sound I most loved in this world, a warm apricot sound shaped like home. We—all of us—watched as Dee appeared at one side of the gargantuan nest, tiptoeing over barbed wire and glittering glass.

*Stay away from the edge, Dee. Climb down the copper beech to me.*

And then Dee was on the very edge of the nest, standing many, many MoFo feet above us all. The towering Insect Creature kept rapt focus on Dee.

"Astee!" she called to the little crow in the maple who could do nothing. Dee had to leave the nest and she had to do it her way. It was too late to stop her now that she was about to throw herself off this aberrational structure. My fledgling who could not fly.

"Dee! No!" I yelled up. And then in crow so she knew I meant it.

*No, Dee. Please.*

"Dannis!" she yelled back at me. "Dannis!"

*I know, Dee.* She wanted to be a hero. She wanted to do the right thing, but strong as she was, her bones would not survive a fall from this height. Every creature here—living and in between—knew this and felt the weight of what would happen. If she was gone, The Changed Ones would stop hunting her. Dee understood this. She knew that everything else would have a better chance without her. She was thinking of her heroic Uncle Dennis luring The Changed Ones into a lake to drown.

"Dee!" I yelled. "Please!"

But I couldn't do this anymore. I couldn't treat her with this

kind of exceptionalism—not at the cost of so many others. I
thought of the words from Onida the walrus...

*She is no more important than a stone. No more vital than bacteria.
Or a virus.*

*If she leaves here, she will die*, I told him.

*Yes*, he'd said.

I could not ask these gorillas and orangutans, survivors and
refugees with their babies and their fragile futures, to lay down
their lives for a one. Even the last. I could not ask the crows for
more lives than they had already given. This is not the law of
nature. The web of reciprocity is a balanced dance of give and
take. And as much as I wanted it to, all of life did not revolve
around this sun.

"Astee!" she yelled back, her words ragged, throat closing up.

And I couldn't do anything. Not from this distance. I
couldn't stop her from being herself anymore, at any cost. I
had to let her go.

I suddenly saw her mother clearly. A MoFo who stood at
the edge of her world's end. A MoFo with Sirius-star eyes
and a dark mane of hair. Tears paint her cheeks. Her bear
heart in tatters; she places Dee in a bundled bassinet. She
stands with her arms outstretched like a great oak—open to
guidance and comfort, open to the whole glittering universe.
She begs under her breath, a prayer, a whisper from the
womb. The prayer is to something she can't see but feels in
her marrow, a plea that the world she had always believed
in, a world of sprouting seeds and yellow-backed bees, will
take care of the tiny, helpless hatchling. A black feather—
soft as a broken heart—flitters down from the evergreens
around her. A last touch, mother and child, skin to skin.
There are no words, but a feeling as powerful as an ocean
inside her compels her to do this, to take off her shoes and
feel the grass beneath her toes. To leave her infant alone

under a shiver of stars. A hair-thin thread between an act of blind faith and an act of unforgivable neglect. She walks, the longest walk of her life—a walk of the plank—from the bassinet to a dark cellar door, its cold metal lock waiting for her. The world crumbles in unison with her heart, craned necks, ruby eyes, snowing ash. A wolf howls. And the moon grieves for a mother who just made the biggest sacrifice of all.

"I love you, Dee!" I called to her.

"I lav you, Astee!" she yelled back. And then she stretched out her wingspan. Beautiful Dee. Seventy percent water like the planet that birthed her. Dee, who had the cunning of a crow and the heart of a musk ox. Formidable as owl, fish quick and filled with the buzzy dynamism of insects. Like her moss, she had survived the end of worlds. She was a hybrid, a mix of things, *akutaq*, soil skinned and stitched together with the stories I shared with her.

And I have never been prouder of anything in my whole life.

Dee looked one more time, down at the dizzying drop and around her at the majestic trees she loved more than life itself. A breeze ruffled her hair and she closed her eyes and emptied her lungs.

Dee jumped.

The crows cried out. The gorillas and the orangutans whooped and hollered. And the Insect Creature hissed— a quick, insistent *sssss*. Two wings jetted out from its back, whirring violently. The Changed Ones heard, responding. One, hawklike and nearest to the Insect Creature, dove from a branch. Dee—made of stone, made of my heart—dropped, down and down, her flightless body clumsy, a mountain goat tossed off the cliff by golden eagle. The Changed One smacked onto rock-hard dirt below Dee. She hit its back with a hard thump. She slid off the greasy plumage above its spine. Dee slumped to the ground. The hawk thing peered down at her with darting head movements.

Dee didn't move.

And then she did.

Her legs whipped her up into a crouch. Her arm swung out in a cobra strike.

Red poured from Dee's beautiful hands. Hands for protecting the ones she loves. The hawk Changed One's eyes rolled. A triangular wedge of glass stuck out the side of its warped head like a surrender flag. Its body crumpled. Dee moved like a cat now, crouch and slink.

The crows all called out to her in a loving cacophony. She called back to them. She scampered, apelike, toward a creature with see-through skin.

It towered above her. A compound eye focused. Claws lifted, open at their hinges. It saw in an optical mosaic; thousands of miniature images made up a picture of Dee using her eagle eyes to scan its head. The Insect Creature whipped out a claw to snatch Dee. She ducked, the claw sailing above her burnt meringue of a hairstyle. She lunged at it, smashing her fist—a fist that had bopped a grizzly's nose, wrecked gymnasium walls, pounded out an earthy hole for orphaned baby bunnies—into the throat of the insect. A sharp snap left the creature's neck dangling unnaturally. That's the problem with transparent skin. It makes finding the most delicate bone of the spine too easy.

But Dee was still surrounded, outnumbered. The dying creature emitted a chemical that rose in warning tendrils. The One In Charge, the Insect Creature by the Chateau doors, was now closer to Dee.

"Go!" came its cold command.

The Changed Ones activated. Dee saw them coming for her. She pulled something from her sealskin jacket. A square vial.

She shook it around, flinging a few drops of liquid toward a heron-like horror that was coming right for her. It recoiled and screeched.

Dee sniffed at the air, adrenaline rocketing through her. Then my head filled with a noxious smell, a smell that breaks into your brain to boop you right behind the eyeballs.

Feral cats burst from the bushes. Some yowled, trotting forward, sniffing the air, keeping their distance from the fray but unable to help themselves. Curiosity nibbled at them like peckish piranhas. They smushed their heads against discarded lumps of trash, rolling around the ground.

Migisi swooped and dove at an imitation raptor.

Another Changed One dropped in front of Dee. I wanted her to run. Dee deepened her squat, claiming the earth beneath her. And then she made a noise.

"Eko."

The Malayan tiger burst from the nearest trash pile in a streak of orange and black. He bit the neck of the Changed One with his fangs, clamping down on the weakest and most delicate part of a thing in transition. Then he tore out its throat. The creature convulsed weakly on the ground. Eko let out a jungle bellow. His brothers leapt from the shadows, taking on other Changed Ones. Red eyes rolled. Tigers dodged and swiped and growled.

I couldn't believe it. Dee had summoned the tigers. Chanel N°5. Those brilliant perfumer MoFos had done an impeccable job of creating synthetic civet piss and Dee had known it would call her cats.

Movement. A descent from the London plane tree. The great male western lowland gorilla was emboldened by the tiger attacks. He armed himself with rusted hedge shears and lumbered forth, his wrath building to a canter. Family called out to him in hoots from the trees. He was running—

a wrecking ball of brawn and brain and blade—full steam toward the largest Insect Creature, who stood at the command center of chaos by the Chateau doors. I should have felt relief at the power of an enraged gorilla, at the slim, see-through joints and thin MoFo bones, but I was filled with dread. If other Changed Ones had appropriated the defense tactics of spiders and hawks, what had this thing mimicked?

The gorilla pounded his chest and roared, brandishing the shears. His mountainous head showcased long fangs. The compound eye took its focus off Dee at the last minute to cock its head at the gorilla. The gorilla, careening toward a boned body, sped up. The transparent creature lifted taller, its claws hanging limp at its side.

*Oh no.*

The gorilla roared, feet away from its target.

The Insect Creature lifted its abdomen—the pointed segment of its body—up between its stick legs. The gorilla, hurtling forth like a runaway truck, slammed into the insect, pinning it to the Chateau doors. The gorilla impaled itself on the spike at the end of the creature's abdomen. They both fell silent. The insect barely moved. The gorilla dropped the shears, searching the Chateau with bark-brown eyes. A twitch. Another. The Changed One pumped the gorilla full of its own fluid with a fucking ovipositor.

*No. Oh god, no.*

The gorilla gained strength and lifted a hulking arm, but the Insect Creature pulled its stinger out of the gorilla's side and struck again, stopping all motion. The gorilla went wide-eyed. And the Insect Creature stepped back, releasing the gorilla of its injection. The gorilla was tranquilized. Quiet.

But I knew better. I knew what this horrible thing had stolen because of a certain after-hours addiction to National Geographic. It had mimicked a wasp, the Voldemort of

*Hymenoptera.* The jewel wasp. A "she," since only female wasps have stingers.

The gorilla was now sedate, glassy-eyed. He started grooming himself compulsively. Close by, so close, three tigers fought Bird Beings, but the gorilla seemed oblivious, as if in a trance. The Wasp Queen waited several feet away, watching the gorilla at first, and then turning her attention to Dee.

The gorilla leapt into action, a quick run and a slap of both palms onto the ground—*thap*! King Kong's roar ripped through the air. The tigers roared back. The gorilla focused on the apes in the trees. Then he charged the base of a London plane tree. He leapt up toward a cluster of gorillas, screaming and shaking his alpine head, slapping his hands against tree trunks. The primates shrieked and cried out in confusion. They hadn't realized that their beloved was under the mind control of a wasp, a soldier commanded by potent neurotoxins. The jewel wasp commandeers cockroaches in this way. This wasp Changed One had created a blank-brained soldier to do its bidding. The apes ushered each other higher into the trees. They called back to the male gorilla in gentle voices, wondering where their father had gone.

Dee roared with the tigers. I looked up. She had fashioned a loop out of rusting copper wire, something she had seen spiders do with their silks. She flung the loop around the neck of a Changed One and pulled hard. The hawk creature was thrust to its side. Olan dismantled its face.

"Dee!" I called to her.

"Astee!" A proud call, a crow's check-in.

I had to keep eyes on everything all at once.

I looked over to the gorilla who was on fire with an anger that wasn't his. He was breaking the limbs off trees, snatching at the apes above him. And then he started to climb. Dee was standing with her face to the sky, where crows mobbed at The

Changed Ones, pecking at their eyes, taunting them with cell phones.

And The Wasp Queen, where was she? The terrifying creature—a female wasp made of MoFo bones—had turned to me on the low maple branch. That compound eye stared through its thousand optical screens at the body of a crow. Her brain made quick calculations. She looked at Dee, then back at me. Migisi saw this predatory focus from the air. She warned us all with a scream, *Look out!* The Wasp Queen commenced a wasp's skittering run. It was fast. And faster. She was closing in. I bolted. I ran from a kaleidoscope eye and gyrating bones and a mandible of mayhem.

A claw clamped down. I was a can of Pabst Blue Ribbon, Big Jim's fingers constricting around me.

I called out. "Dee!"

The claw tightened.

"Dee! Caw! Caw! Caw—" and then I couldn't call out anymore.

The big beautiful blue shuttered black.

# CHAPTER 32

I see little pebbles below. Beautiful black beings lying spiritless above the kingdom of *Web*. I soar above. I block the sight from my eyes. The names their warrior mothers gave them through pearly shell, the sounds they made have lifted me as I fly. I mustn't remember now.

I have to fight.

We swoop between tree limbs, careful of the sharp nest. I shoot past the strength of the maple and strike the head of a Changed One with my beak. It growls and snaps. I'm too quick.

"Blackwings!" I call, and a swarm of black barrels after the Changed One. I snatch up a shard of glass and swoop past the Changed One's beak again. "Come for me, beast! Come for me!"

I must be the bait.

They will have my bones before more of my Blackwing brothers'.

Blackwings—my sisters, my brothers—are faster, lighter. We use the sky light and the trees. The Changed Ones are clumsy in their flight still, bulky and graceless. The wind says to veer right, I do it. Feather to feather, we whip and dive and swoop and curl and they won't snatch us. We are the Sky Sentinels.

It is known.

Below—mouse sized—I see the Last On Two Legs. She stands side by side with brother tigers. A Hollow. I once believed The Hollows to be empty, blind noise makers, space takers governed by unseen forces. Cruel in their treatment of the Blackwings. Marlik, taken from the sky by a Hollow branch that shot fire. Graak, Cottonwood, Mossem, who ate food, a gift from The Hollows, that curled their insides. But not this Hollow. Dee has changed us. Here's a Hollow who speaks the language of the big beautiful blue. A Hollow with eyes open, who sees the Blackwings and loves us each and every and all. Our brother, The One Who Keeps, will keep the darkness at bay.

Graak. Cottonwood. Marlik. Mossem. We forgive and we fly for them.

Migisi loops above. We hear her calls, tight, urgent.

I focus on the skin of *Web* to see the Great Insect. It's moving! It's running, fast on thin legs, across the green and brown.

Dee the Hollow Hatchling turns to see the Great Insect running. Dee screams so loud the whole big beautiful blue can hear.

"The One Who Keeps! The One Who Keeps!" cries our white-headed warrior from above.

"Where, Migisi?" I crow. I scan from the sky and see the Great Insect has something in its claw. I focus.

It's The One Who Keeps. S.T.!

S.T. is in its claw!

Dee runs after it. Her two legs carry her so fast, faster than any Hollow I've ever seen. Her face is on fire.

"Blackwings!" I cry. And they come together, fill the sky like the wings of night, and swoop down the strength of the copper beech. We—Blackwing force—drop down to the grass world, above the kingdom of *Web*. Flying low—so low—for speed, to chase the Great Insect who has stolen our S.T.

"Up ahead! Follow!" I bellow. The crows call out, voices urging one another into faster flight. One Great Black Thing.

We fly at Dee's strong shoulders and she runs as though she's airborne. She has wings, this Hollow. Beside her run the brother tigers.

"The One Who Keeps! The One Who Keeps!" crows cry, filled with legend and hope and love for our Brother Blackwing.

Dee, the Last On Two Legs, roars—a roar from the heart—running, water beads flying from her. The tigers roar. They run like jungle cats. And all the Blackwings call out. We run side by side, ground to air, Hollow to tigers to Blackwing warriors.

The Last Hollow.

Blackwings.

Tigers.

A world of legs and wings but one beating heart.

United by S.T.

We're fury. We're The Wind.

"The One Who Keeps! The One Who Keeps!"

The heart must be light for fast flight. I cannot think of S.T., my brave friend. Straddler of worlds. The One Who Keeps, whom Onida chose to call upon. He's hybrid, a crow hatched for great things. I try not to think of when we watched over him, when he was new from the eggshell—too quick and curious—and he toppled from the maple branch down, down into the Hollow's yard with the fat gnome.

How we all cried out, even me, just a young crow then. How we trusted that he remembered the guidance whispered to him through a sweep of shell, a privilege of the winged. How the Blackwings watched from safe branches, ready to swoop down and take him back. Only we saw the tender Hollow with fat-worm fingers, and the way S.T.'s tiny morning-blue hatchling eyes had imprinted on that big featherless Hollow. So, we watched until the leaves turned coppery crisp and the white blizzard came, and then sun spilled its yolk again. And we knew he'd made his choice to become a Hollow. But we would always be his family—we were all he had after his parents, Graak and Cottonwood, swallowed that wicked Hollow bread. So, we always kept our watch of S.T.; we chased off cats and mobbed marauding owls, even when the blood-hound appeared and stayed and grew into his floppy skin and chased us away. It united our murder; we became strong as guardians. S.T. The Uniter was always destined for something great. Onida told us so. Onida told us that one day we would see. I've always known S.T. was different. Mother Nature is deliberate with her palette. When she paints you with unique colors, it's because she trusts you can handle adversity and inspire others to greatness. I try not to think of the pain inside me, of what we will do without him. Without hope.

The Great Insect is using its clear wings for speed. But there is a white tent ahead. Big billowing home for The Hollows. A fluttering nest. The Great Insect cannot pass, can run no farther. It turns and we see its terrible eye. The Great Insect gets closer as we fly forward. The tigers use their loudest calls. They run in front of Dee, they close in on the Great Insect. They are circling it. The Great Insect is lifting its abdomen through its legs—and we the Blackwings know it will sting that largest tiger. The tiger calls again and readies to use its teeth on the Great Insect.

The Hollow Hatchling yells out. I don't know this call, but

her bald beak is leaky, her face is flower red. She bears the sadness of an ancient oak. The Hollow face can tell so much.

She looks at S.T. in the crush of the Great Insect. She has already lost everything.

The tiger moves toward the Great Insect. Closer. Closer. The stinger is sharp and ready for striped fur. The tiger will soon not know itself. And the Hollow Hatchling, S.T.'s Dee, will not stand a chance.

"Come together, Blackwings, come together!" I call. We are ready to swarm around S.T.'s Hollow. He loves her and we love her too. We'll protect her in the code of murder. In the name of nature.

The Hollow Hatchling calls out so loud the tigers flinch. She jumps in front of the tiger. She is brave as a hummingbird. Fearless as a Sky Sentinel. The Great Insect pauses. It holds back its stinger. S.T. hangs limp in its claw. Dee leaps at the stinger, hurling herself toward the sharp poison.

"No!" I call out. The Blackwings join me. "No, Dee! No! No! No!"

The Great Insect swings its stinger away from Dee, flinging S.T. to the ground. It will not sting The Last's skin. Dee throws herself to where S.T. lies, his beautiful black feathers in her paws. She performs a Hollow ritual, slumping to the ground. She lifts him in the scoops of her strong branches. She pulls our Brother Blackwing to her face. Dee wails, the cries of loss, of hollow longing. Her pain is so heavy, we all fight to fly. Her eyes close and her body suffers an inner earthquake. Her pain dances up around us in jagged bolts like northern lights. S.T. is boneless. His sad wing hangs.

"The Insect!" I yell to the sky sentinels. We swoop around a glassy head and compound eye. The tigers swipe their claws at the Great Insect, but not too close—they know that stinger's power. I zoom in, close to its many frog-egg eyes and it swings a claw at me. *Snap!* I dodge it.

And the Great Insect opens its jaws and it calls out too. A scream. A screech of The Changed Ones.

"Rise, Blackwings! Rise!" I tell them. We spiral above the Great Insect and we see them coming. More bird Changed Ones. They are distant, but there are many of them, flying toward us, calling for our deaths. And behind them, we see The Weavers as they spider across the ground—they are coming too.

The tigers pace. They roar and bite at the quick distance between them and the Great Insect. They cannot get close and so they can do nothing.

And Dee is on the ground, rounded like a rock. She scoops S.T. and she empties out what is inside of her. Her breaths are a wounded rabbit's. A storm passes through her, rain pours from her eyes. She hums in her breast, the hum of the hive. Like S.T., she straddles worlds. They were hybrid together. They were part of each other. I mustn't think of this.

I hear her sing the song of bees.

The Weavers and The Flight Ones and The Beetle Kind are coming.

We cannot stop them, we all know it.

But we will fight with every last feather. Together.

We will always watch out for you, S.T. In life and what flies beyond.

That is the code of murder.

# CHAPTER 33

THE LETTER

Little One,

I know you won't read this, but perhaps, somehow, someone will. Someone who'll see who you are, that you need someone to love you when I'm gone. We don't have the time I thought we did. We were cheated. I guess none of us are guaranteed life, but I still want it so much. Maybe that's a very lovely thing, to suffer so terribly and to still want to breathe the earth's air, to still want to sit and watch the river. After all that's happened, I still believe the earth is worth it. I believe she has a soul, and maybe, I write this to her. I just want to hold you for longer. I want to watch you grow. I'm so hungry to know who you'll be. I know I can't have these things. I can't stop my loved ones from losing their souls. And I can't stop the tears.

Something's happening inside me. I can feel it moving around, cold and angry, hiding behind my eyes, growing and replicating. It's taking over, so I write this quickly as my time runs out. My time runs out.

We met in my body and I knew you were very special. Very special. You were born in our cabin, but I was alone because some of the sick had come to our village and there was fighting. You were born silent. You were born and the winds were strong and the trees rustled. The trees our elders first fought about—foreign trees that grew here so fast, so tall, away from their homeland. Some elders tried to cut the outsiders down, others tied their bodies to trunks and called out for mercy. Now we cherish and honor our strange trees because they were a gift from someone unseen. You were born and there were great white owls sitting outside the window in those trees, watching with yellow eyes. I couldn't leave the bed and then shadow filled the cabin's front door. A moose—the largest I have ever seen, with antlers like a chandelier—stood at the front of the cabin. He tried to get in the door, and shaking, cornered, I aimed a rifle at his head.

"What do you want?" I yelled.

The moose didn't take his eyes off you.

"Go!" I yelled. "You can't have her!"

The moose was not afraid and watched without moving. The great moose and the white owls watched you, Little One. The moose left very slowly, and the night filled with sounds, a night so bright the moon hurt my eyes. And the owls watched you from the window. I was so afraid, but you weren't. You stared at them as if you'd met them before. On the night you were born, an unkindness of ravens flew over our cabin; they sang an eerie song and I knew they were calling for you. I lit a fire and held you close, and I knew then that you were extraordinary.

When the doctor came, she said you were different. I already knew. She said we would need to do tests, but there was no longer anyone to give them. No tests. No labels. Time running out. So, you were just extraordinary.

Everyone in the village fell sick—their eyes, their hands—I don't have time to speak of it. We thought we had survived when the rest of the world hadn't. Even your father lost the light in his eyes. I knew what was coming, so I broke my own heart and tricked them. I locked them in the basement. I'm going to join them before it's too late, but not you. It will kill me, but I am already dying. I feel it. I have to believe that there's a chance for you. Am I insane to think this? Is it my right mind's choice? I'm terrified. I have to believe that the girl who won't stop crying until she hears the birds is where she needs to be. I have to believe that the one I've always spoken to—a whisper I hear in trees, the voice of water, the thing I see in the eyes of animals—is listening. I cry rivers and I give you to the earth.

I did it for you, Little One. I did it for you, Little One. I did it for you, Little One. I knew you were special. I need to find them. They must be close by. My time runs out.

Something's happening inside me. My time runs out.           Runs out.

I'm going to lock us in.      I'm going to lock us all in.

The screens.            I'll just find a screen.            I'll find a screen. I am

rewriting what's inside me.            Changing from the inside.

I'll kill them all.         I'll kill you all.            I'm starving for screens. Starving

for screens.            Starving for screens. I'll kill you all.        I'll kill you all.

I'll kill you.

Changing.            Something's happening inside me.

Find the screens.         Starving. Starving.       My time's run out. I'll kill you

all.         I'm starving for screens.            Starving for screens.


I'm starving for screens.


I have to let you go.

# CHAPTER 34

S.T.
CHATEAU STE. MICHELLE, WOODINVILLE,
WASHINGTON, USA

My nictitating membranes burst open like the velvet curtains at Big Jim's beloved old strip club Jiggles (formally the comedy club, Giggles). Dee's face shone down on me. I was soaked with her tears.

"You're okay, my nestling, everything's okay. I'm here," I told her, just as I did when she waddled in a makeshift moss diaper or when she'd wandered too many tree trunks ahead, wailing because she couldn't see me. I wiggled to feel what was happening in my body. My rib cage throbbed. My gular fluttered like a hawk moth. I felt distinctly like something chewed up and shat out by a dyspeptic giraffe.

Dee, laughing and crying in a complex cabaret of pure emotion, let my name roll from her tongue again and again. "Astee, Astee, Astee!"

I looked around.

Above us, my crow family swarmed and whirled and cawed. To my left, I saw a white MoFo tent, some sort of enormous gathering shelter that ran along the horizon as far as the eye could see. In front of it, The Wasp Queen in a standoff with three tiger brothers, Eko, Liem, Olan. The tigers looked like creatures who knew death was coming for them, its soft fruit scent convening in the clouds. And to my right, the distant bodies of Changed Ones—masses of their strange heads and stolen bodies, bird, spider, beetle—were coming for us.

But above me, The Sun. She hummed the hive song.

We would be together. And it would be okay. The truth is that we are all just little owlets imprinting on one another. When you love someone with your soul, they never really leave you; they are hemmed into your heart. It was this way with Dennis. Big Jim. Nargatha. Tiffany S.

I was glad I was shit at counting. MoFos counted their lives in days and months and years. They got it wrong. Lives aren't measured this way. It's not about how many sunrises we have but how much we fill them with fervor and flight.

Dee shot to her feet. She cradled me carefully in her arms. Then started a vigorous sniffing. She tilted her head, then let out an excited yelp. The Changed Ones grew larger as they neared. Dee looked up to the sky above the white MoFo tent.

Cresting over the top of the fluttering tent was a swarm. Millions of insects formed a pointillism, rendering the whole sky a fuzzy TV screen. Dee hummed louder, calling out to them.

"Astee!" she said. "Sky, Astee!" And the great mass, a veritable cloud formation of bees, descended on her, forming a second skin. Their deafening buzz filled my head; bees landed on my feathers, my beak. I saw their beautiful boiling across Dee's skin. She'd called them to her for comfort. And after the fuzzy tunnel of bees came birds. Not crows this time, but gulls. Glaucous-winged and western gulls swirling the sky in white and silver, splashes of marigold beaks and sugar-pink legs. They called out in questioning keens.

Dee called back to them in gull from the back of her throat, skin buzzing with bees, heart buzzing with excitement.

But The Weavers kept coming. And The Masticators skittered toward us with twitchy mechanical limbs. They were starting to conquer the stretch of open land between us. Coming for us, always coming for us.

The gulls looped in the sky above Dee and she held up her arms and called out to them, her smile blooming. Over an evacuation tent like a white surrender flag came semipalmated plovers, dunlins, and western sandpipers—shorebirds with twig legs and tweezer beaks. They wove their bodies through the tapestry of sky and gull and bee. Black oystercatchers followed them with Vegas-orange bills, and now the sky was speckled with seabirds. Cassin's auklets smudged in charcoal and Leach's storm petrels cut above us with forked tails and ghost colors. Common murres came next, and then the cormorants came—double-crested, Brandt's, pelagic—birds with serpent necks and gorgeous glossy feathers that sang for salt. Then came the arctic terns—the big beautiful blue's migrational marathoners who travel the equivalent of three or more round trips to the moon in their long lives—swirling in white bodies sporting dapper black caps.

Dee screeched in delight. These were birds of *Echo*, the birds that bridge sky and sea. Birds of *Echo* had come, and I thought about the orcas and Onida. *Everything is connected*, I thought. *Life is a breathtaking concatenation.*

At the end, they lifted Dee's heart, and that was enough for me.

The first of The Weavers was now placing spiked legs down on the same grass field we stood on. The Masticators came in a palsied shimmy. They ran fast. Incoming artillery.

I felt a rumble and squinted at a dandelion. Even if we would not, this beautiful weed that flourished in buttery yellow optimism would live on, spinning sunshine into sugar. Imagine getting to live in a world so beautiful that even a weed is a golden treasure. I took comfort in this thought as I saw the dandelion pulse from the shock of something that shook the earth.

And The Weavers filled in all around, taking up space that wasn't theirs, their specialty. The tigers panicked. They formed a striped circle. The Great Insect readied to give its command. And The Changed Ones caught up to us and crouched, poised for violence. Ready to do what their dictator demanded.

Then came music I'd missed as much as the crinkle of a Cheeto® bag.

"Scrreeeeedeeeee, screeeeeeeedeeeeee!"

The call of a snowy owl.

Dee jumped up and down. She sent bright sounds up to the owls who had raised her. We saw Ookpik and Bristle first, side by side in stealth flight. Little Wik burst onto the scene with a screech. The Hook came after like a flat-faced king. Dee held her breath, waiting for her pepper-winged guardian. We heard her first, screaming out for her owlet. And there was Kuupa, her one citrine eye igniting when it found Dee. Dee lifted her arms and Kuupa whooshed by them, a brush with flight feathers.

The calls of barred owls dropped from the air like round, ripe figs. And then owls were everywhere—flammulated, great gray, long- and short-eared, burrowing, and northern pygmy owls. A great parliament with wings that sliced the air like sashimi knives.

You could feel the forgiveness for little Dee.

Kraai and the murder panicked; owls and crows are sworn enemies. But Migisi—incubator of eggs and interspecies diplomat—maintained a steady glide between all the birds, calling out that it was safe. "Mixed up, altogether" was the rough tune of her piccolo notes.

And then a roar convoked the last of our adrenaline. A roar that ran up every spine in a multimile radius. Tigers spun toward the tents. White material rippled as something made its way through them. Another gruff roar. Emerging from the mouth of the tents were great winter-white masses with snowshoe paws. They lumbered forth with undulating shoulders and fur thick as snowdrifts.

Polar bears.

Walking together—twenty or thirty or thirty-five of them. I couldn't believe my beady little hybrid eyes. And then another lance of panic as I remembered the bony polar bear who clamped its jaws on Dee when she was just a hatchling. I was filled with the memory smell of moss and berry and starvation. What had these bears come for?

Dee roared back at the bears with a spring shower of a smile. The bees lifted from her, making intricately morphing patterns above her.

Led by Kuupa and her great peppery wings, the owls screeched and swooped in between the polar bears, and I realized then that the polar bears were on our side. They'd come to help us.

The Wasp Queen swiveled her strange head, watching great white bears. The Changed Ones waited for her command. Bears, birds, bees. But even with the bears, The Changed Ones outnumbered us.

The Queen's antennae lifted. And The Changed Ones charged. Polar bears lifted onto their hind legs, swiping with massive paws. Weavers sank their fangs into white fur. Talons swooped down from the sky and went for the eyes of Masticators. Three tigers spun and lunged. Olan let out a glass-breaking bellow as a Masticator bit off his tail. He retaliated by decapitating the monster. The Changed Ones surged forth in a frenzied swarm. The bears roared, tearing off jittery limbs and gnarled wings, but The Changed Ones kept coming. They poured in from the Chateau grounds. And we could do nothing to stop them.

I looked down at the tenacious dandelion flower. It pulsed. And pulsed again, each time with more vigor. And The Wasp Queen lifted its antennae to the air, ready to conduct chaos.

A hollow sound pounded the earth. The white flags of the wine tent came under attack. Material fluttered and billowed, sharp tearing sounds everywhere as it was shredded, crushed into mud.

*Oh no*, I thought.

The hollow sounds of hooves.

An ambush. Another monster, a hooved hybrid on one side. Bird, beetle, spider, and wasp things on the other. The end had come.

Thousands of birds and bees eddied above us—the bees louder than I'd ever heard—but it wasn't enough. Polar bears, splattered in red, bellowed and lunged at The Changed Ones. One lifted up onto its hind legs like an Arctic King, bringing down his weight onto a Weaver. I looked up at the birds, especially my crow family and the great owls who'd loved Dee from the start. At least there would be winged witnesses to the end. I lifted my beak to them, to their calligraphy in the clouds.

The poles that held the enormous white tent structure couldn't hold. They hit the ground with a metallic clatter.

They were here. There was a wall stretching as wide as the great horizon. A wall of dense, wiry fur, and—I was right— hooves, mighty cloven hooves. Boned horns curling from their skulls. Shaggy-bodied beasts. These were not Changed Ones. These were prehistoric beings who once stormed through an ice age alongside woolly mammoths and short-faced bears.

Like birds, these were the ones who had survived. Here were the soldiers of The Tundra.

Side to side, colossal hoof to hoof, were millions and billions and gazillions of tons of musk oxen. And at the helm of this horizon-wide cloven force was an enormous brute of an ox with a heart the size of Alaska.

Oomingmak.

The whole of Alaska had come for Dee. The Last MoFo On Earth had nestled her way into the hearts of creatures and here were those hearts, beating wildly in a Hollow Kingdom.

Oomingmak saw Dee. Dee saw Oomingmak.

He called to her in a rumble not unlike a Big Jim belch. She bellowed back. Without *Aura*, Dee had somehow summoned her beloved bees, who had called for the birds, who had summoned Alaska—Dee's owls and the bears and Oomingmak. And I suddenly remembered all that time, surely weeks, we hid at the McMenamins sanctuary surrounded by a herd of elephants, the endless hours Dee spent among flowers, humming to the bees that flittered around her and danced across her skin. How I kept dropping stones into Scotch and worrying there was something wrong with her beautiful brain.

Dee had clicked her ruby-red mukluks and called home.

The bees must have taken to the air to spread word of the danger we were in, to get news to her Alaskan guardians. And these beautiful beasts—bird, bear, ox, and bee—must have made a journey of two full moons across tundra and wilderness, braving forests of terrible creatures with destruction in their DNA. An adventure story only they could tell. I'd worried about Dee regressing, but her humming had been cries for help as she tapped into the bee network—a backup for broken *Aura*. I remembered how the Anna's hummingbird had helped Budiwati, Pressa, and me by distracting Changed Ones. "The bees sent me!" she had said. Clever, clever Dee had done it all in a language I'd never known. Just as she'd done with the wolves and ravens when we needed help. She had done it Dee's way.

*The future belongs to the backs of bees.*

Oomingmak lifted his head and roared, and the Great Wall Of Musk Oxen strode forward, their multiton bodies crashing down on the earth below. The tigers bolted. The birds keened. The polar bears started a fearless lumber, driving the mass of Changed Ones backward. The Wasp Queen watched the mass of horned ruminants in motion, her posture changing.

In her mosaic of eyes she had seen the future, a brutal crushing under hooves built to break ice. Here was her greatest fear. Extinction.

"Go!" she cried in a sharp voice, the scratch of steel. And The Changed Ones started to back up, slowly at first, as if unsure, and then, when they saw the Ovipositor in a whirring winged evacuation, they too ran. Skittering back toward the Chateau's entrance and beyond.

A prehistoric bird with the blood of a dinosaur burst onto the scene, pausing to toss back her electric-blue head and roar at the clouds. The feathers of her body shimmied like a saucy 1920s flapper. Budiwati was no longer a beast of burden, but an animal of autonomy. A MoFo named Walt Disney once said that "All our dreams can come true, if we have the courage to pursue them." Budiwati pursued The Changed Ones with the galloping gams of a velociraptor.

Dee ran us fearlessly between the snow-mountain bodies of polar bears, toward the great approaching line of oxen. Toward Oomingmak's enormous nostrils, the bony plate, his fairground–teddy bear ears and eyes—great brown lakes shimmering with love for Dee, a thing that transcended words and worlds. Dee nimbly navigated hulking oxen bodies to swing us up onto Oomingmak's great brown back. A place that felt like home.

The Changed Ones scrambled like illuminated cockroaches ahead. Our bone wall of horns drove them out. We, creatures with hearts free to fly, drove them out with the most powerful force on earth. Love.

And though I was weak and in pain and consumed by that old familiar smell of musty moss and burrito farts, I gave Oomingmak's back a quick stab with my beak for old times' sake. I couldn't help myself.

I was pretty overjoyed to see that furry fuck.

# CHAPTER 35

Dee! Look!" I called out. The sky was a quilted comforter of clouds. I'd found a perfect patch of chanterelles. Dee loved our mushroom foraging. Oomingmak had fallen asleep under a fir a ways back, snoring like a broken buzz saw, no doubt dreaming of his old girlfriend who sat rusting gently in an Alaskan forest. No one could accuse Oomingmak of infidelity. Dee ran her fingers over the mushrooms, releasing sweet, fruitful scents.

"No, Astee. Nat eat." She was right, the chanterelles weren't ready. Nature's circadian rhythms danced inside of Dee. She read the natural world like a book with butterfly wings and beetle bums for pages. This little hybrid who had the admiration of bees and the moss monarch. Dee, the little MoFo who made me a better crow.

Kuupa swooped overhead and screeched in disapproval at my mushroom selection. At the same time, there was a blast of sound, like a musk ox farting in his sleep.

*Overkill,* I thought. *Everyone's a critic.*

Kuupa was hunting too, checking in with her owlet through-out the day with her one omniscient eye. I thought of red-backed fucking voles for the first time in a long while and suddenly lost the will to live. The silver ring on Kuupa's taloned foot glinted above me, rippling my skin into crow bumps. One day I'd ask Kuupa about that ring, about what a MoFo had done for her a long time ago when she was an owlet. The thing, small and seedlike, that unlocked Kuupa's heart for a MoFo nestling. About the small act of kindness that caused a ripple effect in concentric circles through time and saved the last MoFo on earth.

Another story for another time.

Dee and I focused on the golds and gloomy grays of mush-rooms. Later, we would forage for fish and rodents to bring to Migisi and her three brand-new eaglets. You'd be so impressed by the nest Migisi built. My god, it was a monstrous master-piece, a mansion in the sky. It weighed about the same as Big Jim's Ford F-150. Dee had insisted we climb up and watch the eaglets hatch. I thought it would all be a bit intense for me, this birthing business, but it was miraculous. Dee coaxed the little slimy eaglets from their crisp shells with gentle piccolo notes. I became woozy and passed out for part of it, but I did bring Migisi a congratulatory fish head so as not to appear im-polite. Her eaglets were cute little fuckers. Migisi was pleased as pudding.

"They look like tiny silver clouds with fuck-you faces!" I told her.

I watched Dee inspect mushrooms. She took what she needed and not a mushroom more. All things gossamer in the web of reciprocity.

My ribs were still delicate, so I did a lot of hobble-hopping around and pretending to know what I was doing—business as usual, really. Not totally beguiled by mushroom exploration, I slipped into a daydream of a bungalow over turquoise Bora Bora waters and then a recent memory of the musk oxen and polar bears driving out The Changed Ones. We'd claimed our territory back, sending The Changed Ones scattering. There hadn't been a trace of them since. They had just vanished. There were worries about their evolving, coming back in greater numbers—worries as tangible as thorns— but we'd bought ourselves time. Tomorrow was a gift horse's glistening teeth. Against every odd, we'd lived to see another sunrise. I watched Dee, absorbed by the simple pleasures of the soil, thinking, *What an extraordinary luxury to cast a shadow.*

I remembered that soon after The Changed Ones had gone, Pressa had forced me to rest. I had woken up to The Hook's moonflower-white wings.

"They're calling for you," he said.

"Who?" I asked.

"Hoo!" he responded, in owl.

"No…oh, fuck," I said. What the hell. I deserved a lie-in! The early bird might catch the worm, but he also snatches the many adverse symptoms of sleep deprivation. Kuupa swooped down in front of me, incinerating me with the burn from her one great eye.

"I'm coming!" I said, leaping into action. Curiosity—my old nemesis—gnawed away at me and I agreed to talk to the polar bears.

The celebration of Ice Bears was standing in an intimidating mass that looked like the Alps. I gingerly hopped along the ground until Dee scooped me up, walking tall and proud toward a mountain range of white bears. Thankfully I don't wear pants, for I surely would have shit in them.

An old female bear spoke first. "I am The Huntress Of The

Floe. We, Seal's Dread, are so grateful that what we heard was true," she said with a voice as sharp as cracked ice.

"And we're grateful for your help with driving out The Changed Ones," I told her from Dee's smooth fingers. "But, why have you stayed here? Why did you leave Alaska?"

The bear sniffed at the air with a stupendous nose like a moist lump of coal. "The Ice Kingdom melts. The ice always melts now."

I nodded. Their home was warming, turning to a water world. *Echo* would expand and The Ice Bears had no choice but to pad south.

"But that's not why we came," she said. "We are here because of The One Who Keeps."

"Aha!" I puffed up with pride. "That's me!"

"No," she said. She turned her gargantuan white body to make room for another. A polar bear twice as big as The Huntress Of The Floe lumbered to the front of the bear clan. I felt Dee's knees buckle at the sight of him.

"This is my son," she said, her sounds filled with a glacial loneliness. I pictured a landscape of ice, sharp peaks, and sparkling surfaces. I pictured refracted rainbows, a hollow longing, a polar bear's endless searching. "This is Tornassuk. He is The One Who Keeps."

*Oh no,* I thought. She's confused, maybe unstable. There was quite enough identity theft going on around here. I'd set her straight.

The enormous male bear towered over Dee. He stared at the last MoFo and winced as if it pained him. Dee reached her hand out.

"Careful, Dee!" I said. But her hand, fingers splayed like a peacock fan, hovered steady. The enormous bear took a hard sniff. He pressed his moist nose to her palm.

"Uh, sorry guys, you're mistaken," I told the bears. "My

name is Shit Turd and I'm an American crow. I am The One Who Keeps."

Tornassuk spoke. His voice was booming, rattling like ice in a globe-sized glass. "And so, we have the same name. We have come a long way. The owls knew to follow the summoning of the bees. We know she called them. She is your cub?" he asked, staring hard at Dee. Dee was shiny-eyed, mesmerized by his mountainous presence.

"She is Dee," I said. "She belongs to no one."

The great bear nodded his blocky head. "I too am the keeper of a Skinner cub," he said. My heart froze. His mother, the great white bear, let out a low rumble, urging him to tell the whole truth. He continued. "When the storms worsened and the seas became angry, The Ice Bears moved into the land. We saw what had happened to the Skinners. Some of us perished."

Another bear behind them bellowed in bleak pain. It clung to us all like cold wet clothes. Grief.

"We found a small Skinner cub. I knew because I saw it written in the ice lights—I was The One Who Keeps—and I took in the little cub, a tiny furless boy, and I cared for him."

"We, The Hunters Of The Floe, Seal's Dread, knew to listen to Onida. We protected him as if he were an ice cub," said his mother.

Tornassuk took over. "He was growing fast. We fed him the sweetest slips of our meals. We taught him the way of The Ice Bears..." He stopped, his sad eyes scanning the length of Dee's arms.

His mother continued. "Our cub ventured out on his own to fish. He was old enough then—his muscles and skin had thickened. He could handle the ice. But there was another out in the ice fields. An alone. A wild-eyed bear who had not recovered from the days of starvation, a bear with murder on her mind. A Seal Slayer who hated the Skinners for everything they'd done to her. And she took him from us. Left us with nothing of him, barely even bones. We believed he was the Last Of The Skinner Cubs, gone." The bears went quiet. Their sorrow hit me like an icy front.

*There had been another MoFo. There had been a boy out there in the tundra. How far away had he been from the owls, Migisi, and me in Toksook? What if I had known? What could I have done to save him?*

"Many years ago, I almost lost my son, Tornassuk. We know the pain of loss," said The Huntress Of The Floe.

"What happened to the bear who…did this?" I asked, remembering the musty lichen smell of her, how she'd clamped her jaw on Dee's tiny skull. Only now I knew that there had been more than frigid hunger at play—she'd been out for vengeance. I thought of why she'd stopped, backing away from Dee. How I'd screamed that she was my cub. Had she lost her cubs at the hands of the MoFos? Had she heard me in the softest part of her heart? I'd never know. But I suddenly felt colder than I'd ever felt.

"I brought her a seal's end," said Tornassuk, The One Who Keeps. He said this without hate. He said it as it is done in the animal kingdom, a necessity to survive. I imagined bright scarlet snow. "When the owls told us of the other Skinner cub, that she was the true last and that she was in grave danger, we came. We did it for our sea bear, for the cub we lost," said Tornassuk, The One Who Keeps. "And we did it because the Beasts must be stopped. When A Kind becomes too great in number, the whole of nature conspires to swipe it back to balance. To freeze the flow. We must do this to survive."

I thought of the wolves and ravens working together. Genghis and his Orange. Me and Dee. Dee and three tigers. My friendship with an entire parliament of owls. Me and penguins for shit sakes. Trees with a million differences in the golden spray of their leaves in sylvan alliance. Big Jim and Nargatha. Survival didn't have to be stolen adaptations and horror—it could be friendships. He was right. We were stronger *akutaq*. Unlikely alliances were the very cornerstone of survival.

The polar bears didn't return to Alaska. The territory the musk oxen had afforded us was big enough for predators and prey under their aegis, all creatures furred, feathered, and scaled trying to survive. The Ice Bears liked being close to Dee; it helped with the glacial weight of losing a cub. They spoke to us about the dangers ravaging *Echo*. The Darwinian War. About a tide that was about to turn...

I shook off that old MoFo habit of memories to enjoy mushroom foraging with Dee. We'd wandered deeper into the trees, so that the sky soon became a viridescent patchwork of leaves. Without the threat of The Changed Ones, creatures had come out of hiding. The sky sang in blue, the grass grinned in green. Butterflies and dragonflies danced in a daydream. And then Dee made a sharp *cheenk!*—a robin's alert chirp. I was on a rock in between the jutting phalluses of mushrooms. Dee was up ahead. Up among the glittering green of leaves, I saw that the trees were filled with squirrels. The squirrels were eerily still. I saw their shining eyes, their focused stares. And I started to worry.

Dee was a rabbit. Slight squat. A coiled spring. Staring up ahead at the trunk of a large western red cedar with focused feline eyes. I tracked her eyes again. And I saw him.

I blinked my eyes. I windshield-wiped with my nictitating membranes to be sure.

There, next to the trunk was a MoFo.

Standing on two legs with a straight spine. His hair was fawn brown, lodging to a single leaf. Sweat glistening on pale, mud-mottled skin that wasn't green. Thick beard like a dense clump of dried moss. He had a classic male MoFo shape, the shape of a bartender or Michael Angelo's David or Jon Bon Jovi! A grown male MoFo, maybe the age of Big Jim. Clear eyes, not a trace of red. A ripped shirt. Dirt-colored shorts exposed knobby knees like two shiny baseballs. A bite mark throbbed on his arm—two smiles and a blooming bruise— telltale tooth emblem of a raccoon. Pressa would later help stave off this infection. His left hand was balled nervously at his side. Thunderstruck, he stared at Dee as if he'd found the mythical thing of a fairy tale. He had.

So here it was. I'd never given up hope. When you've waited for something so long and it finally arrives, you can taste it, sweet as sap. I resurrected words I'd rehearsed every drunken night in Toksook Bay.

"Hello," I said as I'd rehearsed to a chubby old stove so many, many times. "We've been looking for you. Thank god you're alive."

The MoFo stared at a silver-tongued crow, surely wondering if this was a trick of the forest, the misfirings of a lonely mind. I balanced on one foot, offering the other foot to shake, though a bit too far away, because that is a polite way to say hello if you're a MoFo meeting another MoFo and I have never been good at fist bumps.

And then I said, "You are not the last one. This is Dee."

A MoFo about to meet another MoFo—the dream, utopia, paradise.

His eyes widened. He was understandably shocked to discover he wasn't utterly alone as the singular biped on this planet. Here was a young female MoFo who moved like a wild animal. An especially handsome crow was talking to him and this was clearly disorientating. I hopped toward him.

Dee was in motion.

"Handshake, Dee!" I prompted, in case she'd forgotten her

manners and my impeccable etiquette coaching. And then Dee was in front of the MoFo. There were two on this big beautiful blue! Imagine the last two rhinos on earth finding one another, no longer breaking under the burden of being the last. It was as if a curse had been lifted, an enchantment settling like cottonwood on all our skins. We all, even the lecherous lothario squirrels, I'm sure of it, felt a bright magic lighting up the future.

I would have screamed in joy but didn't want to startle this male MoFo. First impressions were everything; Big Jim learned this the first and only time he met Sarah M. from Tinder as he shook her hand and simultaneously farted.

Squirrels salivated from the branches like Pavlov's dogs, if they'd been plush-tailed perverts.

"Hello!" I said again. And Dee was in front of the MoFo and her hand was out, clever girl. He buckled, emotion getting the better of him. He dropped to baseball knees, weak with relief. Only as I neared, I saw that his stomach was smiling.

Dee kept aloof eyes on his entrails as they slipped to the ground. They made an *Echo* purple-blue sound, the sound of an eel flopping on land. His eyes turned to glass.

*No. No, no, no.*

I scanned in horror, searching for sense. Dee held a jagged shard of glass slick with blood.

*What had she done? What had she done?*

But I knew.

Dee had used the cold defense strategy of a cassowary.

She turned to me, already anticipating my shock. She watched my last pea weevil's worth of patience pack its bags and hail an Uber.

"Astee, danger!" She lifted up the MoFo's right hand, un-clasping a switchblade from his death grip. She hopped over the pale body that posed so many questions, its stories slashed into extinction. Dee ripped open the MoFo's bag, pouring out the contents.

A lump of meat, old and rubbery. A necklace of MoFo teeth fell out. A tattered notebook. A makeshift ax. Dee pointed at a mound of black twigs.

"Astee!" She gestured violently at the twigs.

Not twigs but severed crow feet. Black beaks scattered in between. Dee's face wrinkled into snarls. The notebook was littered with the ramblings of a madman. But the last page made my beak hairs stand on end.

THE MONSTERS ABOVE THE BUNKER ARE DEAD. SOMETHING KILLED THEM IN THE NIGHT. LEFT THE BUNKER. STRANGE MI-GRATIONS HAPPENING ANIMALS BIRDS ALL FOLLOWING SOMETHING. TRACKED A SKY FULL OF CROWS AND SAW A CREATURE LIKE A GIRL BUT NOT. CROWS ALL AROUND IT. MUST BE A GHOST. CANNOT BE REAL, CHILDREN IN THE BUNKER ARE LONG DEAD. EVERYONE IS DEAD. HUNTING THE GHOST GIRL. KILLING CROWS TO LURE HER. WILL CAPTURE THE GHOST GIRL.

I took it all in. The squirrels looked utterly disappointed. And I used my MoFo mind to make deductions, remembering that squirrels have only one thing on their filthy minds. The squirrels had been waiting for a show. The squirrels were a clear, Windex-ed window into this MoFo's dark intentions.

I squinted into the branches and saw our owls. Kuupa, Wik, Ookpik, Bristle, and The Hook had seen it all with citrine eyes. They'd seen this play out before it happened. They trusted Dee could handle it.

This is how it is done in the animal kingdom, a necessity to survive. Dee lived by the quiet storm of senses inside her. She'd seen what he was underneath his camouflage before I had—an animal. Oh, the pelts we wear. Dee had never needed Big Jim's hands to protect her. The female of the species is more deadly than the male.

Eyes up at Dee, who waited for my response. I gave a head bob. Relief escaped her through a soft sigh.

I had been wrong to call Dee a flower. Dee was not a flower; she was a fucking weed. Beautiful and tenacious as a tiger. Misunderstood and mislabeled. Spiny and spiraling unapologetically toward life. Flowers live in short, delicate bursts, but Dee had thorns and tangled roots and would fight for every chance at a life. Blackberry bush's darling pride. My, my, what a beautiful and deadly thing she was growing into.

She picked me up and nuzzled my beak, feeling the hollow ache and terrible longing of my disappointment.

"Gisi," she said, gesturing in the direction of Migisi's sky mansion. The sun started to sink in a bright burst of sherbet-pink tatters. I took a deep breath. We'd get to savor another sunrise, the light hours offering up a whole banquet of possibility and adventure. A future.

There were three eaglets waiting for us. Our brave crows. A parliament of owls. A cantankerous cassowary. An aurora of protective polar bears. A lake-eyed musk ox who'd scoured the tundra and the taiga for Dee, finally following the wisdom of bees. Three tigers who craved the comfort of Dee's warm, biscuity smell. Family doesn't have to look like you; they can have feathers and scales and scutes. What matters is that you're loved for who you are in your heart. We survive when we are seen.

The deep rasp of a tiger claiming his territory revved into a chorus of fierce music.

*All the world's a stage. The show must go on.*

The big beautiful blue is filled with secrets and hidden lives waiting to be discovered. Far, far away, shivers of hammerheads gathered in a swirling sea, grasshopper mice howled at dark desert moons, horned tahrs tackled the stoic face of a Himalayan mountain, sloths sustained a kingdom of algae in the digestive system of a rainforest. Wild creatures, all fighting for a sunrise.

What a wonderful world.

And who knows what or who else was out there? Something dawned on me right then—why we hadn't seen a trace of The Changed Ones since the oxen had driven them away.

Dee shared my thoughts. She pointed at the horizon and then at herself.

"MoFo, Astee," she said, her eyes meeting mine. "Like Dee. Danger." She pointed at the horizon again. Could it be that The Changed Ones had been driven away by Dee's allies, but they had stayed away because they were hunting? Because there was another out there. Another like Dee.

I thought of all the creatures I'd met since I left my little Ravenna nest. They were all worth fighting for. Dee and I would no longer hide or live in fear. We would no longer stand by as an abominable horde destroyed our big beautiful blue. Our purpose landed in front of me, not delicately like the alighting of a Eurasian wren, but rather like a wasp crashlanding upon an eyeball. We had to eradicate the monsters that were ravaging our home.

Dee and I shared a sly look. Yes, we felt the big beautiful blue calling for us.

Maybe I'd get to see some of the wonders of the world after all.

Winner winner chicken dinner.

Dee strode like something nature had dreamed up in bold

brushstrokes. Fruit of the imagination, plucked from a star-kissed sky. She was an evolutionary masterpiece, the little seed that could, eternity's sunrise, forever perched in my soul. She claimed each footfall, as confident as the earth that held her.

And I hopped along after her. Just a little thing with feathers.

# ACKNOWLEDGMENTS

To my agent, the one and only Bill Clegg, who continues to astound and inspire me with his literary intuition and graceful guidance. Thank you for making me a better writer and for not batting an eye when I brought a real live talking crow to your house.

Thank you to my Clegg Agency family, especially Lilly Sandberg, David Kambhu, and Simon Toop for their cunning corvid minds, and to Marion Duvert for helping S.T. to fly farther than he ever could have dreamed.

My immeasurable gratitude to my Grand Central Publishing family. To my magnificent editor, Karen Kosztolnyik, who is not only a writer's Glinda the Good Witch but an all-around brilliant MoFo and my dear friend. Thank you for waving your magic wand over every word and making the editorial process an utter joy, all while rocking out to Bon Jovi.

Thank you to Rachael Kelly for your professionalism and endless patience as we battled internet goblins together.

What an extraordinarily lucky duck I am to have worked with Anjuli Johnson, production editor extraordinaire, and Alayna Johnson, copyedit queen, who took every S.T.ism in stride.

Editing the wordplay of a logophile corvid is no easy feat. You are both spectacular and unrivaled goddesses of grammar.

My eternal thanks to Grand Central geniuses Thomas Louie, Andrew Duncan, Joseph Benincase, Ali Cutrone, Alison Lazarus, Chris Murphy, Karen Torres, Matthew Ballast, Brian McLendon, and Alana Spendley. And a very special supersized thank you to Ben Sevier.

Thank you to Tom McIntyre and Shawn Donley for your kindness and for being so very good at what you do.

To my peerless publicists, Andy Dodds and Jordan Rubinstein, who champion books with a ferocity seen only in adult male bull sharks. I'm so lucky to work with you both. Andy, thank you for always being there.

An elephantine thanks to GCP's indelibly talented art director, Jarrod Taylor, whose cover art continues to stop traffic.

Thank you to my friends and family who have shown up for me in every way a MoFo could hope for.

To my writerly tribe, Stacy Lawson, Susan Urban, Shoshana Levenberg, Corry Venema-Weiss, Janet Yoder, Billie Condon, Susan Knox, Geri Gale, and our beloved Randy Hale, who is in our hearts as we write every word. An extra special thank you to Susan Urban, whose expert literary eyes I trust to handle the chaos of early drafts. And to Stacy Lawson for working tirelessly to make sure no one discovers I'm actually a female Mr. Bean.

Thank you to Sara Lucas for your Alaskan expertise and for the work that you do. Teachers are true heroes.

To the booksellers who have welcomed me into your stores as though I were family, I am perpetually grateful.

To all the readers, writers, and animal lovers I have been so fortunate to connect with in person and virtually, thank you for the inspiration and kindness. The love that has been shown to my characters is astonishing. And to the artists who have brought S.T. to life with their incomparable talent—I am humbled and in awe. Our waggish little crow has become tattoos, cross-stitches, a purse, a great many paintings, sketches, cakes, cookies, felt art, 3D printings, Halloween costumes, decor, sculptures, cocktails, jewelry, and songs. Your art has inspired me, proving that creativity is bewitchingly contagious.

Thank you to every person protecting our wildlife and our planet. With special thanks to my lovely bird-savior friend, Margie Hanrahan, and the world's greatest talking crow, Jimini Crowket. And to Petra Link and her darling little budding wildlife ambassador crow, Grover. And boundless gratitude to my friends at Discovery Bay Wild Bird Rescue for everything that you do for Washington wildlife.

To Jpeg, you are the tonic to my gin, the Orange to my Genghis. Thank you for being my partner in crime, creativity, and life, and for not divorcing me over the way I load the dishwasher.

Thank you to the real animals who inspired these characters and the ones who inspire me every day, especially T the crow, who never fails to lift my spirits. And to all the very good creatures who have been a comfort to their MoFos during a global pandemic—well done, darlings.

And to Miso, the real-life Genghis Cat and tiny tiger who ruled my home and heart for fourteen years. I love you, Pip Pip.

# ABOUT THE AUTHOR

**Kira Jane Buxton**'s debut novel, *Hollow Kingdom*, was a finalist for the Thurber Prize for American Humor, the Audie Awards, and the Washington State Book Awards, and was named a best book of 2019 by NPR, *Book Riot*, and *Good Housekeeping*. She spends her time with three cats, a dog, two crows, a charm of hummingbirds, five Steller's jays, two dark-eyed juncos, two squirrels, and a husband.

Facebook.com/KiraJaneBuxton
Twitter @KiraJaneWrites
KiraJaneBuxton.com